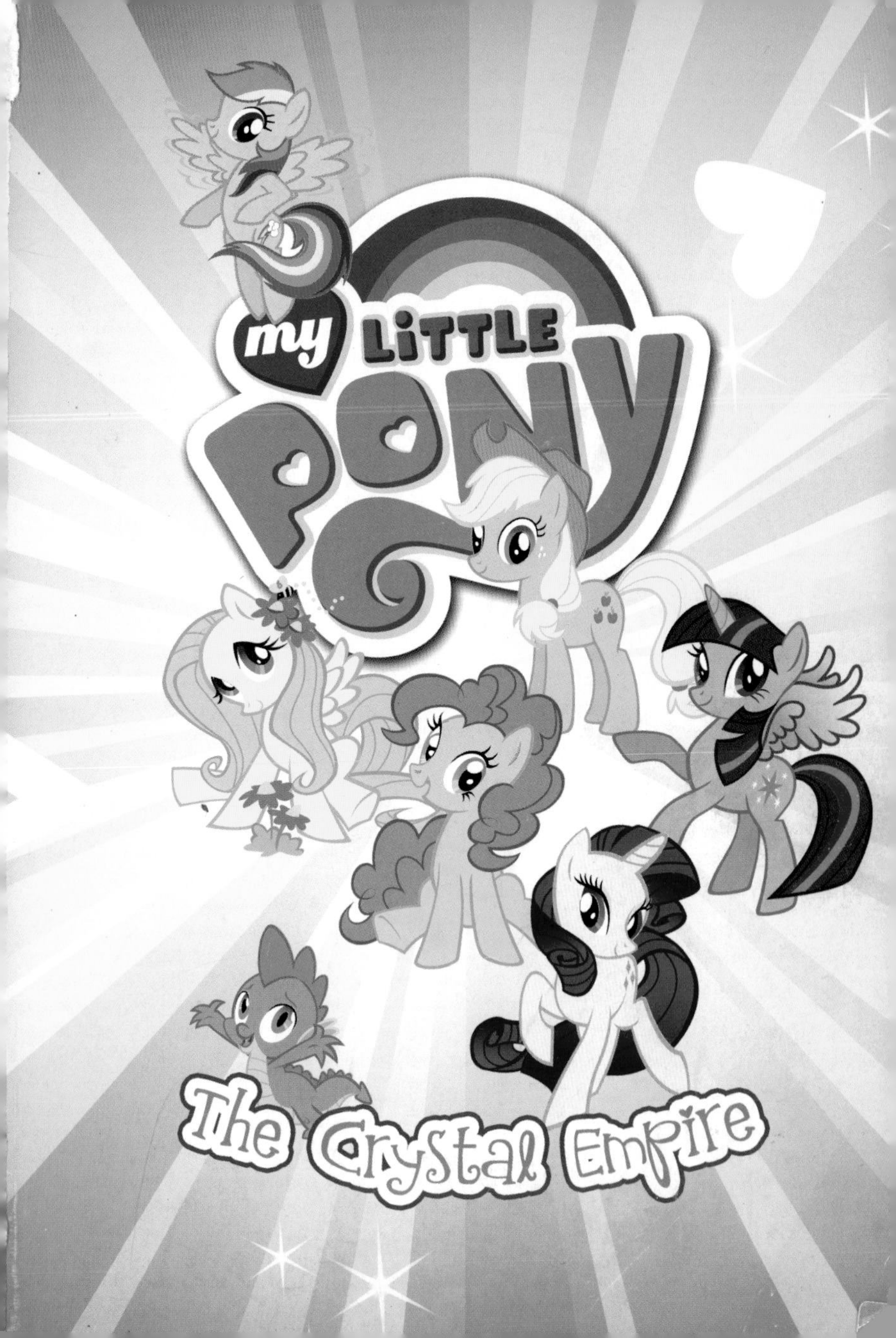
my LITTLE PONY
The Crystal Empire

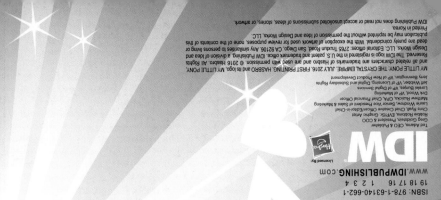

Special thanks to Hasbro's Ben Montano, David Erwin,
Josh Feldman, Ed Lane, Beth Artale, and Michael Kelly.

ISBN: 978-1-63140-662-1

19 18 17 16   1 2 3 4

www.IDWPUBLISHING.com

IDW

Licensed By:

Ted Adams, CEO & Publisher
Greg Goldstein, President & COO
Robbie Robbins, EVP/Sr. Graphic Artist
Chris Ryall, Chief Creative Officer/Editor-in-Chief
Laurie Windrow, Senior Vice President of Sales & Marketing
Matthew Ruzicka, CPA, Chief Financial Officer
Dirk Wood, VP of Marketing
Lorelei Bunjes, VP of Digital Services
Jeff Webber, VP of Licensing, Digital and Subsidiary Rights
Jerry Bennington, VP of New Product Development

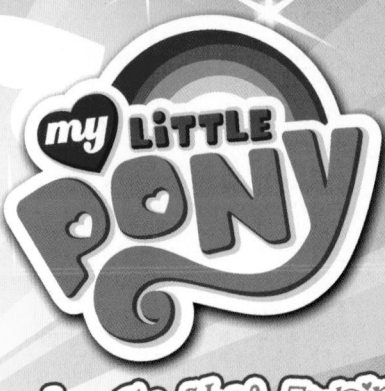

The Crystal Empire

Written by
Meghan McCarthy

Adaptation by
Justin Eisinger

Edits by
Alonzo Simon

Lettering and Design by
Gilberto Lazcano

Production Assistance by
Amauri Osario

MEET THE PONIES

Twilight Sparkle

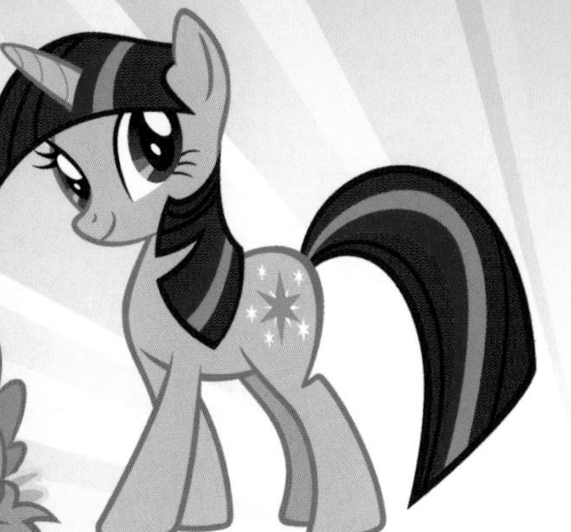

TWILIGHT SPARKLE TRIES TO FIND THE ANSWER TO EVERY QUESTION! WHETHER STUDYING A BOOK OR SPENDING TIME WITH PONY FRIENDS, SHE ALWAYS LEARNS SOMETHING NEW!

Spike

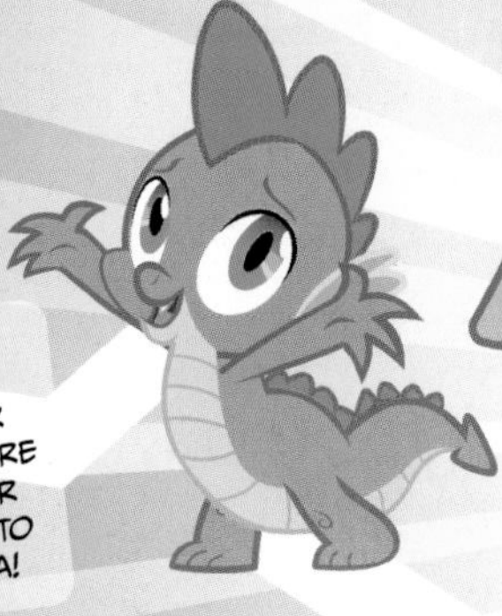

SPIKE IS TWILIGHT SPARKLE'S BEST FRIEND AND NUMBER ONE ASSISTANT. HIS FIRE BREATH CAN DELIVER SCROLLS DIRECTLY TO PRINCESS CELESTIA!

Applejack

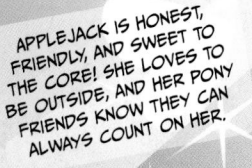

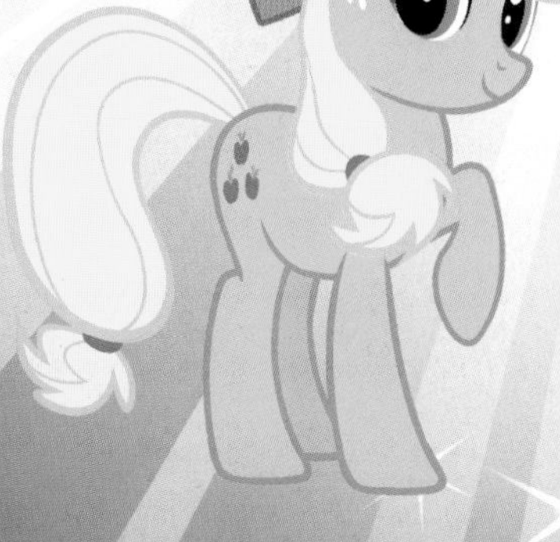

APPLEJACK IS HONEST, FRIENDLY, AND SWEET TO THE CORE! SHE LOVES TO BE OUTSIDE, AND HER PONY FRIENDS KNOW THEY CAN ALWAYS COUNT ON HER.

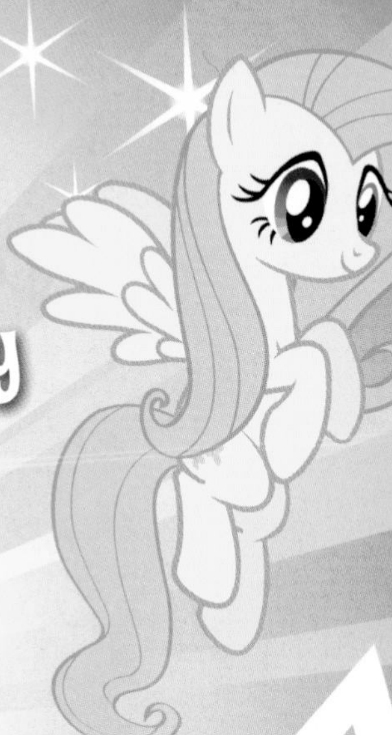

Fluttershy

FLUTTERSHY IS A KIND AND GENTLE PONY WITH A BIG HEART. SHE LIKES TO TAKE CARE OF OTHERS, ESPECIALLY HER LITTLE ANIMAL FRIENDS.

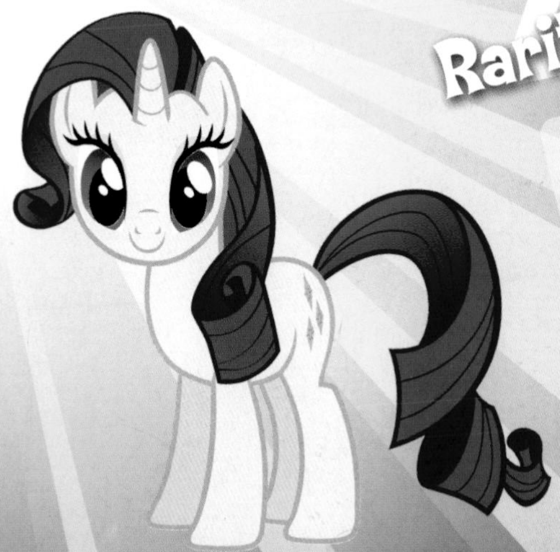

Rarity

RARITY KNOWS HOW TO ADD SPARKLE TO ANY OUTFIT! SHE LOVES TO GIVE HER PONY FRIENDS ADVICE ON THE LATEST PONY FASHIONS AND HAIRSTYLES.

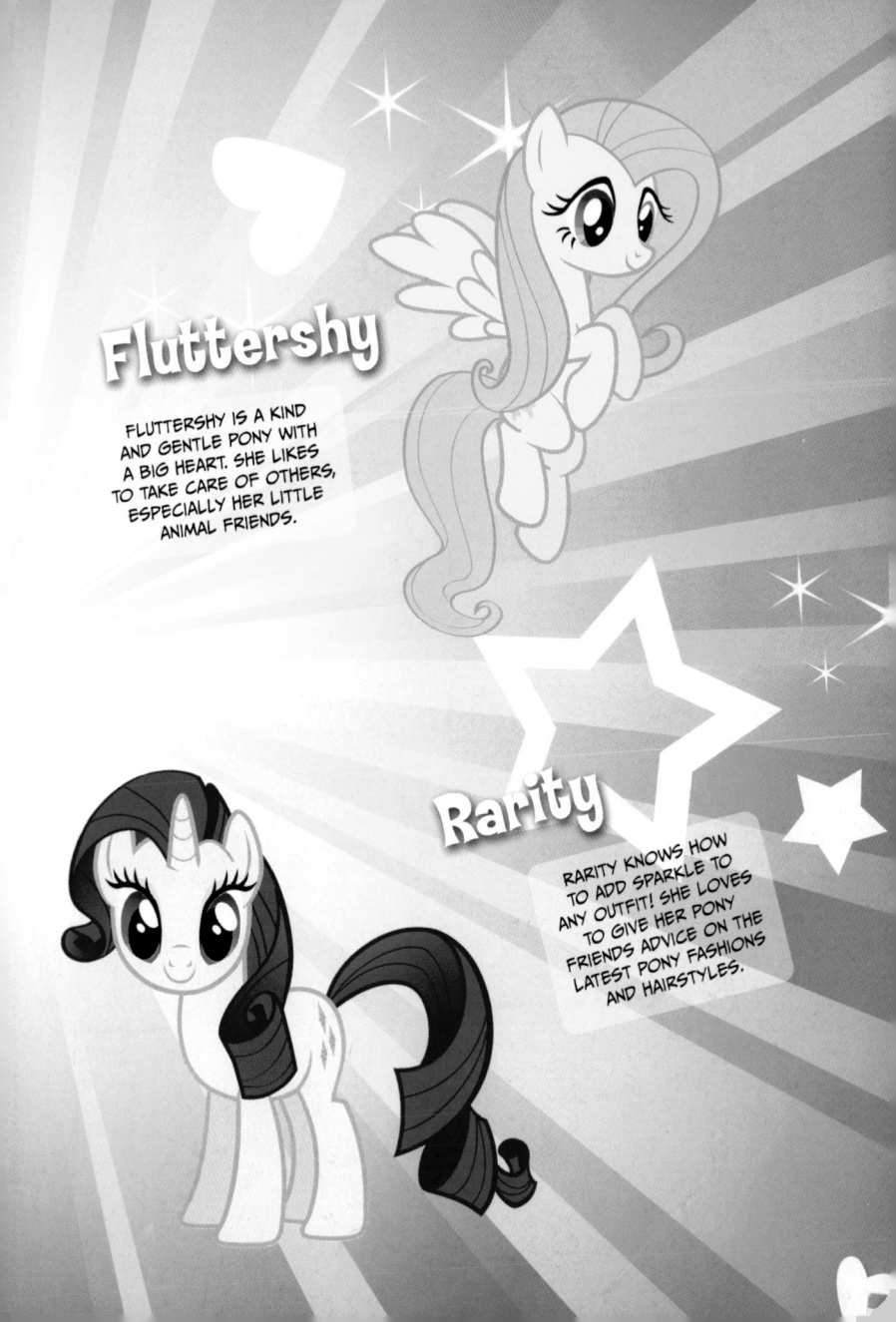

Pinkie Pie

PINKIE PIE KEEPS HER PONY FRIENDS LAUGHING AND SMILING ALL DAY! CHEERFUL AND PLAYFUL, SHE ALWAYS LOOKS ON THE BRIGHT SIDE.

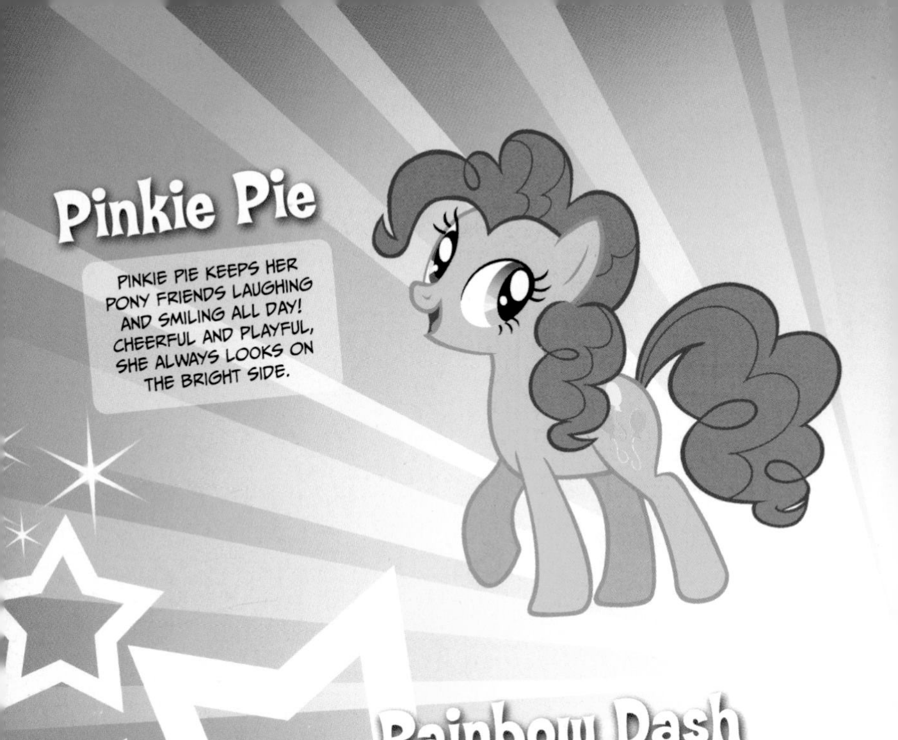

Rainbow Dash

RAINBOW DASH LOVES TO FLY AS FAST AS SHE CAN! SHE IS ALWAYS READY TO PLAY A GAME, GO ON AN ADVENTURE, OR HELP OUT ONE OF HER PONY FRIENDS.

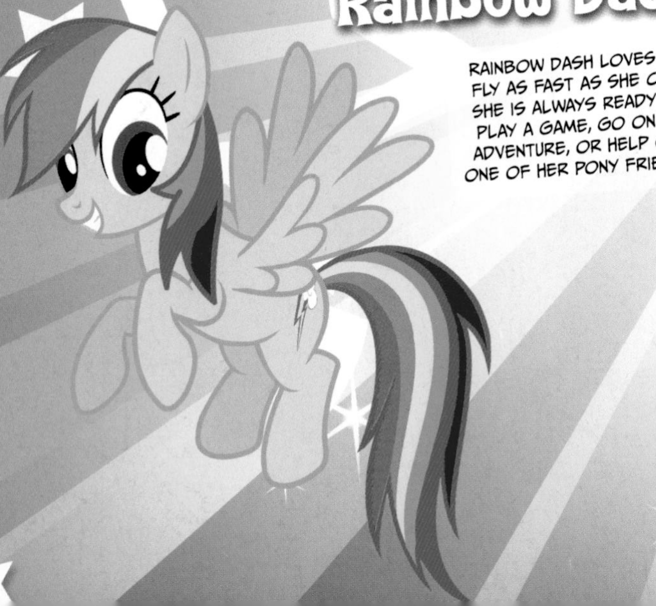

Princess Celestia

PRINCESS CELESTIA IS
A MAGICAL AND BEAUTIFUL
PONY WHO RULES THE LAND
OF EQUESTRIA. ALL OF THE
PONIES IN PONYVILLE LOOK
UP TO HER!

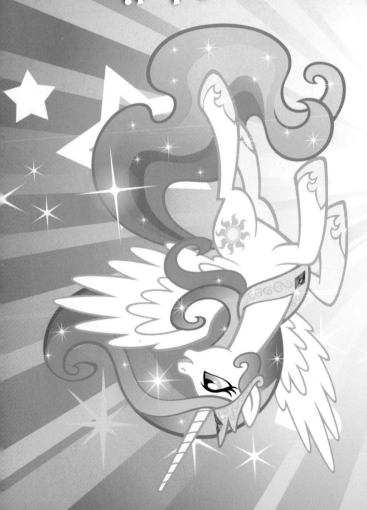

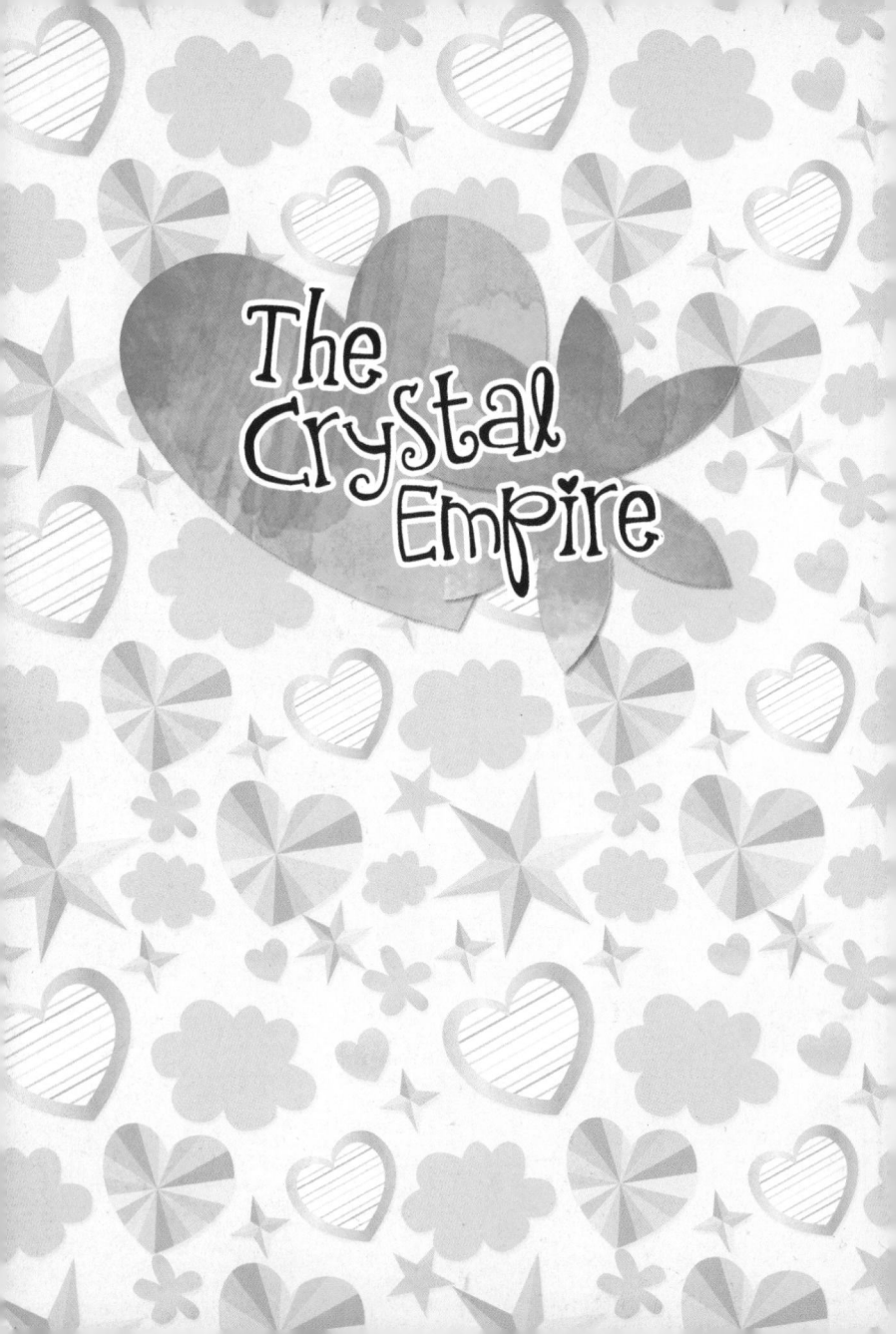

The Crystal Empire

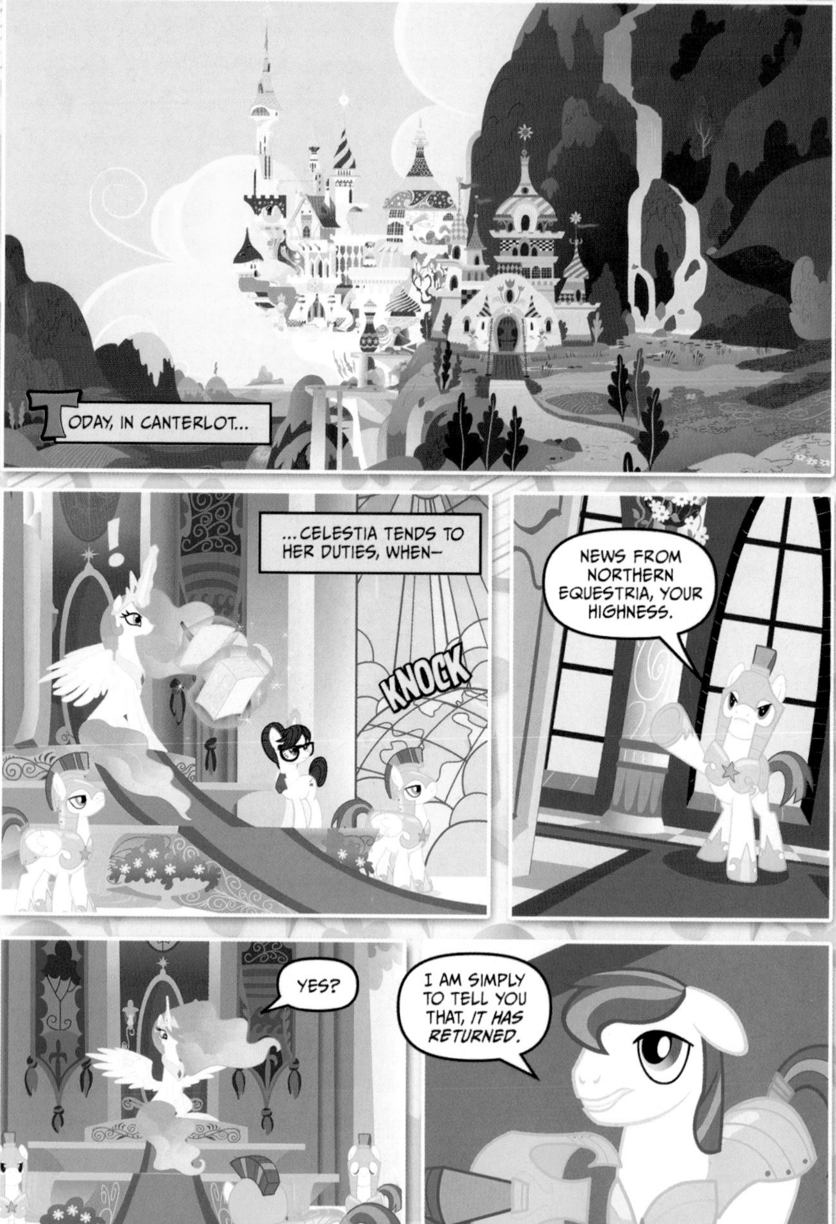
TODAY, IN CANTERLOT...
...CELESTIA TENDS TO HER DUTIES, WHEN—
KNOCK
NEWS FROM NORTHERN EQUESTRIA, YOUR HIGHNESS.
YES?
I AM SIMPLY TO TELL YOU THAT, *IT HAS RETURNED*.

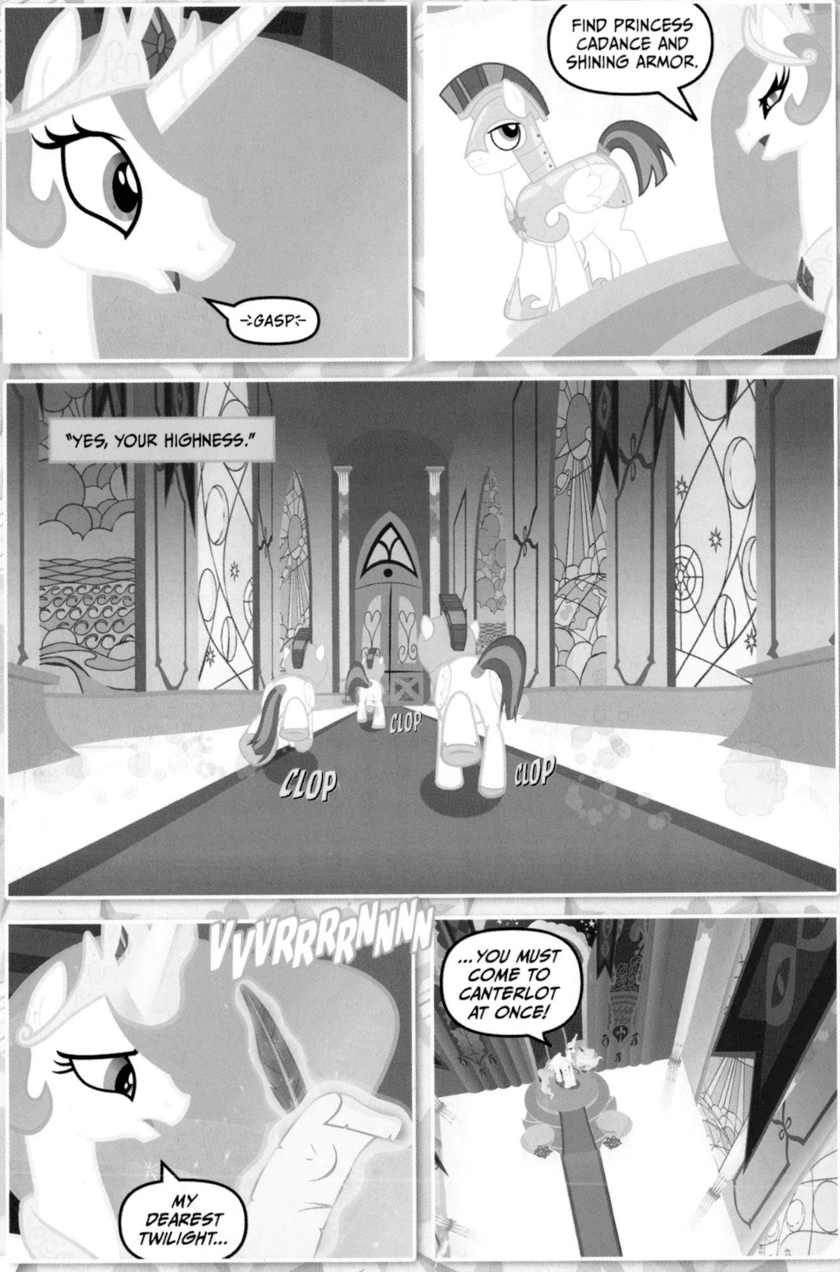
-GASP-
FIND PRINCESS CADANCE AND SHINING ARMOR.
"YES, YOUR HIGHNESS."
CLOP
CLOP
CLOP
VVVRRRRNNNN
MY DEAREST TWILIGHT...
...YOU MUST COME TO CANTERLOT AT ONCE!

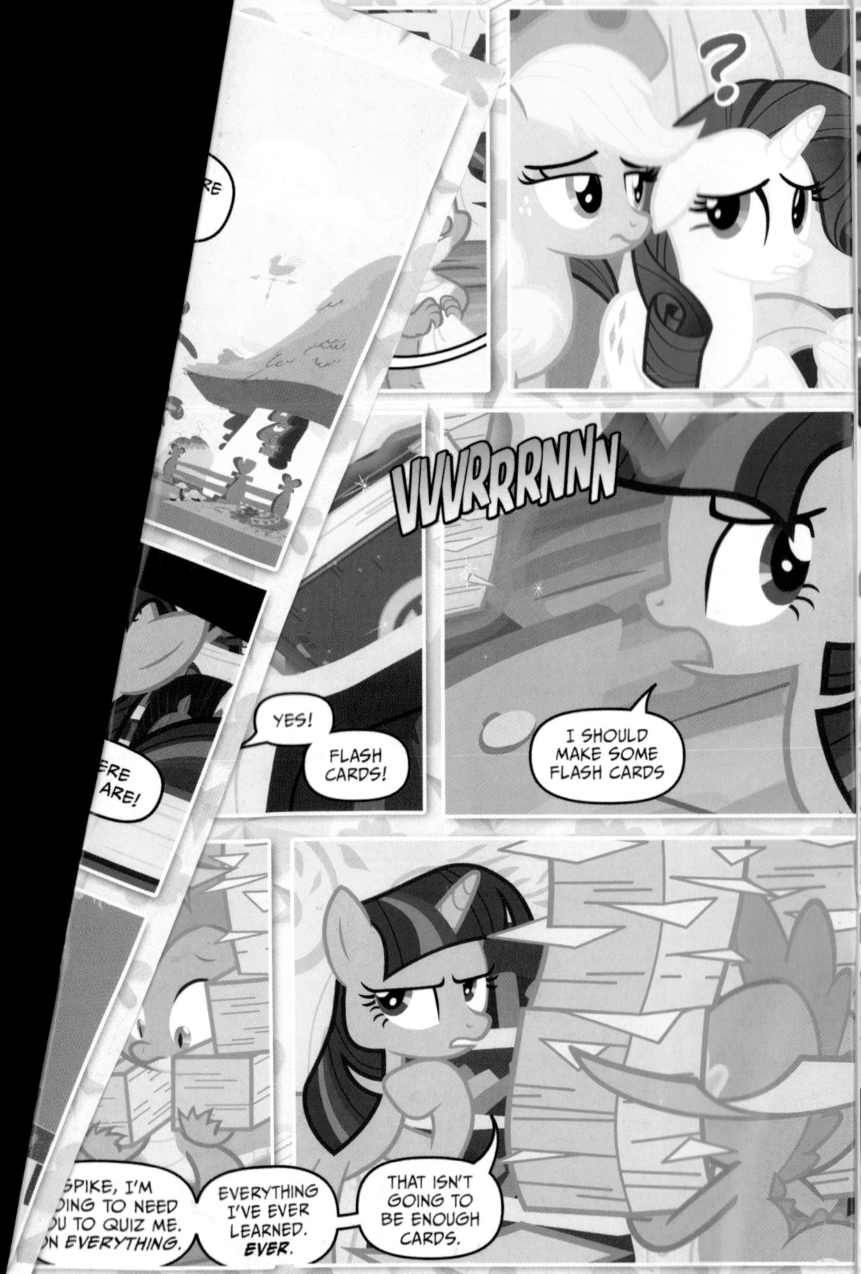
?
VVVRRRNNN
YES!
FLASH CARDS!
I SHOULD MAKE SOME FLASH CARDS
EVERYTHING I'VE EVER LEARNED. EVER.
THAT ISN'T GOING TO BE ENOUGH CARDS.
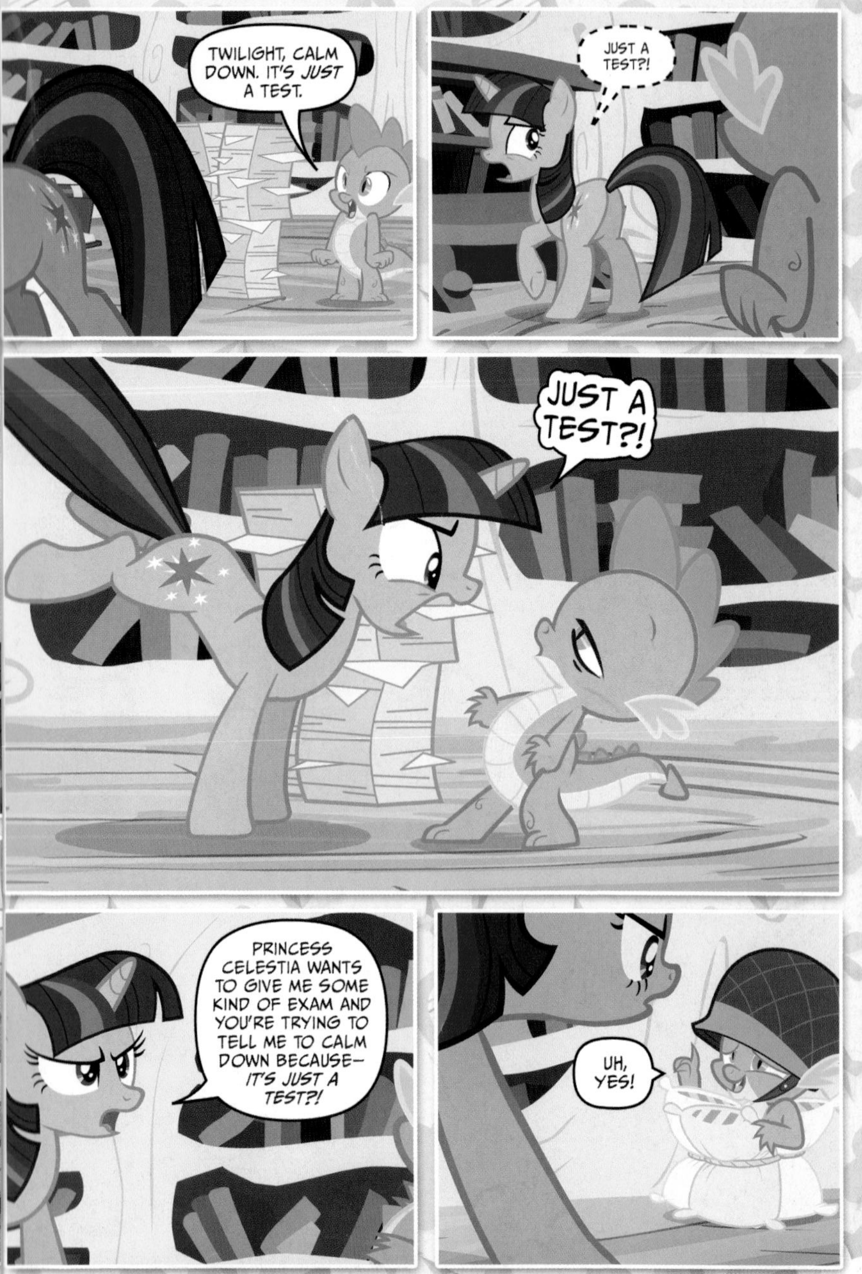
TWILIGHT, CALM DOWN. IT'S JUST A TEST.
JUST A TEST?!
JUST A TEST?!
PRINCESS CELESTIA WANTS TO GIVE ME SOME KIND OF EXAM AND YOU'RE TRYING TO TELL ME TO CALM DOWN BECAUSE— IT'S JUST A TEST?!
UH, YES!

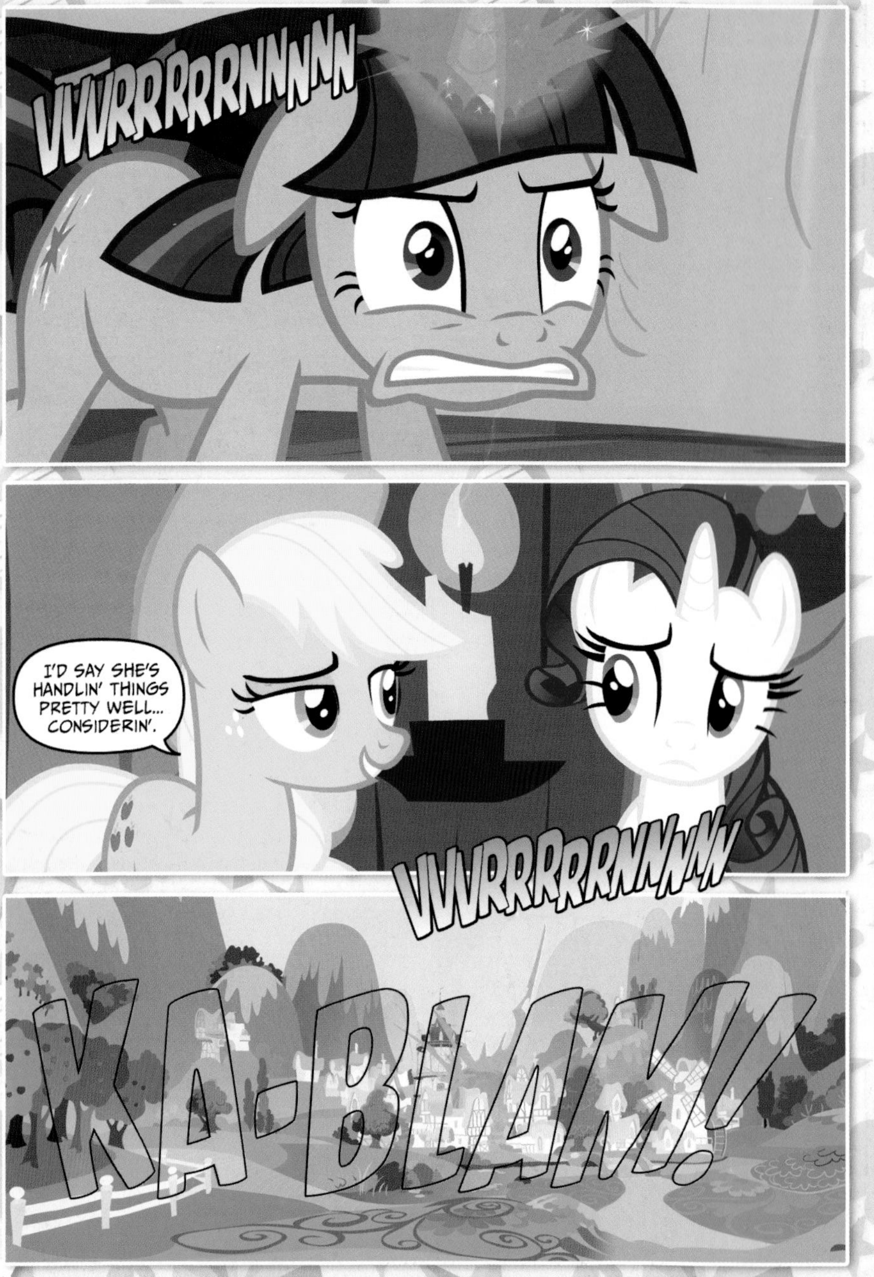
VVVRRRRRNNNNN
I'D SAY SHE'S HANDLIN' THINGS PRETTY WELL... CONSIDERIN'.
VVVRRRRRNNNNN
KA-BLAM!!

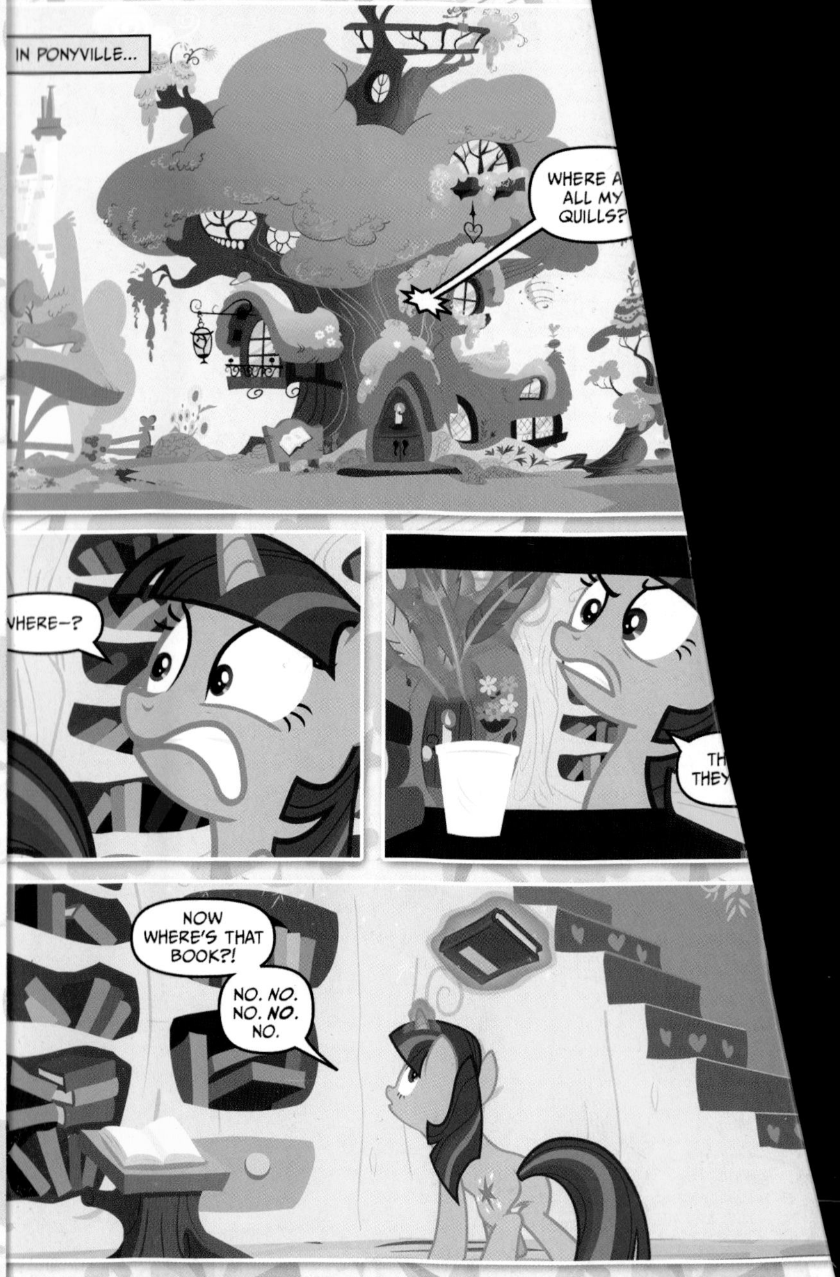
IN PONYVILLE...
WHERE-?
NOW WHERE'S THAT BOOK?!
NO. NO. NO. NO. NO.

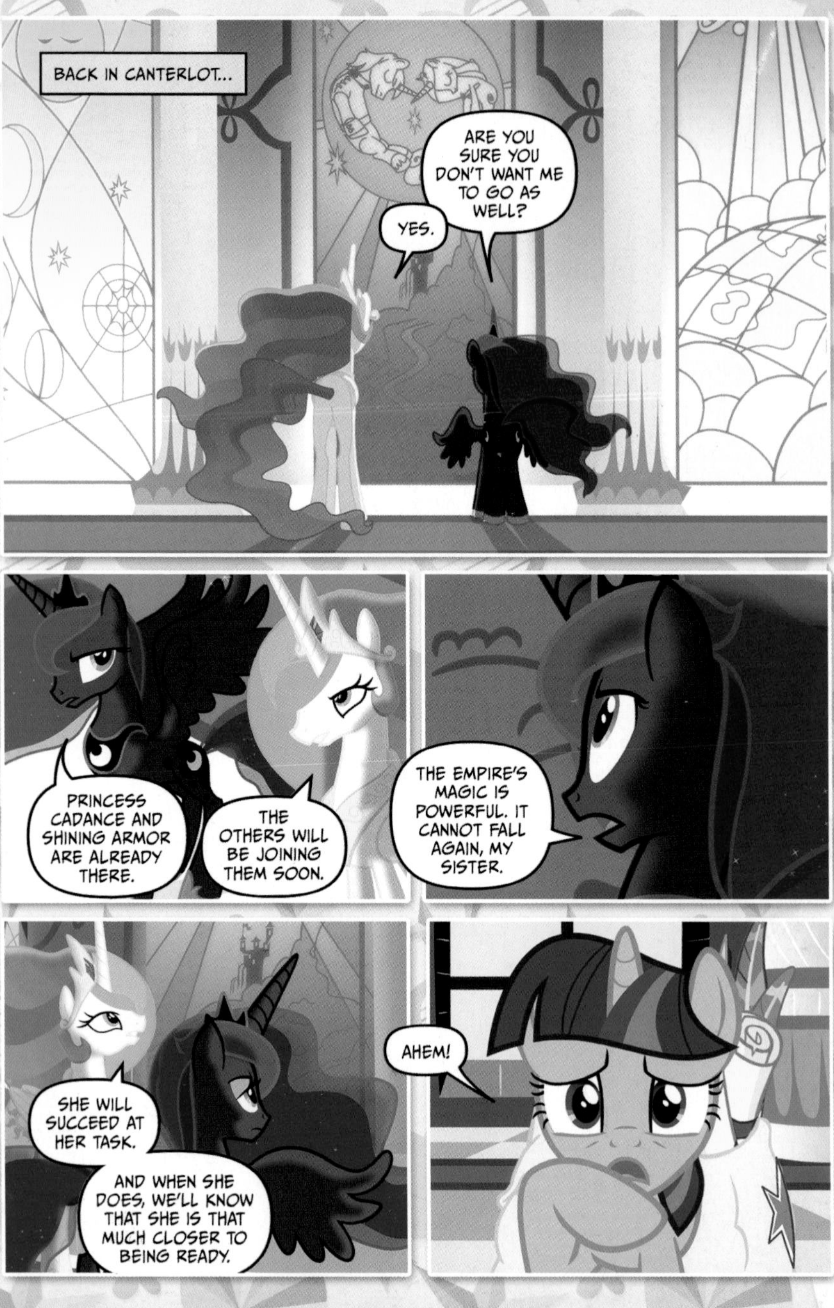
BACK IN CANTERLOT...
ARE YOU SURE YOU DON'T WANT ME TO GO AS WELL?
YES.
PRINCESS CADANCE AND SHINING ARMOR ARE ALREADY THERE.
THE OTHERS WILL BE JOINING THEM SOON.
THE EMPIRE'S MAGIC IS POWERFUL. IT CANNOT FALL AGAIN, MY SISTER.
SHE WILL SUCCEED AT HER TASK.
AND WHEN SHE DOES, WE'LL KNOW THAT SHE IS THAT MUCH CLOSER TO BEING READY.
AHEM!

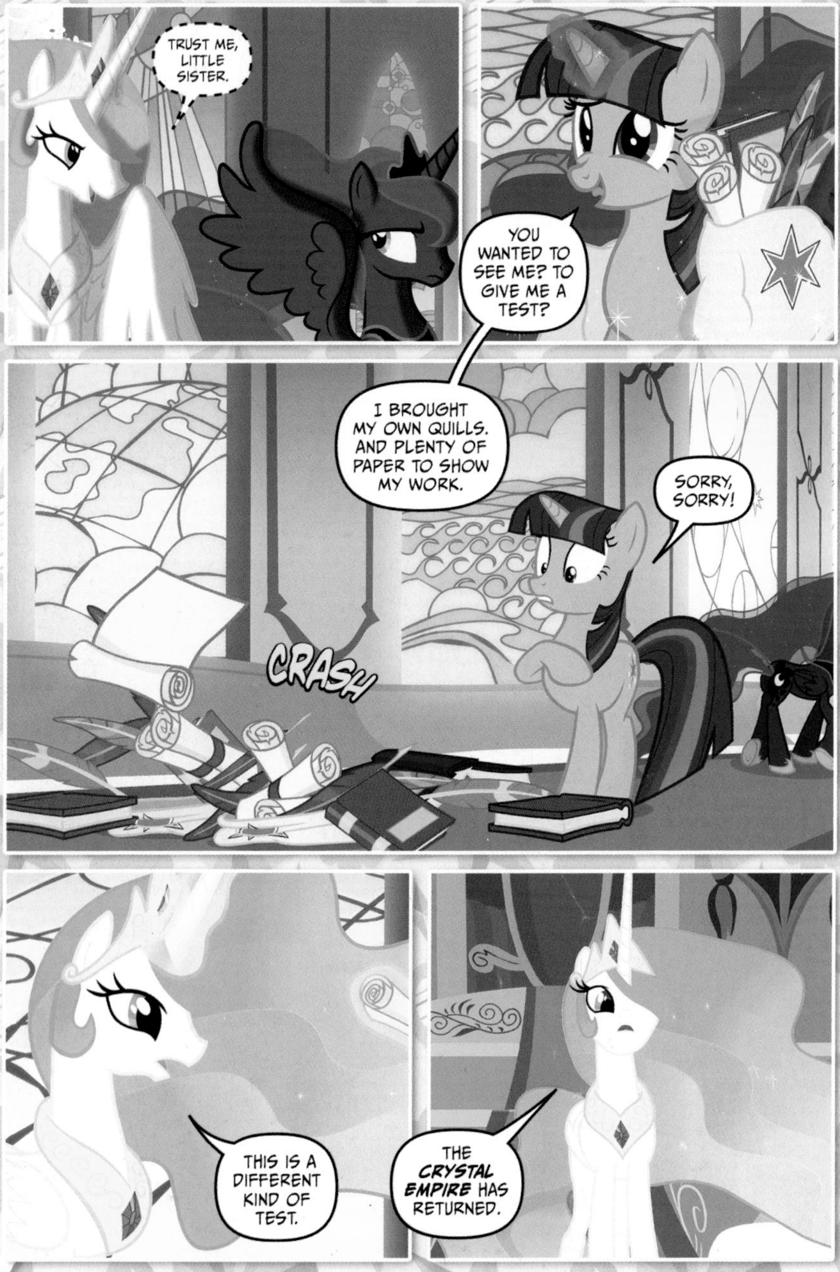
TRUST ME, LITTLE SISTER.
YOU WANTED TO SEE ME? TO GIVE ME A TEST?
I BROUGHT MY OWN QUILLS. AND PLENTY OF PAPER TO SHOW MY WORK.
SORRY, SORRY!
CRASH
THIS IS A DIFFERENT KIND OF TEST.
THE *CRYSTAL EMPIRE* HAS RETURNED.

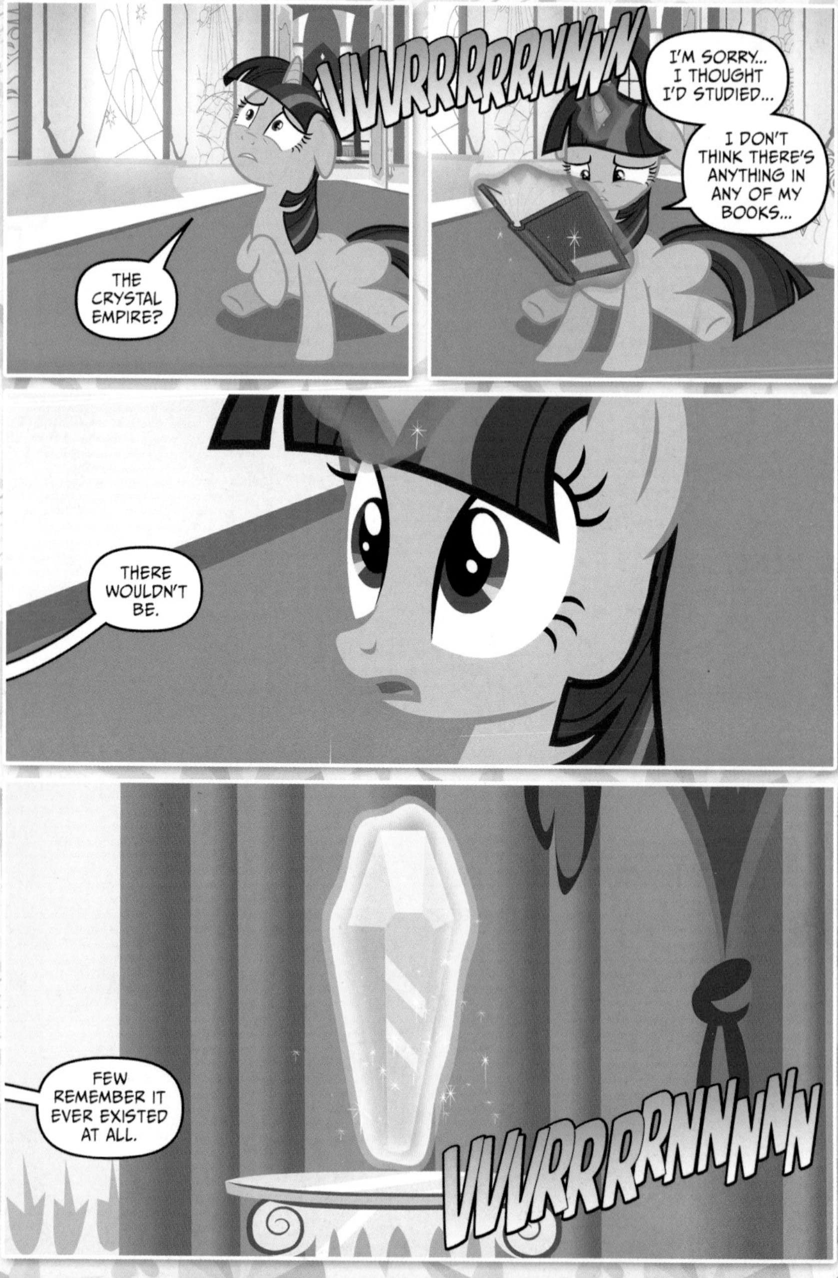
THE CRYSTAL EMPIRE?
VVVRRRRRNNNN
I'M SORRY... I THOUGHT I'D STUDIED...
I DON'T THINK THERE'S ANYTHING IN ANY OF MY BOOKS...
THERE WOULDN'T BE.
FEW REMEMBER IT EVER EXISTED AT ALL.
VVVRRRRRNNNNNN

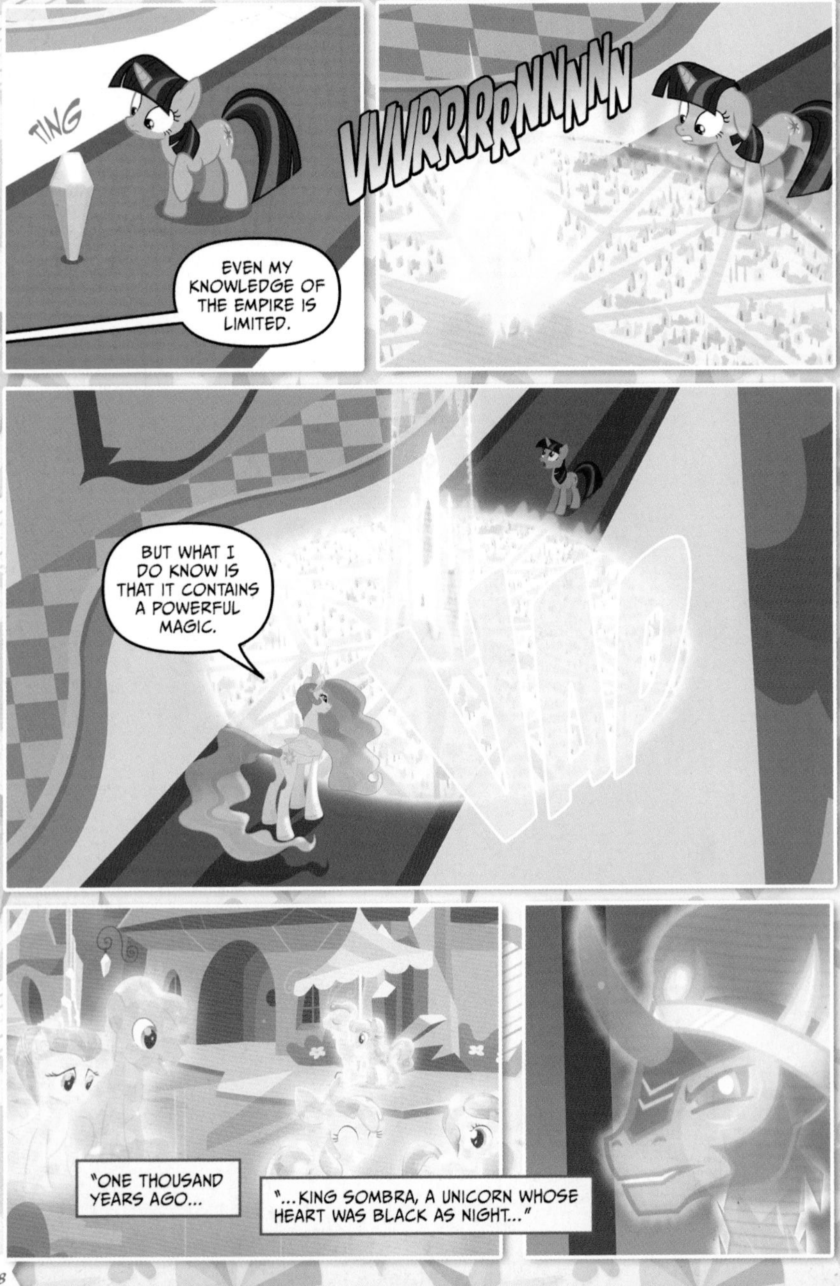
TING
EVEN MY KNOWLEDGE OF THE EMPIRE IS LIMITED.
VVVRRRRNNNNN
BUT WHAT I DO KNOW IS THAT IT CONTAINS A POWERFUL MAGIC.
"ONE THOUSAND YEARS AGO...
"...KING SOMBRA, A UNICORN WHOSE HEART WAS BLACK AS NIGHT..."

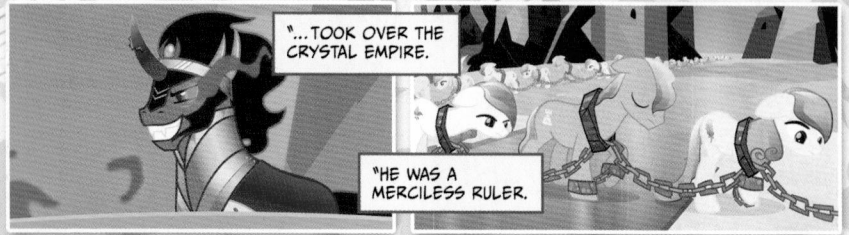

"...TOOK OVER THE CRYSTAL EMPIRE.

"HE WAS A MERCILESS RULER.

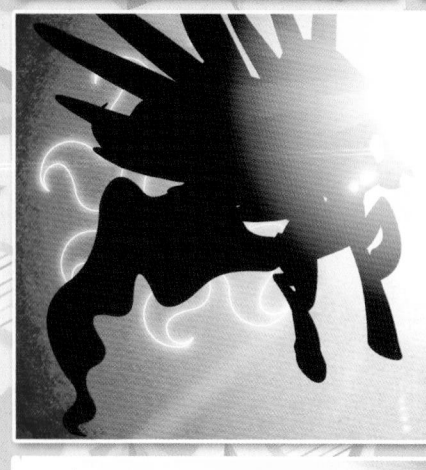

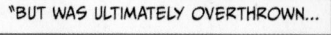

"BUT WAS ULTIMATELY OVERTHROWN...

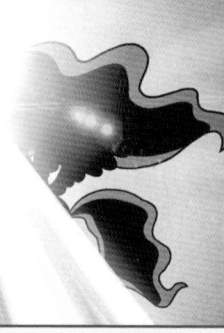

"...TURNED TO SHADOW...

"...AND BANISHED TO THE ICE OF THE ARCTIC NORTH."

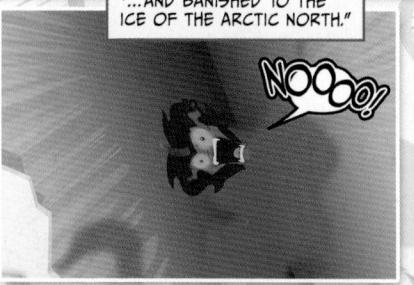

NOOOO!

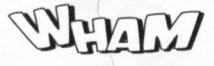

WHAM

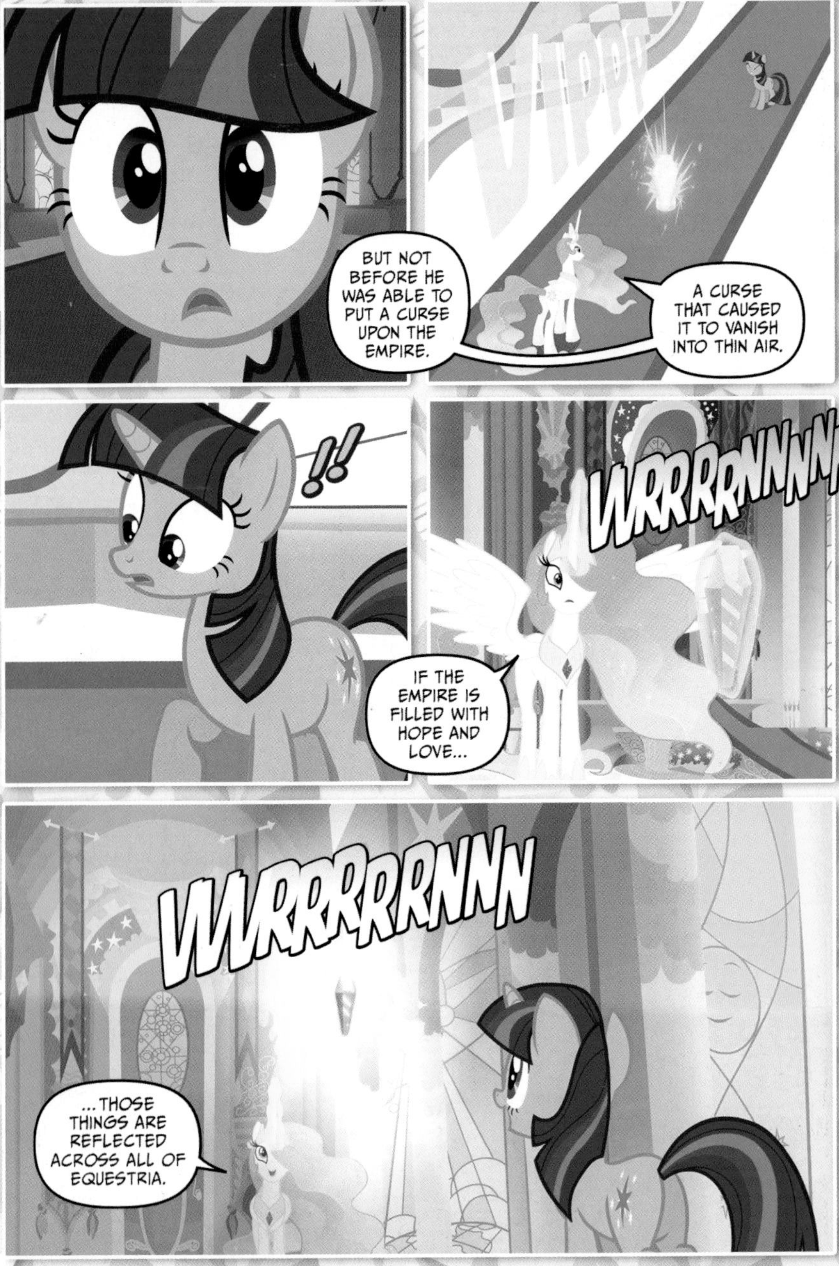
VIPPP
BUT NOT BEFORE HE WAS ABLE TO PUT A CURSE UPON THE EMPIRE.
A CURSE THAT CAUSED IT TO VANISH INTO THIN AIR.
!!
VVRRRRNNNN
IF THE EMPIRE IS FILLED WITH HOPE AND LOVE...
VVRRRRNNN
...THOSE THINGS ARE REFLECTED ACROSS ALL OF EQUESTRIA.

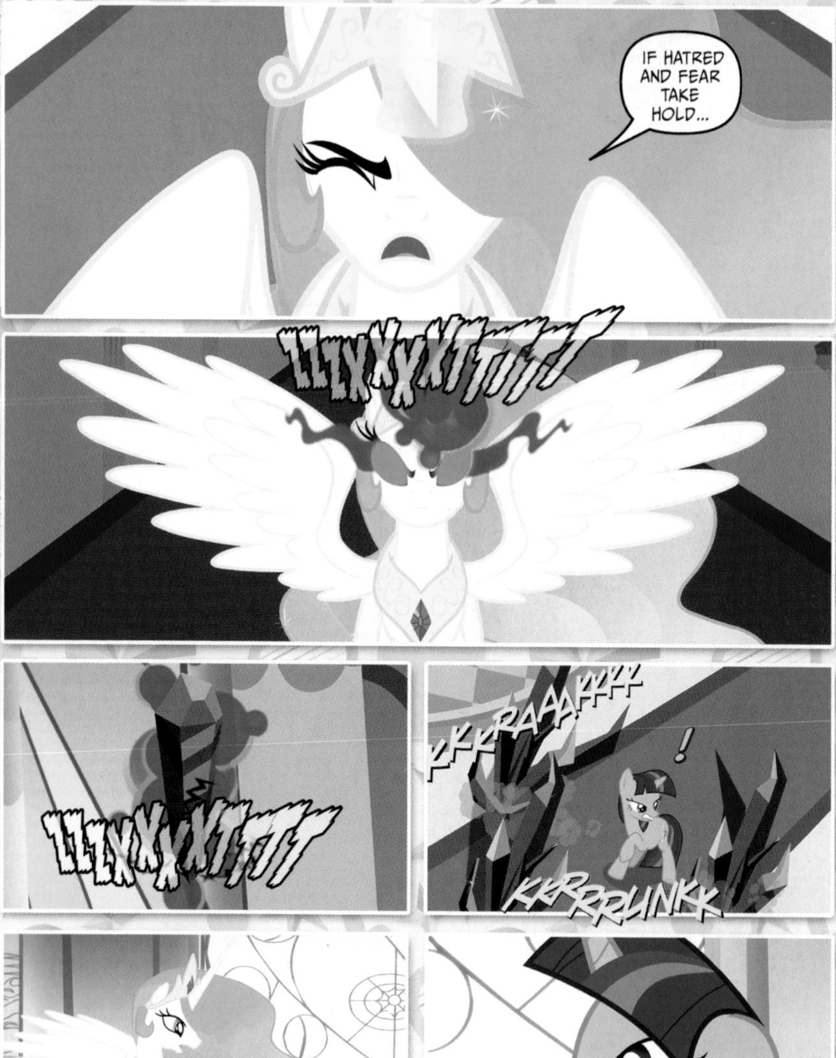
IF HATRED AND FEAR TAKE HOLD...
ZZZXXXXTTTTT
ZZZXXXXTTTTT
KKKRAAAKKKK
!
KKRRRRUNKK
WHICH IS WHY I NEED YOUR HELP FINDING A WAY TO PROTECT IT.
YOU WANT ME TO HELP PROTECT AN ENTIRE EMPIRE?

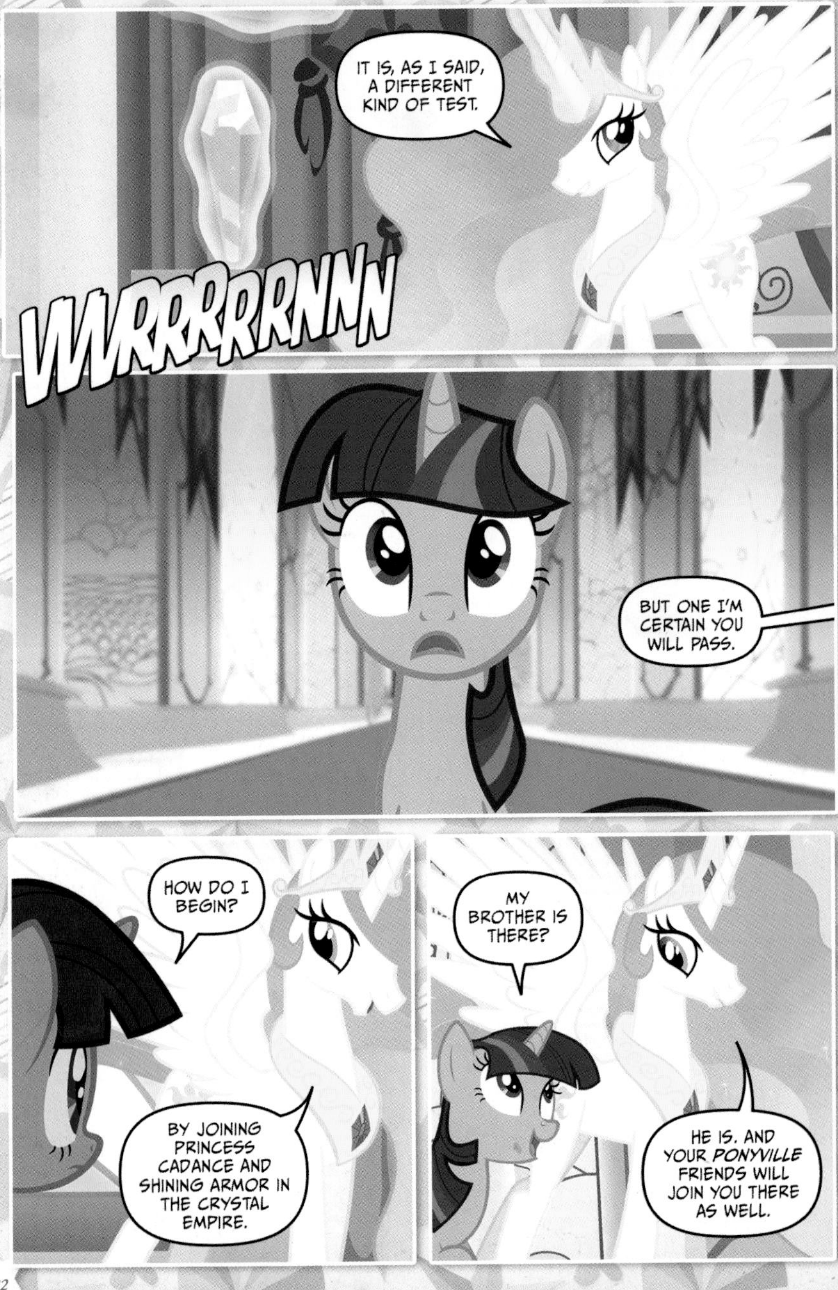
IT IS, AS I SAID, A DIFFERENT KIND OF TEST.
VWRRRRRNNN
BUT ONE I'M CERTAIN YOU WILL PASS.
HOW DO I BEGIN?
BY JOINING PRINCESS CADANCE AND SHINING ARMOR IN THE CRYSTAL EMPIRE.
MY BROTHER IS THERE?
HE IS. AND YOUR *PONYVILLE* FRIENDS WILL JOIN YOU THERE AS WELL.

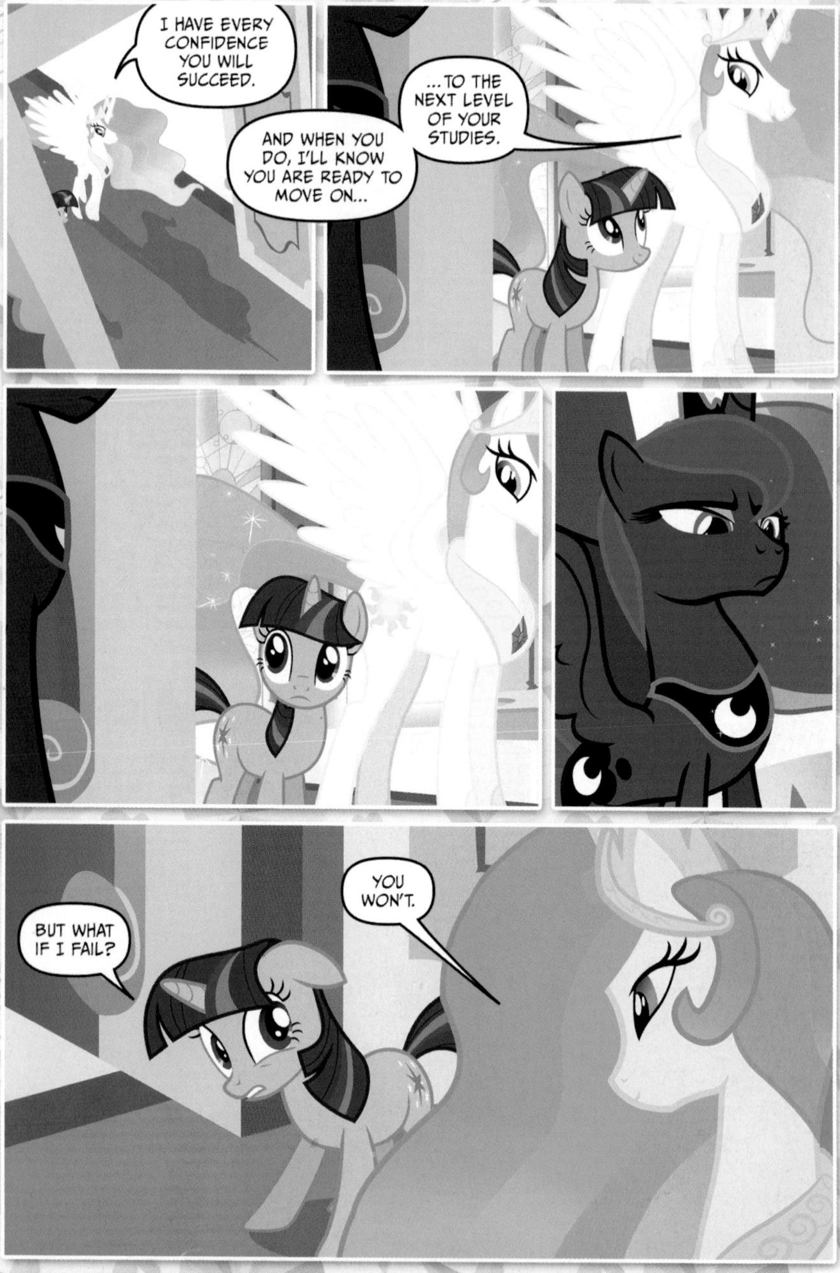
I HAVE EVERY CONFIDENCE YOU WILL SUCCEED.
AND WHEN YOU DO, I'LL KNOW YOU ARE READY TO MOVE ON...
...TO THE NEXT LEVEL OF YOUR STUDIES.
BUT WHAT IF I FAIL?
YOU WON'T.

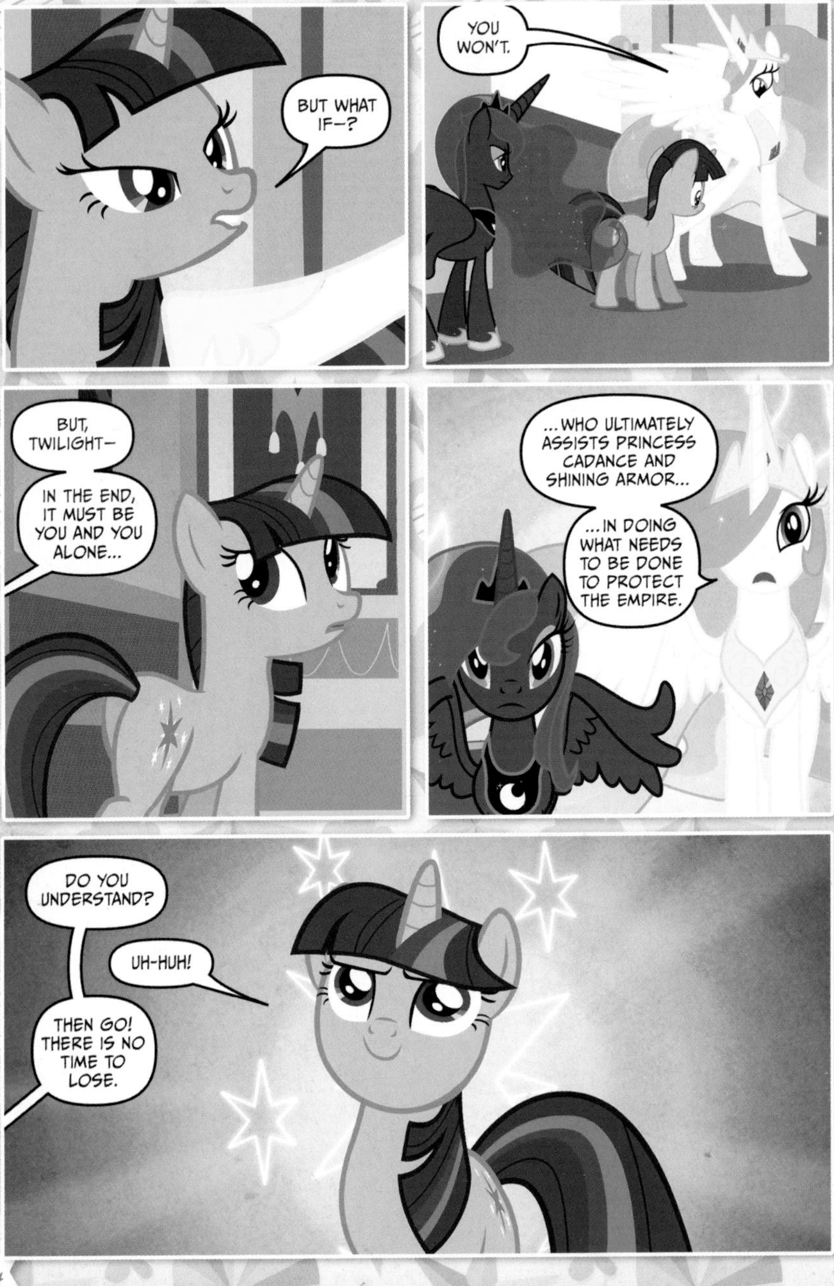
BUT WHAT IF–?
YOU WON'T.
BUT, TWILIGHT–
IN THE END, IT MUST BE YOU AND YOU ALONE...
...WHO ULTIMATELY ASSISTS PRINCESS CADANCE AND SHINING ARMOR...
...IN DOING WHAT NEEDS TO BE DONE TO PROTECT THE EMPIRE.
DO YOU UNDERSTAND?
UH-HUH!
THEN GO! THERE IS NO TIME TO LOSE.

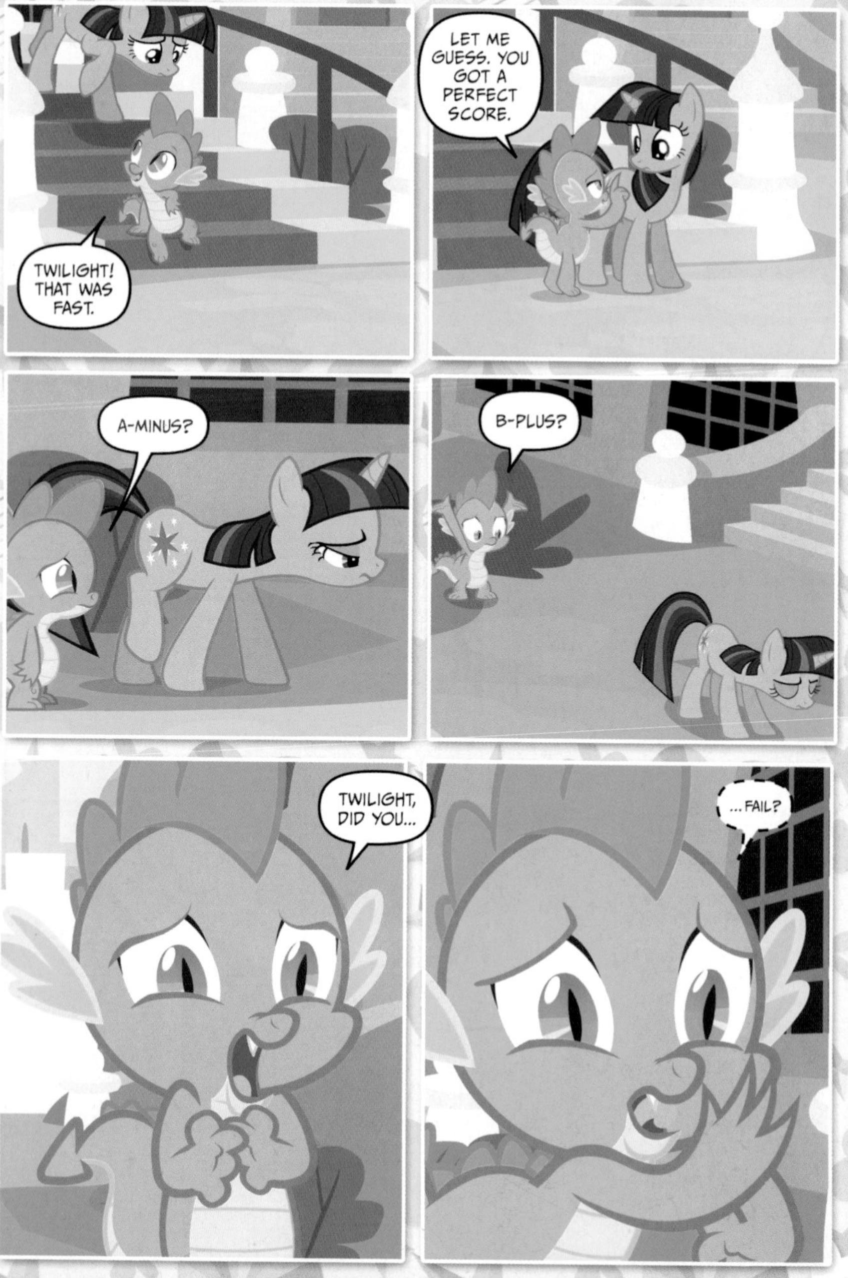
TWILIGHT! THAT WAS FAST.
LET ME GUESS. YOU GOT A PERFECT SCORE.
A-MINUS?
B-PLUS?
TWILIGHT, DID YOU...
...FAIL?

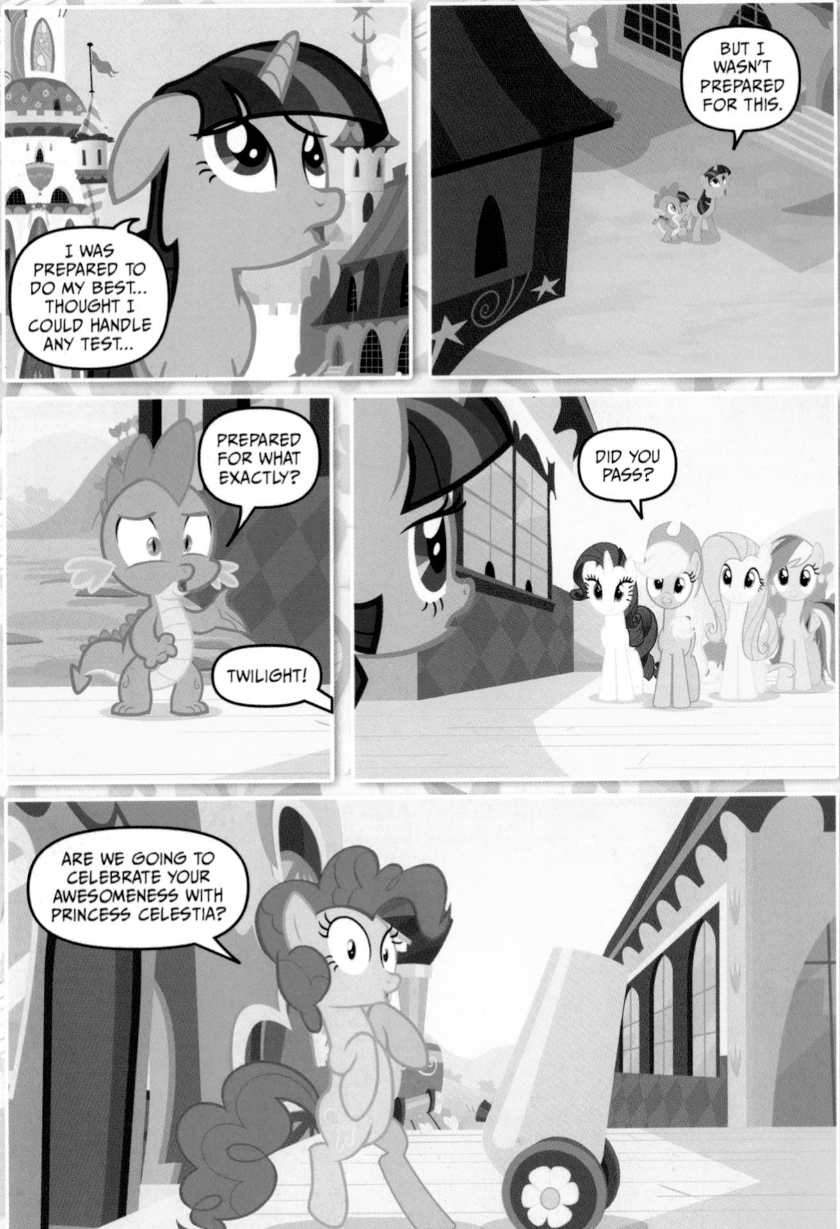
I WAS PREPARED TO DO MY BEST... THOUGHT I COULD HANDLE ANY TEST...
BUT I WASN'T PREPARED FOR THIS.
TWILIGHT!
PREPARED FOR WHAT EXACTLY?
DID YOU PASS?
ARE WE GOING TO CELEBRATE YOUR AWESOMENESS WITH PRINCESS CELESTIA?

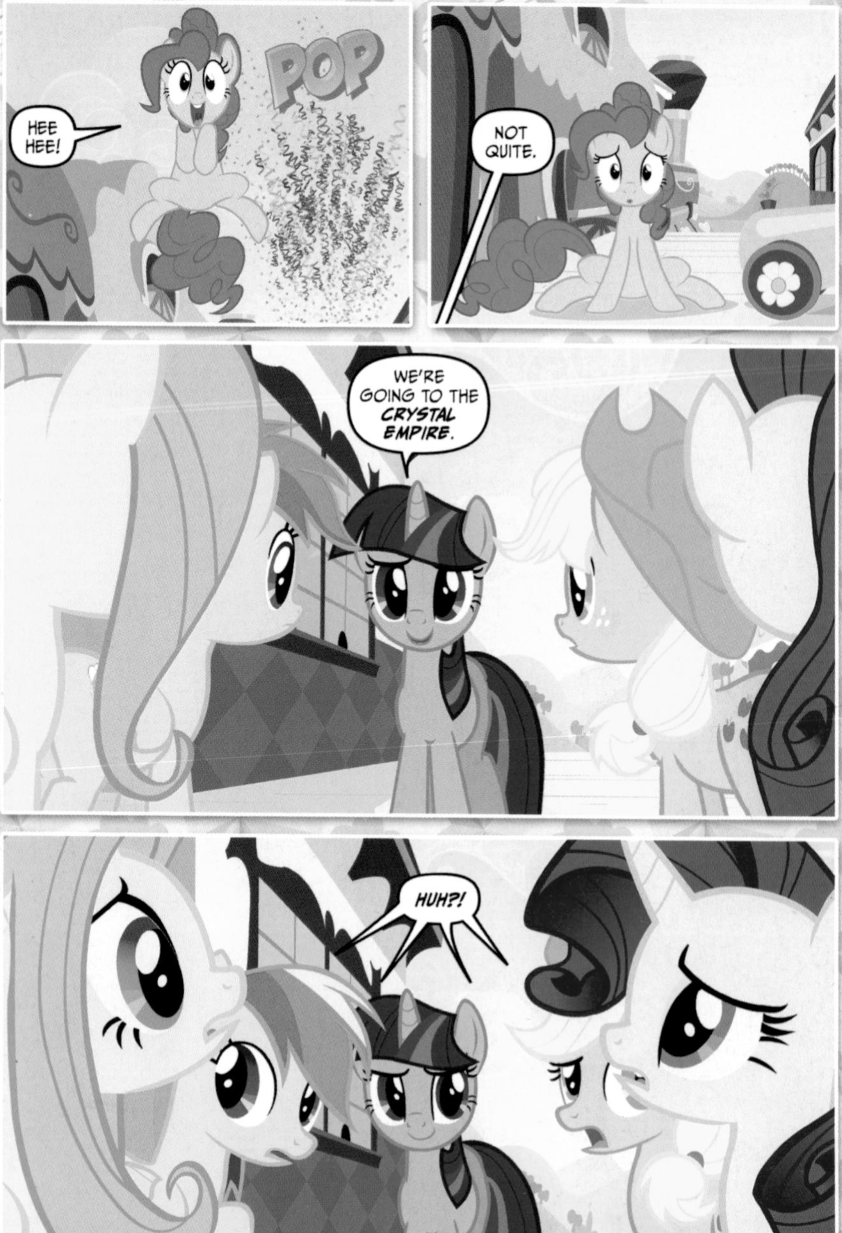
HEE HEE!
POP
NOT QUITE.
WE'RE GOING TO THE CRYSTAL EMPIRE.
HUH?!

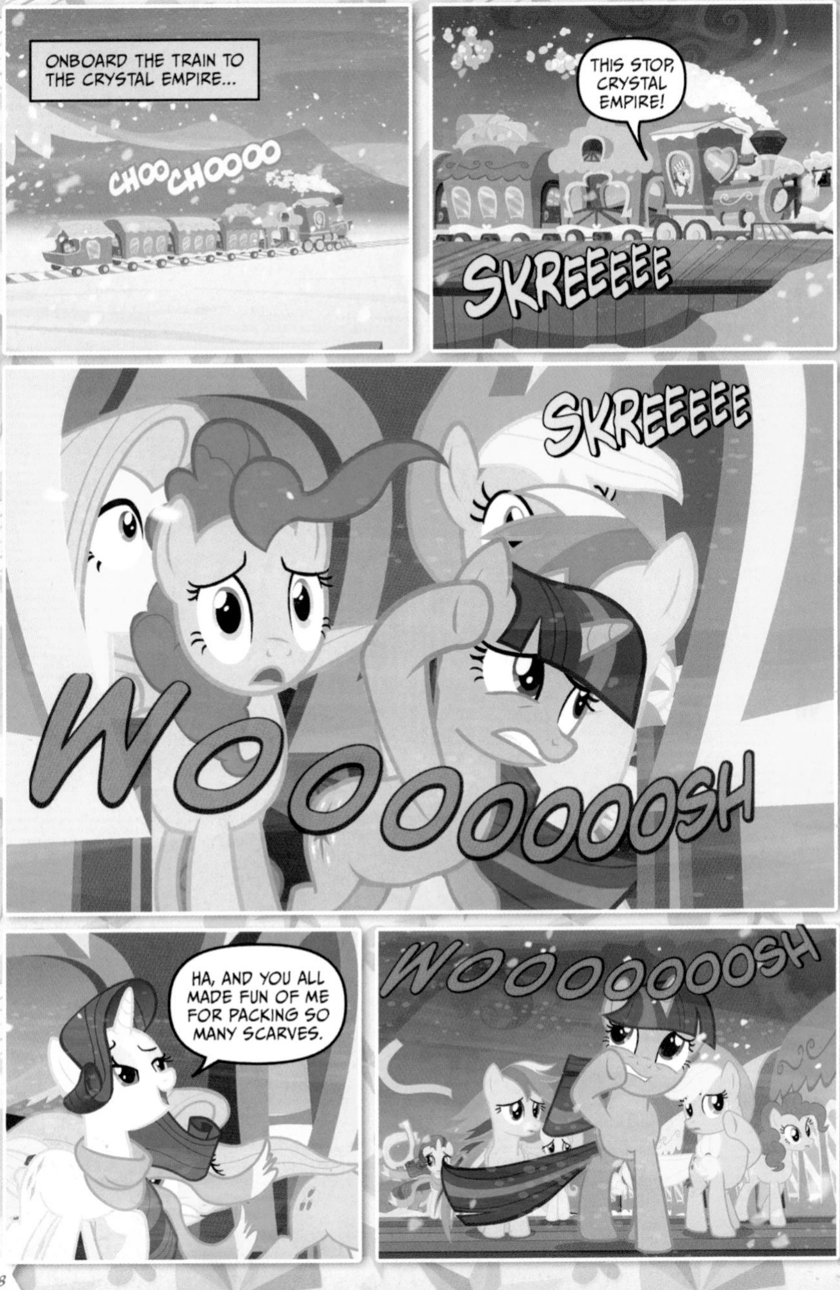
ONBOARD THE TRAIN TO THE CRYSTAL EMPIRE...
CHOOCHOOOO
THIS STOP, CRYSTAL EMPIRE!
SKREEEEE
SKREEEEE
WOOOOOOOSH
HA, AND YOU ALL MADE FUN OF ME FOR PACKING SO MANY SCARVES.
WOOOOOOOOSH

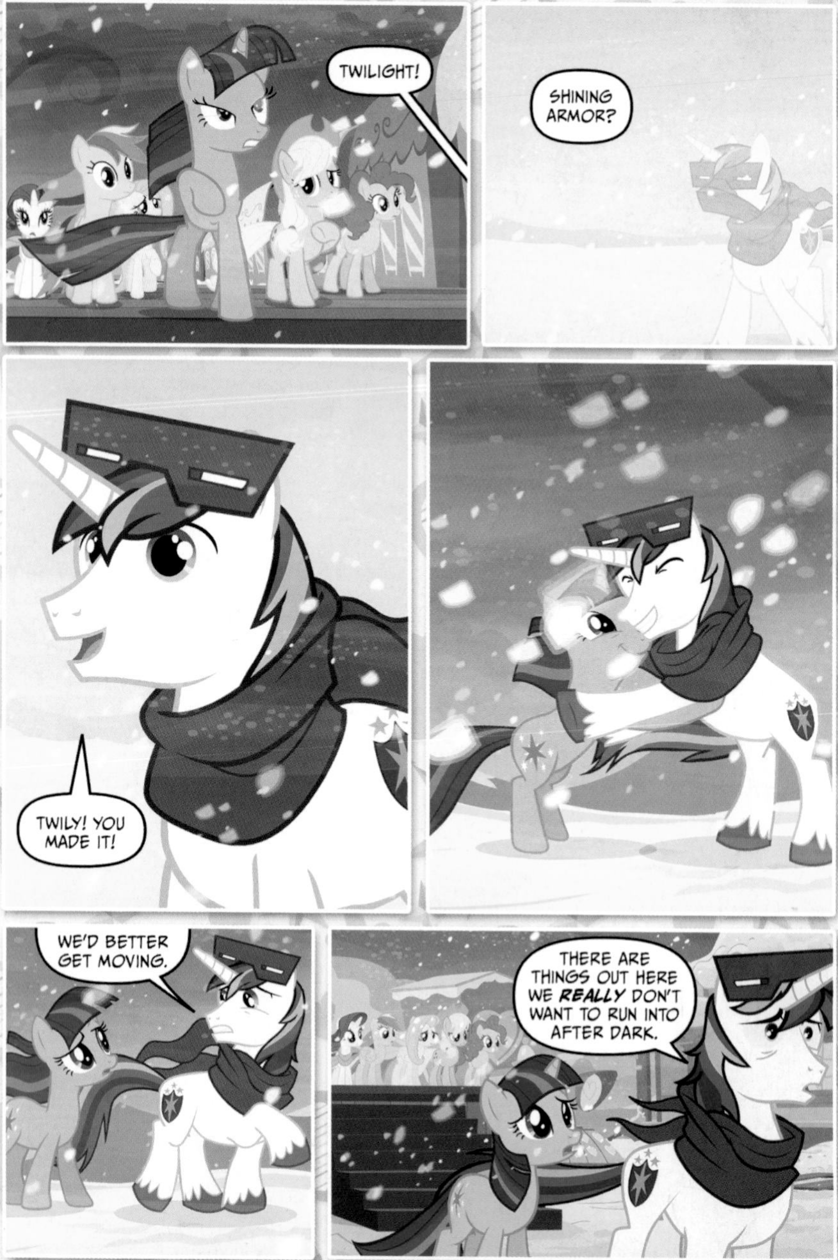
TWILIGHT!
SHINING ARMOR?
TWILY! YOU MADE IT!
WE'D BETTER GET MOVING.
THERE ARE THINGS OUT HERE WE **REALLY** DON'T WANT TO RUN INTO AFTER DARK.

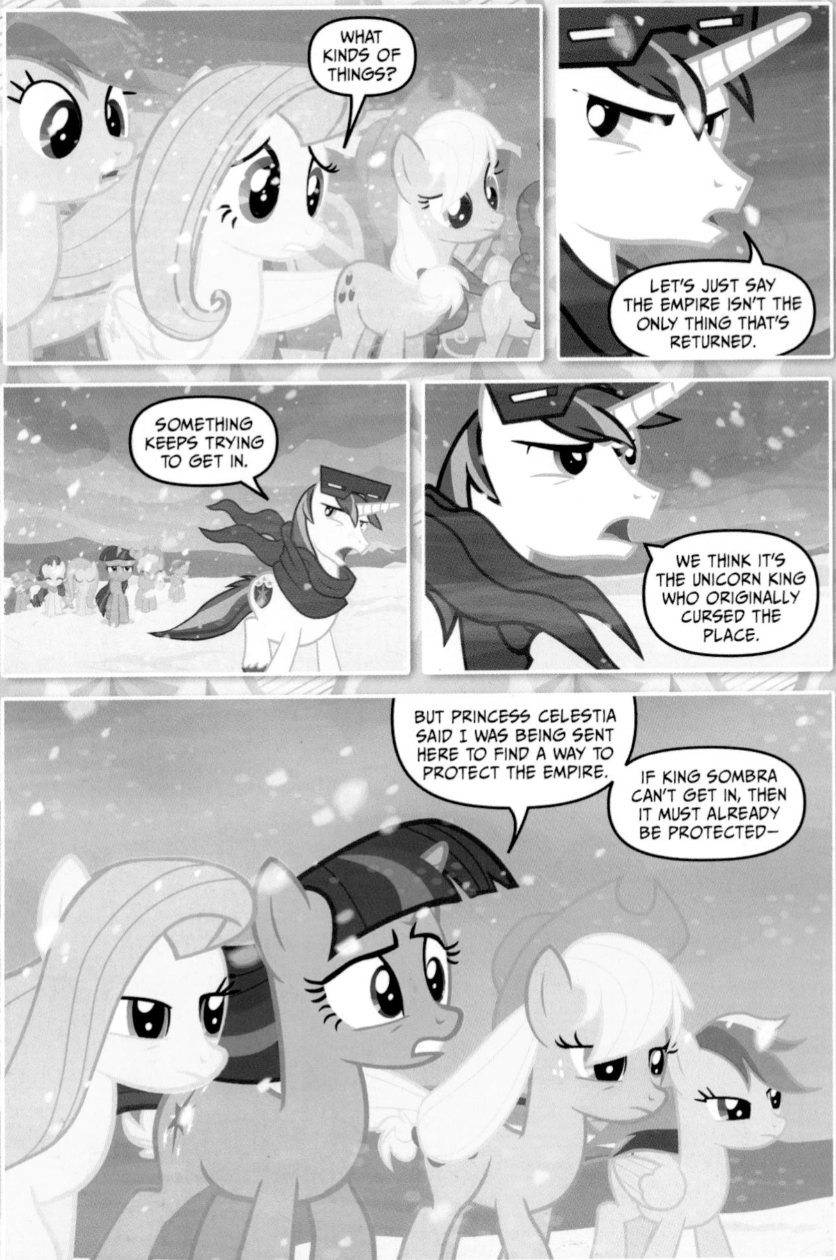
WHAT KINDS OF THINGS?
LET'S JUST SAY THE EMPIRE ISN'T THE ONLY THING THAT'S RETURNED.
SOMETHING KEEPS TRYING TO GET IN.
WE THINK IT'S THE UNICORN KING WHO ORIGINALLY CURSED THE PLACE.
BUT PRINCESS CELESTIA SAID I WAS BEING SENT HERE TO FIND A WAY TO PROTECT THE EMPIRE.
IF KING SOMBRA CAN'T GET IN, THEN IT MUST ALREADY BE PROTECTED—

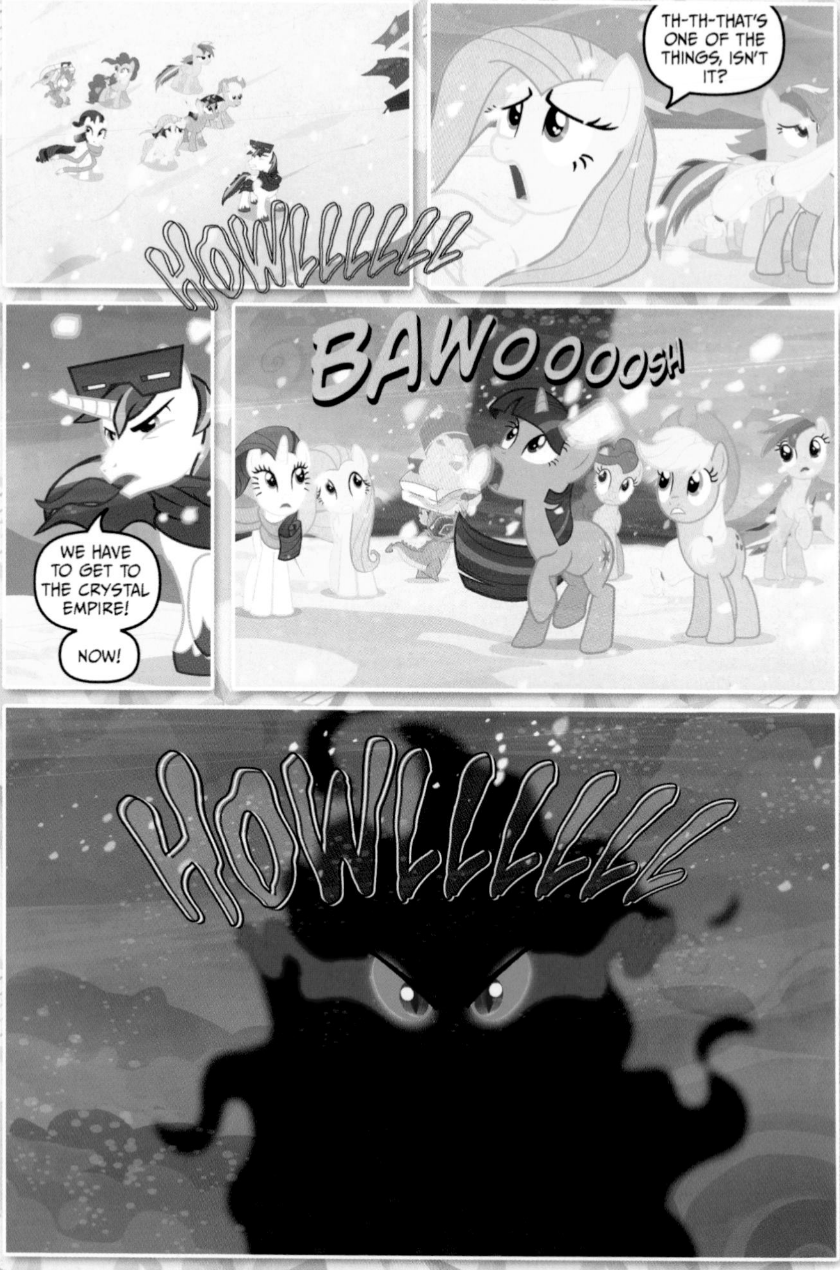
HOWLLLLLL
TH-TH-THAT'S ONE OF THE THINGS, ISN'T IT?
WE HAVE TO GET TO THE CRYSTAL EMPIRE!
NOW!
BAWOOOOOSH
HOWLLLLLLL

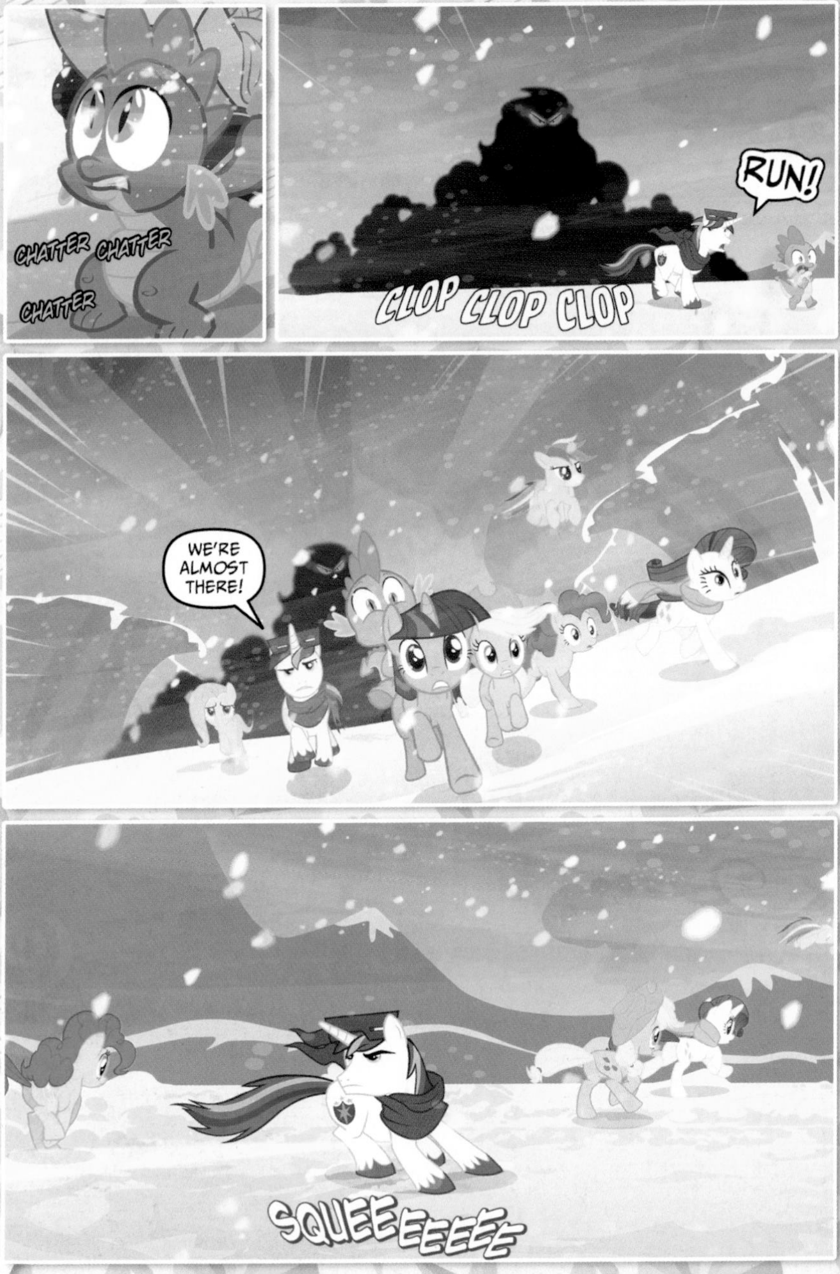
CHATTER CHATTER
CHATTER
CLOP CLOP CLOP
RUN!
WE'RE ALMOST THERE!
SQUEEEEEEEE

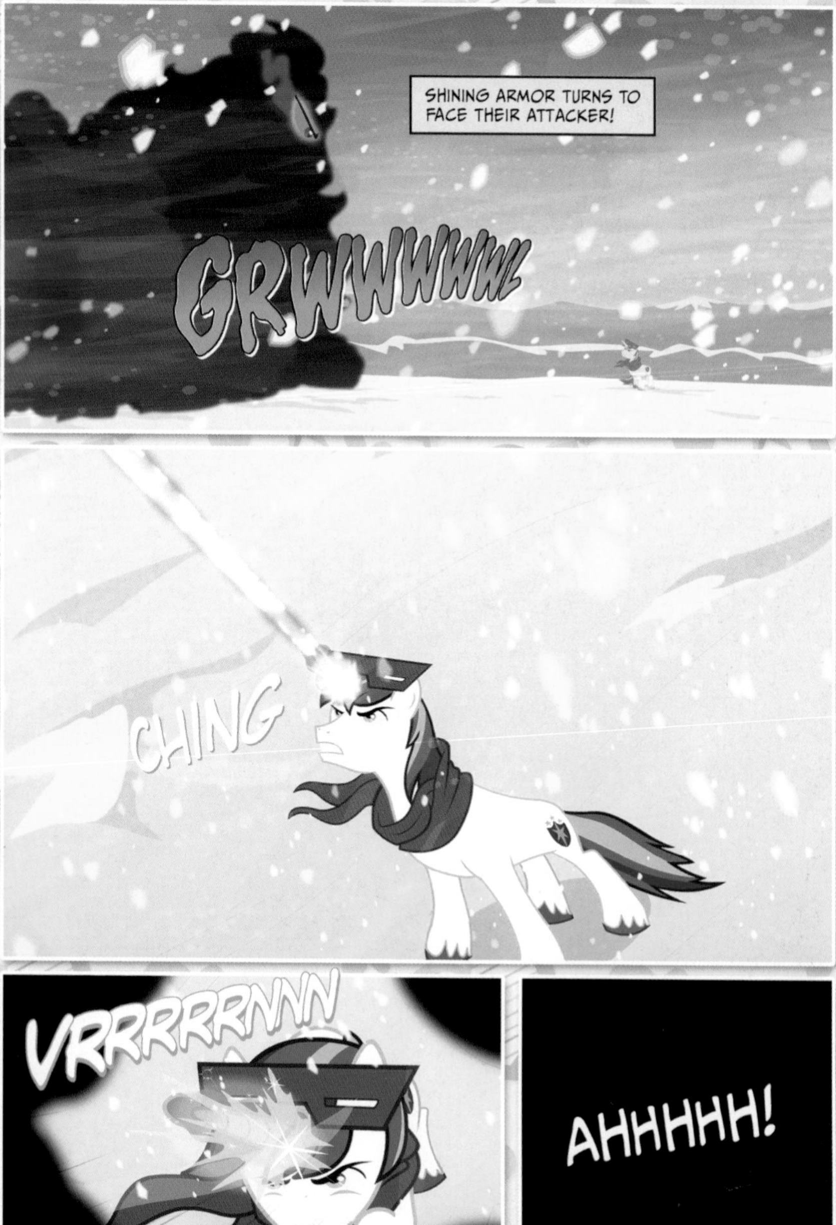
SHINING ARMOR TURNS TO FACE THEIR ATTACKER!
GRWWWWWL
CHING
VRRRRRNNN
AHHHHH!

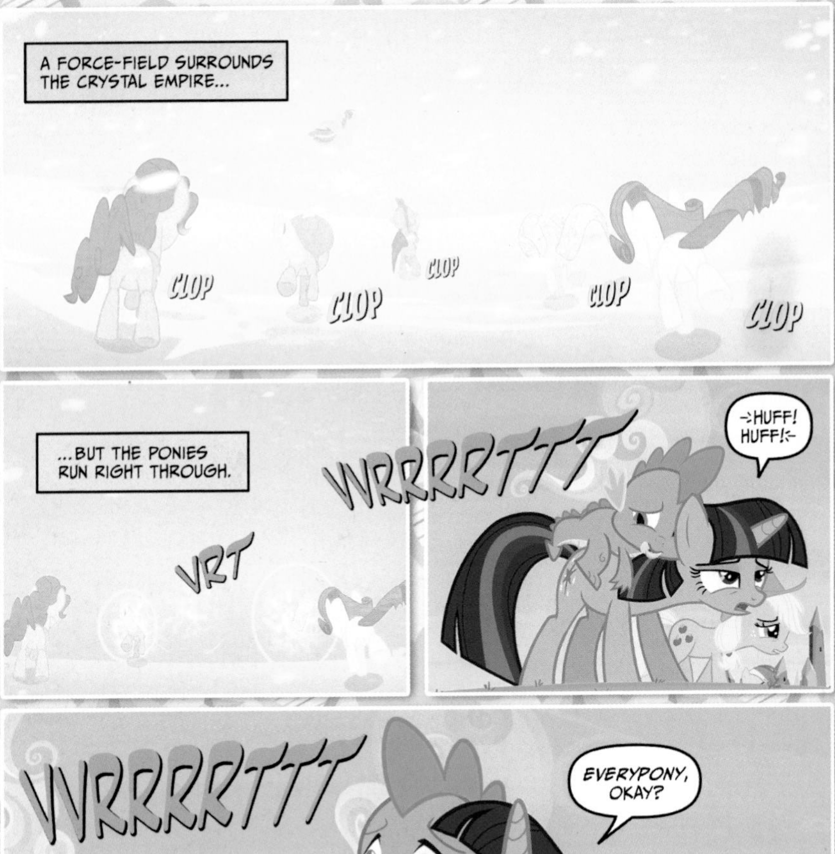
A FORCE-FIELD SURROUNDS THE CRYSTAL EMPIRE...
CLOP
CLOP
CLOP
CLOP
CLOP
...BUT THE PONIES RUN RIGHT THROUGH.
VRT
VVRRRRTTTT
-›HUFF! HUFF!‹-
VVRRRRTTTT
EVERYPONY, OKAY?
I—I THINK SO.

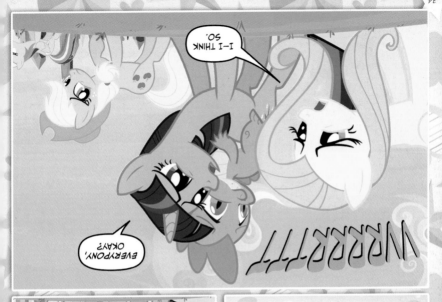

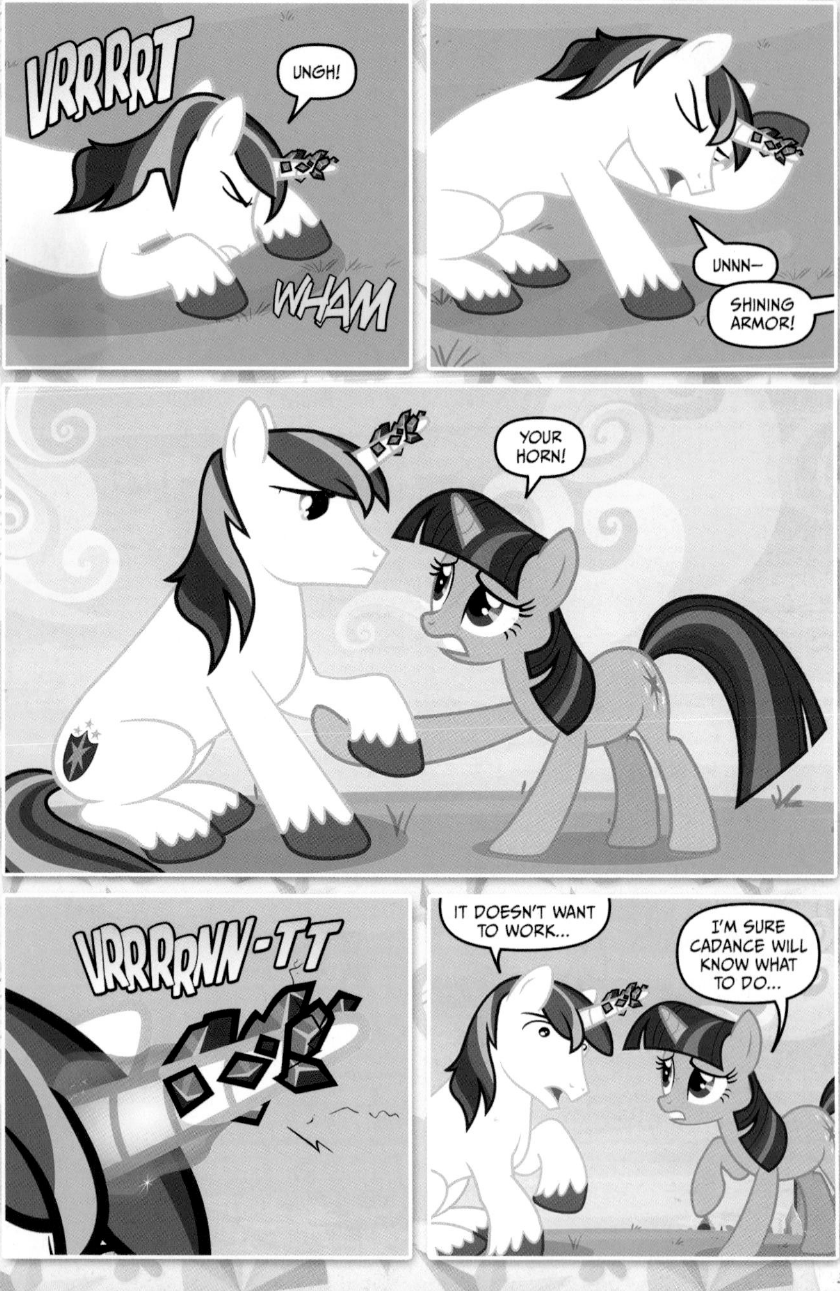
VRRRRT
UNGH!
WHAM
UNNN—
SHINING ARMOR!
YOUR HORN!
VRRRRNN-TT
IT DOESN'T WANT TO WORK...
I'M SURE CADANCE WILL KNOW WHAT TO DO...

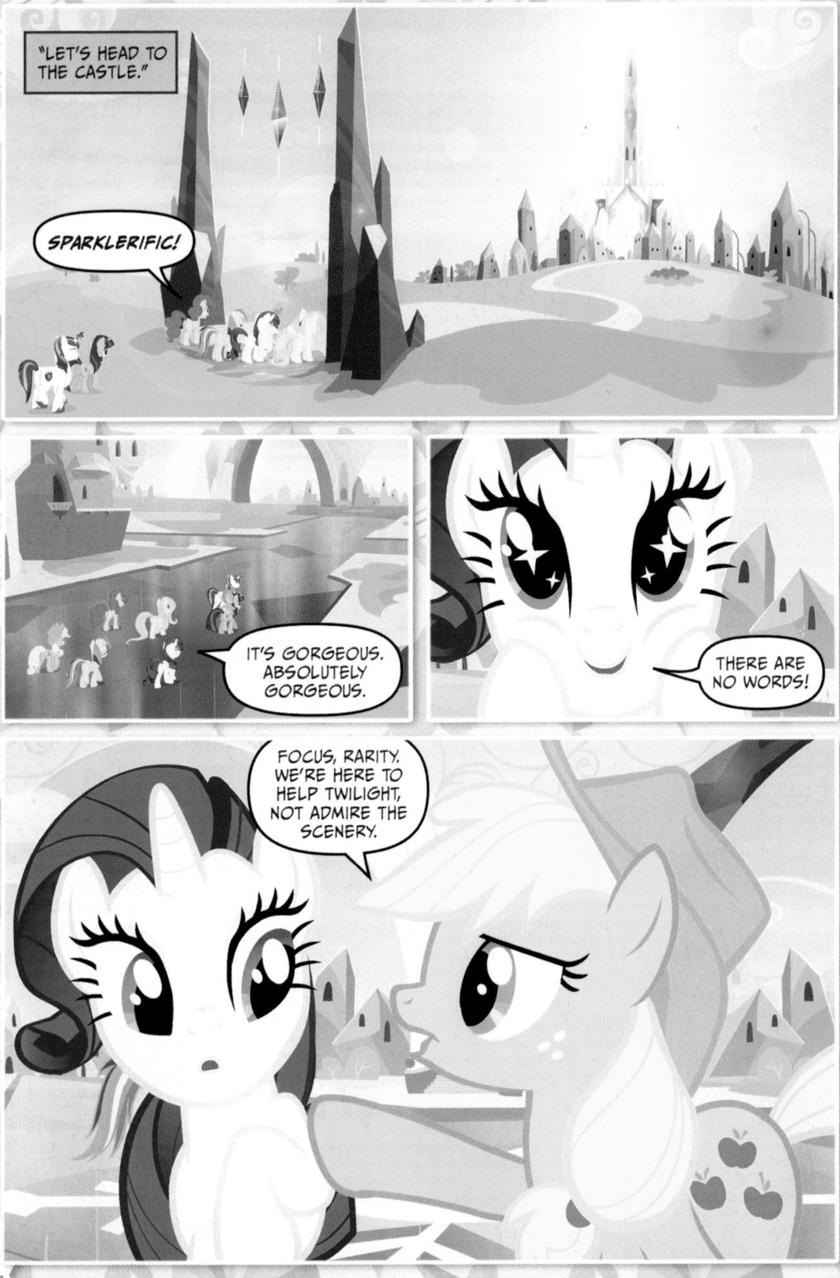
"LET'S HEAD TO THE CASTLE."
SPARKLERIFIC!
IT'S GORGEOUS. ABSOLUTELY GORGEOUS.
THERE ARE NO WORDS!
FOCUS, RARITY. WE'RE HERE TO HELP TWILIGHT, NOT ADMIRE THE SCENERY.

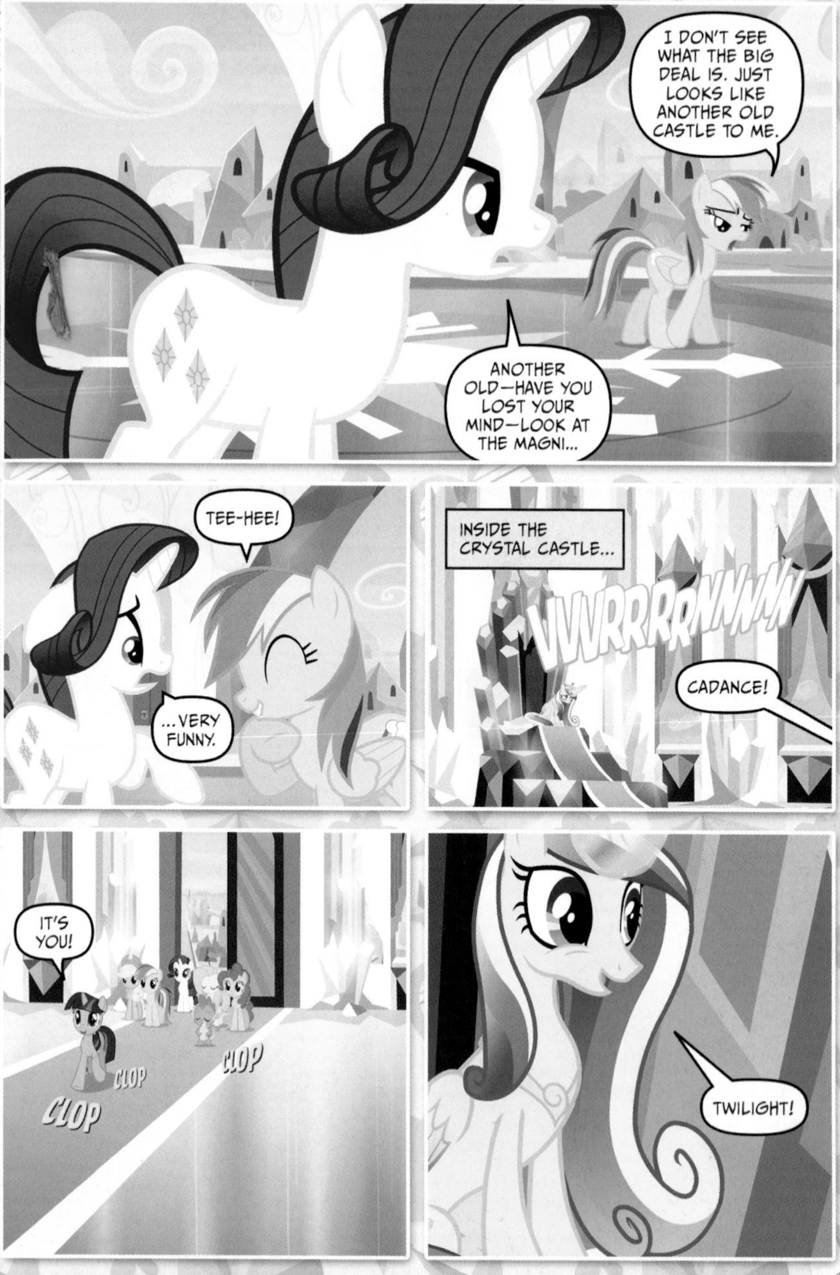
I DON'T SEE WHAT THE BIG DEAL IS. JUST LOOKS LIKE ANOTHER OLD CASTLE TO ME.
ANOTHER OLD—HAVE YOU LOST YOUR MIND—LOOK AT THE MAGNI...
TEE-HEE!
...VERY FUNNY.
INSIDE THE CRYSTAL CASTLE...
VVVRRRRNNNNN
CADANCE!
IT'S YOU!
CLOP
CLOP
CLOP
TWILIGHT!

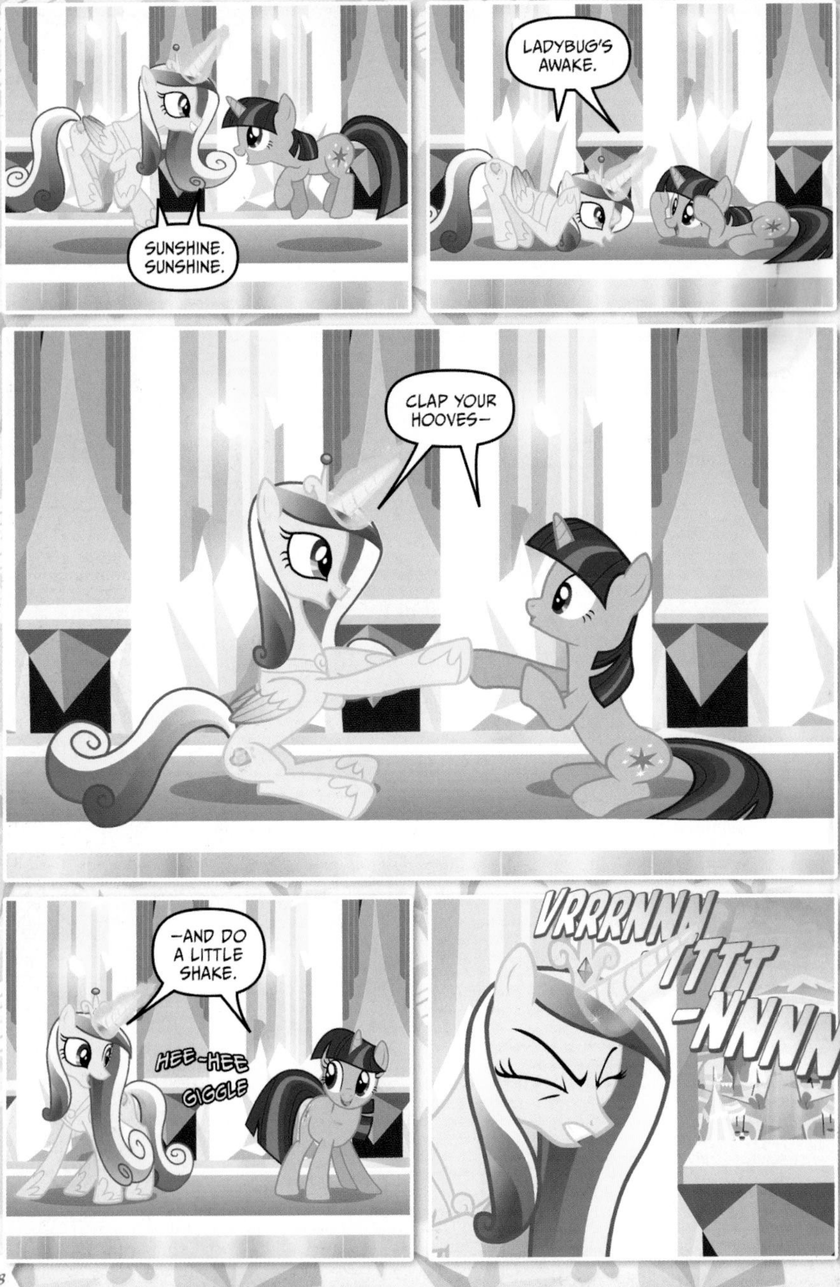
SUNSHINE. SUNSHINE.
LADYBUG'S AWAKE.
CLAP YOUR HOOVES—
—AND DO A LITTLE SHAKE.
HEE-HEE
GIGGLE
VRRRNNN ITTT -NNNN

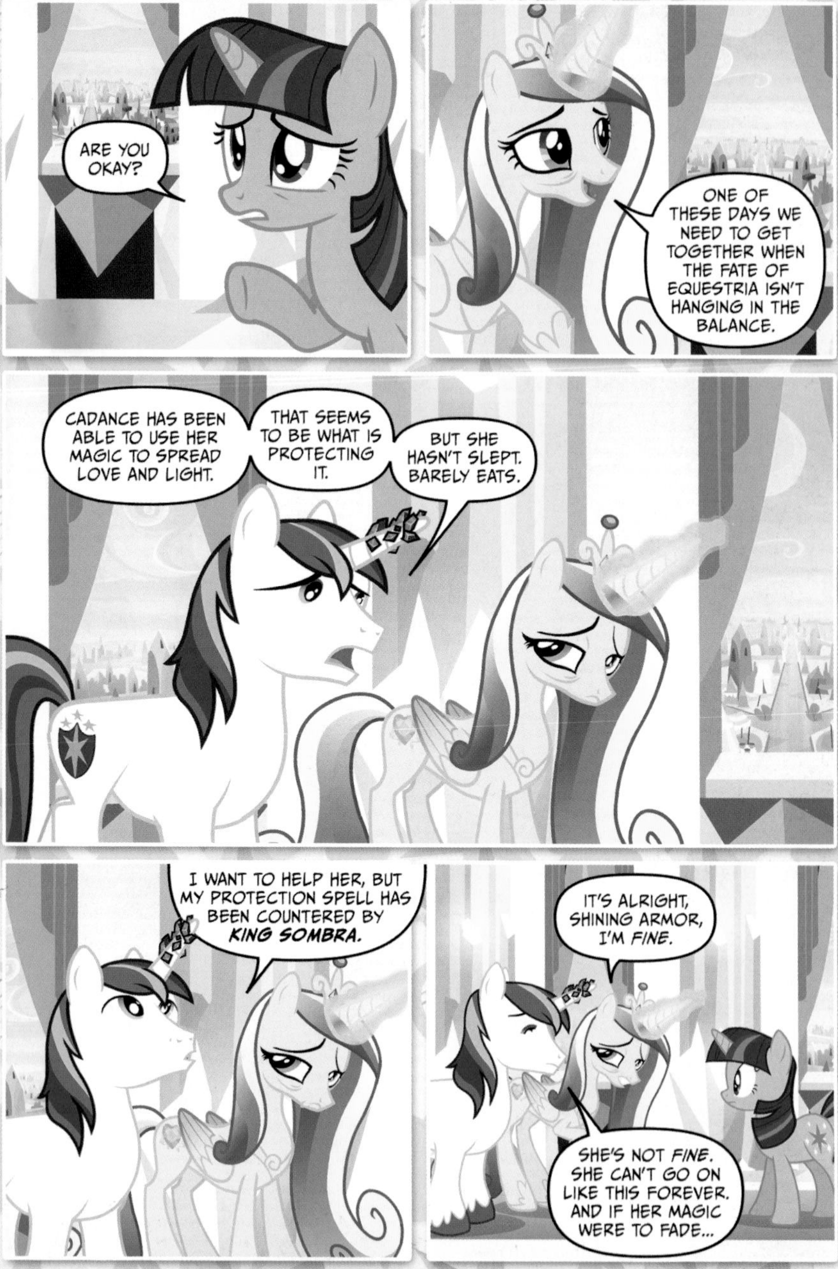

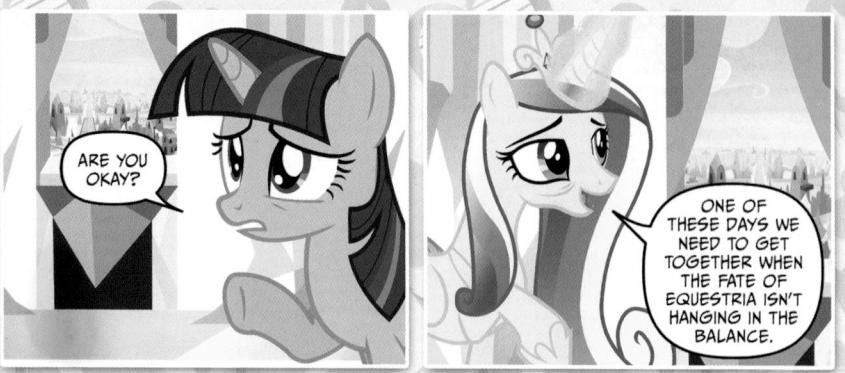

ARE YOU OKAY?

ONE OF THESE DAYS WE NEED TO GET TOGETHER WHEN THE FATE OF EQUESTRIA ISN'T HANGING IN THE BALANCE.

CADANCE HAS BEEN ABLE TO USE HER MAGIC TO SPREAD LOVE AND LIGHT.

THAT SEEMS TO BE WHAT IS PROTECTING IT.

BUT SHE HASN'T SLEPT. BARELY EATS.

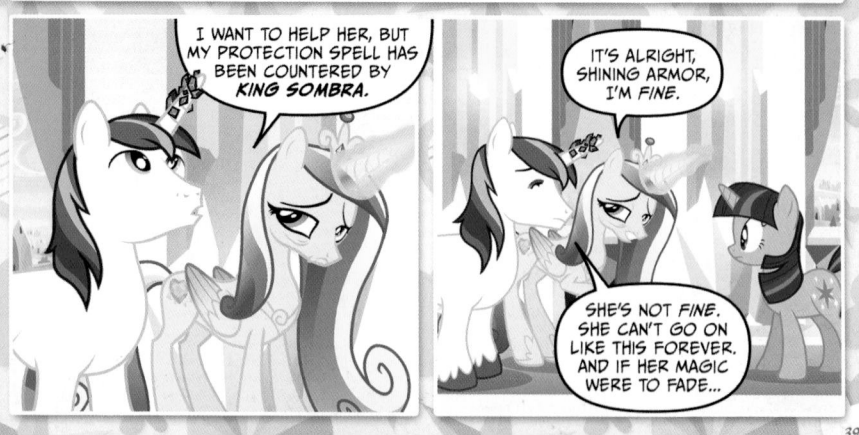

I WANT TO HELP HER, BUT MY PROTECTION SPELL HAS BEEN COUNTERED BY *KING SOMBRA.*

IT'S ALRIGHT, SHINING ARMOR, I'M *FINE.*

SHE'S NOT *FINE.* SHE CAN'T GO ON LIKE THIS FOREVER. AND IF HER MAGIC WERE TO FADE...

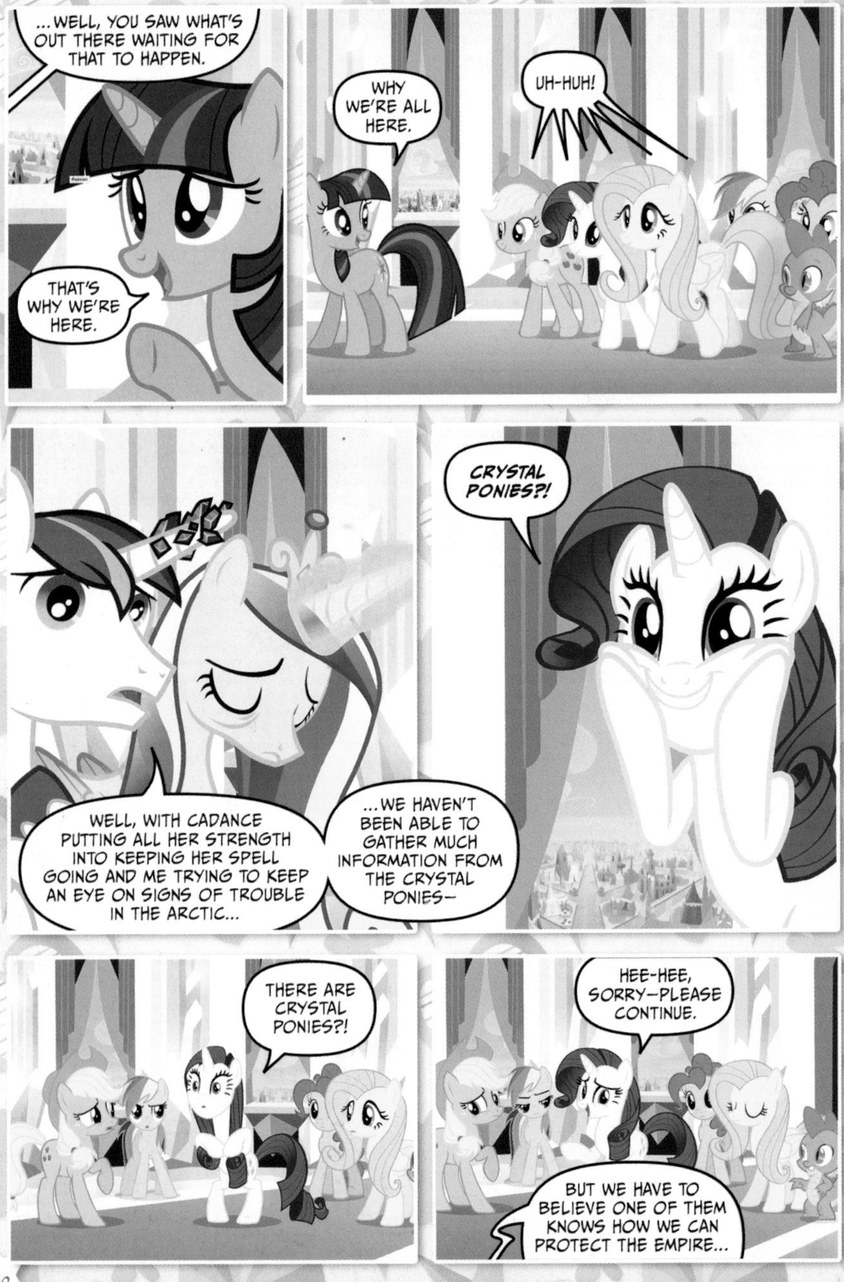
...WELL, YOU SAW WHAT'S OUT THERE WAITING FOR THAT TO HAPPEN.
THAT'S WHY WE'RE HERE.
WHY WE'RE ALL HERE.
UH-HUH!
WELL, WITH CADANCE PUTTING ALL HER STRENGTH INTO KEEPING HER SPELL GOING AND ME TRYING TO KEEP AN EYE ON SIGNS OF TROUBLE IN THE ARCTIC...
...WE HAVEN'T BEEN ABLE TO GATHER MUCH INFORMATION FROM THE CRYSTAL PONIES—
CRYSTAL PONIES?!
THERE ARE CRYSTAL PONIES?!
HEE-HEE, SORRY—PLEASE CONTINUE.
BUT WE HAVE TO BELIEVE ONE OF THEM KNOWS HOW WE CAN PROTECT THE EMPIRE...

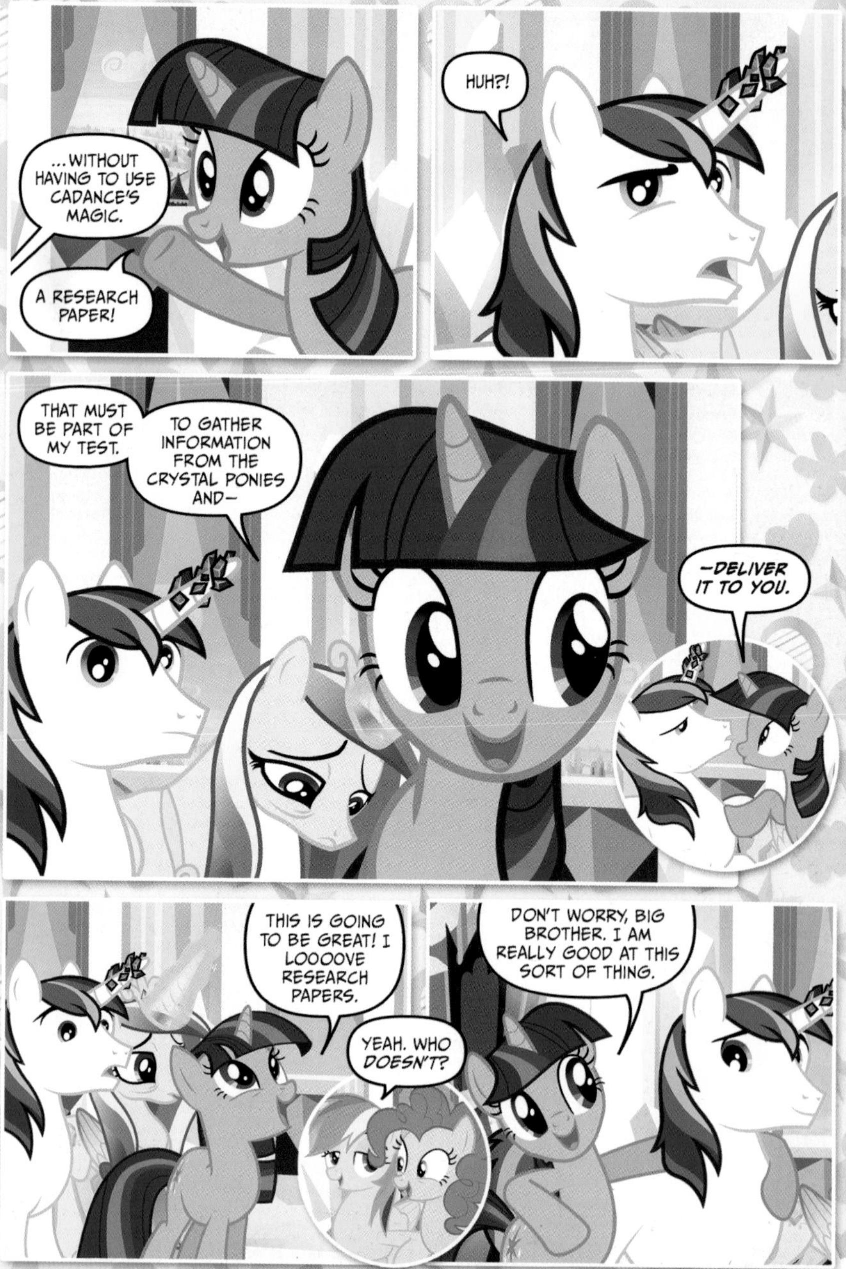
...WITHOUT HAVING TO USE CADANCE'S MAGIC.
A RESEARCH PAPER!
HUH?!
THAT MUST BE PART OF MY TEST.
TO GATHER INFORMATION FROM THE CRYSTAL PONIES AND—
—DELIVER IT TO YOU.
THIS IS GOING TO BE GREAT! I LOOOOVE RESEARCH PAPERS.
YEAH. WHO DOESN'T?
DON'T WORRY, BIG BROTHER. I AM REALLY GOOD AT THIS SORT OF THING.

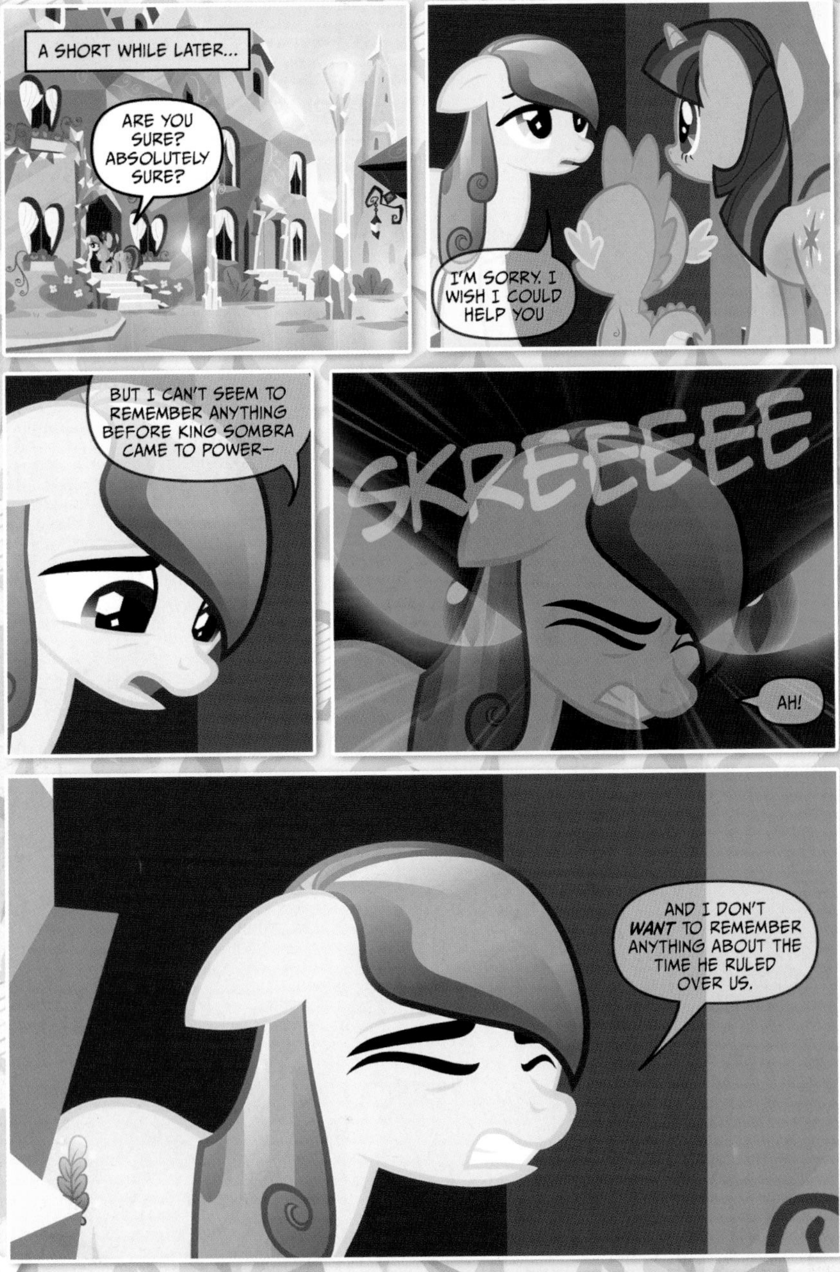
A SHORT WHILE LATER...
ARE YOU SURE? ABSOLUTELY SURE?
I'M SORRY. I WISH I COULD HELP YOU
BUT I CAN'T SEEM TO REMEMBER ANYTHING BEFORE KING SOMBRA CAME TO POWER–
SKREEEEEE
AH!
AND I DON'T *WANT* TO REMEMBER ANYTHING ABOUT THE TIME HE RULED OVER US.

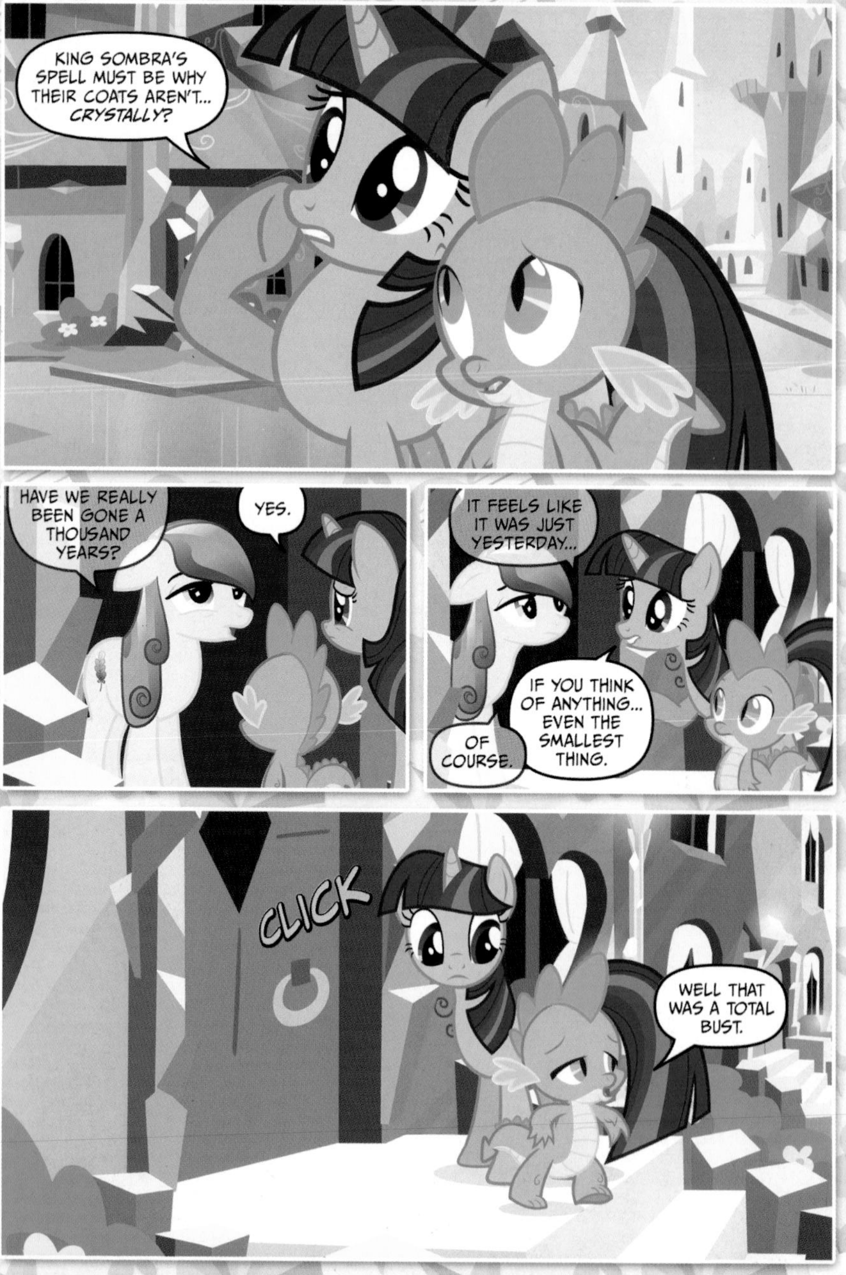
KING SOMBRA'S SPELL MUST BE WHY THEIR COATS AREN'T... *CRYSTALLY?*
HAVE WE REALLY BEEN GONE A THOUSAND YEARS?
YES.
IT FEELS LIKE IT WAS JUST YESTERDAY...
IF YOU THINK OF ANYTHING... EVEN THE SMALLEST THING.
OF COURSE.
CLICK
WELL THAT WAS A TOTAL BUST.

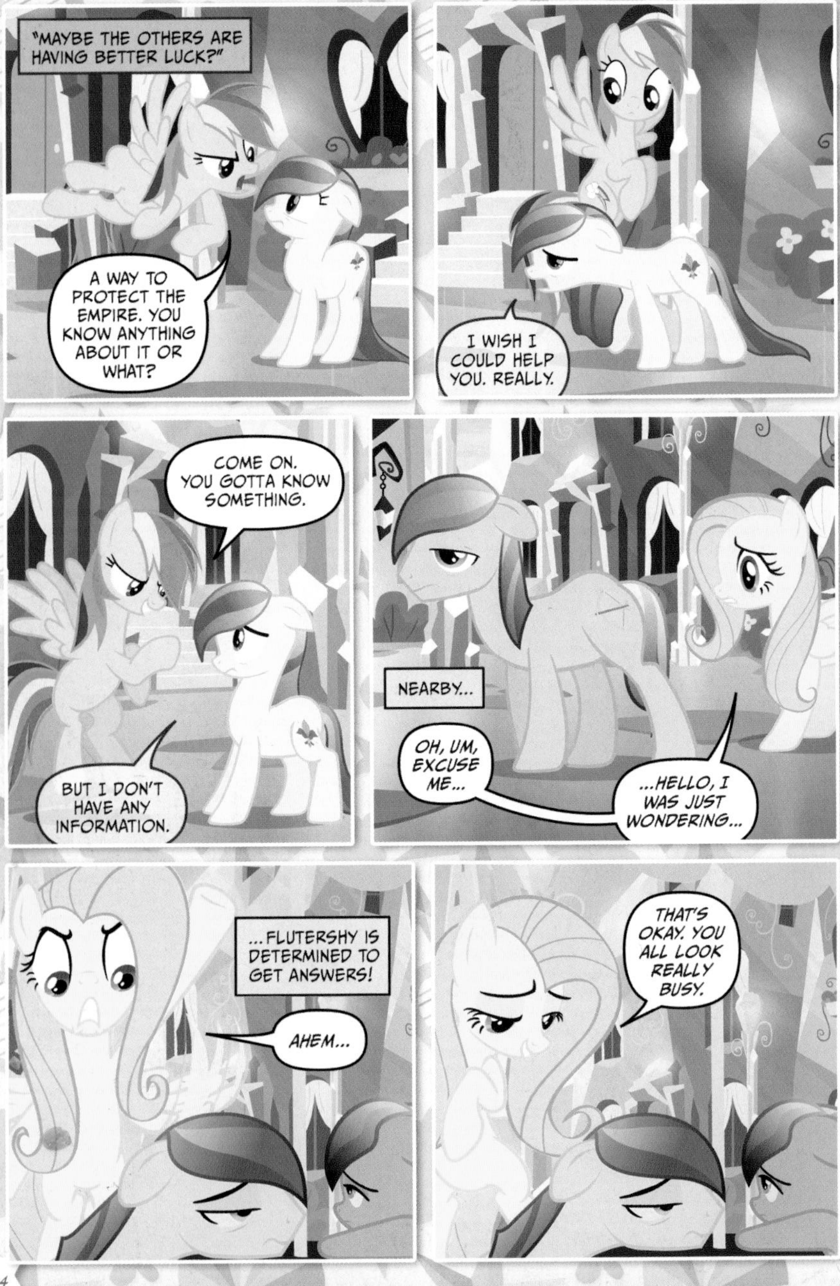
"MAYBE THE OTHERS ARE HAVING BETTER LUCK?"
A WAY TO PROTECT THE EMPIRE. YOU KNOW ANYTHING ABOUT IT OR WHAT?
I WISH I COULD HELP YOU. REALLY.
COME ON. YOU GOTTA KNOW SOMETHING.
BUT I DON'T HAVE ANY INFORMATION.
NEARBY...
OH, UM, EXCUSE ME...
...HELLO, I WAS JUST WONDERING...
...FLUTERSHY IS DETERMINED TO GET ANSWERS!
AHEM...
THAT'S OKAY. YOU ALL LOOK REALLY BUSY.

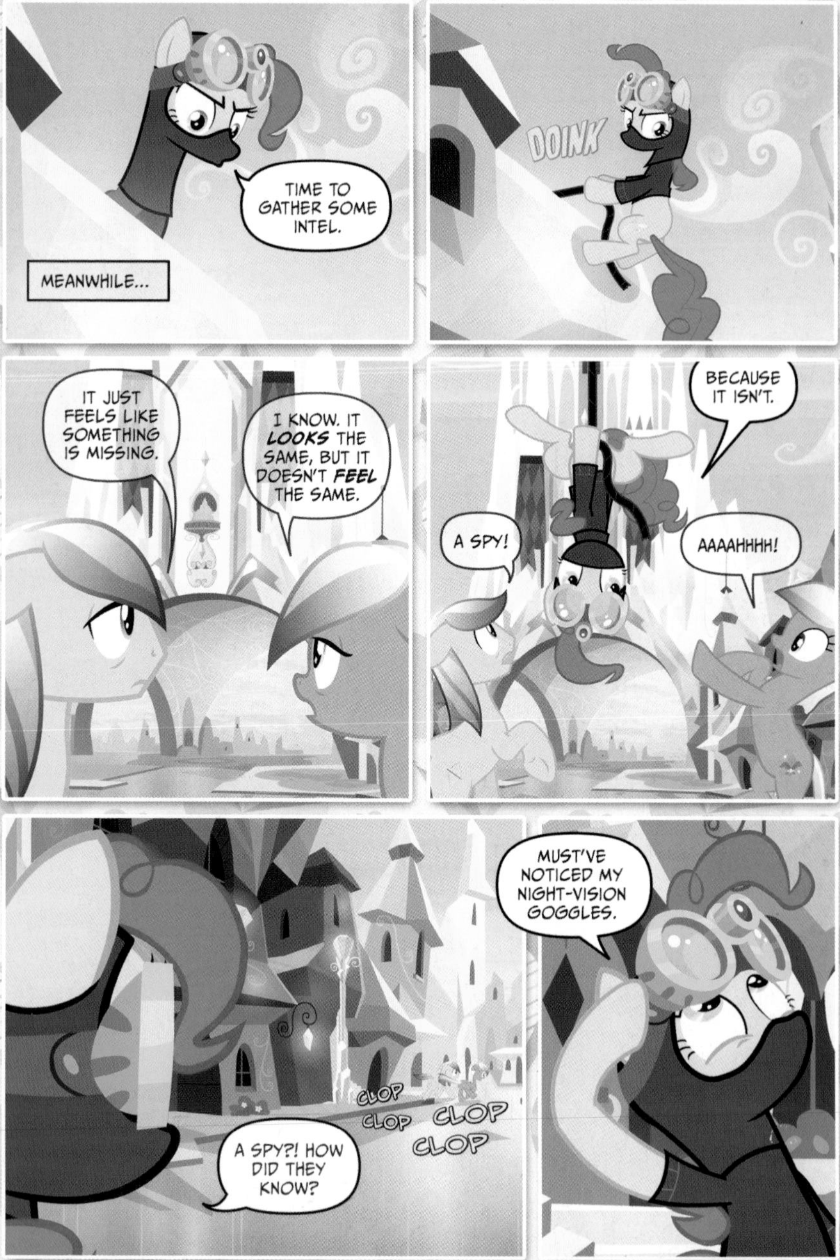

TIME TO GATHER SOME INTEL.
MEANWHILE...
DOINK
IT JUST FEELS LIKE SOMETHING IS MISSING.
I KNOW. IT **LOOKS** THE SAME, BUT IT DOESN'T **FEEL** THE SAME.
BECAUSE IT ISN'T.
A SPY!
AAAAHHHH!
CLOP
CLOP
CLOP
CLOP
A SPY?! HOW DID THEY KNOW?
MUST'VE NOTICED MY NIGHT-VISION GOGGLES.

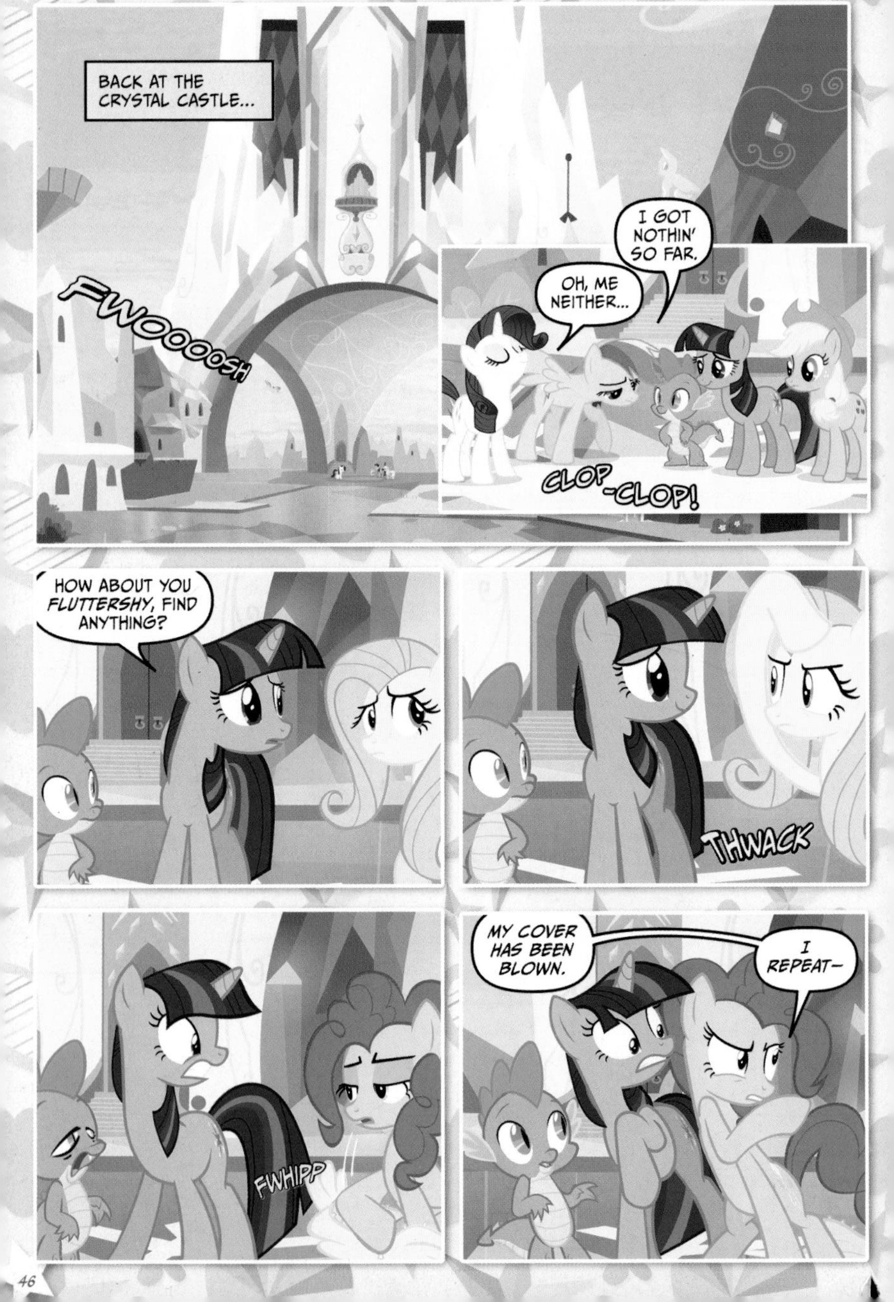
BACK AT THE CRYSTAL CASTLE...
FWOOOOSH
I GOT NOTHIN' SO FAR.
OH, ME NEITHER...
CLOP-CLOP!
HOW ABOUT YOU FLUTTERSHY, FIND ANYTHING?
THWACK
FWHIPP
MY COVER HAS BEEN BLOWN.
I REPEAT–

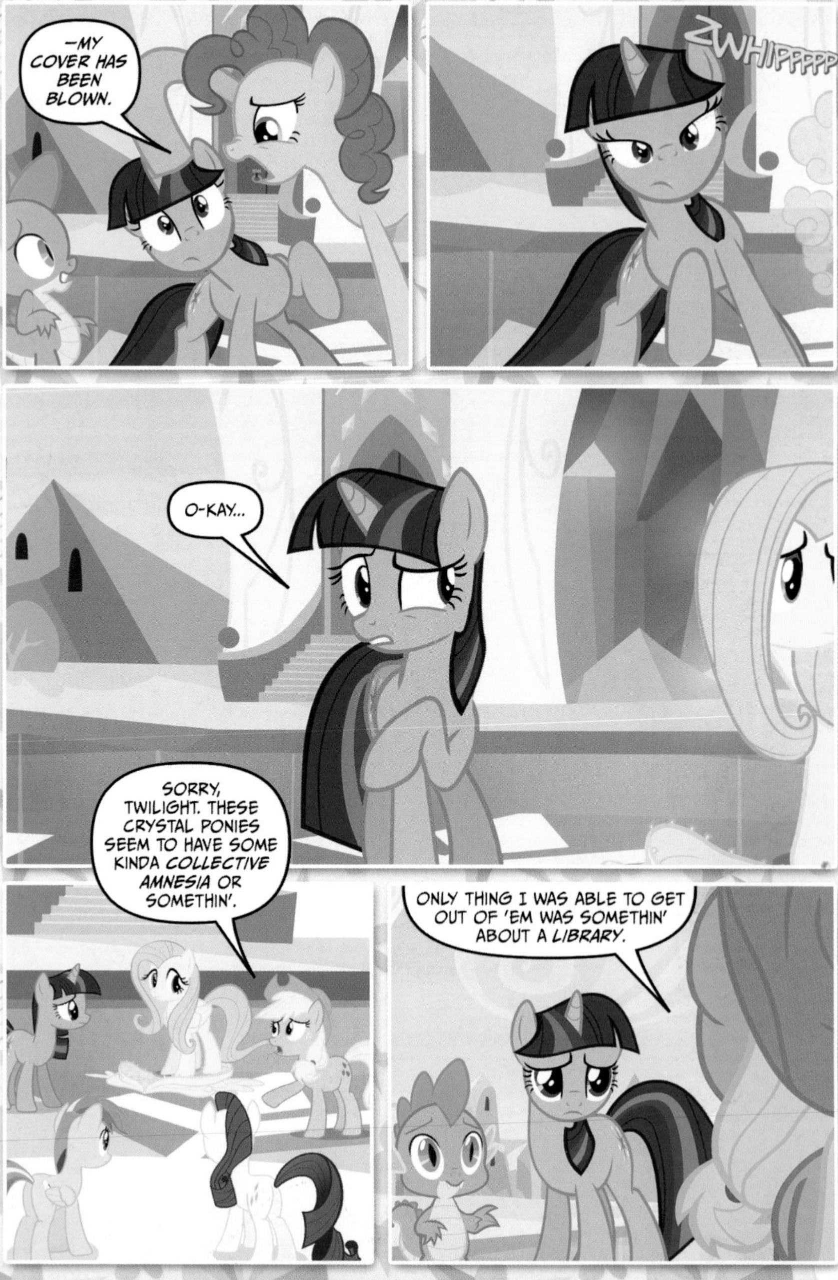

—MY COVER HAS BEEN BLOWN.
ZWHIPPPPP
O-KAY...
SORRY, TWILIGHT. THESE CRYSTAL PONIES SEEM TO HAVE SOME KINDA *COLLECTIVE AMNESIA* OR SOMETHIN'.
ONLY THING I WAS ABLE TO GET OUT OF 'EM WAS SOMETHIN' ABOUT A *LIBRARY*.

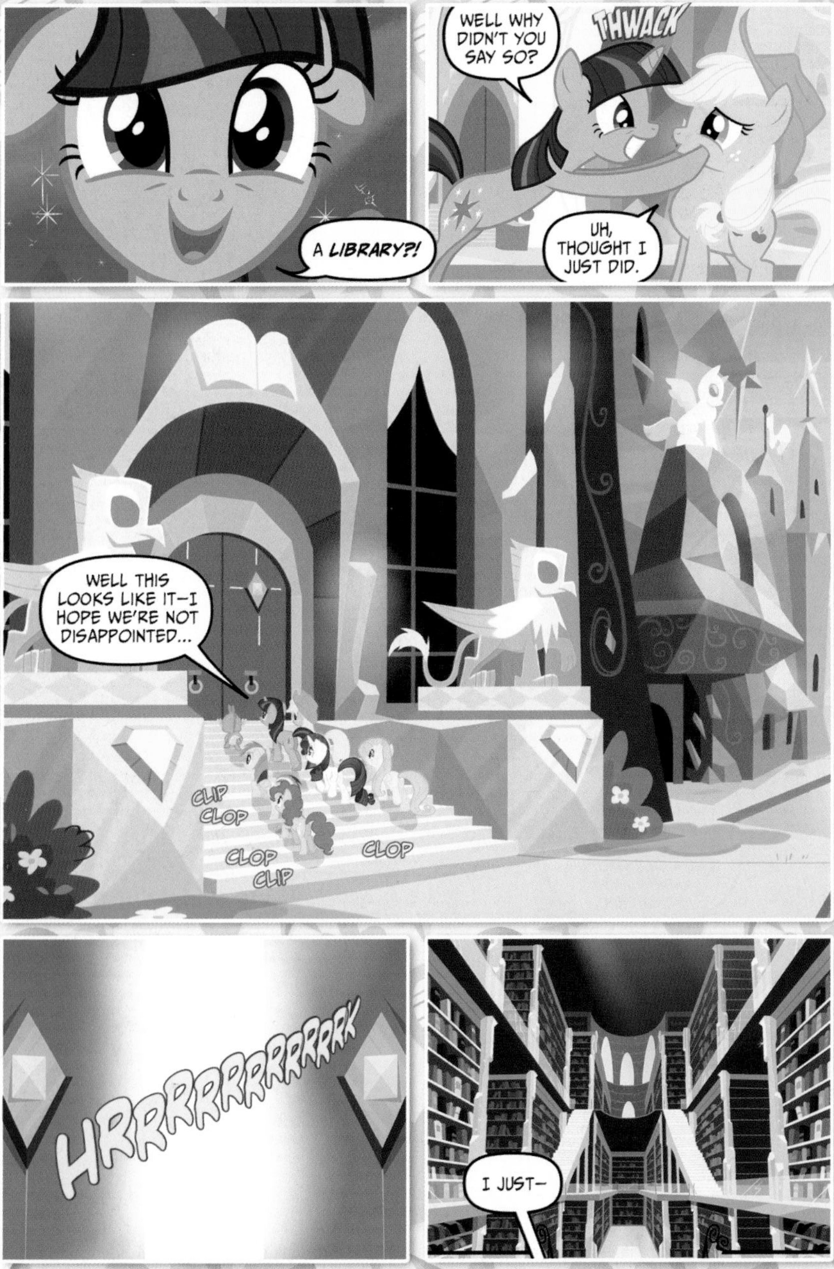
A LIBRARY?!
WELL WHY DIDN'T YOU SAY SO?
THWACK
UH, THOUGHT I JUST DID.
WELL THIS LOOKS LIKE IT—I HOPE WE'RE NOT DISAPPOINTED...
CLIP
CLOP
CLOP
CLIP
CLOP
HRRRRRRRRRRRK
I JUST—

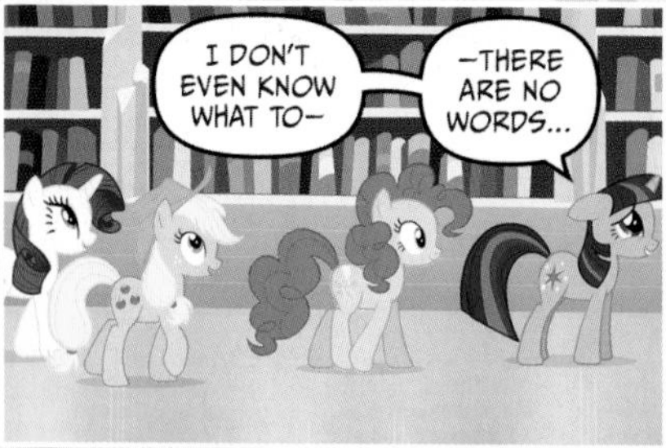
I DON'T EVEN KNOW WHAT TO—
—THERE ARE NO WORDS...
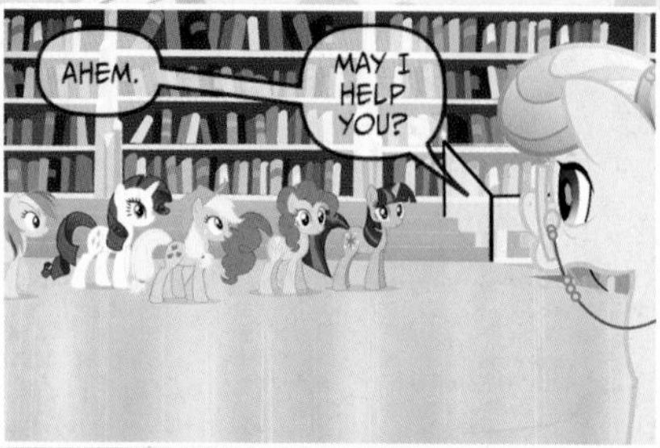
AHEM.
MAY I HELP YOU?
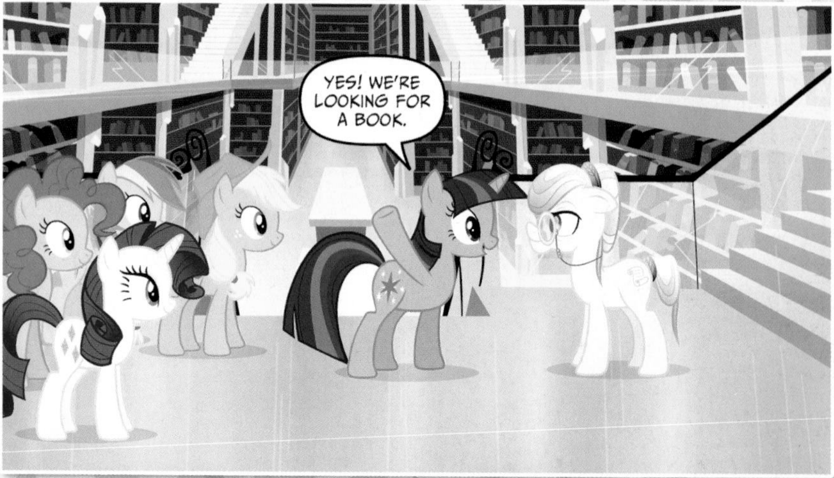
YES! WE'RE LOOKING FOR A BOOK.
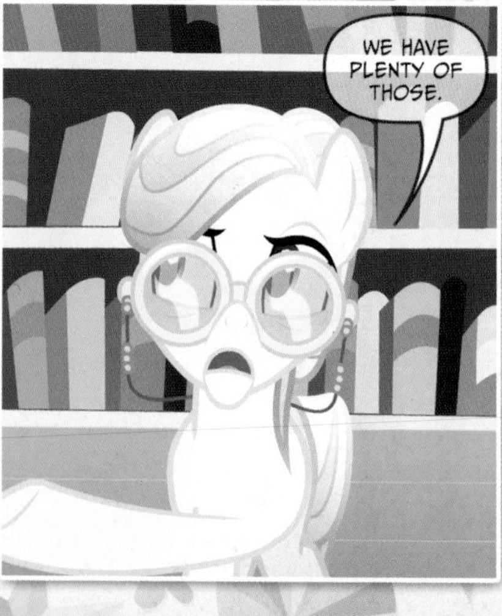
WE HAVE PLENTY OF THOSE.
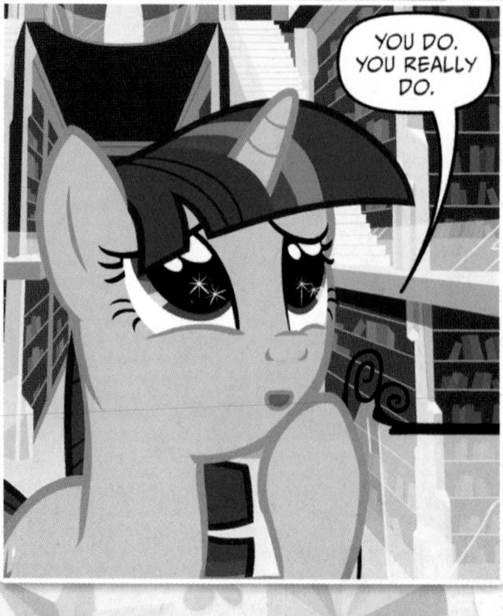
YOU DO. YOU REALLY DO.

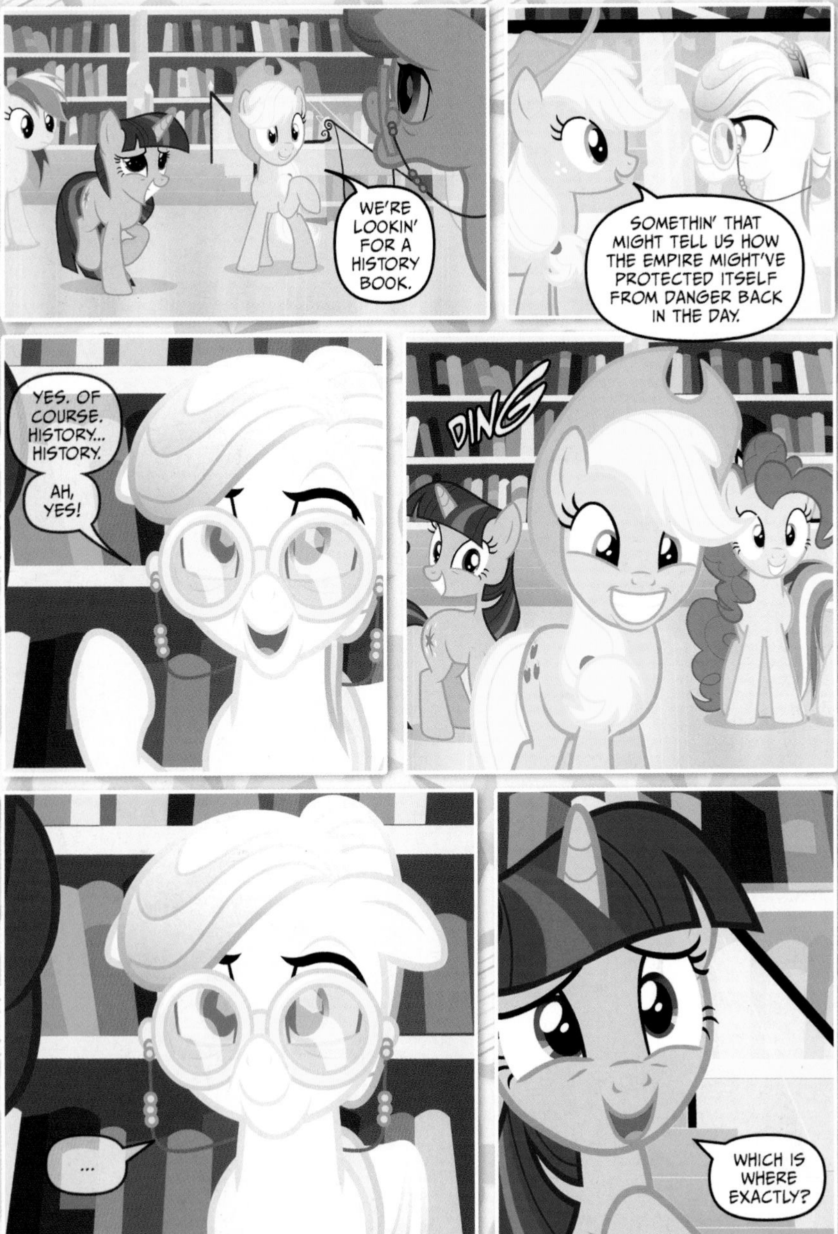
WE'RE LOOKIN' FOR A HISTORY BOOK.
SOMETHIN' THAT MIGHT TELL US HOW THE EMPIRE MIGHT'VE PROTECTED ITSELF FROM DANGER BACK IN THE DAY.
YES. OF COURSE. HISTORY... HISTORY.
AH, YES!
DING
...
WHICH IS WHERE EXACTLY?

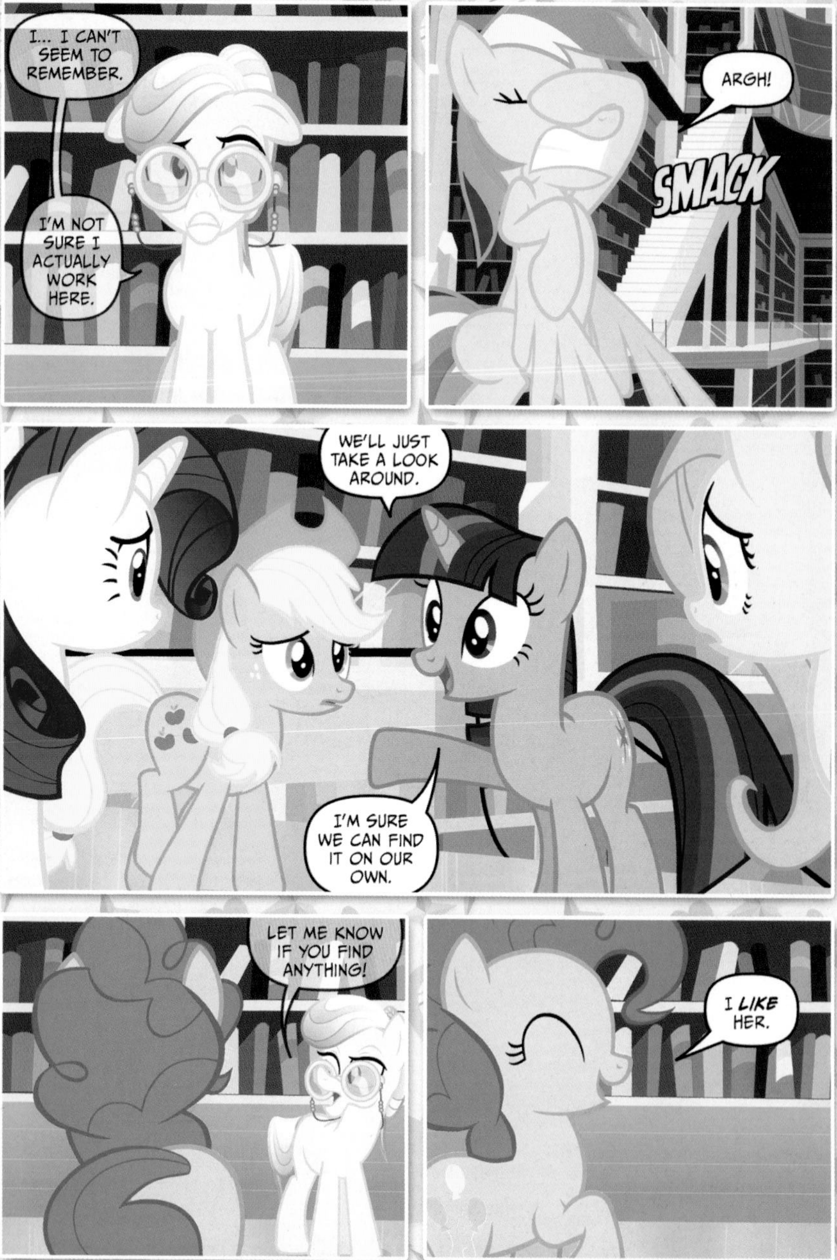
I... I CAN'T SEEM TO REMEMBER.
I'M NOT SURE I ACTUALLY WORK HERE.
ARGH!
SMACK
WE'LL JUST TAKE A LOOK AROUND.
I'M SURE WE CAN FIND IT ON OUR OWN.
LET ME KNOW IF YOU FIND ANYTHING!
I *LIKE* HER.

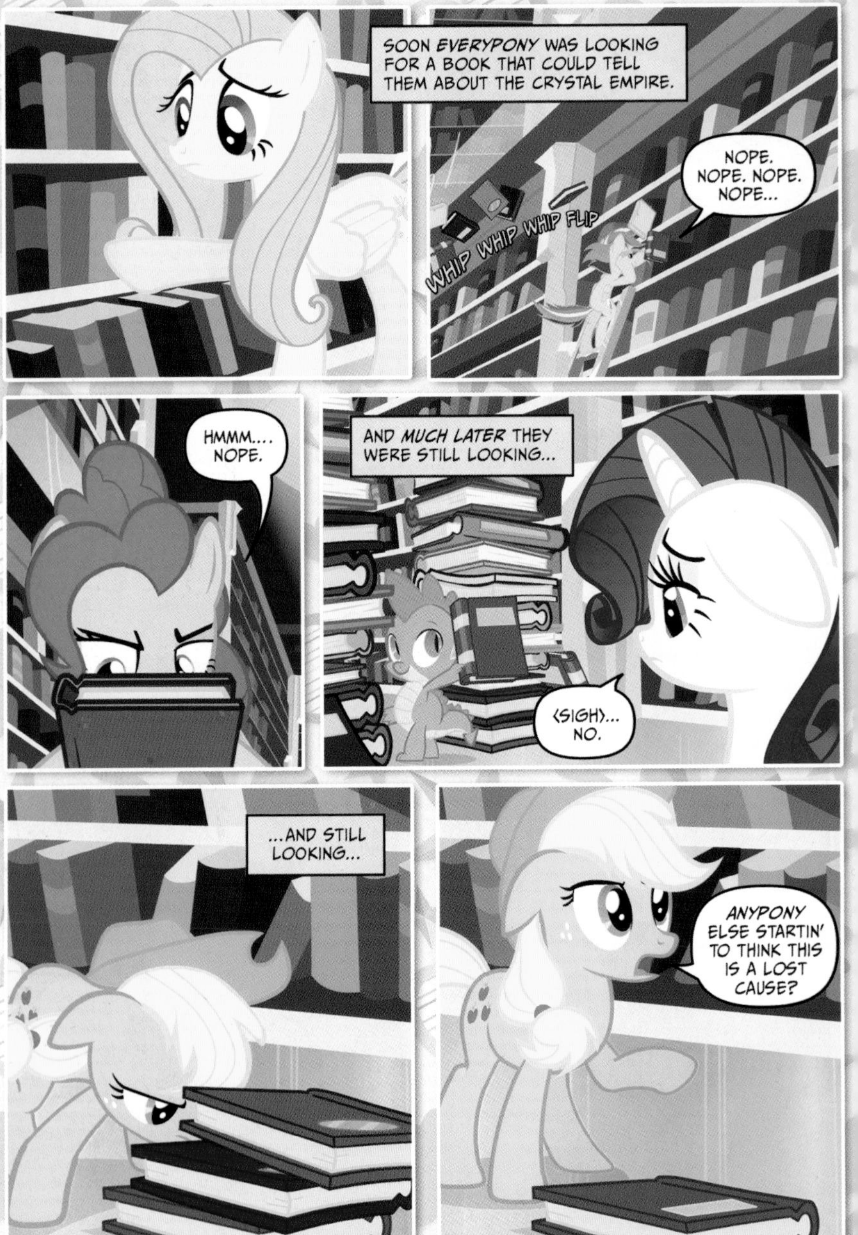
SOON *EVERYPONY* WAS LOOKING FOR A BOOK THAT COULD TELL THEM ABOUT THE CRYSTAL EMPIRE.
NOPE. NOPE. NOPE. NOPE...
WHIP WHIP WHIP FLIP
HMMM.... NOPE.
AND *MUCH LATER* THEY WERE STILL LOOKING...
‹SIGH›... NO.
...AND STILL LOOKING...
ANYPONY ELSE STARTIN' TO THINK THIS IS A LOST CAUSE?

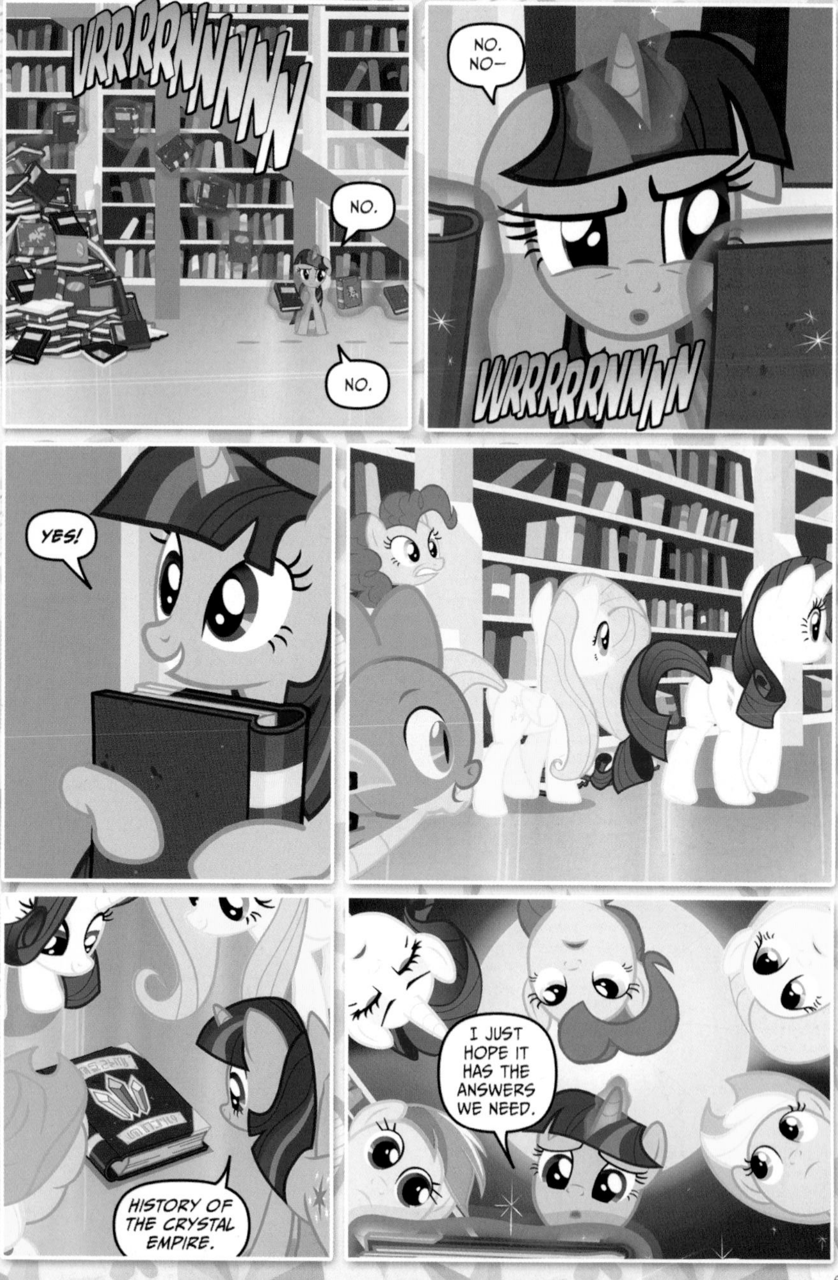
VRRRRNNNNN
NO.
NO.
NO.
NO–
VVRRRRNNNNN
YES!
HISTORY OF THE CRYSTAL EMPIRE.
I JUST HOPE IT HAS THE ANSWERS WE NEED.

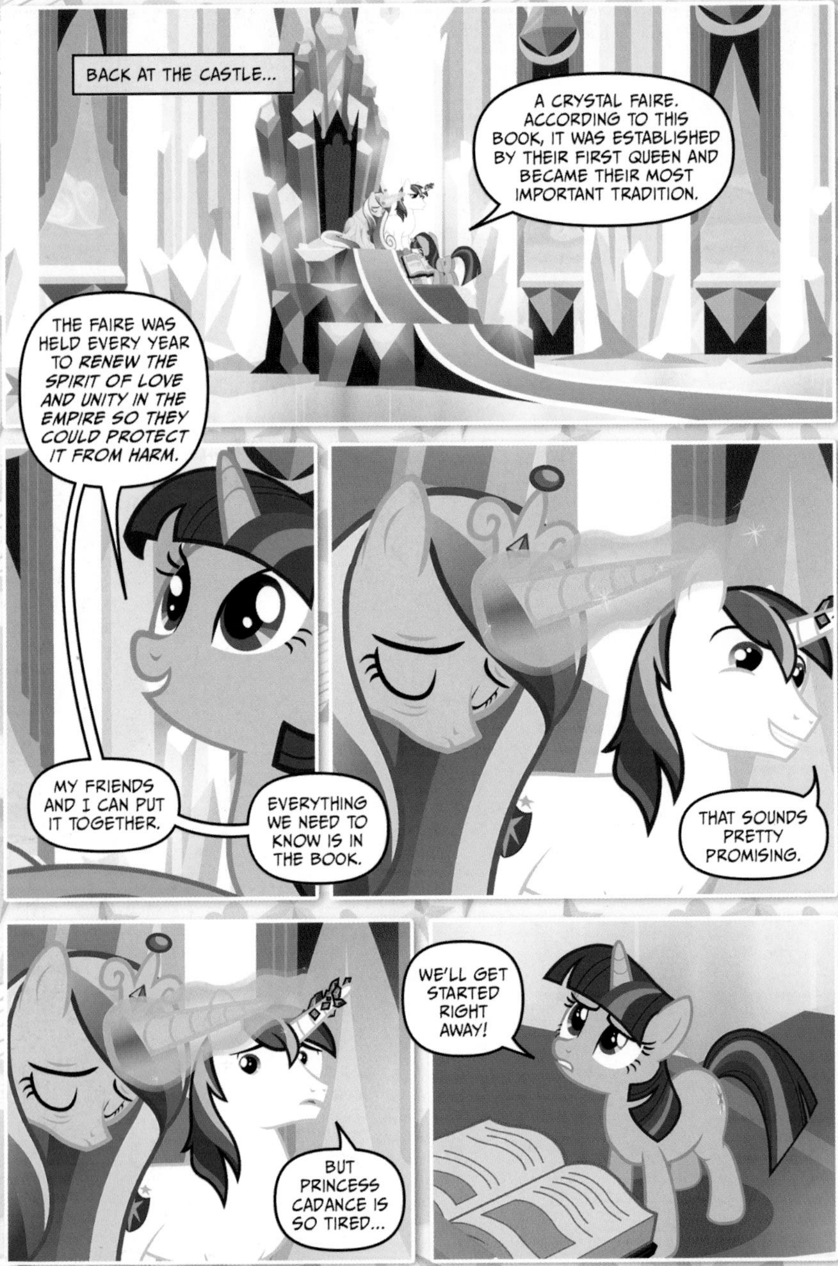
BACK AT THE CASTLE...
A CRYSTAL FAIRE. ACCORDING TO THIS BOOK, IT WAS ESTABLISHED BY THEIR FIRST QUEEN AND BECAME THEIR MOST IMPORTANT TRADITION.
THE FAIRE WAS HELD EVERY YEAR TO RENEW THE SPIRIT OF LOVE AND UNITY IN THE EMPIRE SO THEY COULD PROTECT IT FROM HARM.
MY FRIENDS AND I CAN PUT IT TOGETHER.
EVERYTHING WE NEED TO KNOW IS IN THE BOOK.
THAT SOUNDS PRETTY PROMISING.
BUT PRINCESS CADANCE IS SO TIRED...
WE'LL GET STARTED RIGHT AWAY!

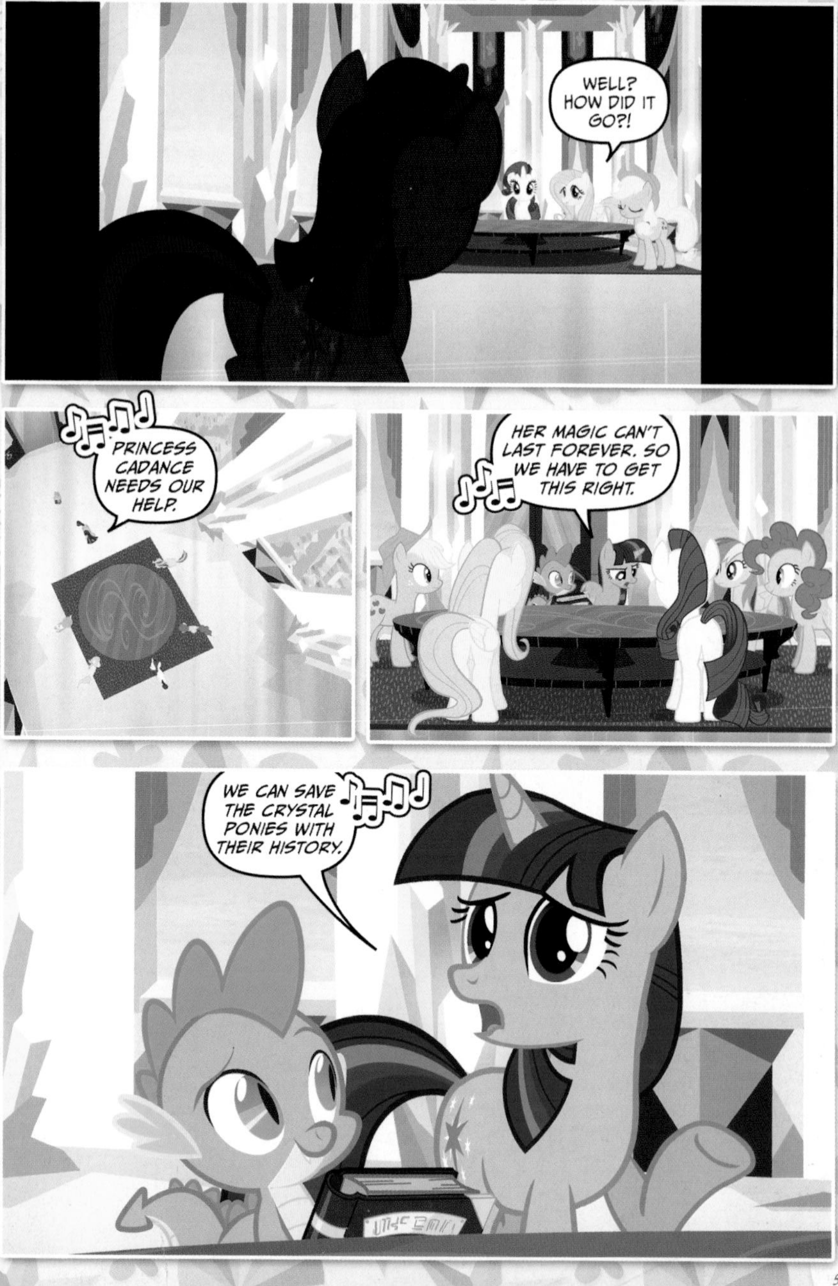
WELL? HOW DID IT GO?!
PRINCESS CADANCE NEEDS OUR HELP.
HER MAGIC CAN'T LAST FOREVER. SO WE HAVE TO GET THIS RIGHT.
WE CAN SAVE THE CRYSTAL PONIES WITH THEIR HISTORY.

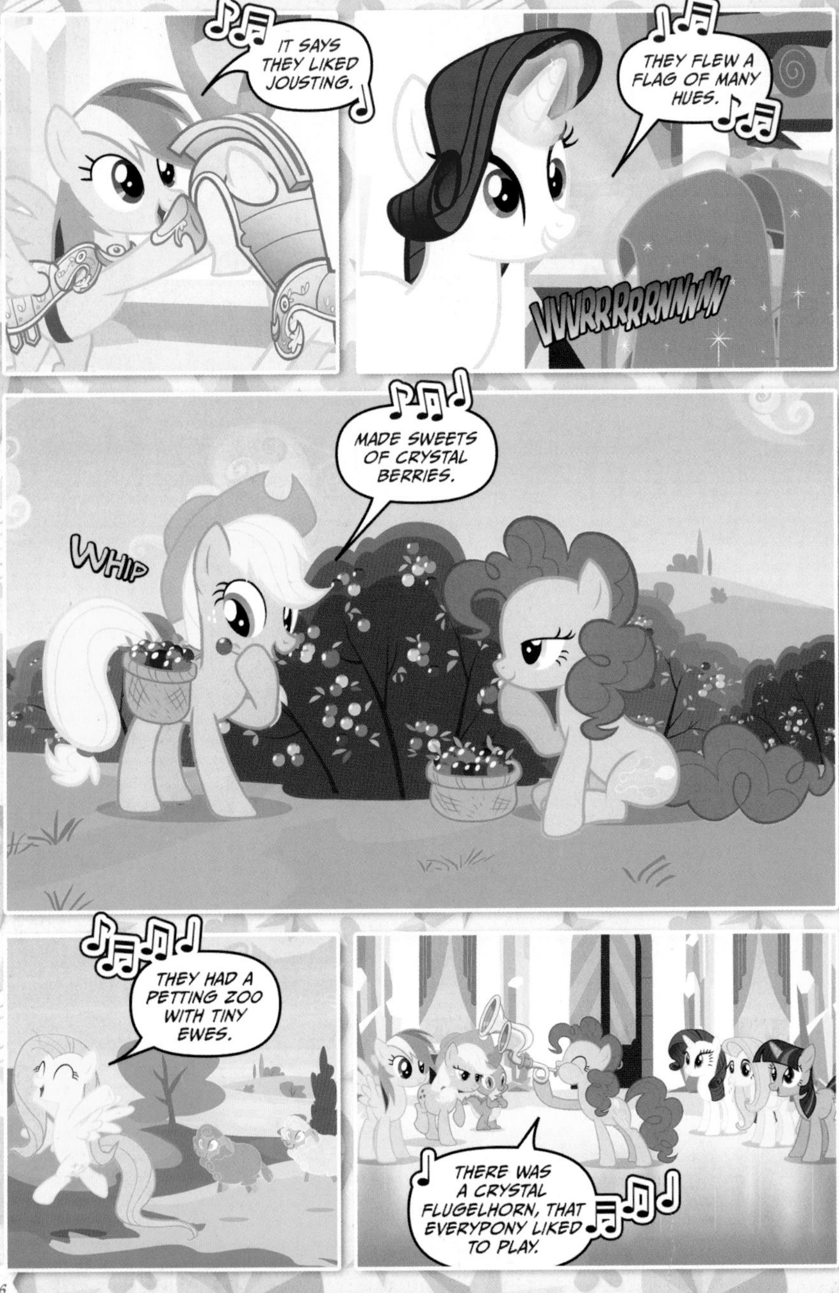
IT SAYS THEY LIKED JOUSTING.
THEY FLEW A FLAG OF MANY HUES.
VVVRRRRRNNNNN
MADE SWEETS OF CRYSTAL BERRIES.
WHIP
THEY HAD A PETTING ZOO WITH TINY EWES.
THERE WAS A CRYSTAL FLUGELHORN, THAT EVERYPONY LIKED TO PLAY.

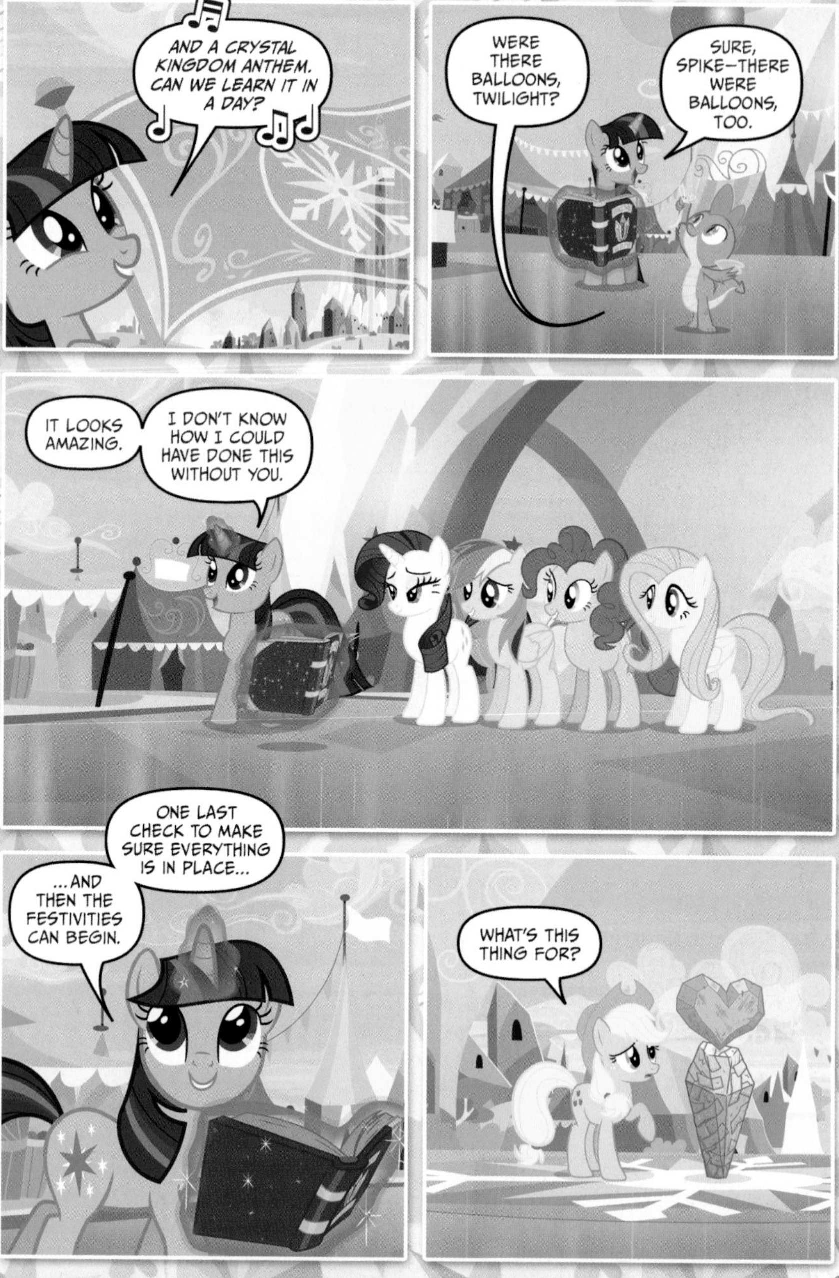
AND A CRYSTAL KINGDOM ANTHEM. CAN WE LEARN IT IN A DAY?
WERE THERE BALLOONS, TWILIGHT?
SURE, SPIKE—THERE WERE BALLOONS, TOO.
IT LOOKS AMAZING.
I DON'T KNOW HOW I COULD HAVE DONE THIS WITHOUT YOU.
ONE LAST CHECK TO MAKE SURE EVERYTHING IS IN PLACE...
...AND THEN THE FESTIVITIES CAN BEGIN.
WHAT'S THIS THING FOR?

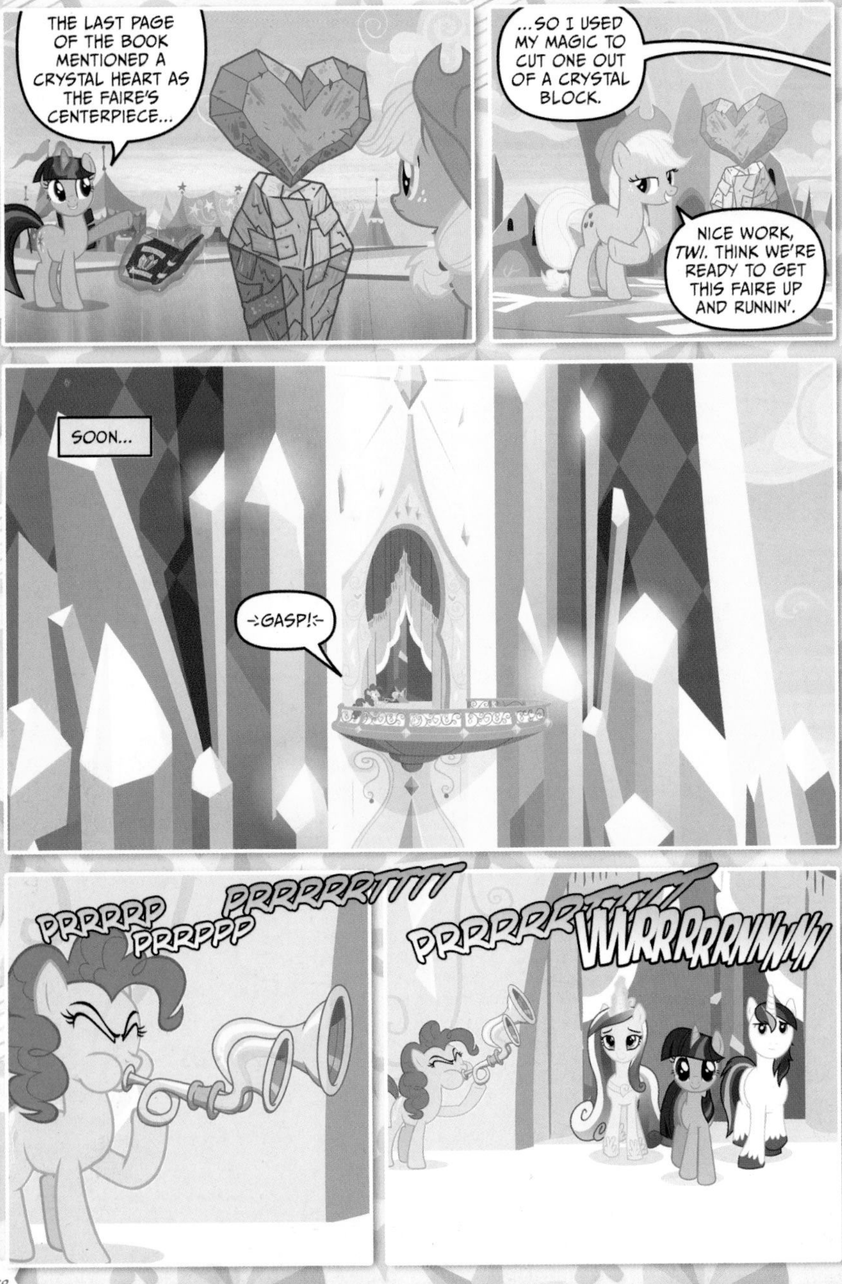
THE LAST PAGE OF THE BOOK MENTIONED A CRYSTAL HEART AS THE FAIRE'S CENTERPIECE...
...SO I USED MY MAGIC TO CUT ONE OUT OF A CRYSTAL BLOCK.
NICE WORK, TWI. THINK WE'RE READY TO GET THIS FAIRE UP AND RUNNIN'.
SOON...
-GASP!-
PRRRRP
PRRPPP
PRRRRRTTTTT
PRRRRRTTTTT
VVVRRRRRNNNNN

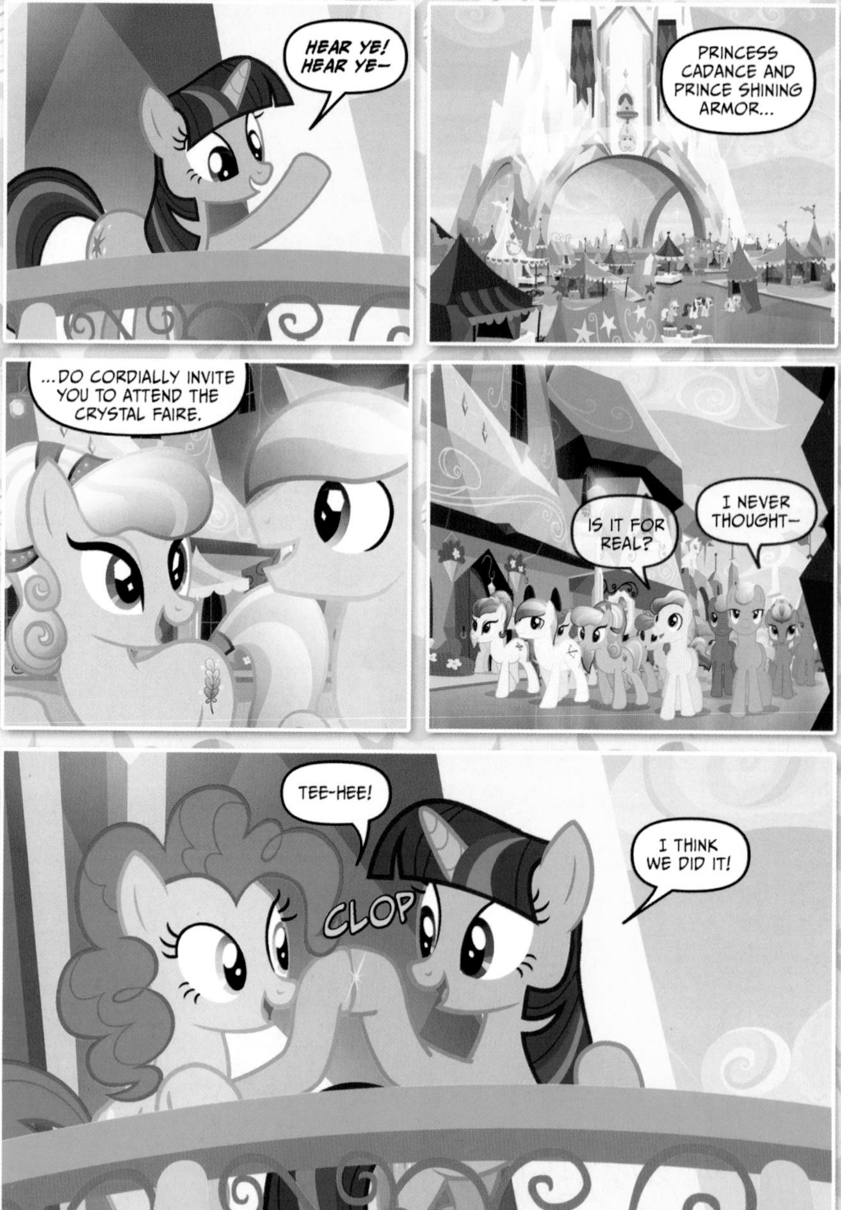
HEAR YE! HEAR YE—
PRINCESS CADANCE AND PRINCE SHINING ARMOR...
...DO CORDIALLY INVITE YOU TO ATTEND THE CRYSTAL FAIRE.
IS IT FOR REAL?
I NEVER THOUGHT—
TEE-HEE!
CLOP
I THINK WE DID IT!

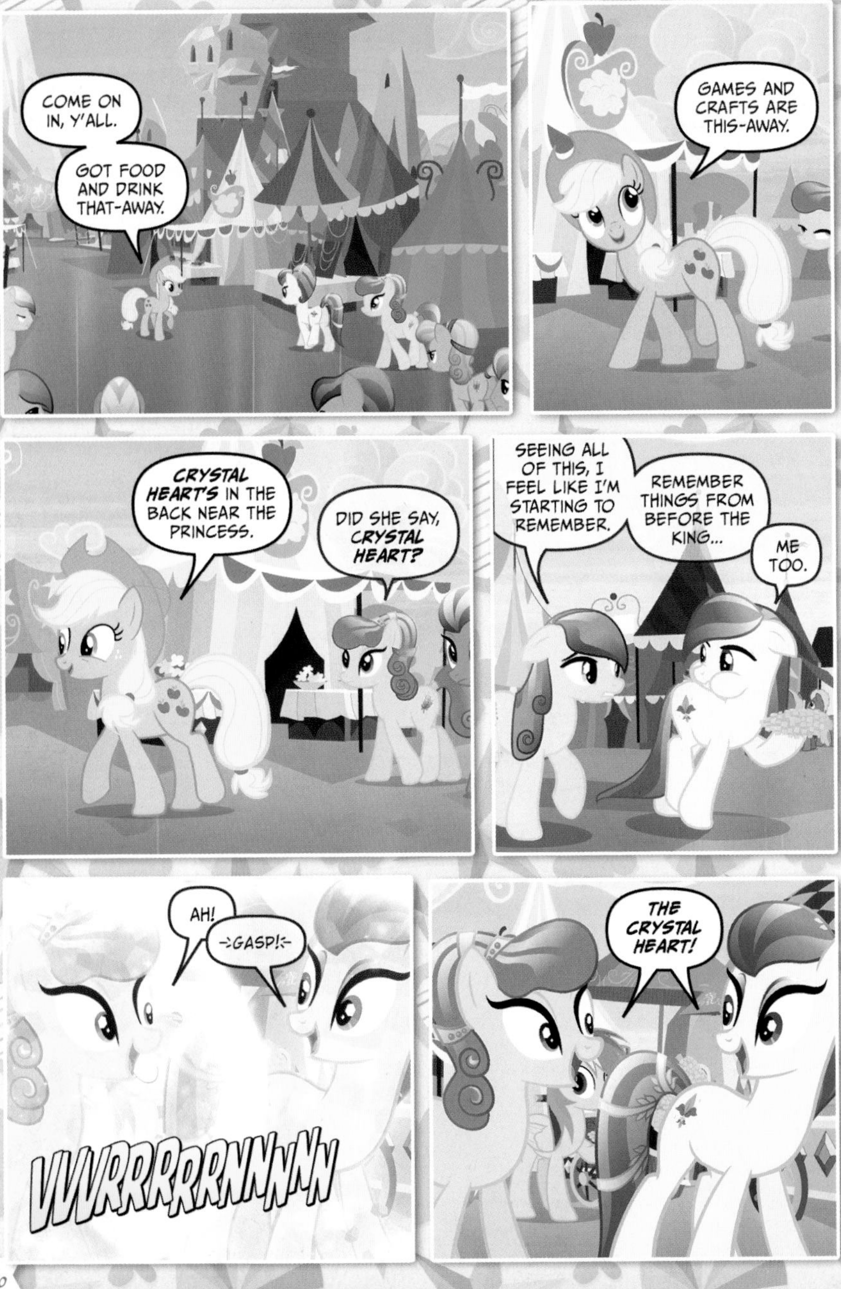
COME ON IN, Y'ALL.
GOT FOOD AND DRINK THAT-AWAY.
GAMES AND CRAFTS ARE THIS-AWAY.
CRYSTAL HEART'S IN THE BACK NEAR THE PRINCESS.
DID SHE SAY, CRYSTAL HEART?
SEEING ALL OF THIS, I FEEL LIKE I'M STARTING TO REMEMBER.
REMEMBER THINGS FROM BEFORE THE KING...
ME TOO.
AH!
-GASP!-
VVVRRRRRNNNNN
THE CRYSTAL HEART!

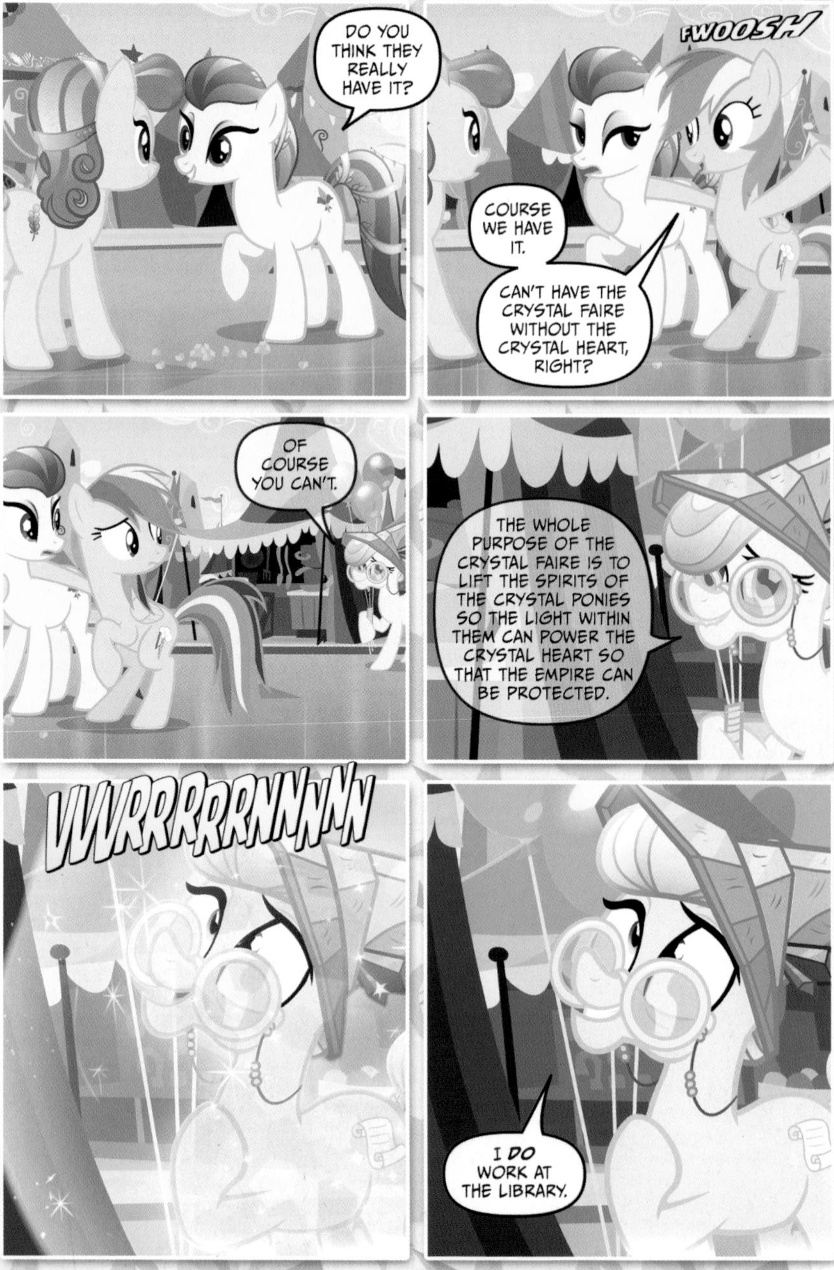
DO YOU THINK THEY REALLY HAVE IT?
FWOOSH
COURSE WE HAVE IT.
CAN'T HAVE THE CRYSTAL FAIRE WITHOUT THE CRYSTAL HEART, RIGHT?
OF COURSE YOU CAN'T.
THE WHOLE PURPOSE OF THE CRYSTAL FAIRE IS TO LIFT THE SPIRITS OF THE CRYSTAL PONIES SO THE LIGHT WITHIN THEM CAN POWER THE CRYSTAL HEART SO THAT THE EMPIRE CAN BE PROTECTED.
VVVRRRRRNNNNN
I *DO* WORK AT THE LIBRARY.

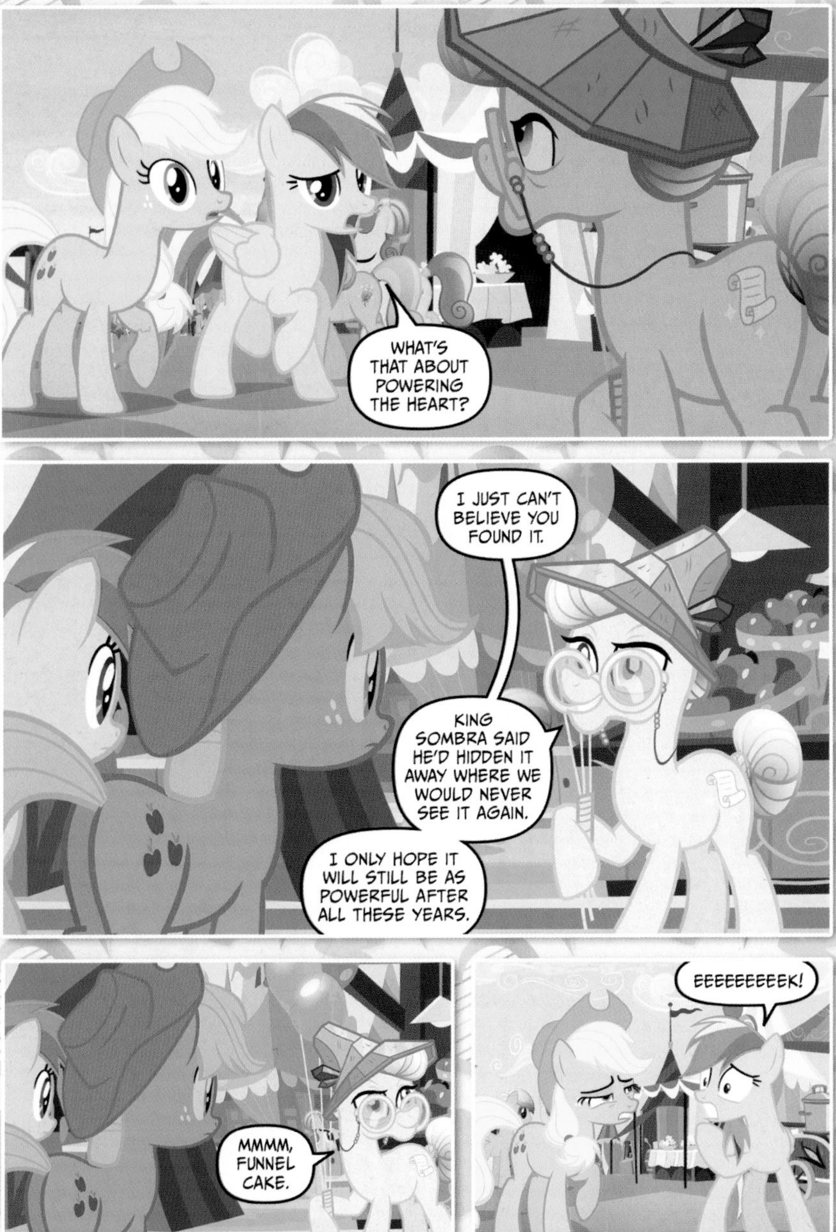
WHAT'S THAT ABOUT POWERING THE HEART?
I JUST CAN'T BELIEVE YOU FOUND IT.
KING SOMBRA SAID HE'D HIDDEN IT AWAY WHERE WE WOULD NEVER SEE IT AGAIN.
I ONLY HOPE IT WILL STILL BE AS POWERFUL AFTER ALL THESE YEARS.
MMMM, FUNNEL CAKE.
EEEEEEEEEK!

FWOOOOOOOOSH
YOINK
WHY DID YOU–?
I THINK WE MAY HAVE A PROBLEM.

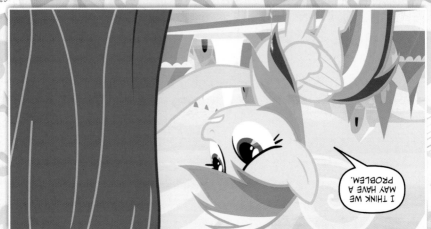

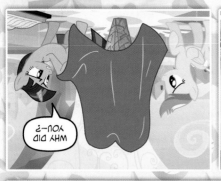

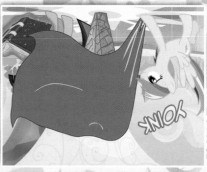

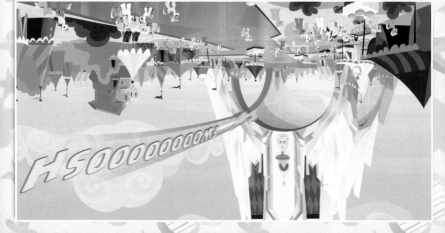

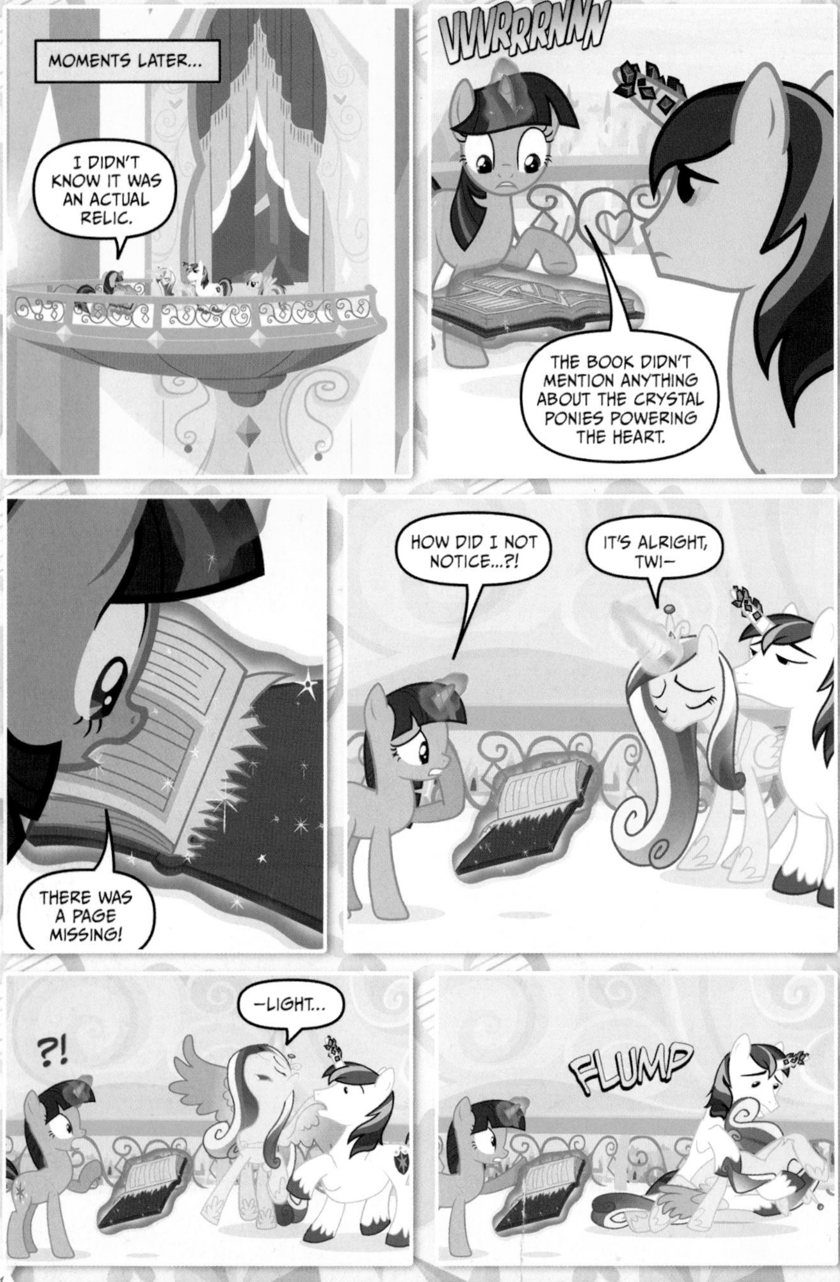
MOMENTS LATER...
I DIDN'T KNOW IT WAS AN ACTUAL RELIC.
VVVRRRNNN
THE BOOK DIDN'T MENTION ANYTHING ABOUT THE CRYSTAL PONIES POWERING THE HEART.
THERE WAS A PAGE MISSING!
HOW DID I NOT NOTICE...?!
IT'S ALRIGHT, TWI—
?!
—LIGHT...
FLUMP

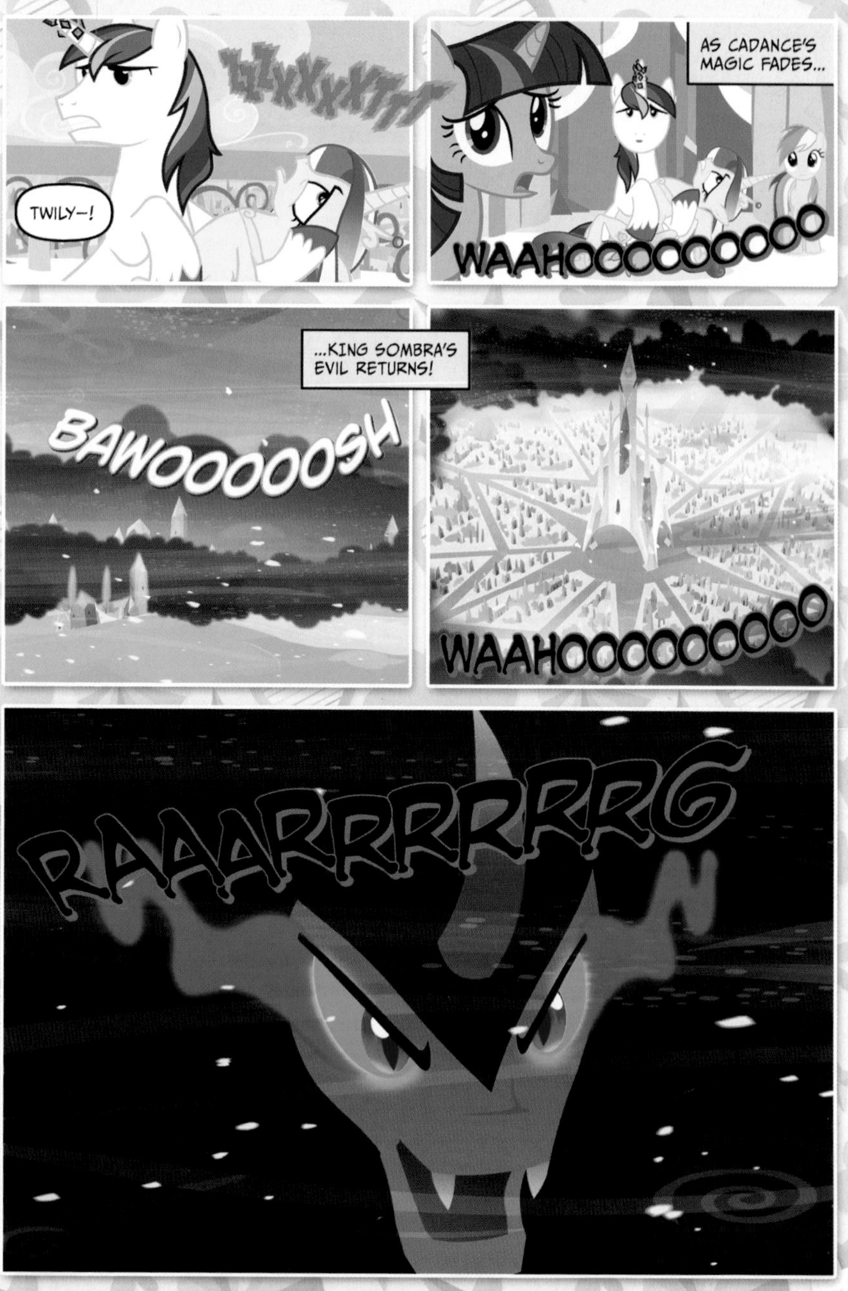
TWILY–!
TZZXXXXTT!
AS CADANCE'S MAGIC FADES...
WAAHOOOOOOOOOOO
...KING SOMBRA'S EVIL RETURNS!
BAWOOOOOOSH
WAAHOOOOOOOOOOO
RAAARRRRRRG

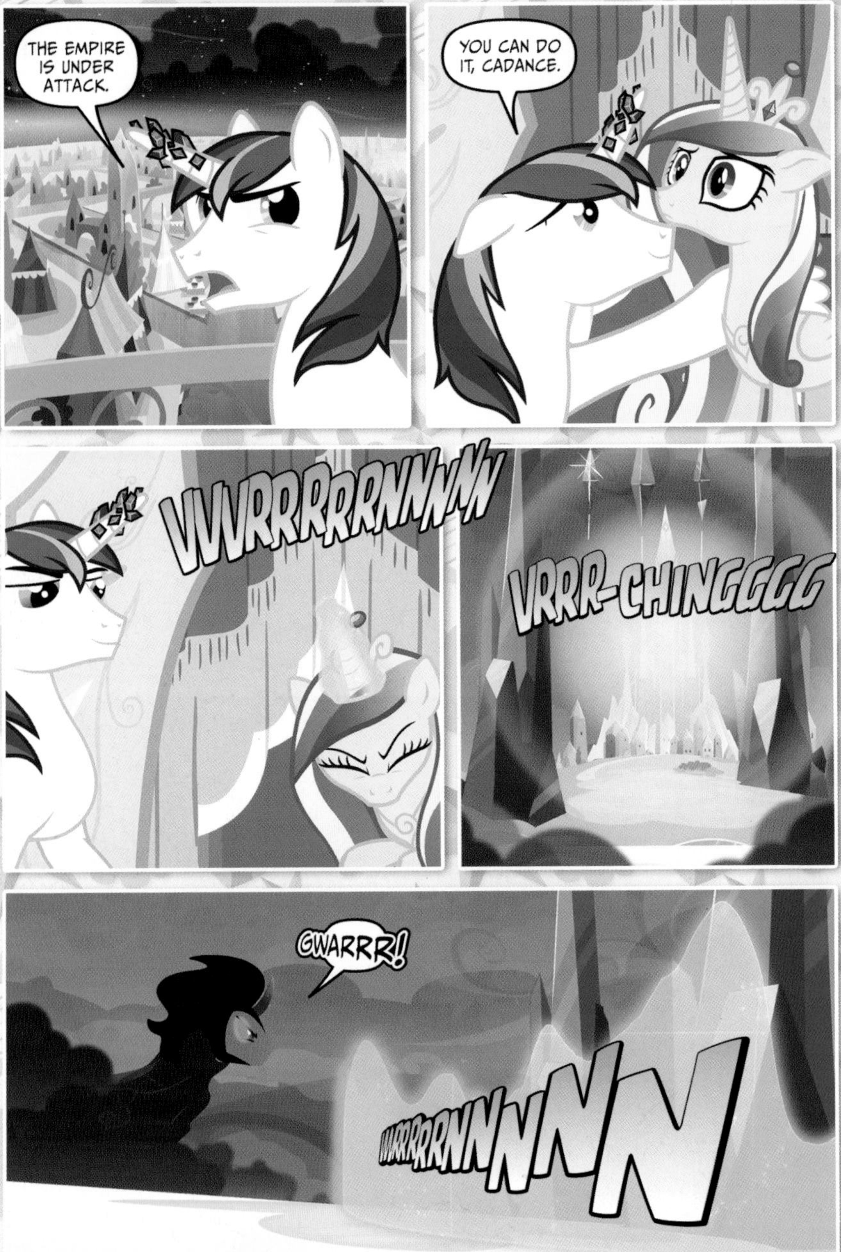
THE EMPIRE IS UNDER ATTACK.
YOU CAN DO IT, CADANCE.
VVVRRRRRNNNNN
VRRR-CHINGGGG
GWARRR!
VVRRRRNNNNNN

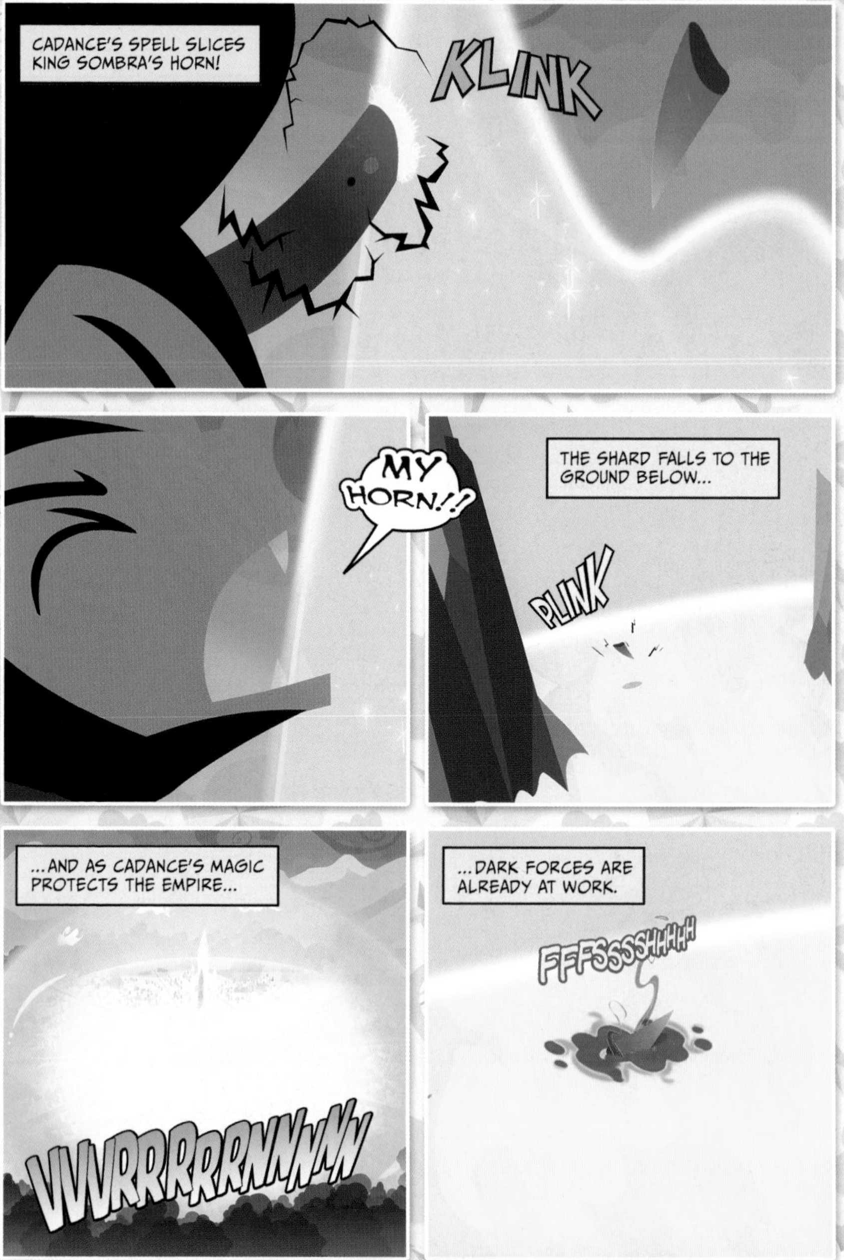
CADANCE'S SPELL SLICES KING SOMBRA'S HORN!
KLINK
MY HORN!!
THE SHARD FALLS TO THE GROUND BELOW...
PLINK
...AND AS CADANCE'S MAGIC PROTECTS THE EMPIRE...
VVVRRRRRNNNNN
...DARK FORCES ARE ALREADY AT WORK.
FFFSSSSHHHHH

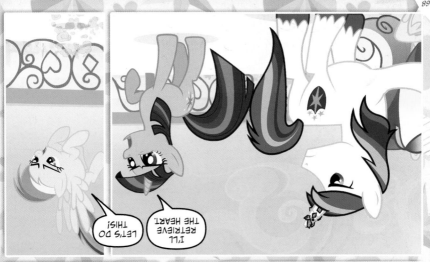

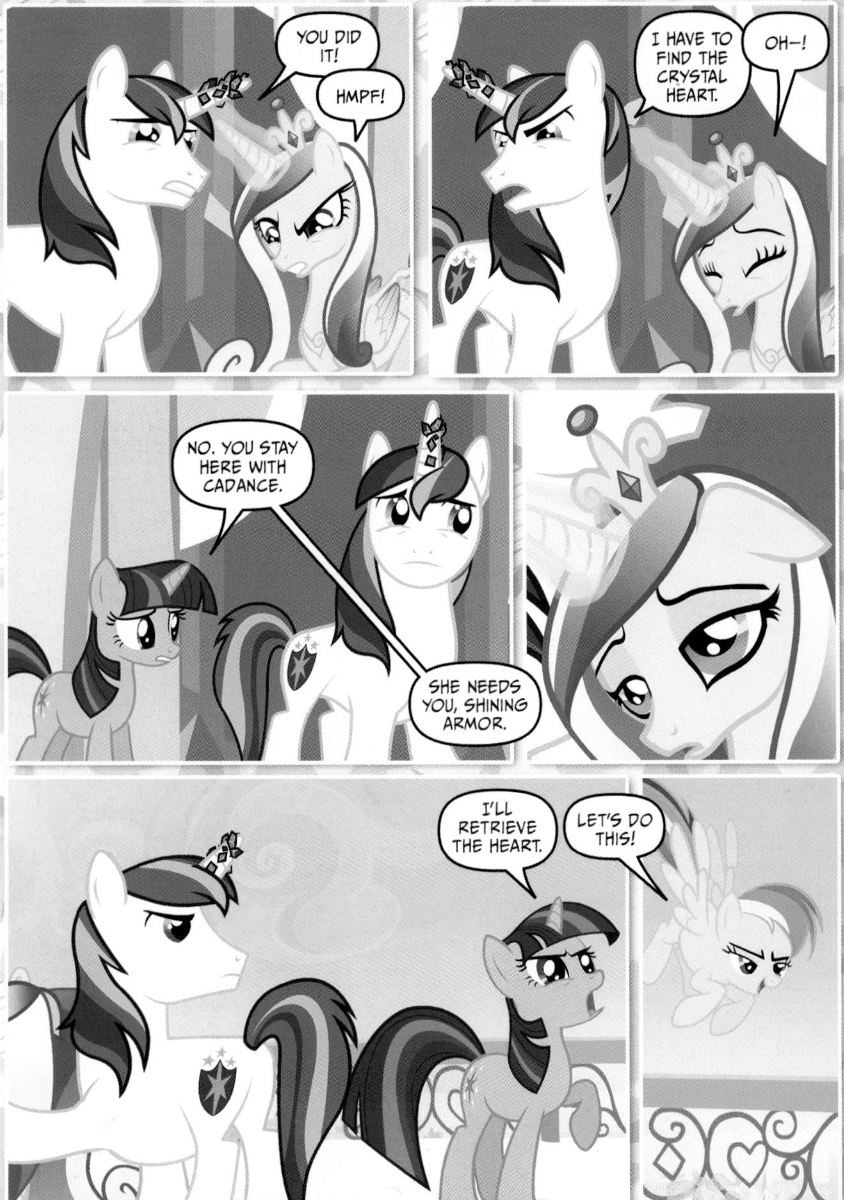
YOU DID IT!
HMPF!
I HAVE TO FIND THE CRYSTAL HEART.
OH—!
NO. YOU STAY HERE WITH CADANCE.
SHE NEEDS YOU, SHINING ARMOR.
I'LL RETRIEVE THE HEART.
LET'S DO THIS!

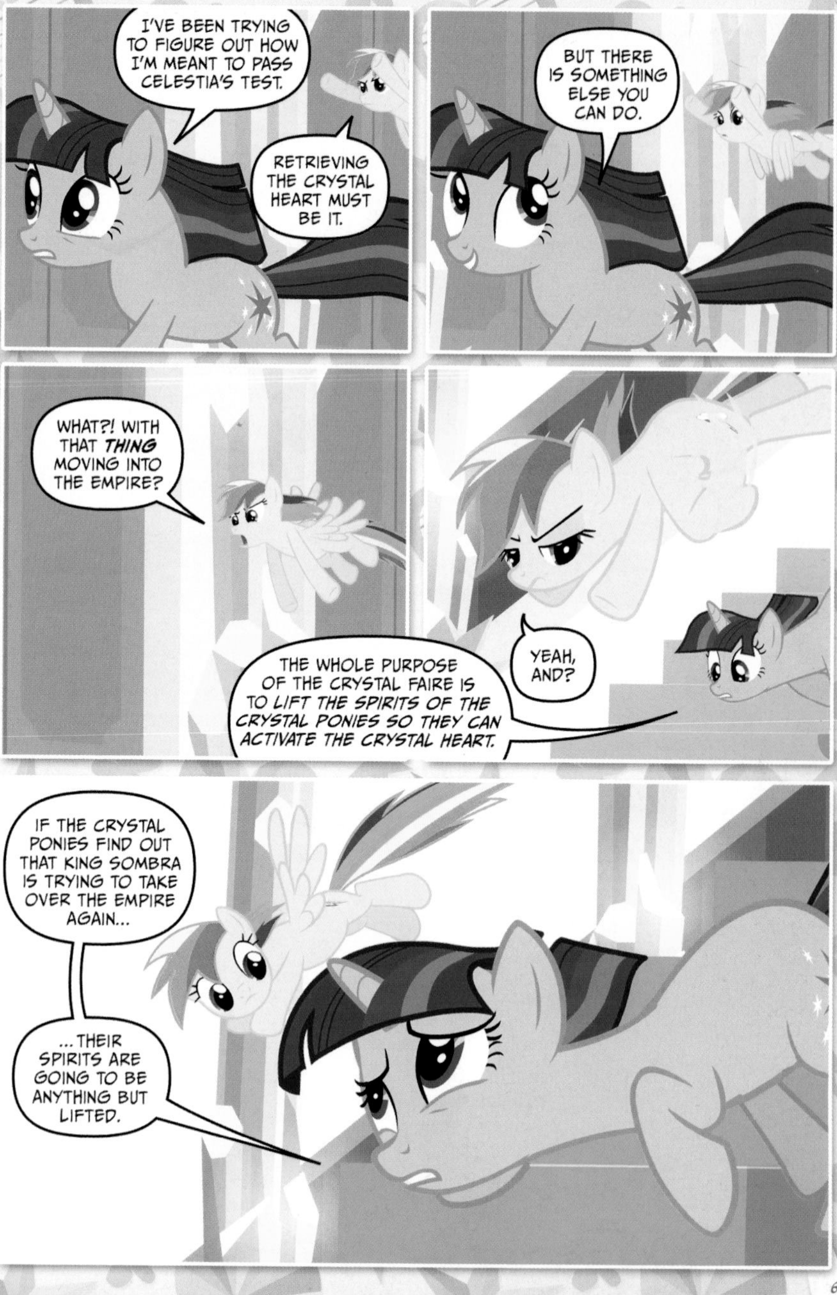
I'VE BEEN TRYING TO FIGURE OUT HOW I'M MEANT TO PASS CELESTIA'S TEST.
RETRIEVING THE CRYSTAL HEART MUST BE IT.
BUT THERE IS SOMETHING ELSE YOU CAN DO.
WHAT?! WITH THAT *THING* MOVING INTO THE EMPIRE?
YEAH, AND?
THE WHOLE PURPOSE OF THE CRYSTAL FAIRE IS TO *LIFT THE SPIRITS OF THE CRYSTAL PONIES SO THEY CAN ACTIVATE THE CRYSTAL HEART.*
IF THE CRYSTAL PONIES FIND OUT THAT KING SOMBRA IS TRYING TO TAKE OVER THE EMPIRE AGAIN...
...THEIR SPIRITS ARE GOING TO BE ANYTHING BUT LIFTED.

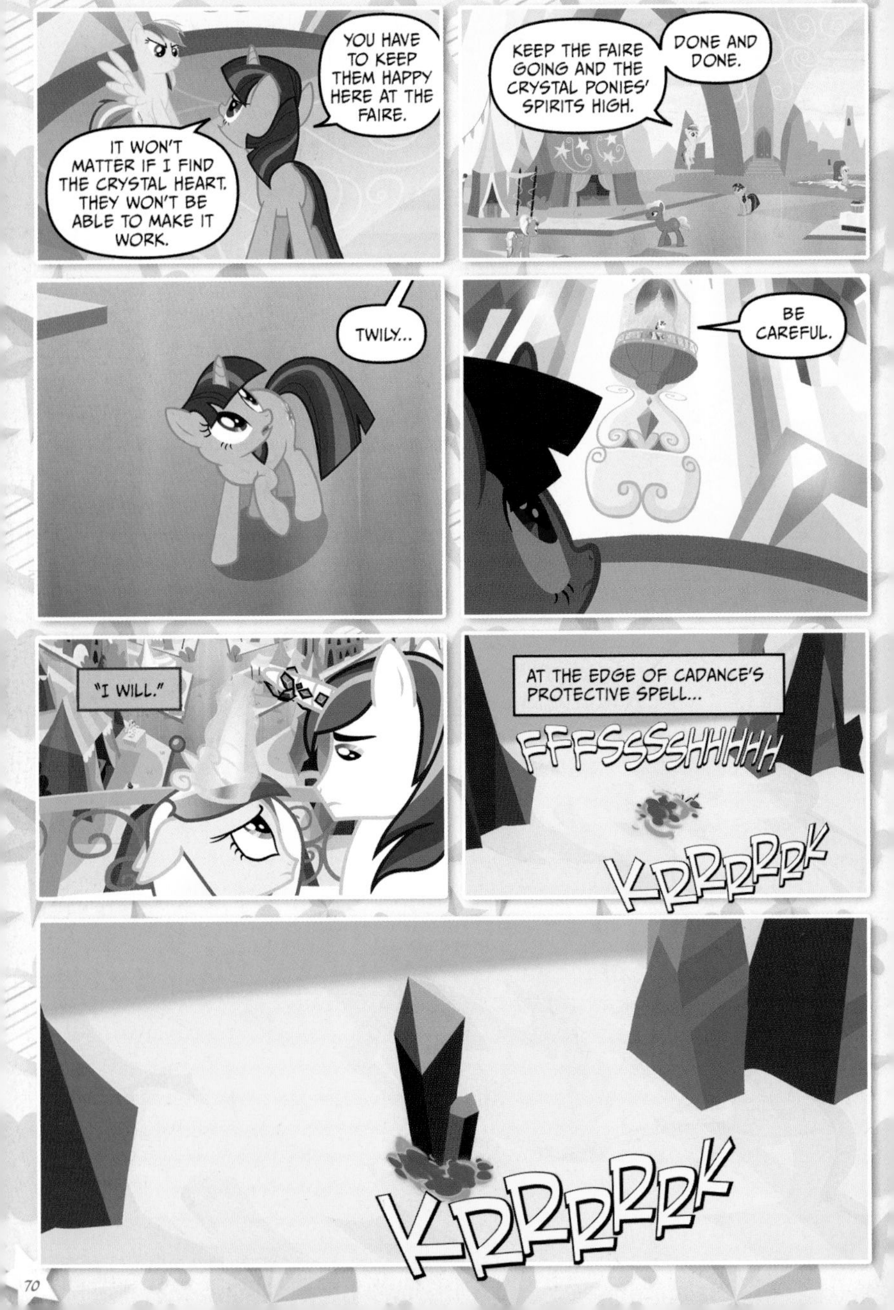
YOU HAVE TO KEEP THEM HAPPY HERE AT THE FAIRE.
IT WON'T MATTER IF I FIND THE CRYSTAL HEART. THEY WON'T BE ABLE TO MAKE IT WORK.
KEEP THE FAIRE GOING AND THE CRYSTAL PONIES' SPIRITS HIGH.
DONE AND DONE.
TWILY...
BE CAREFUL.
"I WILL."
AT THE EDGE OF CADANCE'S PROTECTIVE SPELL...
FFFSSSSHHHHH
KRRRRRK
KRRRRRK

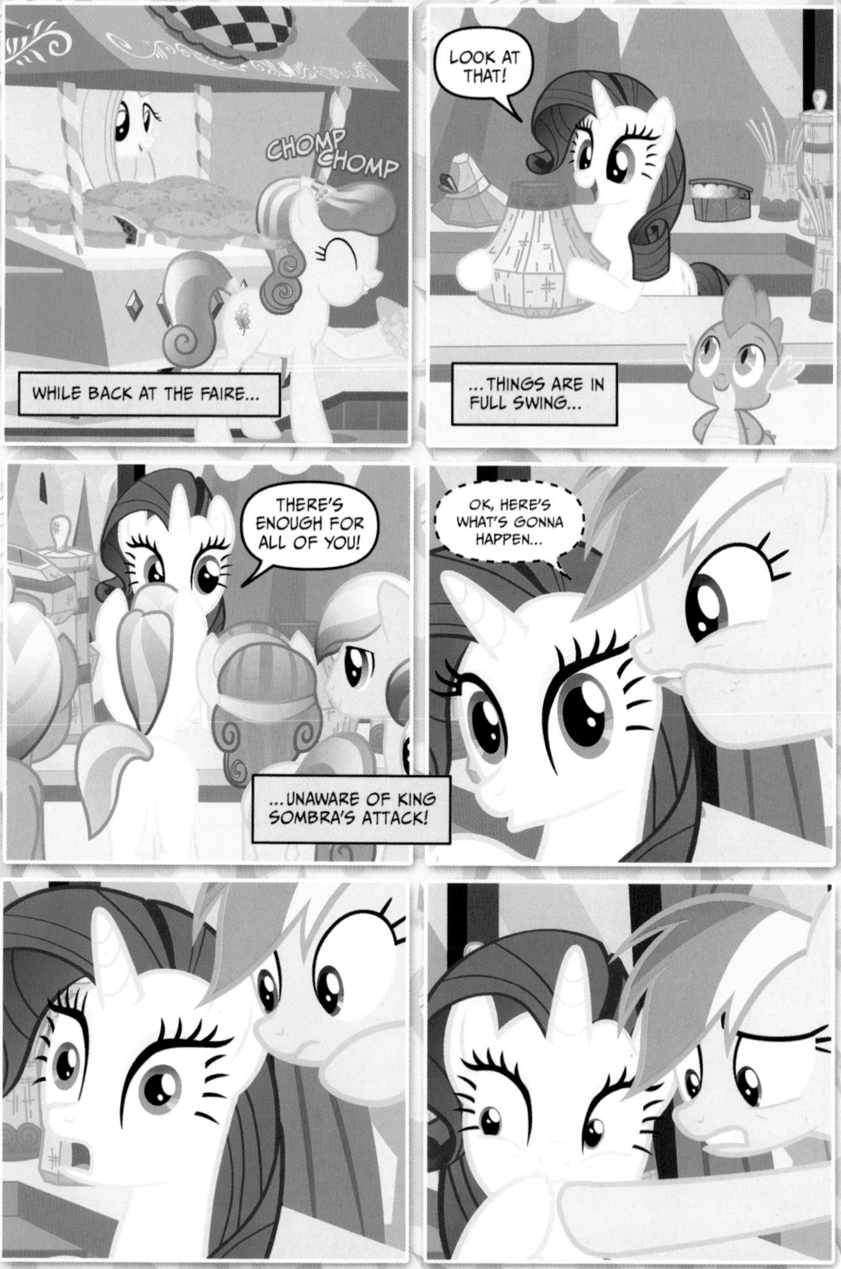
CHOMP CHOMP
WHILE BACK AT THE FAIRE...
LOOK AT THAT!
...THINGS ARE IN FULL SWING...
THERE'S ENOUGH FOR ALL OF YOU!
...UNAWARE OF KING SOMBRA'S ATTACK!
OK, HERE'S WHAT'S GONNA HAPPEN...

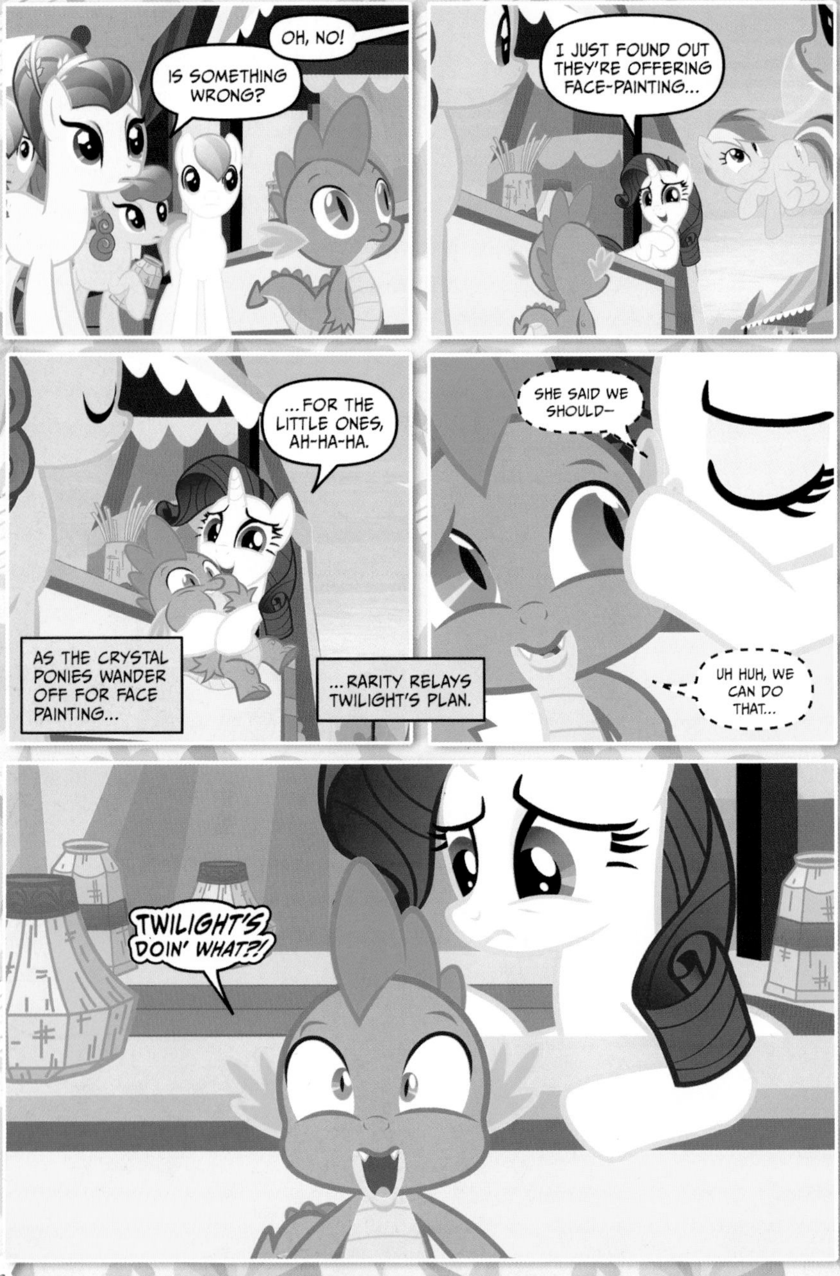
OH, NO!
IS SOMETHING WRONG?
I JUST FOUND OUT THEY'RE OFFERING FACE-PAINTING...
...FOR THE LITTLE ONES, AH-HA-HA.
AS THE CRYSTAL PONIES WANDER OFF FOR FACE PAINTING...
...RARITY RELAYS TWILIGHT'S PLAN.
SHE SAID WE SHOULD–
UH HUH, WE CAN DO THAT...
TWILIGHT'S DOIN' WHAT?!

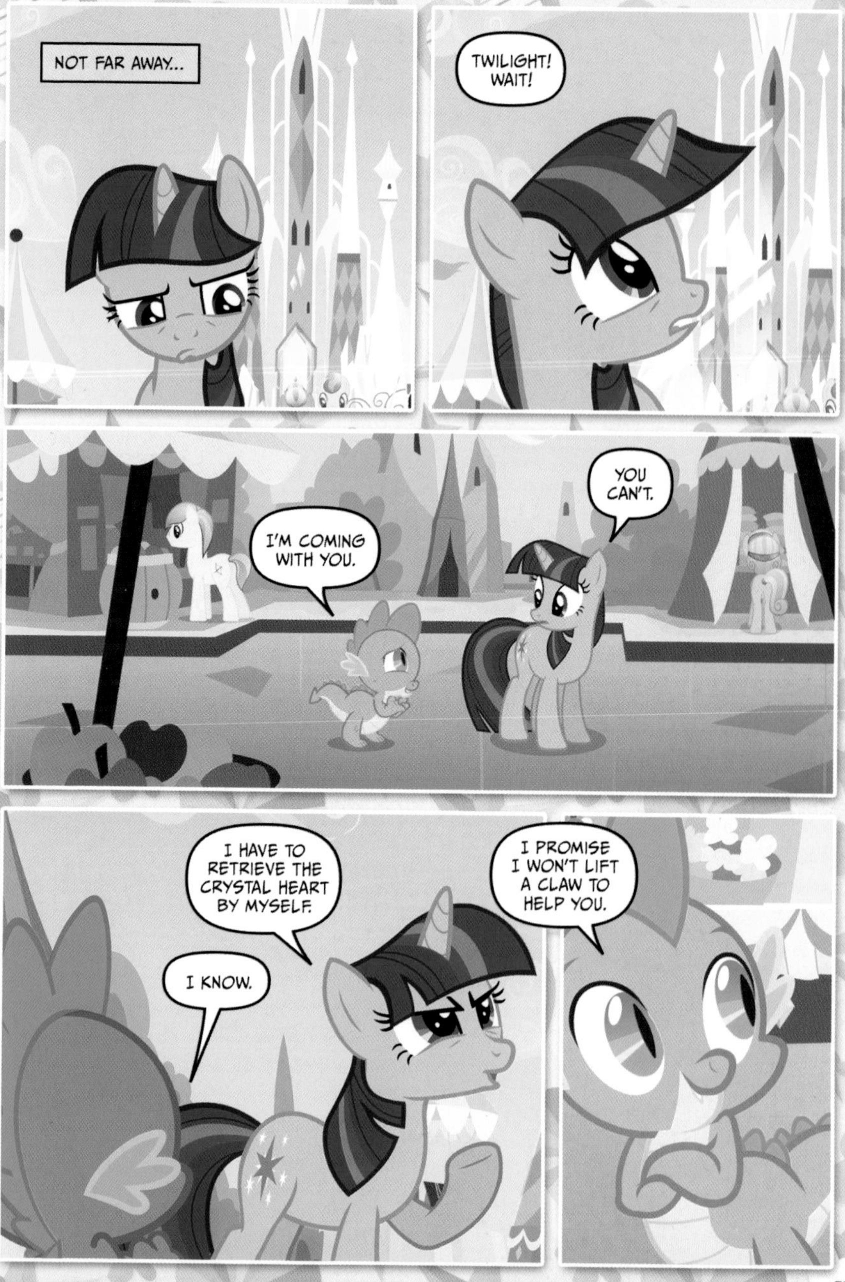
NOT FAR AWAY...
TWILIGHT! WAIT!
I'M COMING WITH YOU.
YOU CAN'T.
I HAVE TO RETRIEVE THE CRYSTAL HEART BY MYSELF.
I KNOW.
I PROMISE I WON'T LIFT A CLAW TO HELP YOU.

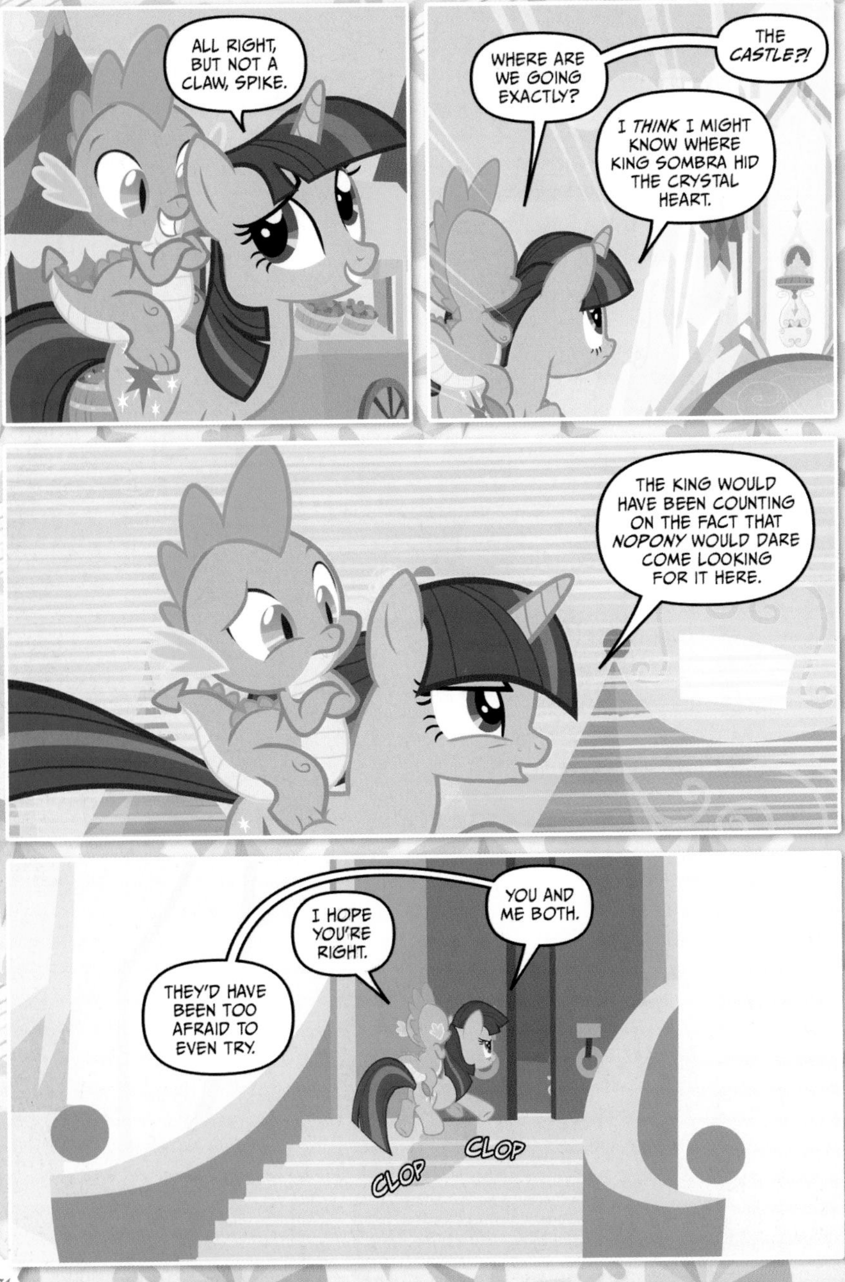
ALL RIGHT, BUT NOT A CLAW, SPIKE.
WHERE ARE WE GOING EXACTLY?
THE *CASTLE?!*
I *THINK* I MIGHT KNOW WHERE KING SOMBRA HID THE CRYSTAL HEART.
THE KING WOULD HAVE BEEN COUNTING ON THE FACT THAT *NOPONY* WOULD DARE COME LOOKING FOR IT HERE.
I HOPE YOU'RE RIGHT.
THEY'D HAVE BEEN TOO AFRAID TO EVEN TRY.
YOU AND ME BOTH.
CLOP
CLOP

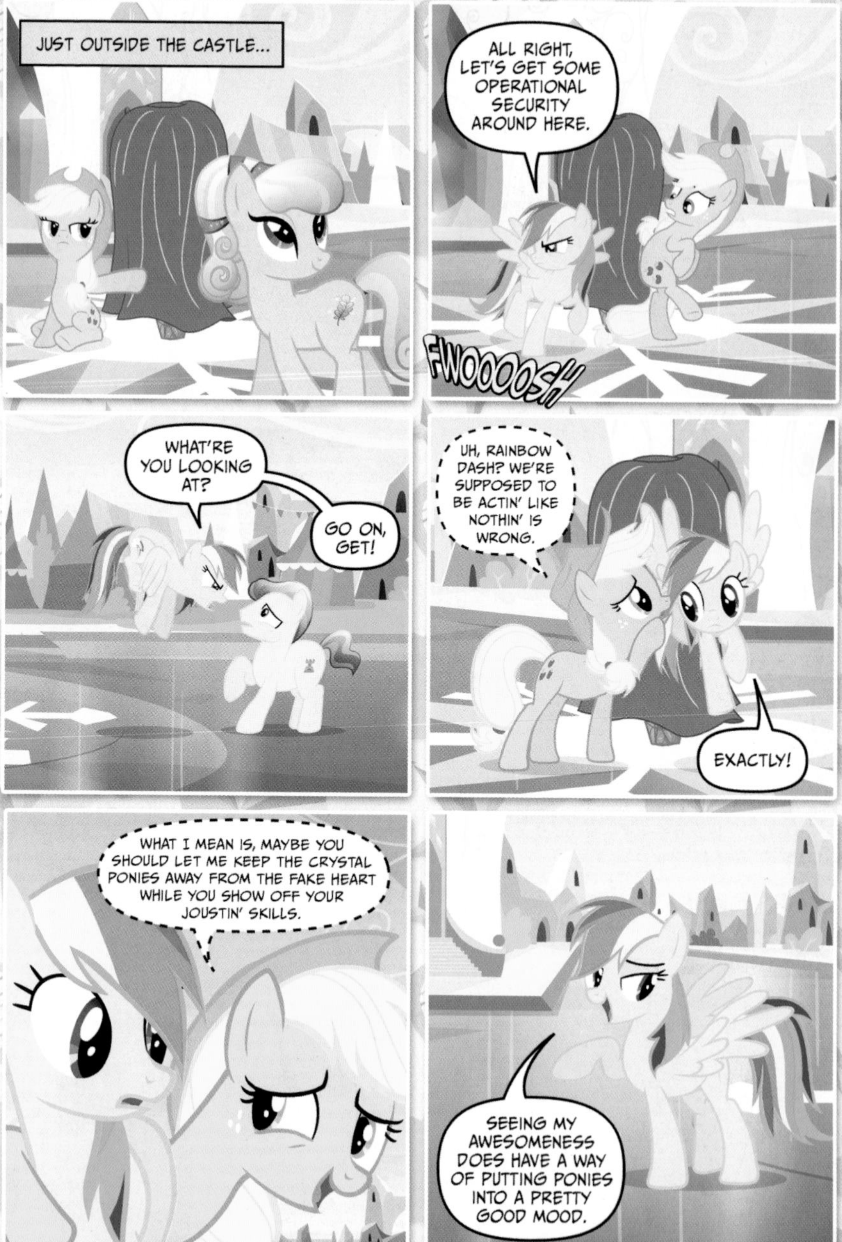
JUST OUTSIDE THE CASTLE...
ALL RIGHT, LET'S GET SOME OPERATIONAL SECURITY AROUND HERE.
FWOOOOSH!
WHAT'RE YOU LOOKING AT?
GO ON, GET!
UH, RAINBOW DASH? WE'RE SUPPOSED TO BE ACTIN' LIKE NOTHIN' IS WRONG.
EXACTLY!
WHAT I MEAN IS, MAYBE YOU SHOULD LET ME KEEP THE CRYSTAL PONIES AWAY FROM THE FAKE HEART WHILE YOU SHOW OFF YOUR JOUSTIN' SKILLS.
SEEING MY AWESOMENESS DOES HAVE A WAY OF PUTTING PONIES INTO A PRETTY GOOD MOOD.

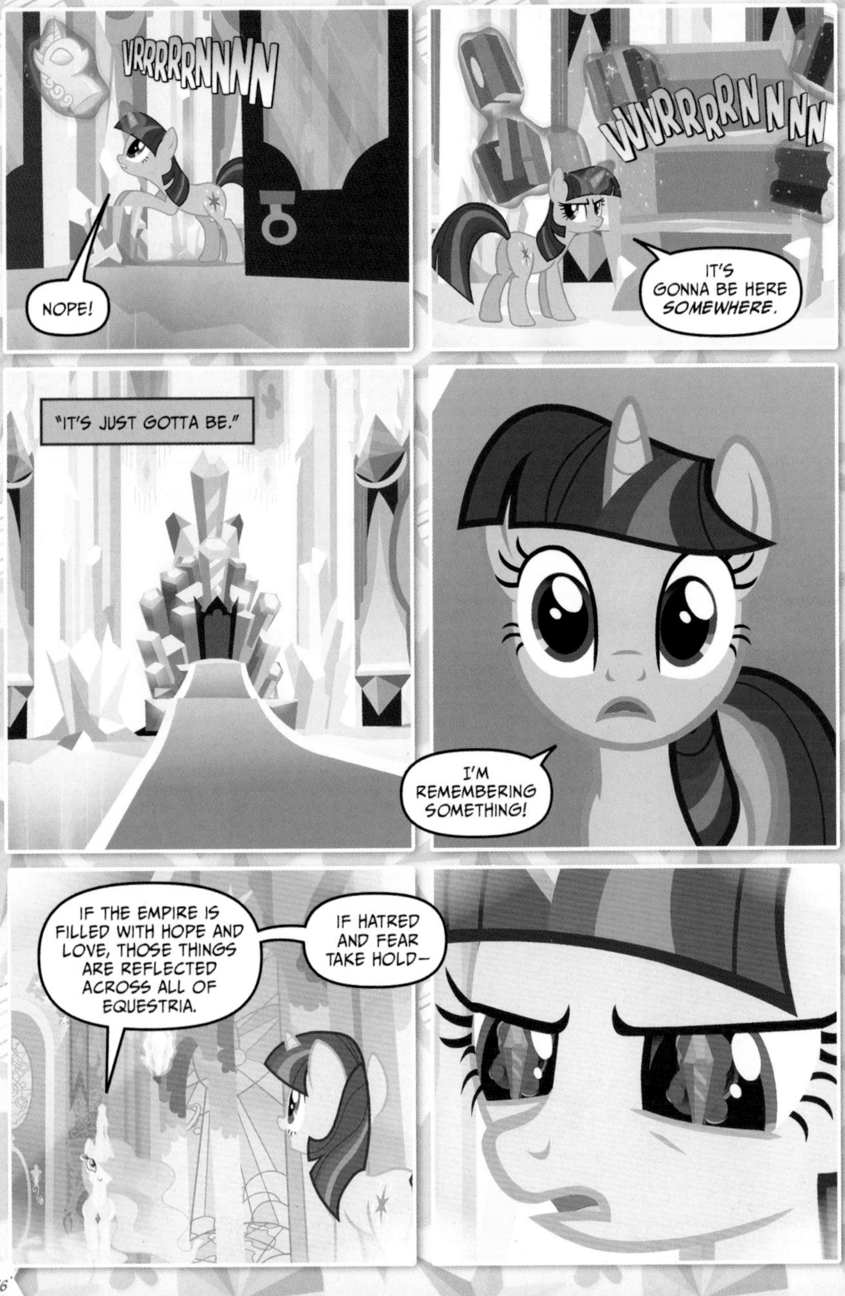
VRRRRRNNNN
NOPE!
VVVRRRRNNNN
IT'S GONNA BE HERE SOMEWHERE.
"IT'S JUST GOTTA BE."
I'M REMEMBERING SOMETHING!
IF THE EMPIRE IS FILLED WITH HOPE AND LOVE, THOSE THINGS ARE REFLECTED ACROSS ALL OF EQUESTRIA.
IF HATRED AND FEAR TAKE HOLD–

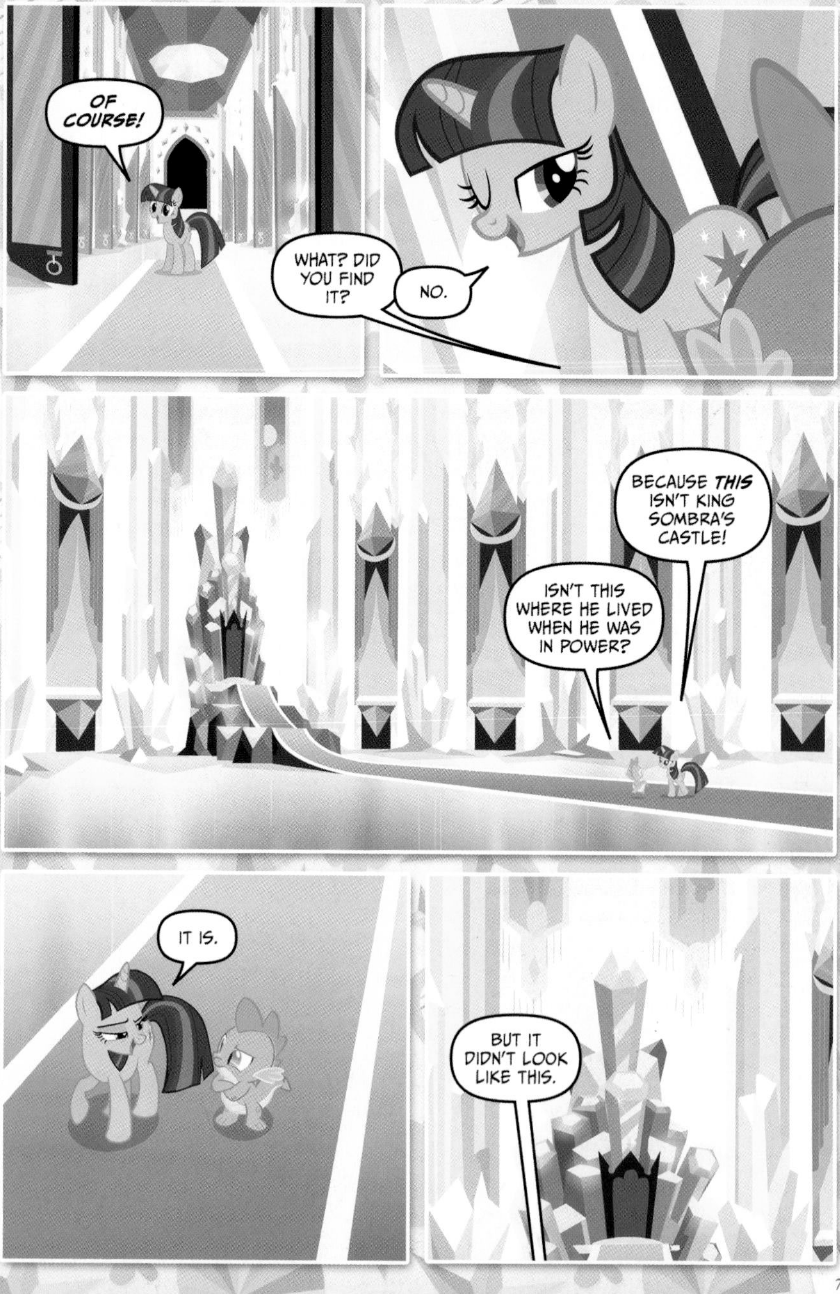
OF COURSE!
WHAT? DID YOU FIND IT?
NO.
ISN'T THIS WHERE HE LIVED WHEN HE WAS IN POWER?
BECAUSE **THIS** ISN'T KING SOMBRA'S CASTLE!
IT IS.
BUT IT DIDN'T LOOK LIKE THIS.

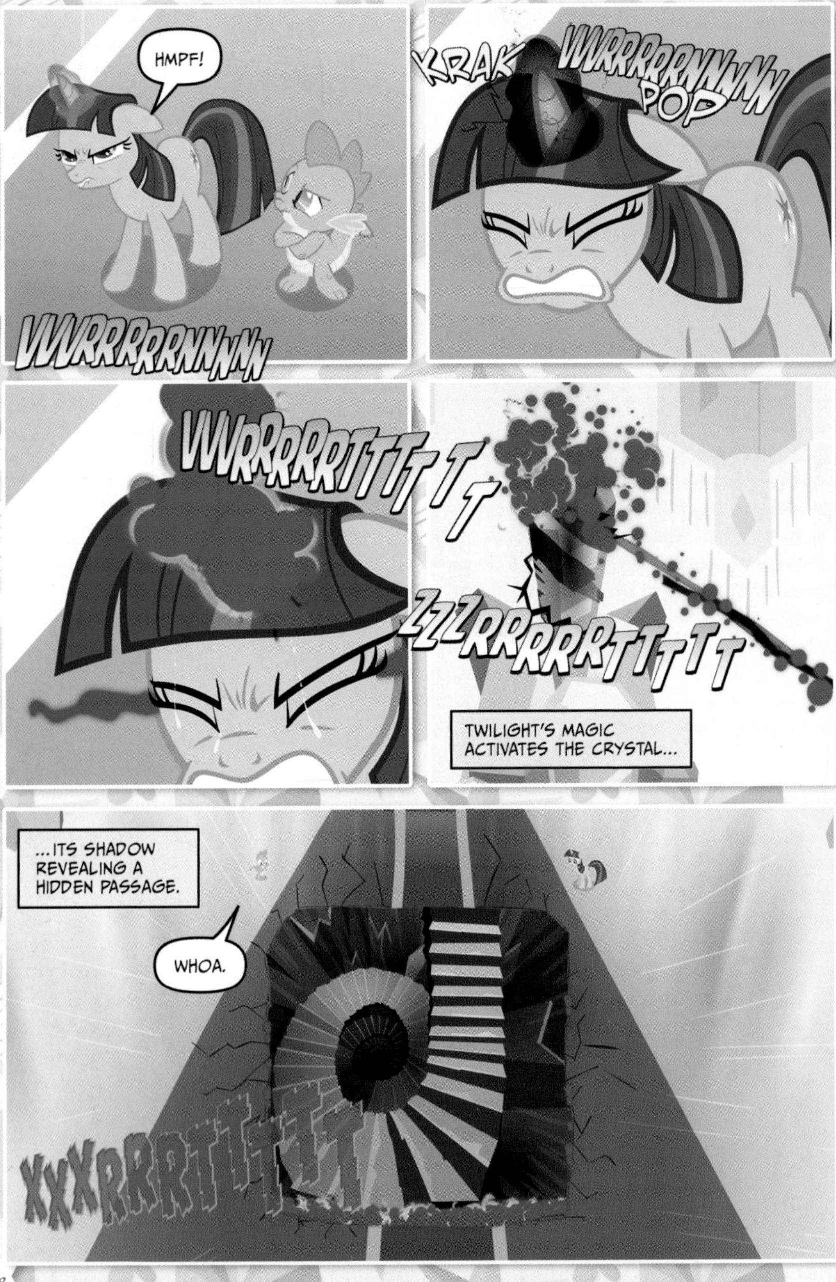
HMPF!
VVVVRRRRRRNNNNNN
KRAK
VVVVRRRRRRNNNNNN
POP
VVVVRRRRRRTTTTTT
ZZZRRRRRRTTTTTT
TWILIGHT'S MAGIC ACTIVATES THE CRYSTAL...
...ITS SHADOW REVEALING A HIDDEN PASSAGE.
WHOA.
XXXRRRTTTTT

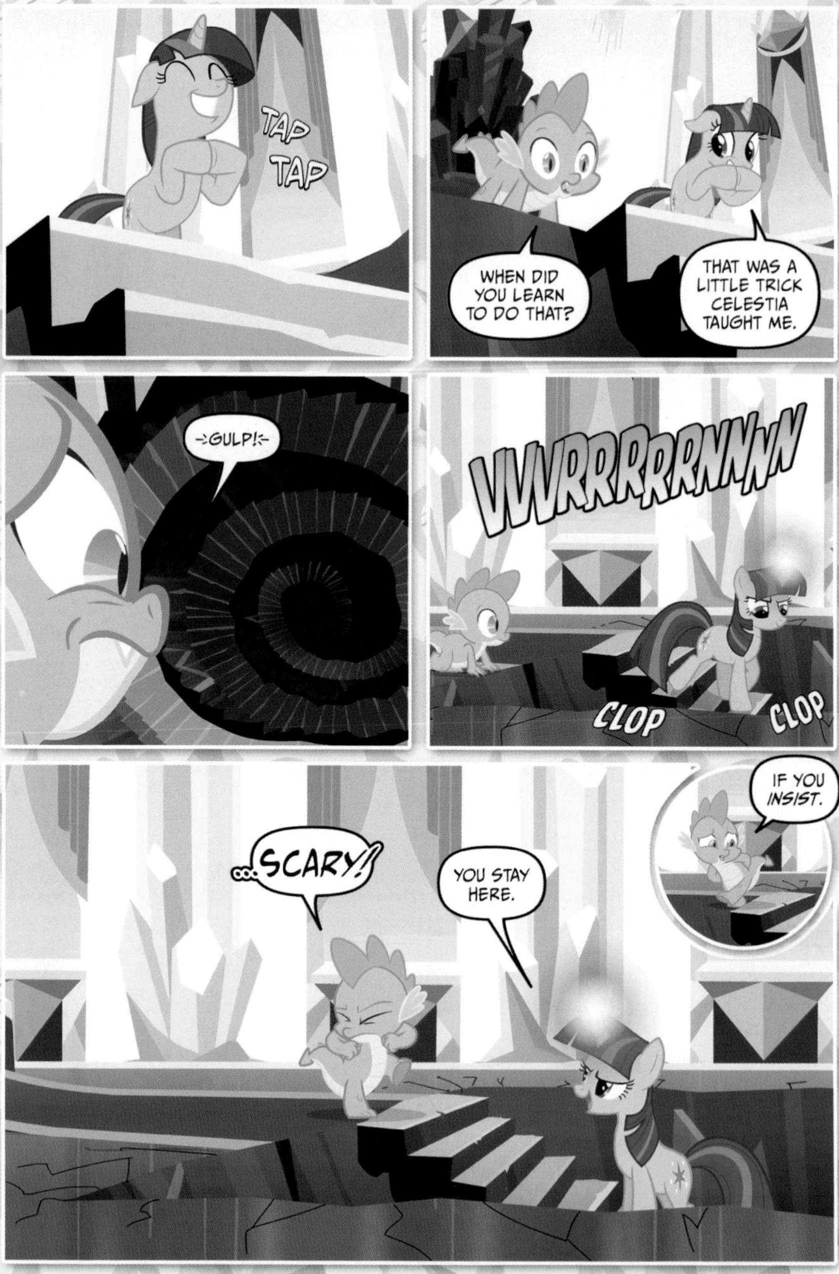
TAP
TAP
WHEN DID YOU LEARN TO DO THAT?
THAT WAS A LITTLE TRICK CELESTIA TAUGHT ME.
-GULP!-
VVVRRRRRNNNN
CLOP
CLOP
...SCARY!
YOU STAY HERE.
IF YOU INSIST.

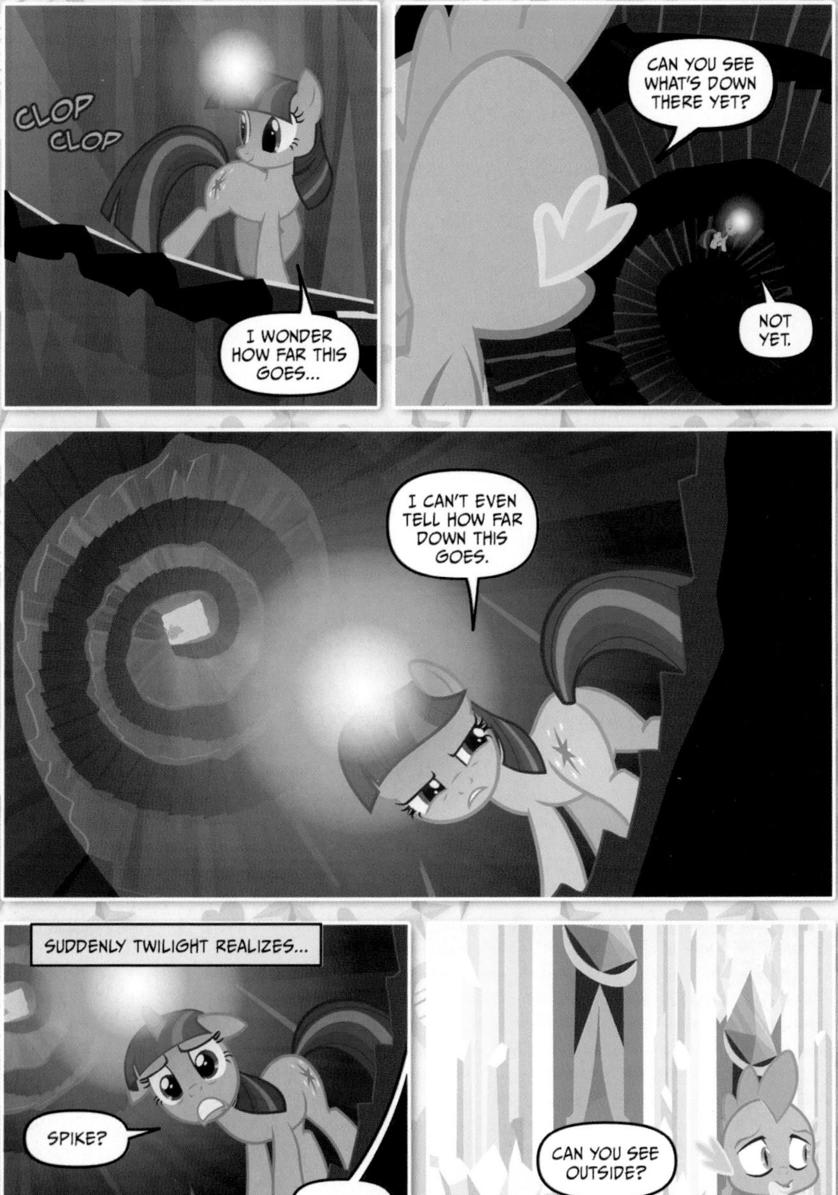
CLOP
CLOP
I WONDER HOW FAR THIS GOES...
CAN YOU SEE WHAT'S DOWN THERE YET?
NOT YET.
I CAN'T EVEN TELL HOW FAR DOWN THIS GOES.
SUDDENLY TWILIGHT REALIZES...
SPIKE?
YEAH?
CAN YOU SEE OUTSIDE?

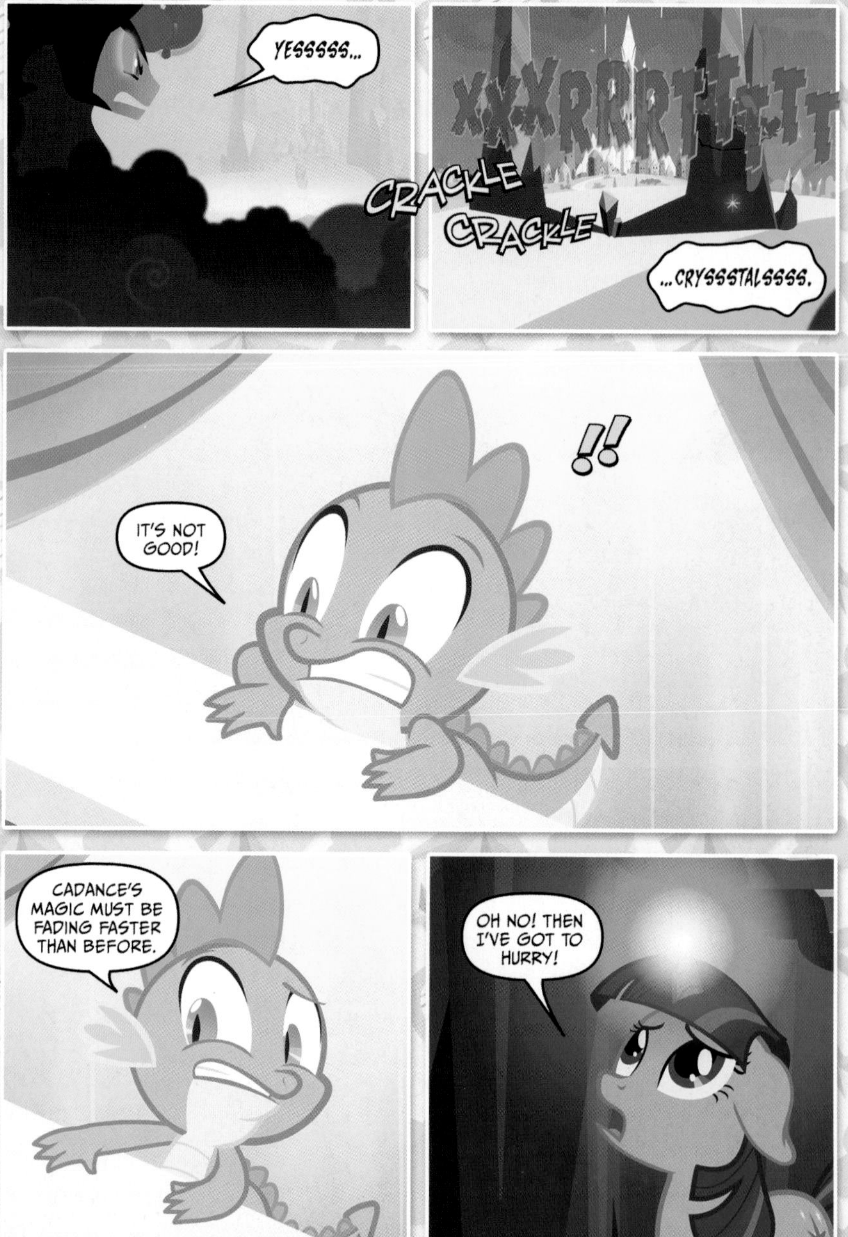
YESSSSS...
XXXRRRTTTTTT
CRACKLE
CRACKLE
...CRYSSSTALSSSS.
IT'S NOT GOOD!
!!
CADANCE'S MAGIC MUST BE FADING FASTER THAN BEFORE.
OH NO! THEN I'VE GOT TO HURRY!

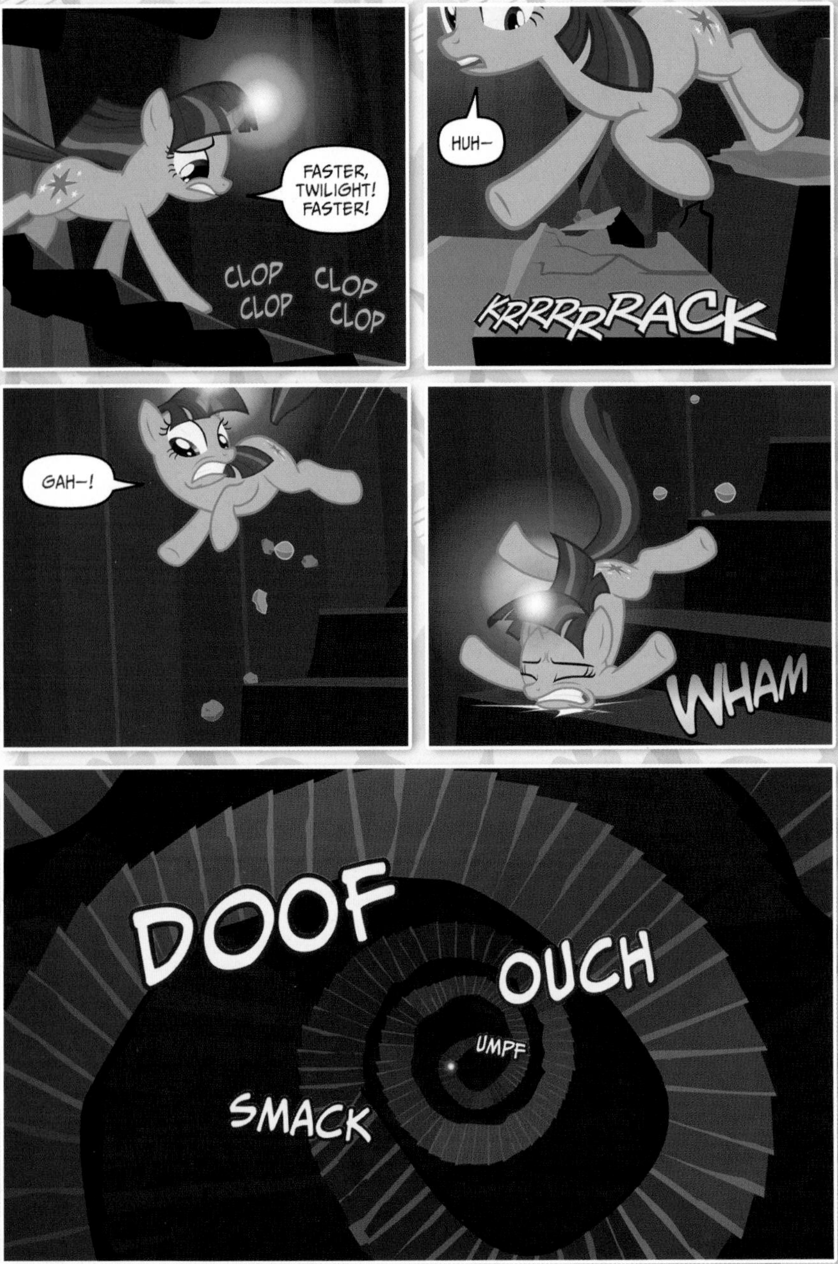
FASTER, TWILIGHT! FASTER!
CLOP CLOP
CLOP CLOP
HUH—
KRRRRRACK
GAH—!
WHAM
DOOF
OUCH
UMPF
SMACK

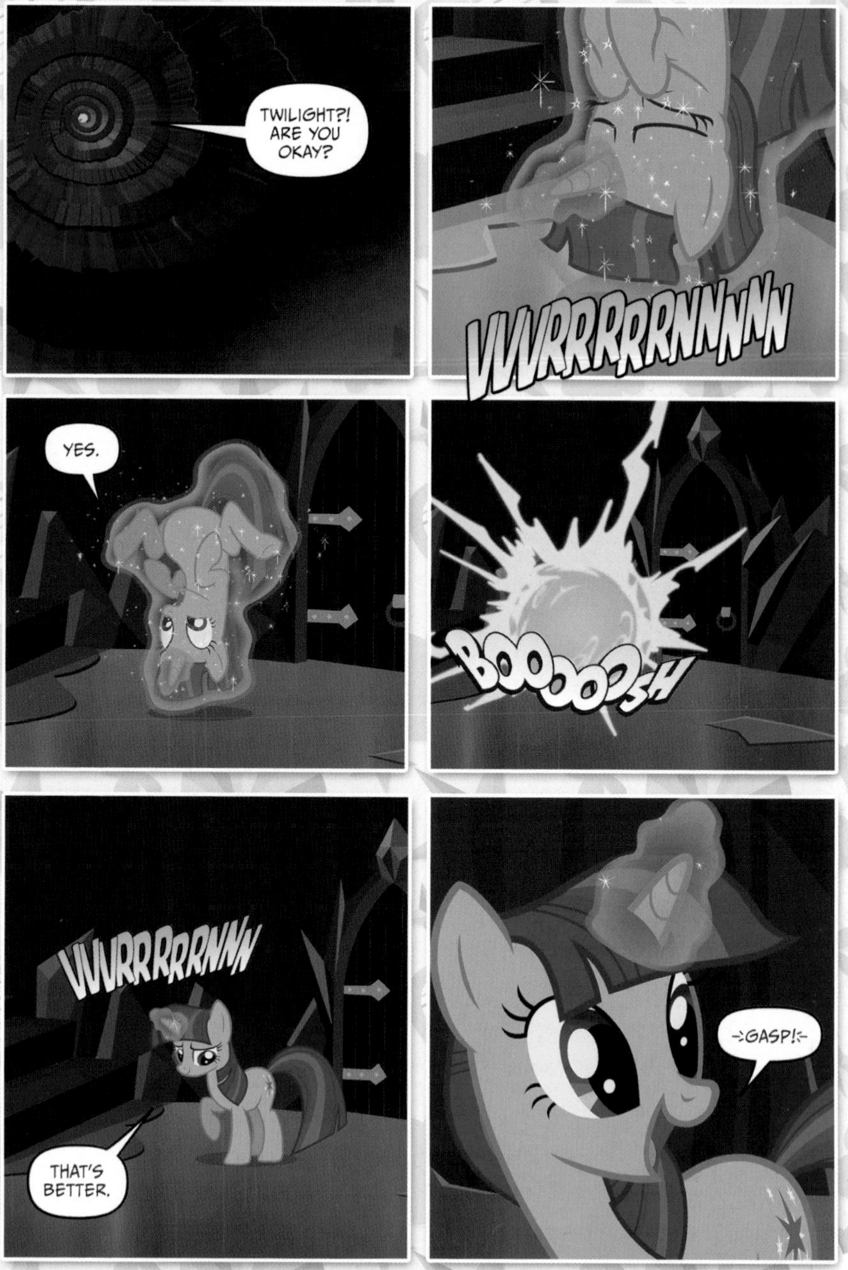
TWILIGHT?! ARE YOU OKAY?
VVVRRRRRNNNNN
YES.
BOOOOOOSH
VVVRRRRRNNN
THAT'S BETTER.
-GASP!-

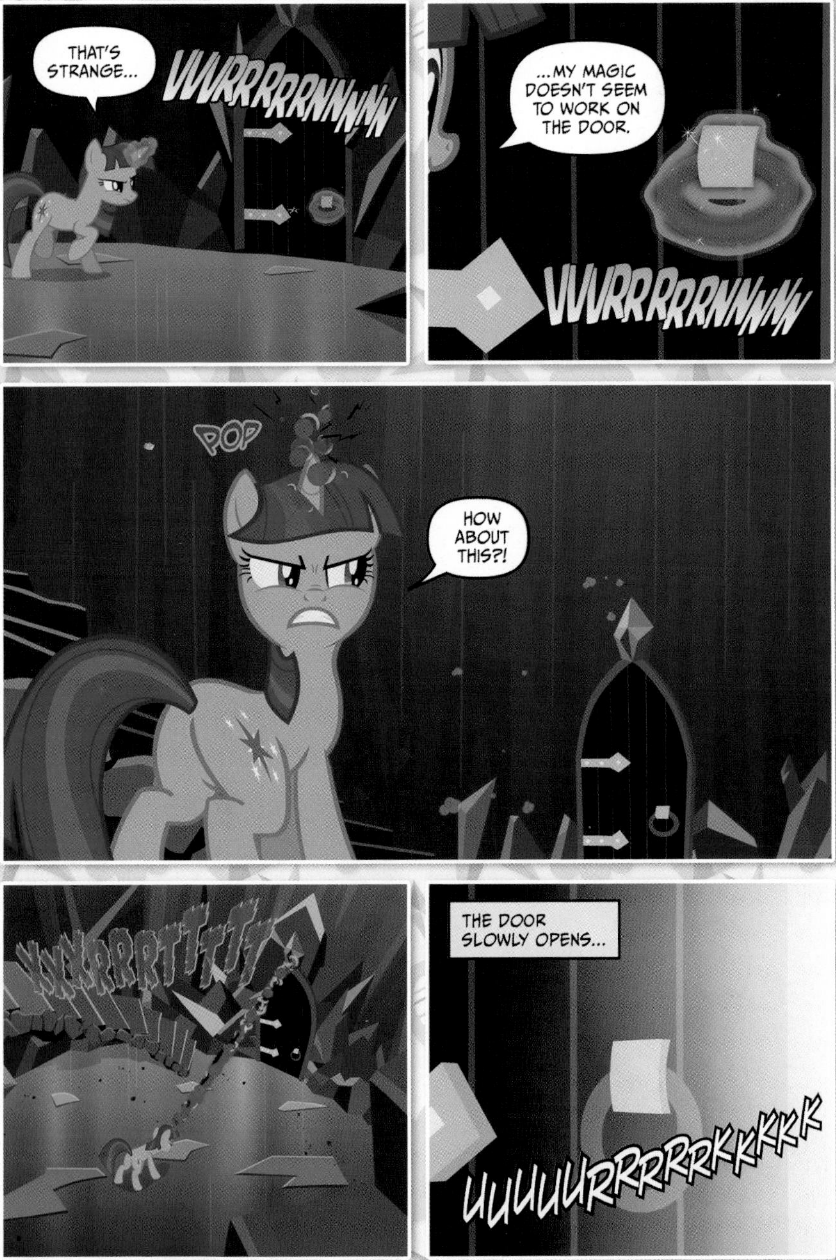
THAT'S STRANGE...
VVVRRRRRNNNNN
...MY MAGIC DOESN'T SEEM TO WORK ON THE DOOR.
VVVRRRRRNNNNN
POP
HOW ABOUT THIS?!
THE DOOR SLOWLY OPENS...
UUUUURRRRRKKKKK

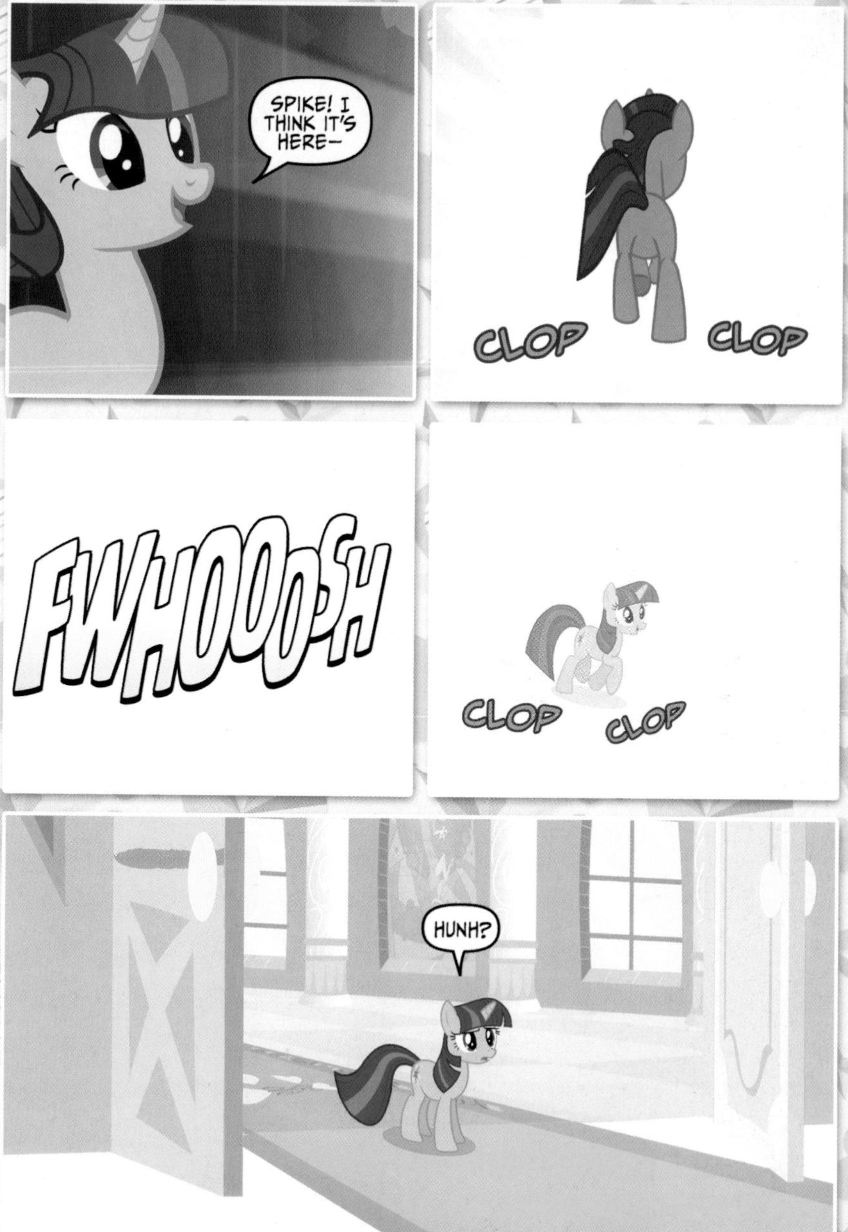
SPIKE! I THINK IT'S HERE—
CLOP
CLOP
FWHOOOSH
CLOP
CLOP
HUNH?

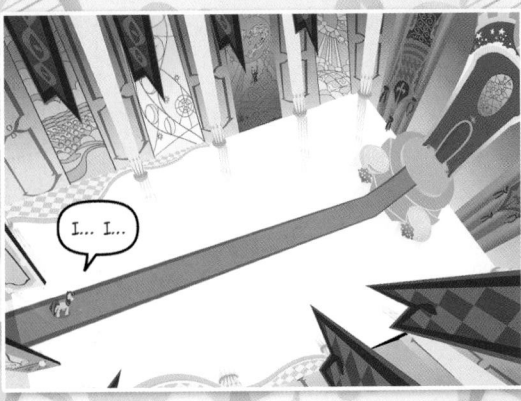

I... I...

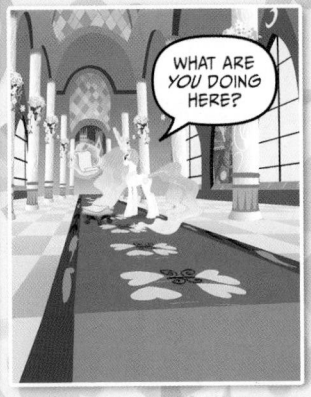

WHAT ARE *YOU* DOING HERE?

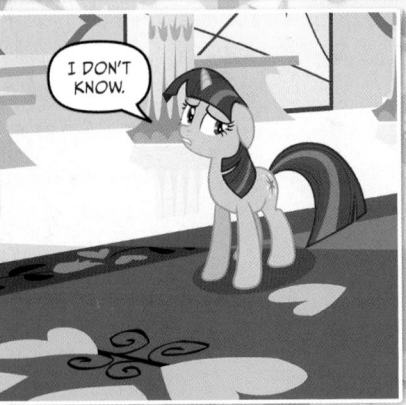

I DON'T KNOW.

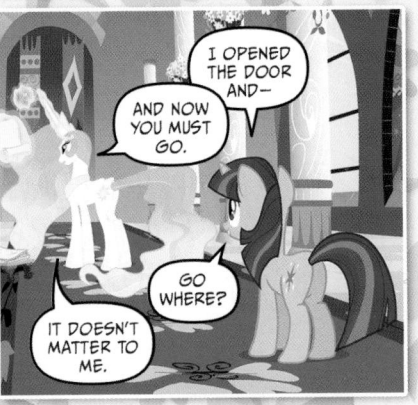

I OPENED THE DOOR AND—

AND NOW YOU MUST GO.

GO WHERE?

IT DOESN'T MATTER TO ME.

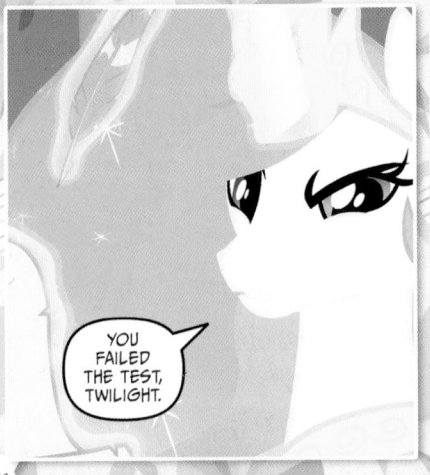

YOU FAILED THE TEST, TWILIGHT.

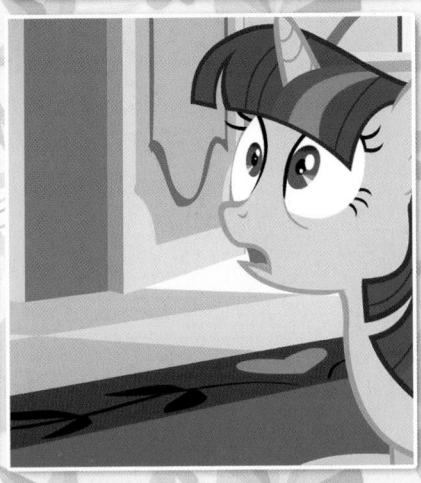

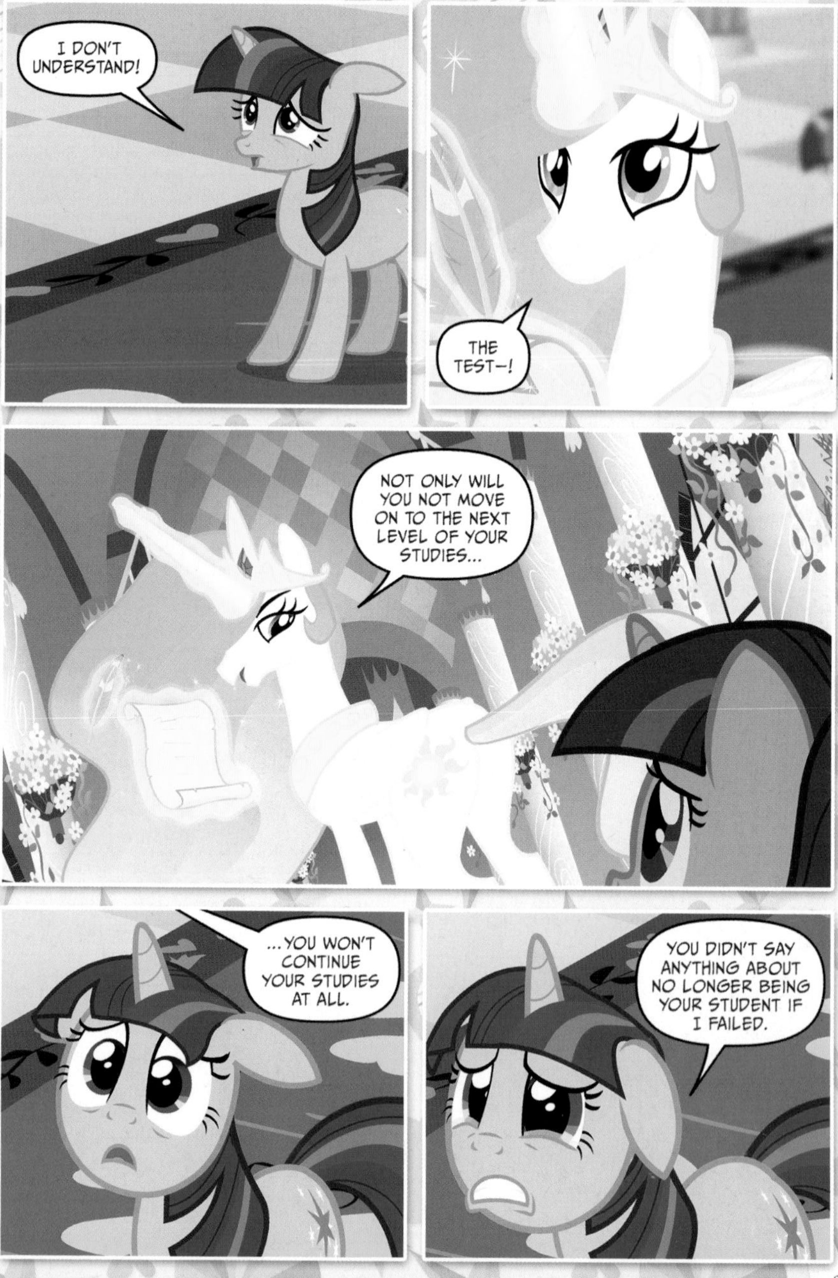
I DON'T UNDERSTAND!
THE TEST—!
NOT ONLY WILL YOU NOT MOVE ON TO THE NEXT LEVEL OF YOUR STUDIES...
...YOU WON'T CONTINUE YOUR STUDIES AT ALL.
YOU DIDN'T SAY ANYTHING ABOUT NO LONGER BEING YOUR STUDENT IF I FAILED.

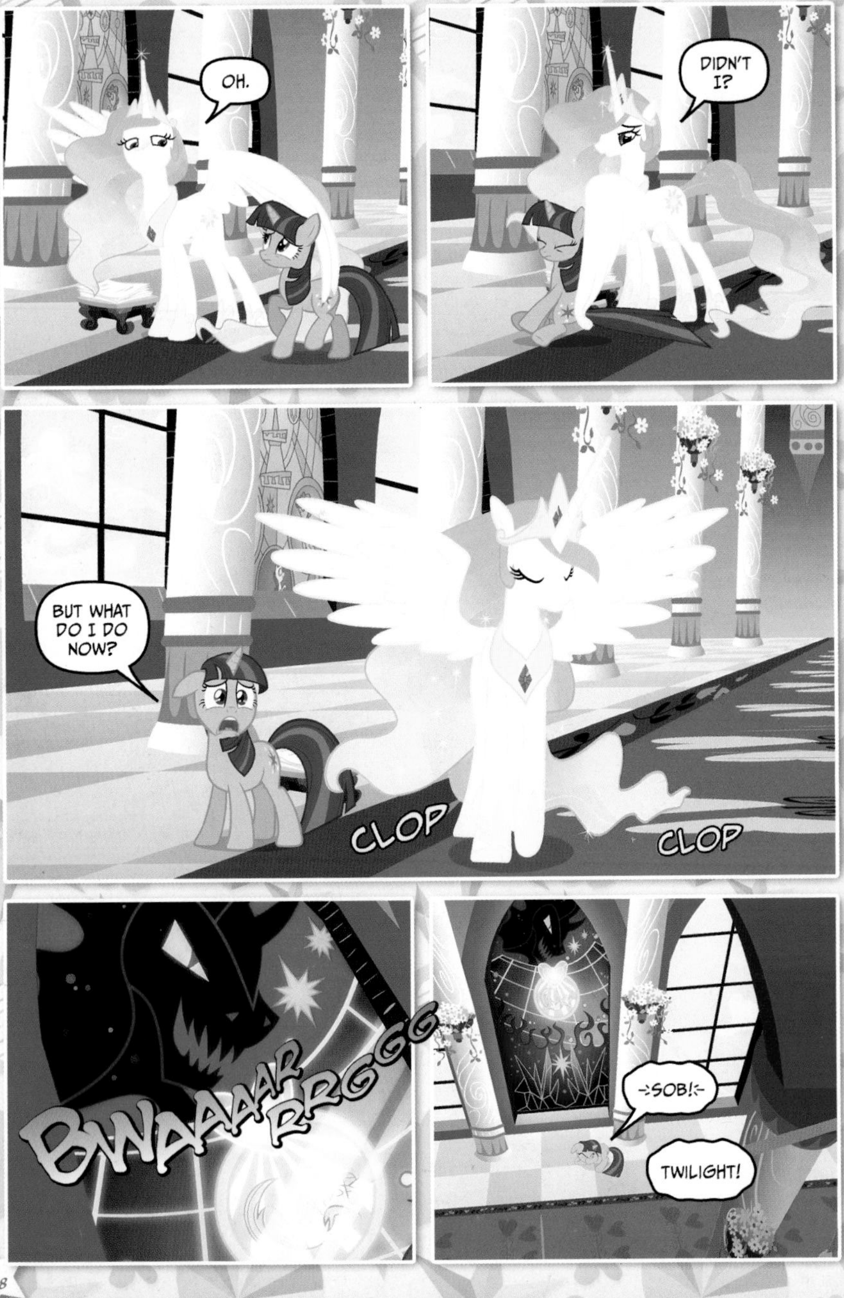
OH.
DIDN'T I?
BUT WHAT DO I DO NOW?
CLOP
CLOP
BWAAAAR RRGGG
-SOB!-
TWILIGHT!

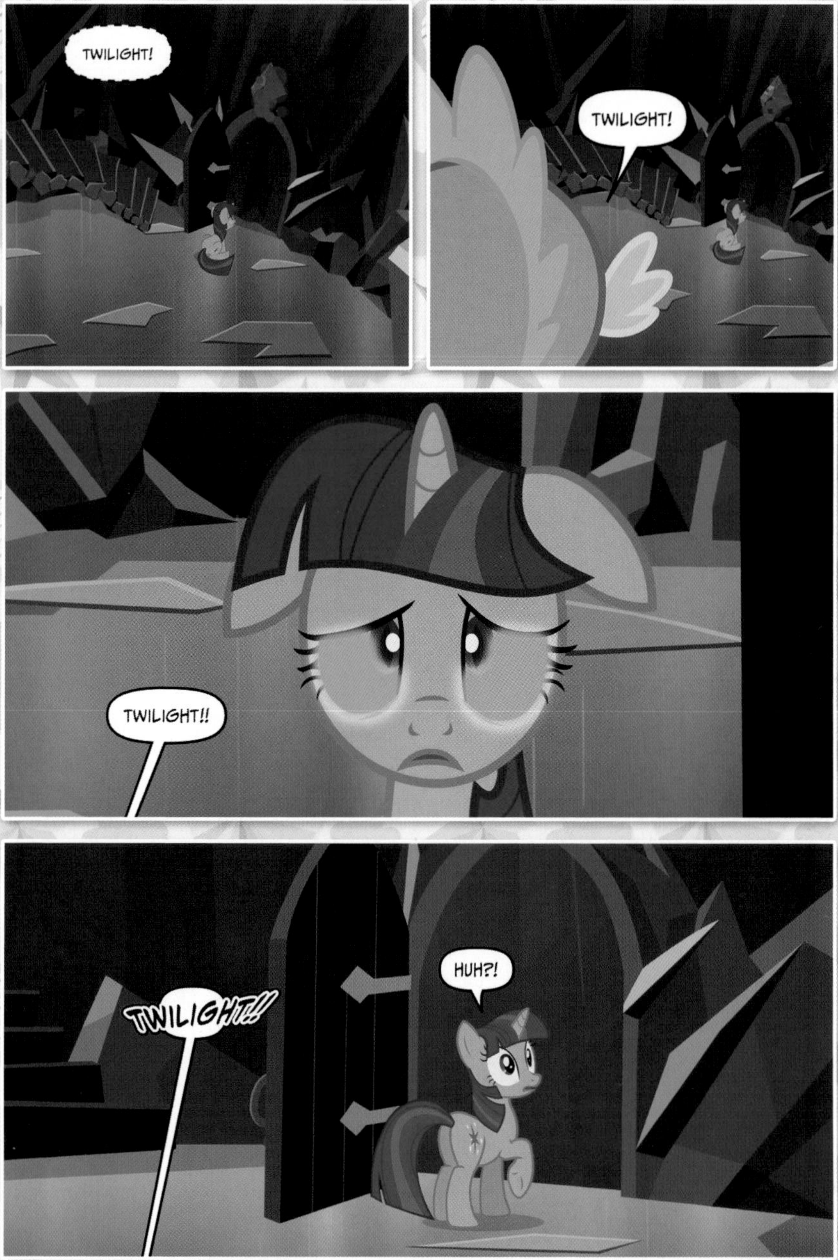
TWILIGHT!
TWILIGHT!
TWILIGHT!!
TWILIGHT!!
HUH?!

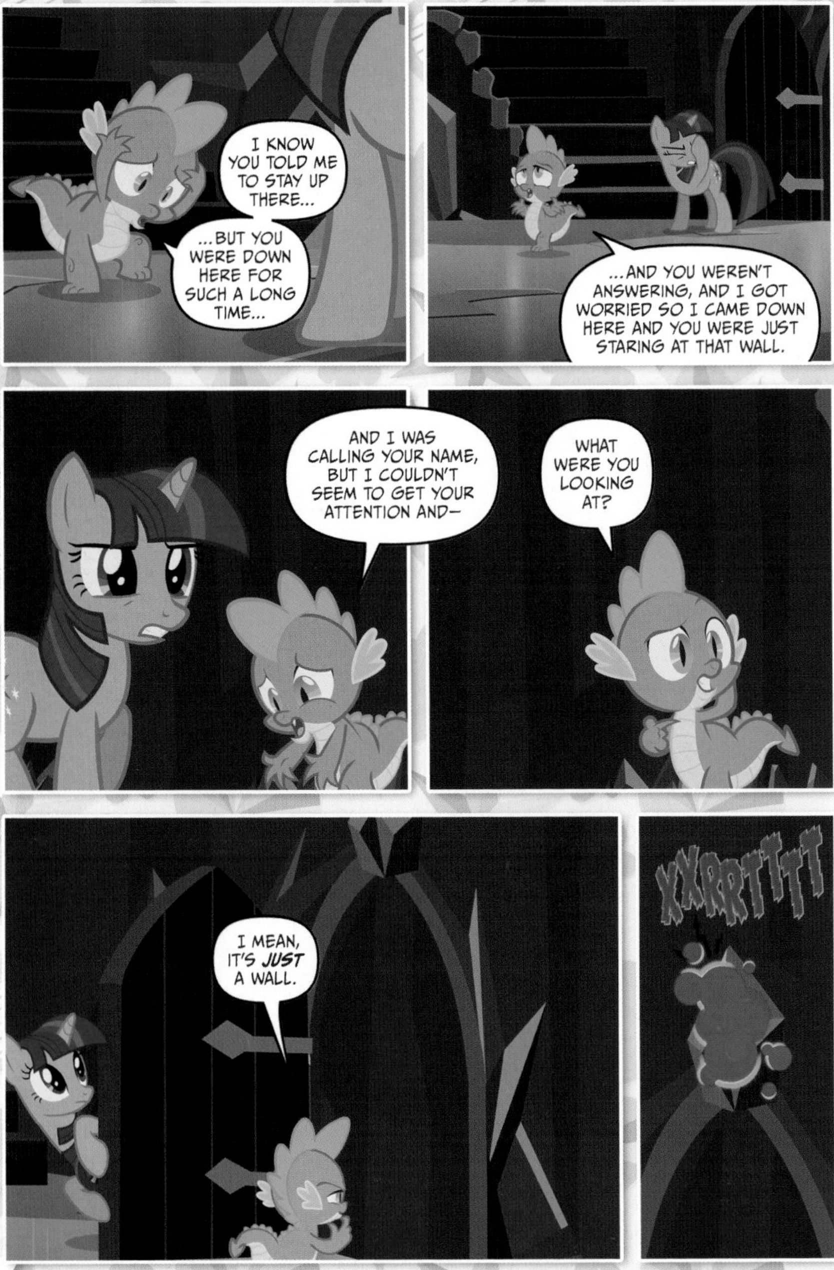
I KNOW YOU TOLD ME TO STAY UP THERE...
...BUT YOU WERE DOWN HERE FOR SUCH A LONG TIME...
...AND YOU WEREN'T ANSWERING, AND I GOT WORRIED SO I CAME DOWN HERE AND YOU WERE JUST STARING AT THAT WALL.
AND I WAS CALLING YOUR NAME, BUT I COULDN'T SEEM TO GET YOUR ATTENTION AND—
WHAT WERE YOU LOOKING AT?
I MEAN, IT'S *JUST* A WALL.
XXRRTTTT

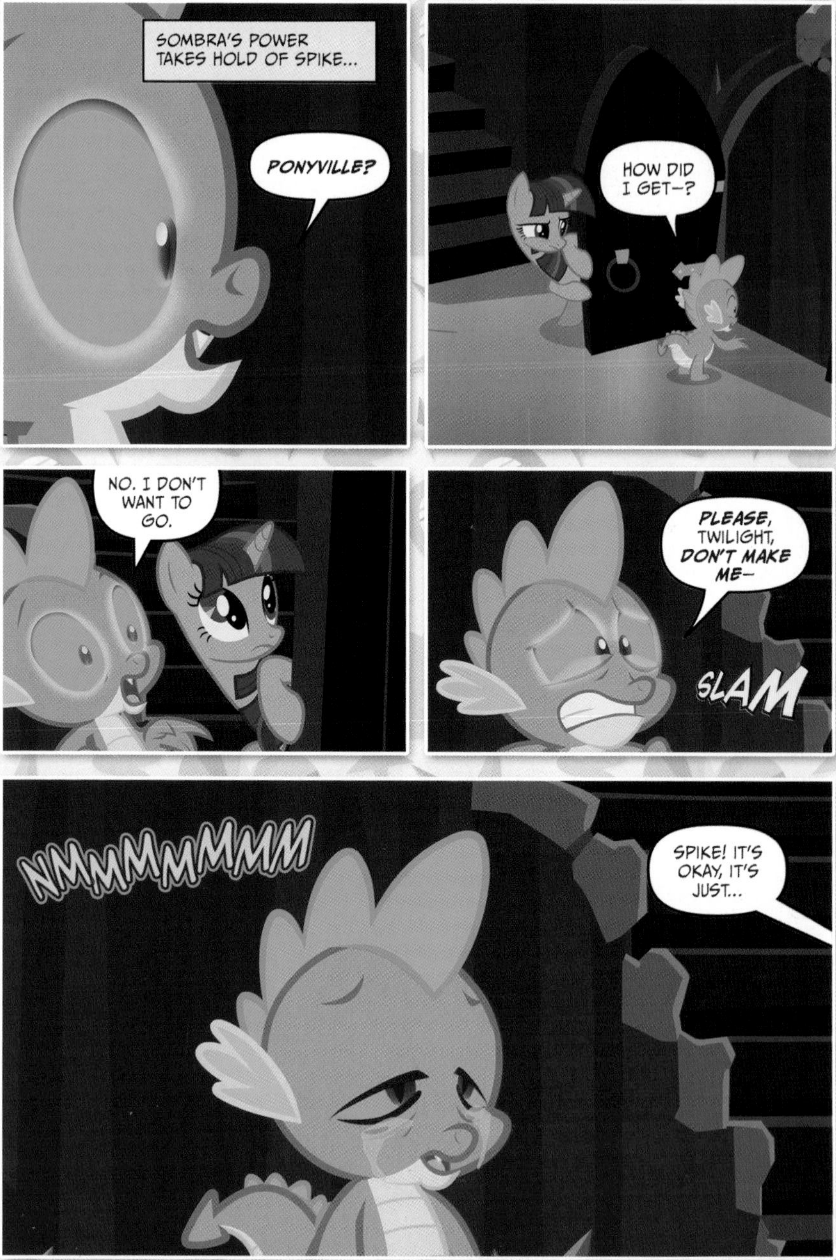
SOMBRA'S POWER TAKES HOLD OF SPIKE...
PONYVILLE?
HOW DID I GET—?
NO. I DON'T WANT TO GO.
PLEASE, TWILIGHT, ***DON'T MAKE ME—***
SLAM
NMMMMMMMM
SPIKE! IT'S OKAY, IT'S JUST...

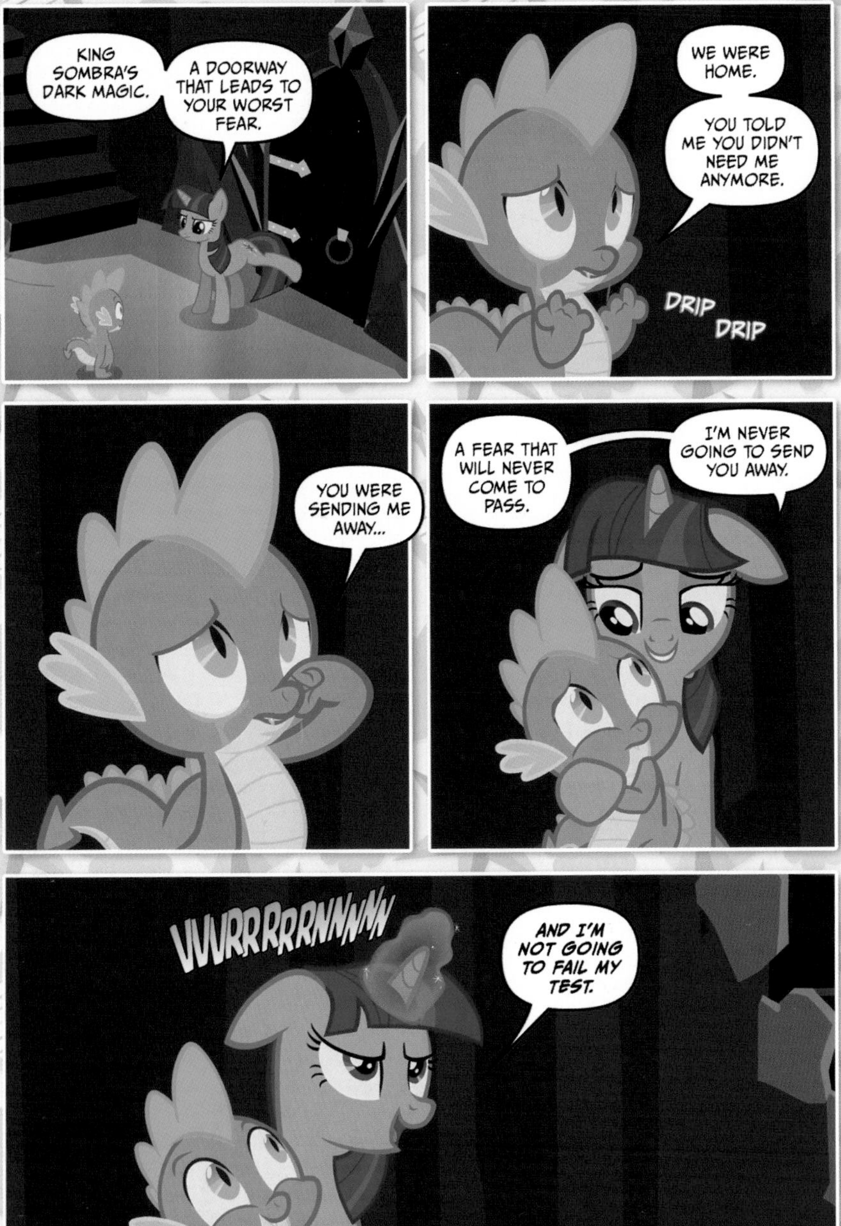
KING SOMBRA'S DARK MAGIC.
A DOORWAY THAT LEADS TO YOUR WORST FEAR.
WE WERE HOME.
YOU TOLD ME YOU DIDN'T NEED ME ANYMORE.
DRIP
DRIP
YOU WERE SENDING ME AWAY...
A FEAR THAT WILL NEVER COME TO PASS.
I'M NEVER GOING TO SEND YOU AWAY.
VVURRRRRNNNNN
AND I'M NOT GOING TO FAIL MY TEST.

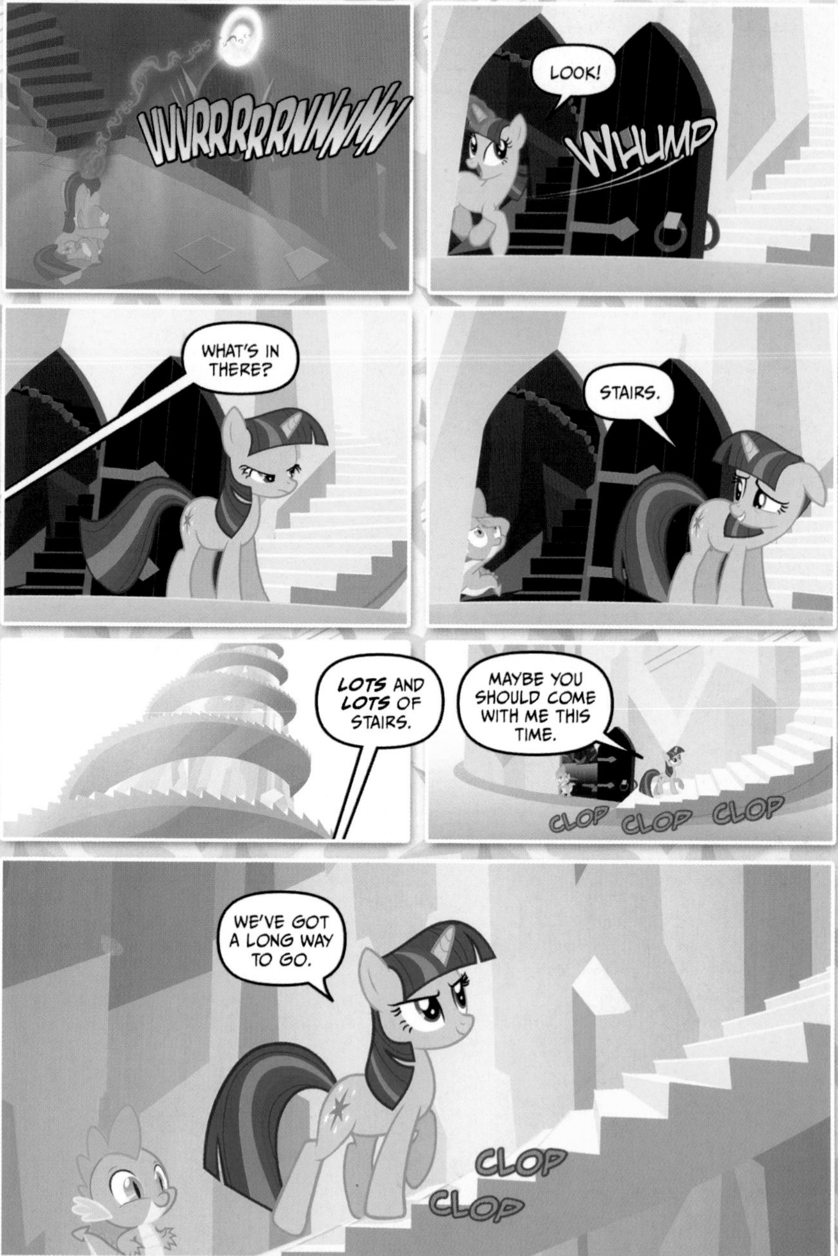
VVVRRRRRNNNNN
LOOK!
WHUMP
WHAT'S IN THERE?
STAIRS.
LOTS AND LOTS OF STAIRS.
MAYBE YOU SHOULD COME WITH ME THIS TIME.
CLOP CLOP CLOP
WE'VE GOT A LONG WAY TO GO.
CLOP
CLOP

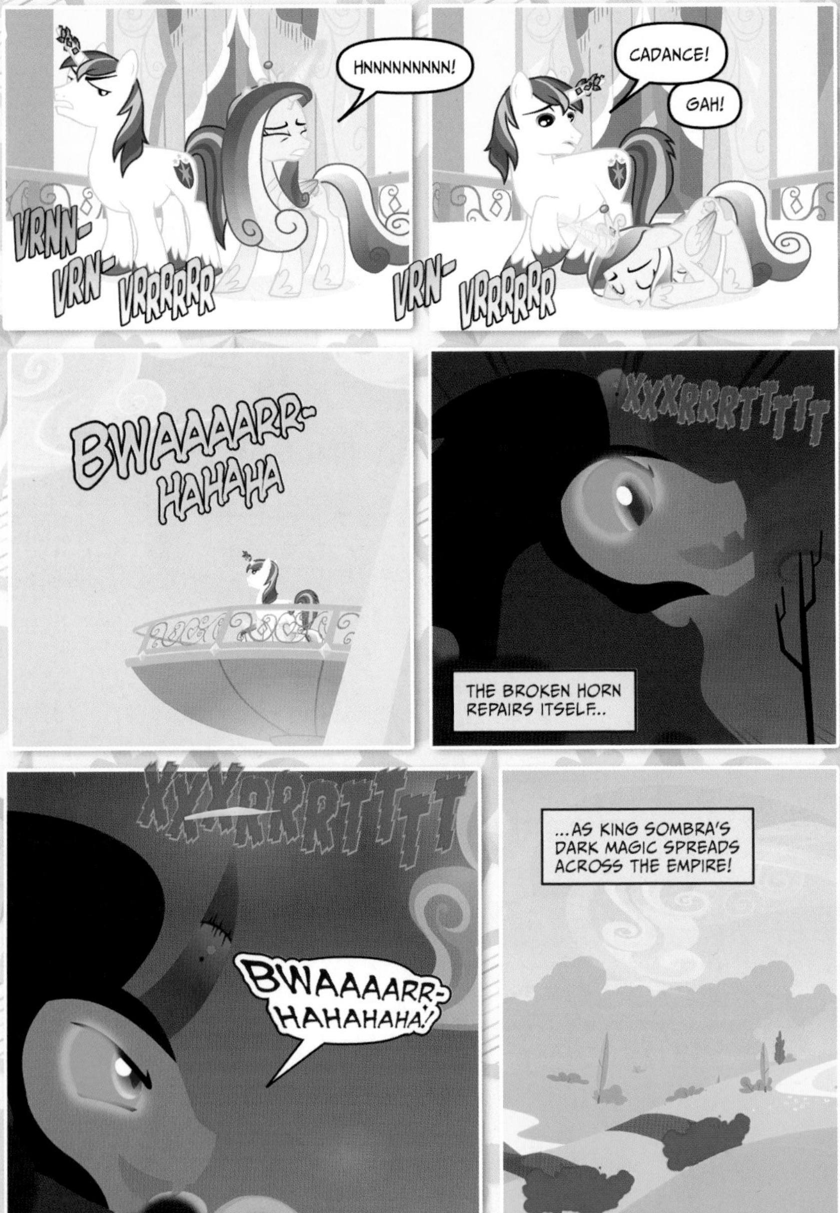
HNNNNNNNNN!
VRNN-
VRN-
VRRRRRR
CADANCE!
GAH!
VRN-
VRRRRRR
BWAAAARR-
HAHAHA
XXXRRRTTTTT
THE BROKEN HORN
REPAIRS ITSELF...
XXXRRRTTTTT
BWAAAARR-
HAHAHAHA!
...AS KING SOMBRA'S
DARK MAGIC SPREADS
ACROSS THE EMPIRE!

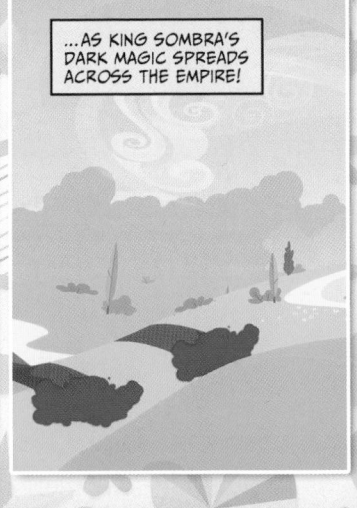

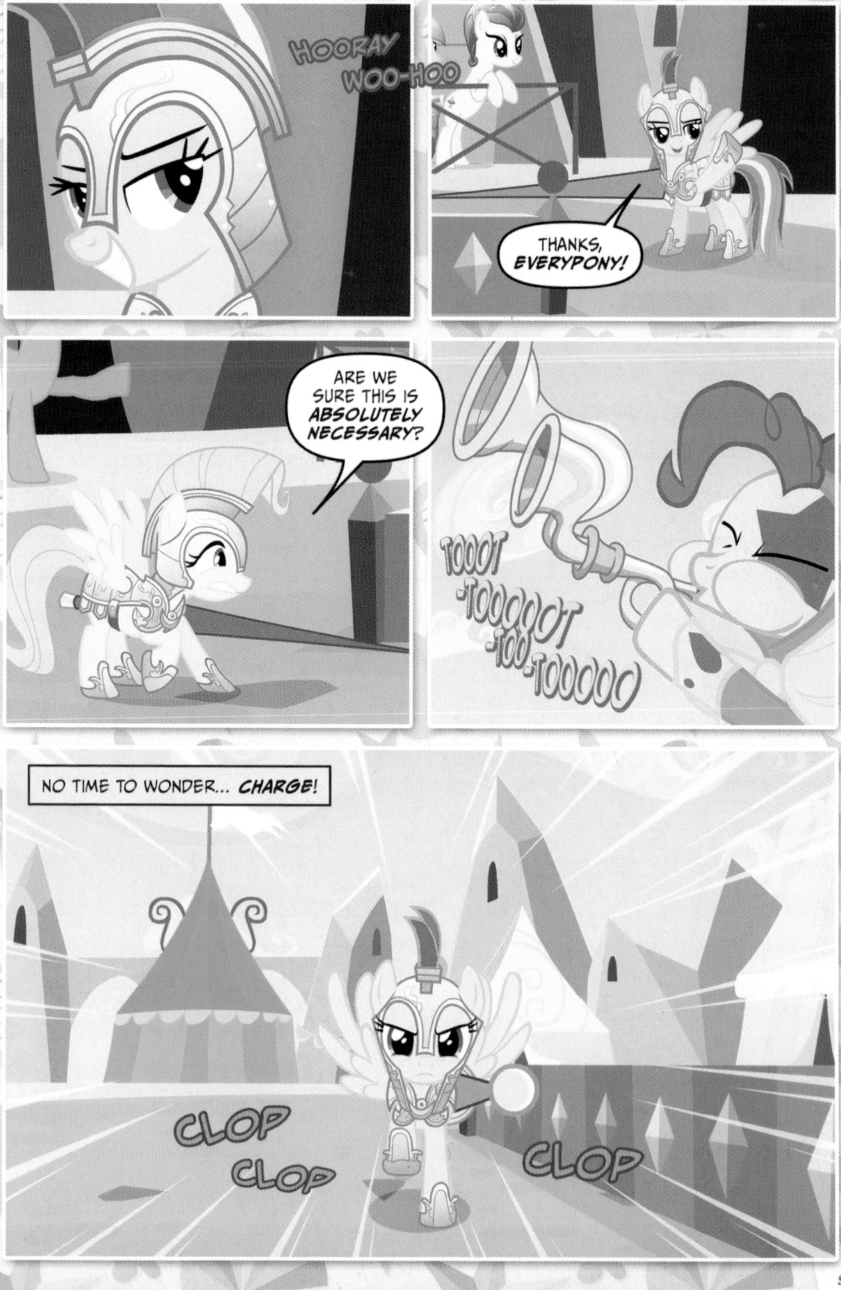
HOORAY
WOO-HOO
THANKS, *EVERYPONY!*
ARE WE SURE THIS IS *ABSOLUTELY NECESSARY?*
TOOOT -TOOOOOT -TOO-TOOOOO
NO TIME TO WONDER... *CHARGE!*
CLOP
CLOP
CLOP

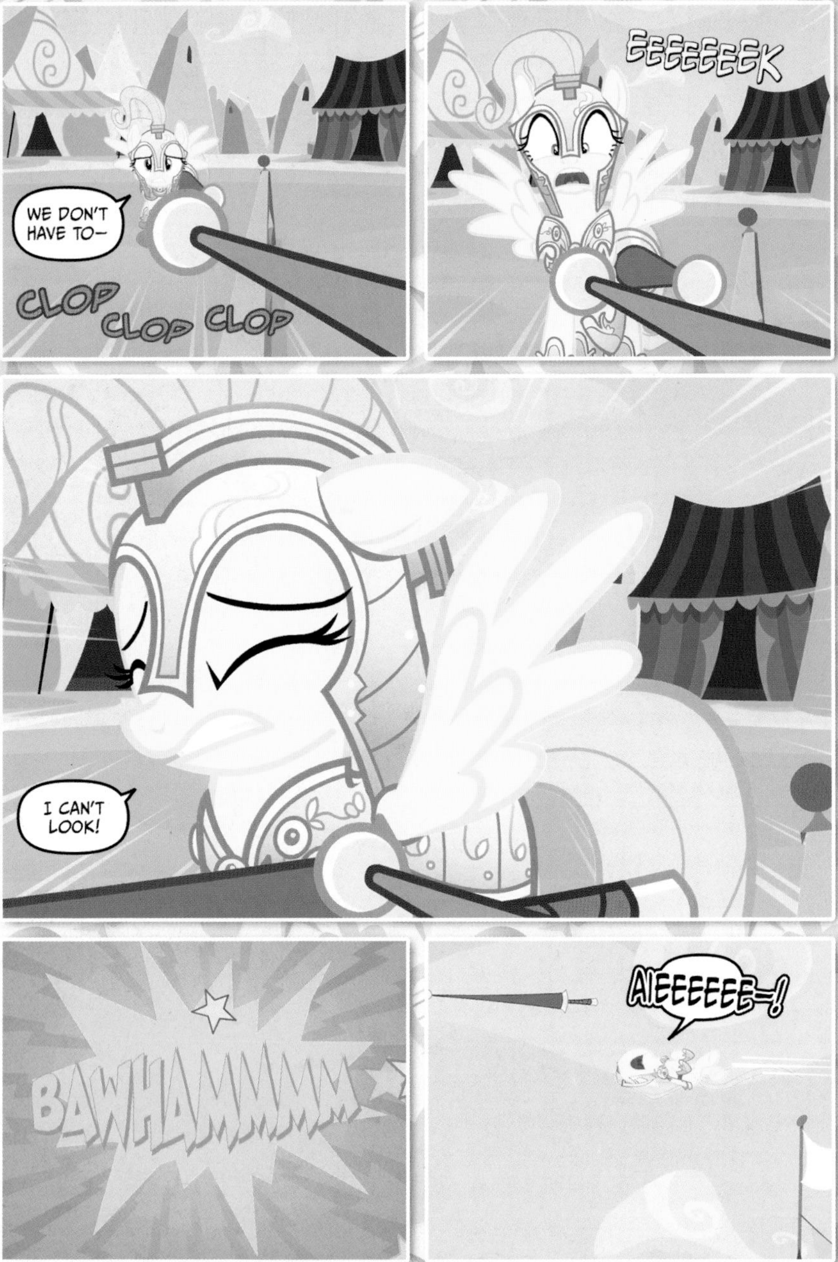
WE DON'T HAVE TO—
CLOP CLOP CLOP
EEEEEEEK
I CAN'T LOOK!
BAWHAMMMM
AIEEEEEE—!

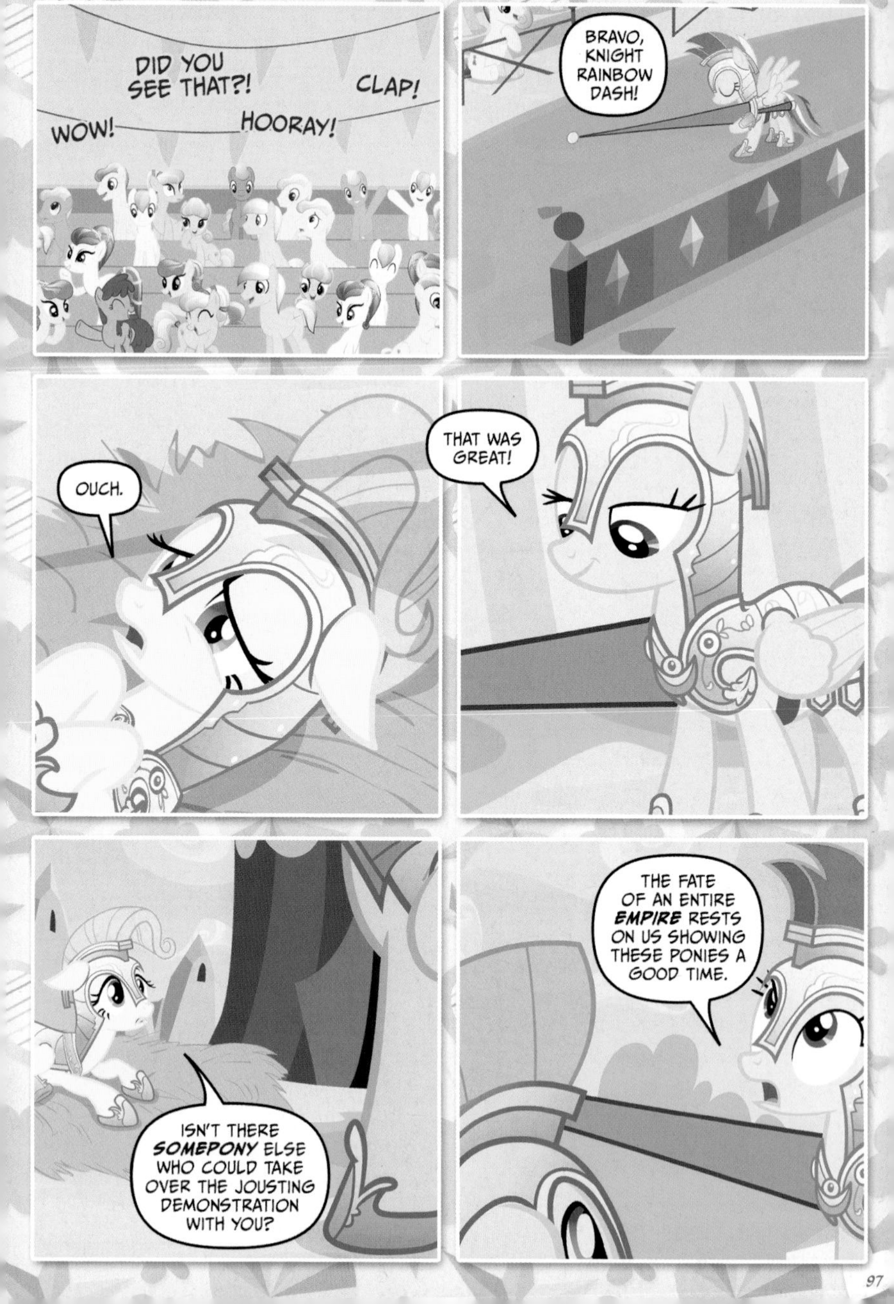
DID YOU SEE THAT?!
CLAP!
WOW!
HOORAY!
BRAVO, KNIGHT RAINBOW DASH!
OUCH.
THAT WAS GREAT!
ISN'T THERE **SOMEPONY** ELSE WHO COULD TAKE OVER THE JOUSTING DEMONSTRATION WITH YOU?
THE FATE OF AN ENTIRE **EMPIRE** RESTS ON US SHOWING THESE PONIES A GOOD TIME.

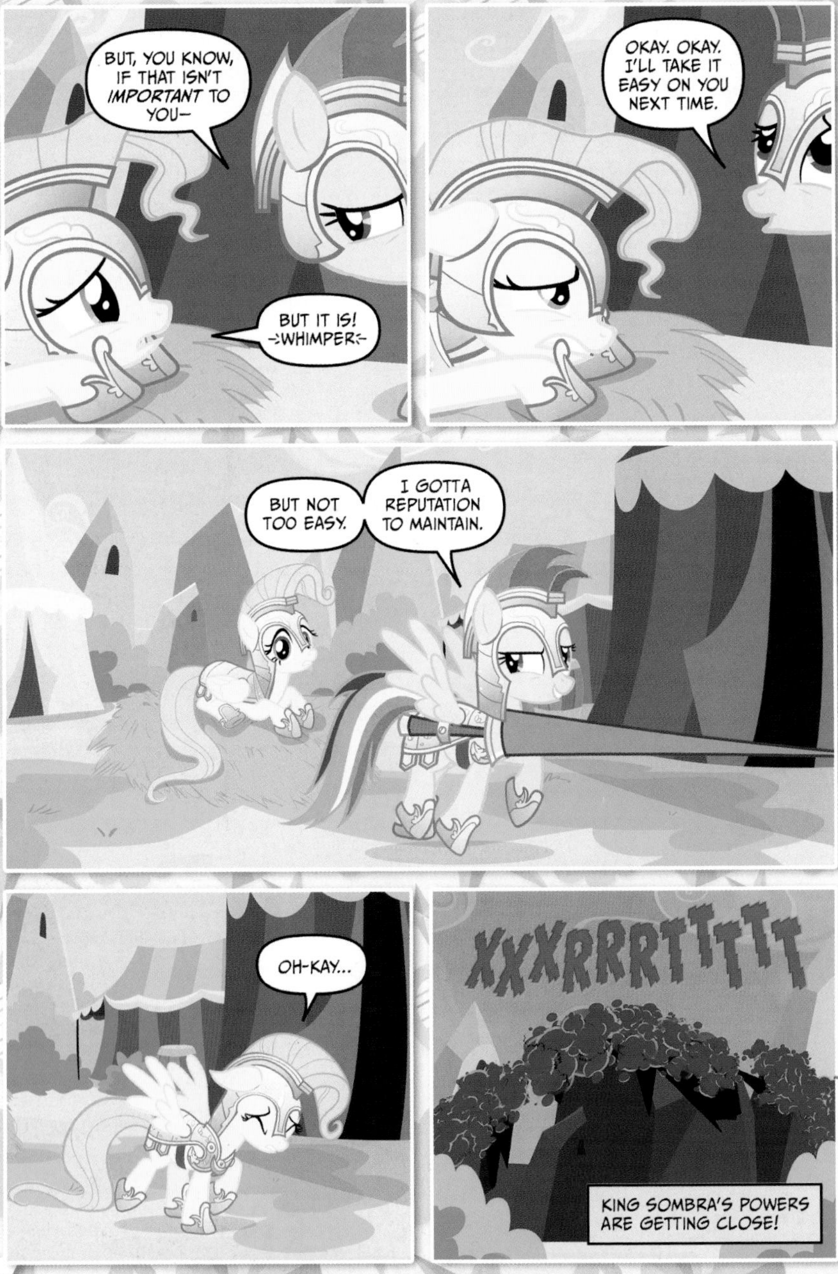
BUT, YOU KNOW, IF THAT ISN'T *IMPORTANT* TO YOU—
BUT IT IS! -:-WHIMPER-:-
OKAY. OKAY. I'LL TAKE IT EASY ON YOU NEXT TIME.
BUT NOT TOO EASY.
I GOTTA REPUTATION TO MAINTAIN.
OH-KAY...
XXXRRRTTTTT
KING SOMBRA'S POWERS ARE GETTING CLOSE!

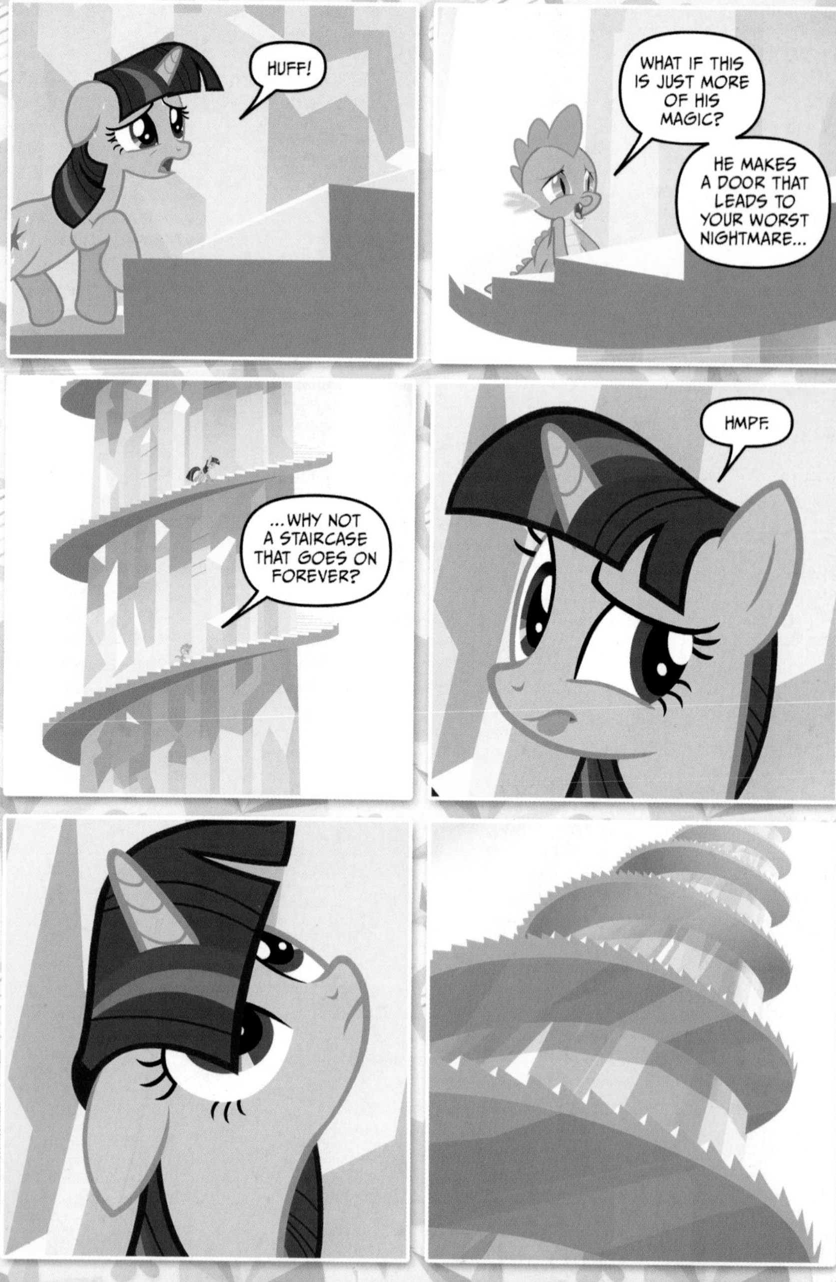
HUFF!
WHAT IF THIS IS JUST MORE OF HIS MAGIC?
HE MAKES A DOOR THAT LEADS TO YOUR WORST NIGHTMARE...
...WHY NOT A STAIRCASE THAT GOES ON FOREVER?
HMPF.

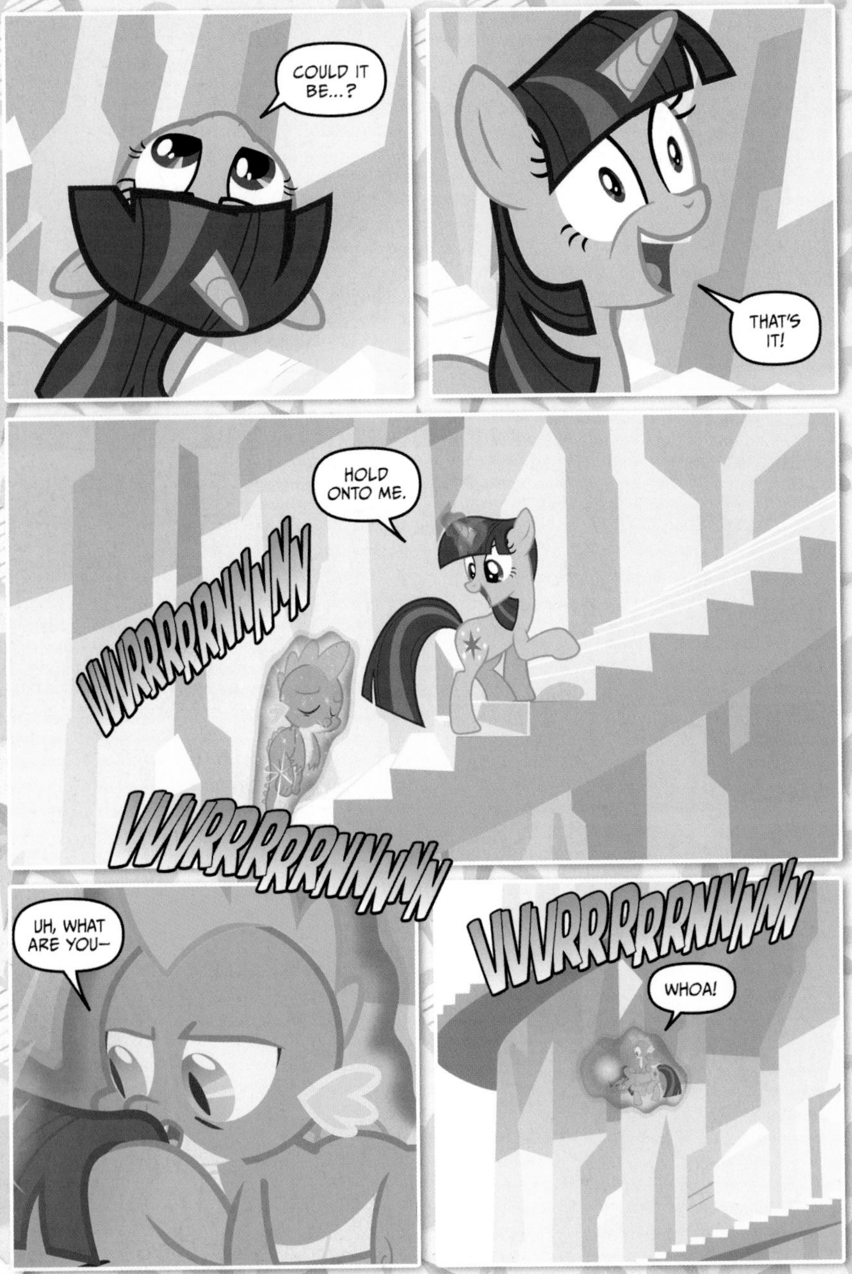
COULD IT BE...?
THAT'S IT!
HOLD ONTO ME.
VVVRRRRRNNNNN
VVVRRRRRNNNNNN
UH, WHAT ARE YOU–
VVVRRRRRNNNNN
WHOA!

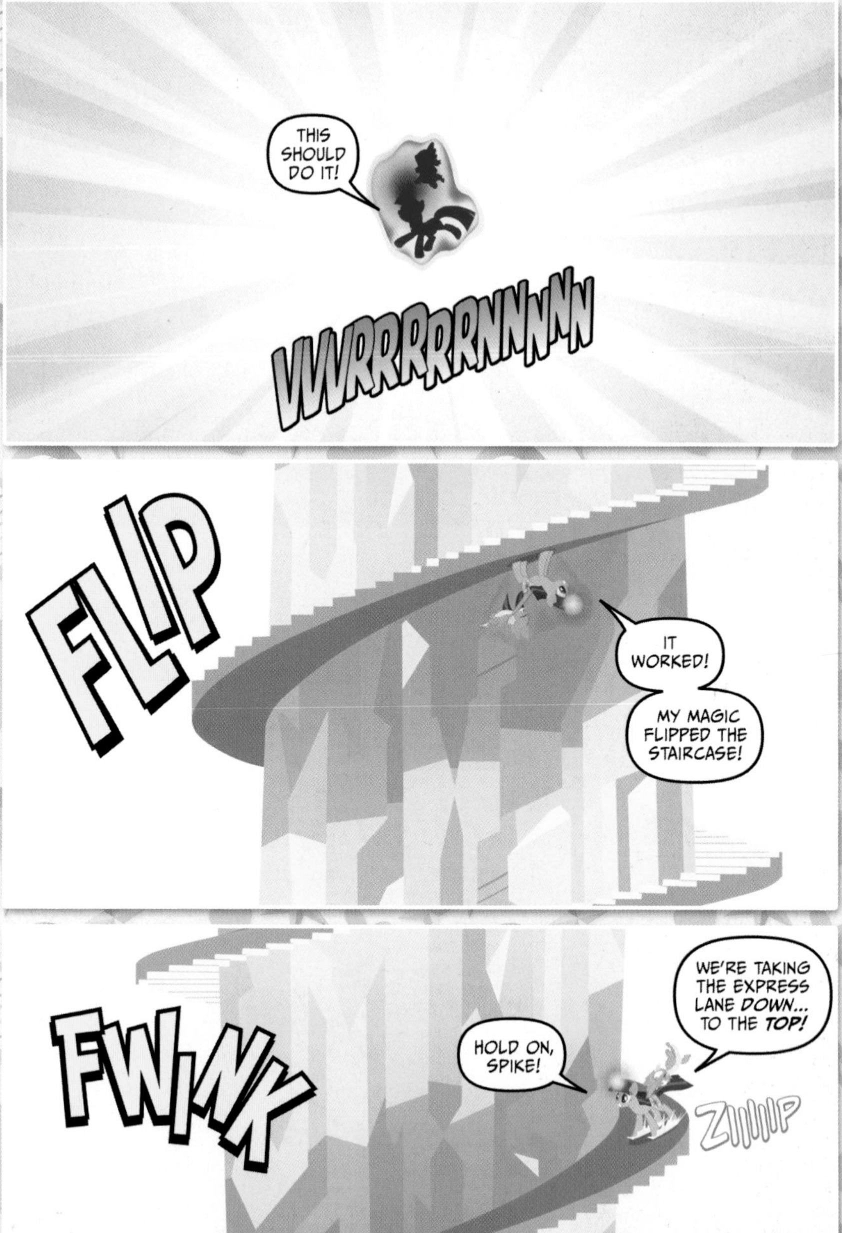
THIS SHOULD DO IT!
VVVRRRRRNNNNN
FLIP
IT WORKED!
MY MAGIC FLIPPED THE STAIRCASE!
FWINK
HOLD ON, SPIKE!
WE'RE TAKING THE EXPRESS LANE *DOWN*... TO THE ***TOP!***
ZIIIIIP

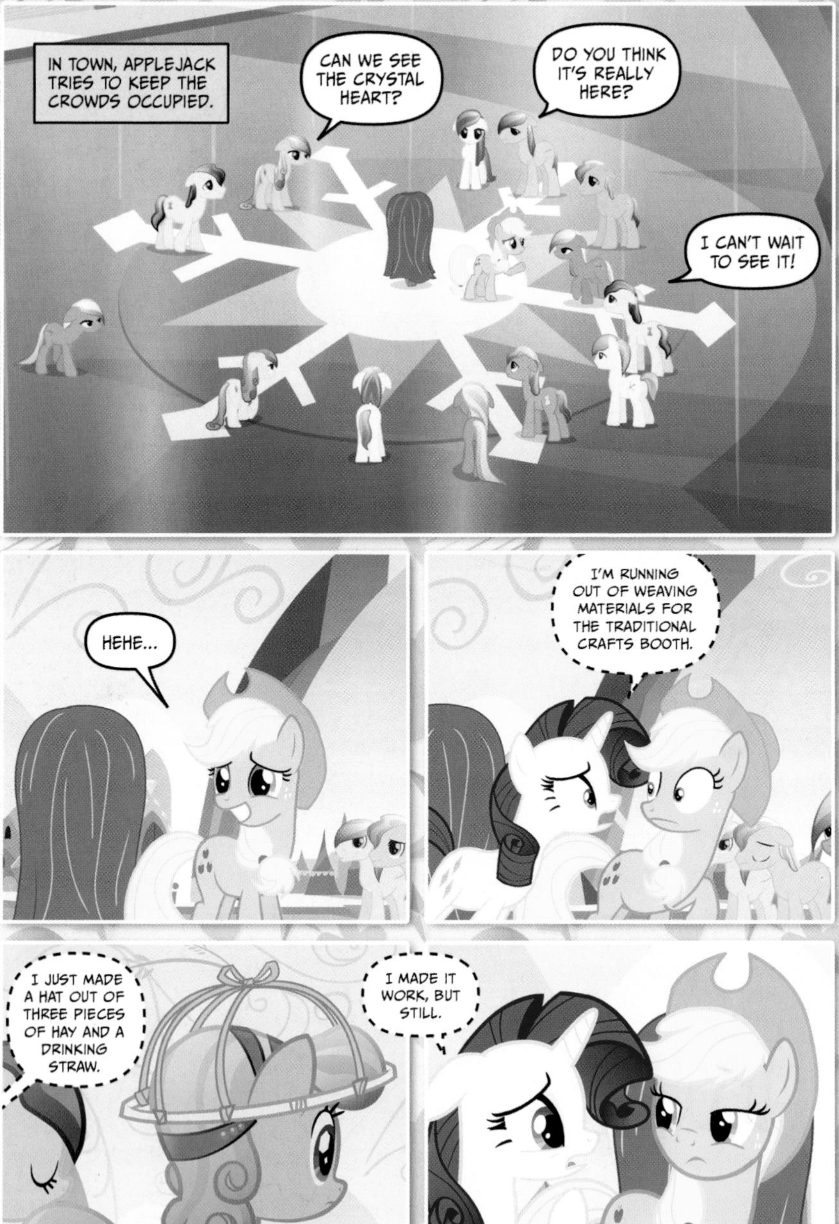
IN TOWN, APPLEJACK TRIES TO KEEP THE CROWDS OCCUPIED.
CAN WE SEE THE CRYSTAL HEART?
DO YOU THINK IT'S REALLY HERE?
I CAN'T WAIT TO SEE IT!
HEHE...
I'M RUNNING OUT OF WEAVING MATERIALS FOR THE TRADITIONAL CRAFTS BOOTH.
I JUST MADE A HAT OUT OF THREE PIECES OF HAY AND A DRINKING STRAW.
I MADE IT WORK, BUT STILL.

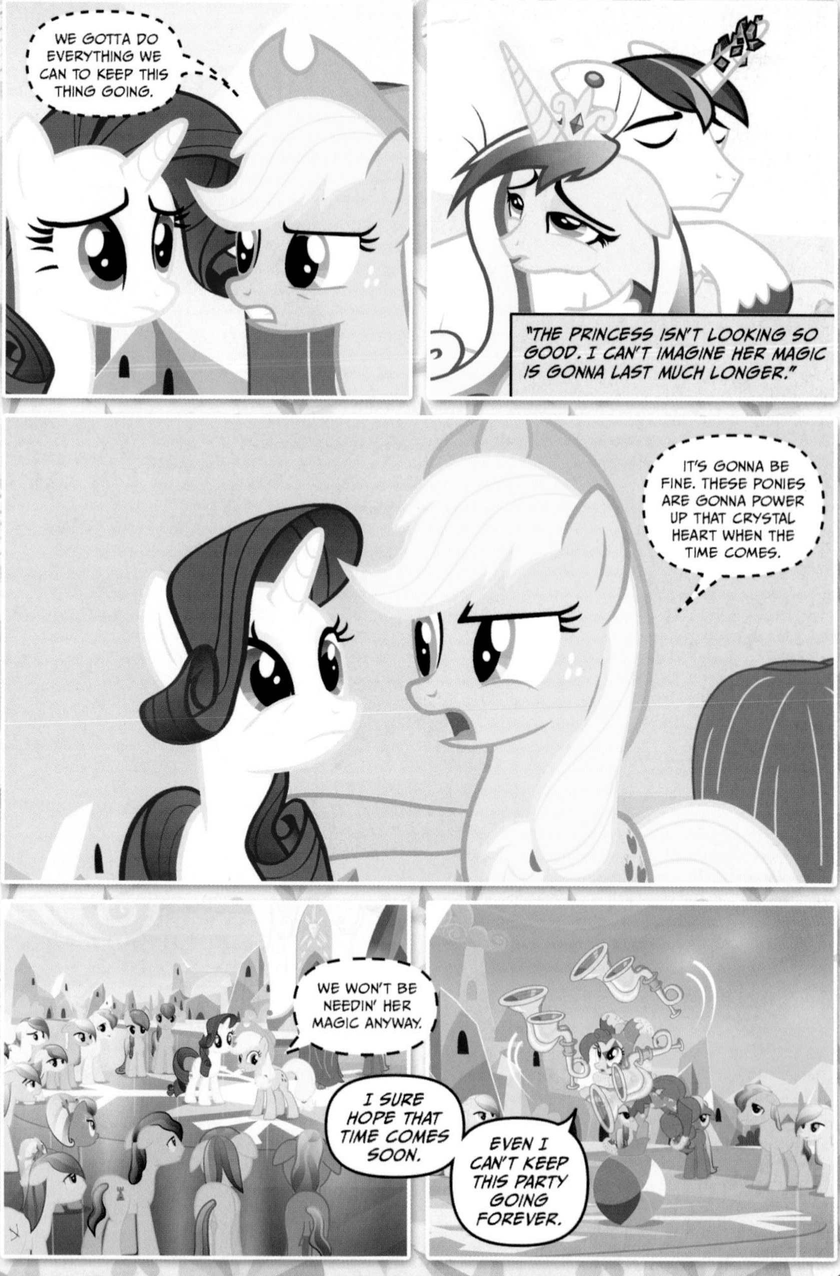
WE GOTTA DO EVERYTHING WE CAN TO KEEP THIS THING GOING.
"THE PRINCESS ISN'T LOOKING SO GOOD. I CAN'T IMAGINE HER MAGIC IS GONNA LAST MUCH LONGER."
IT'S GONNA BE FINE. THESE PONIES ARE GONNA POWER UP THAT CRYSTAL HEART WHEN THE TIME COMES.
WE WON'T BE NEEDIN' HER MAGIC ANYWAY.
I SURE HOPE THAT TIME COMES SOON.
EVEN I CAN'T KEEP THIS PARTY GOING FOREVER.

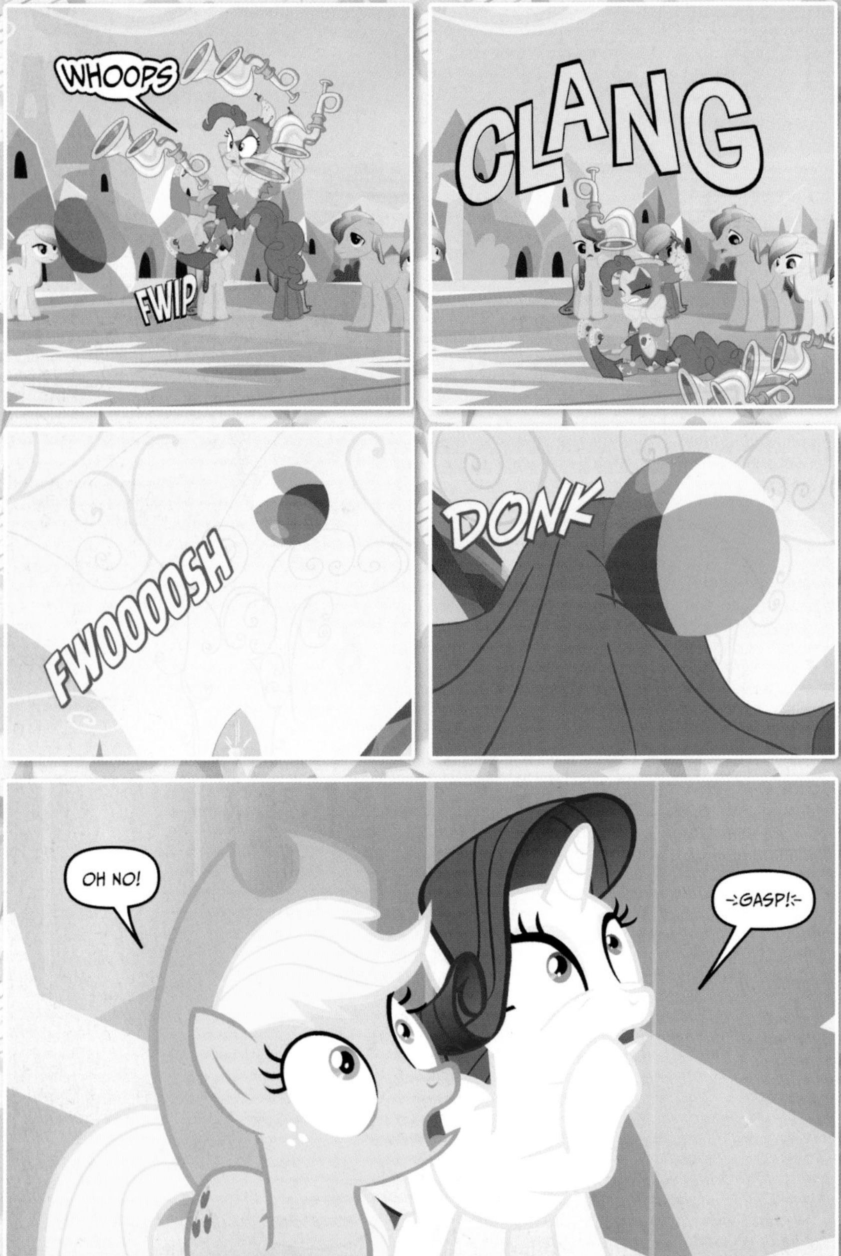
WHOOPS
FWIP
CLANG
FWOOOOSH
DONK
OH NO!
-GASP!-

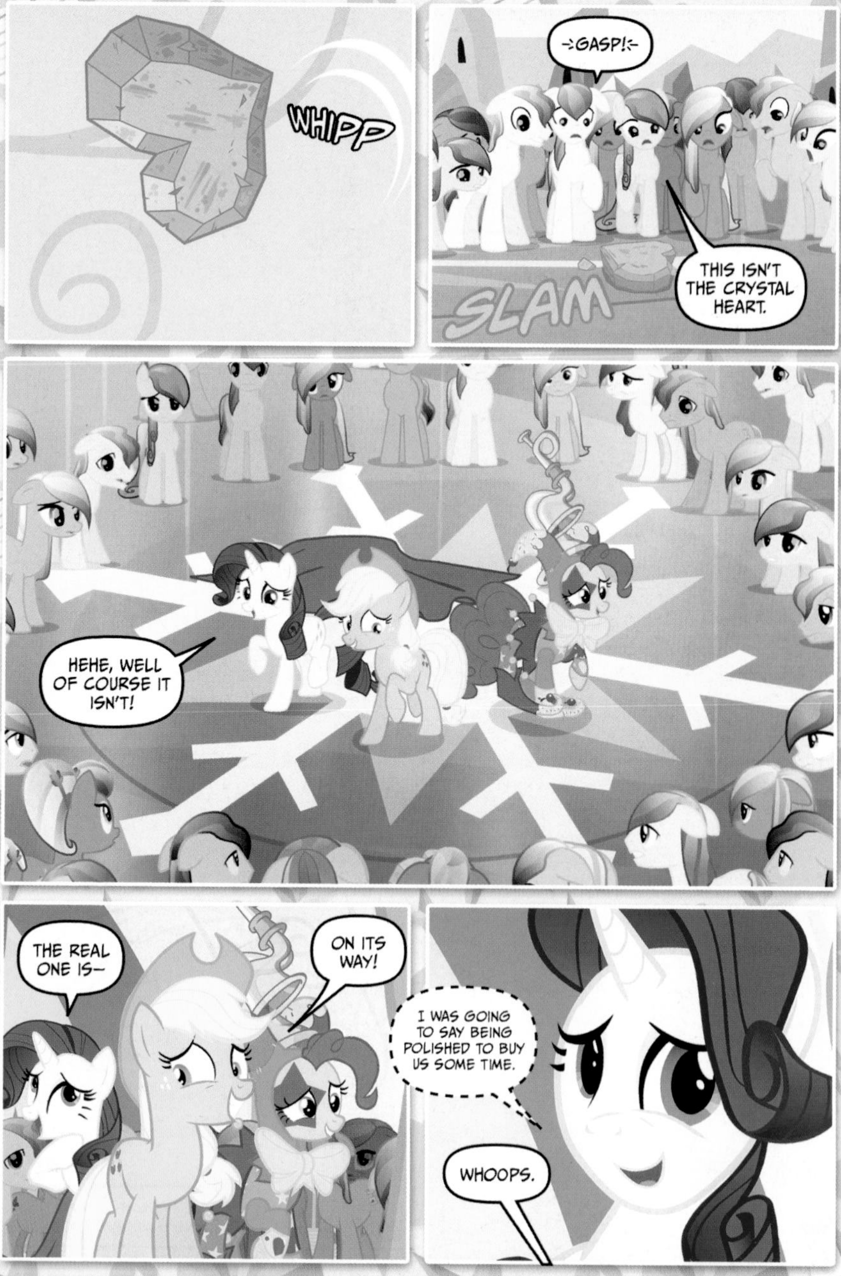
WHIPP
-:-GASP!-:-
SLAM
THIS ISN'T THE CRYSTAL HEART.
HEHE, WELL OF COURSE IT ISN'T!
THE REAL ONE IS—
ON ITS WAY!
I WAS GOING TO SAY BEING POLISHED TO BUY US SOME TIME.
WHOOPS.

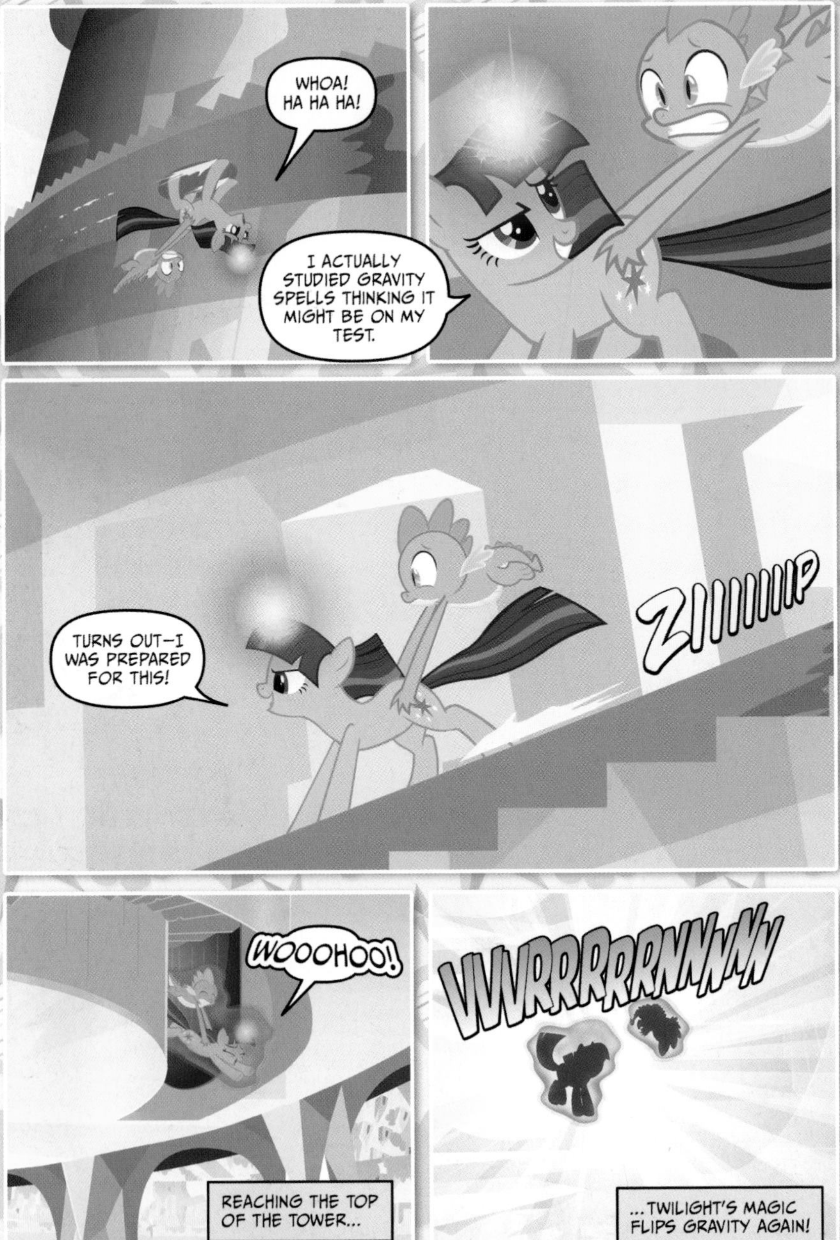
WHOA! HA HA HA!
I ACTUALLY STUDIED GRAVITY SPELLS THINKING IT MIGHT BE ON MY TEST.
TURNS OUT—I WAS PREPARED FOR THIS!
ZIIIIIIIP
WOOOHOO!
REACHING THE TOP OF THE TOWER...
VVVRRRRRNNNNN
...TWILIGHT'S MAGIC FLIPS GRAVITY AGAIN!

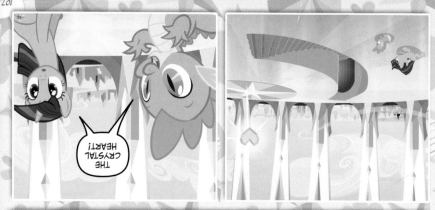

THE CRYSTAL HEART!

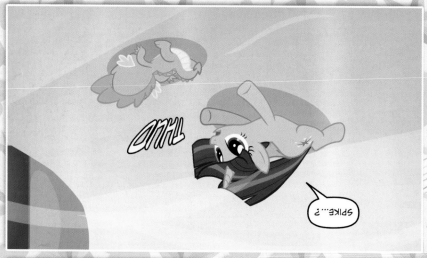

THUD

SPIKE...?

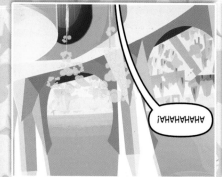

AHAHAHAHA!

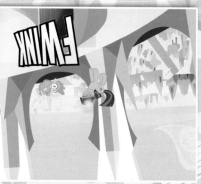

FWINK

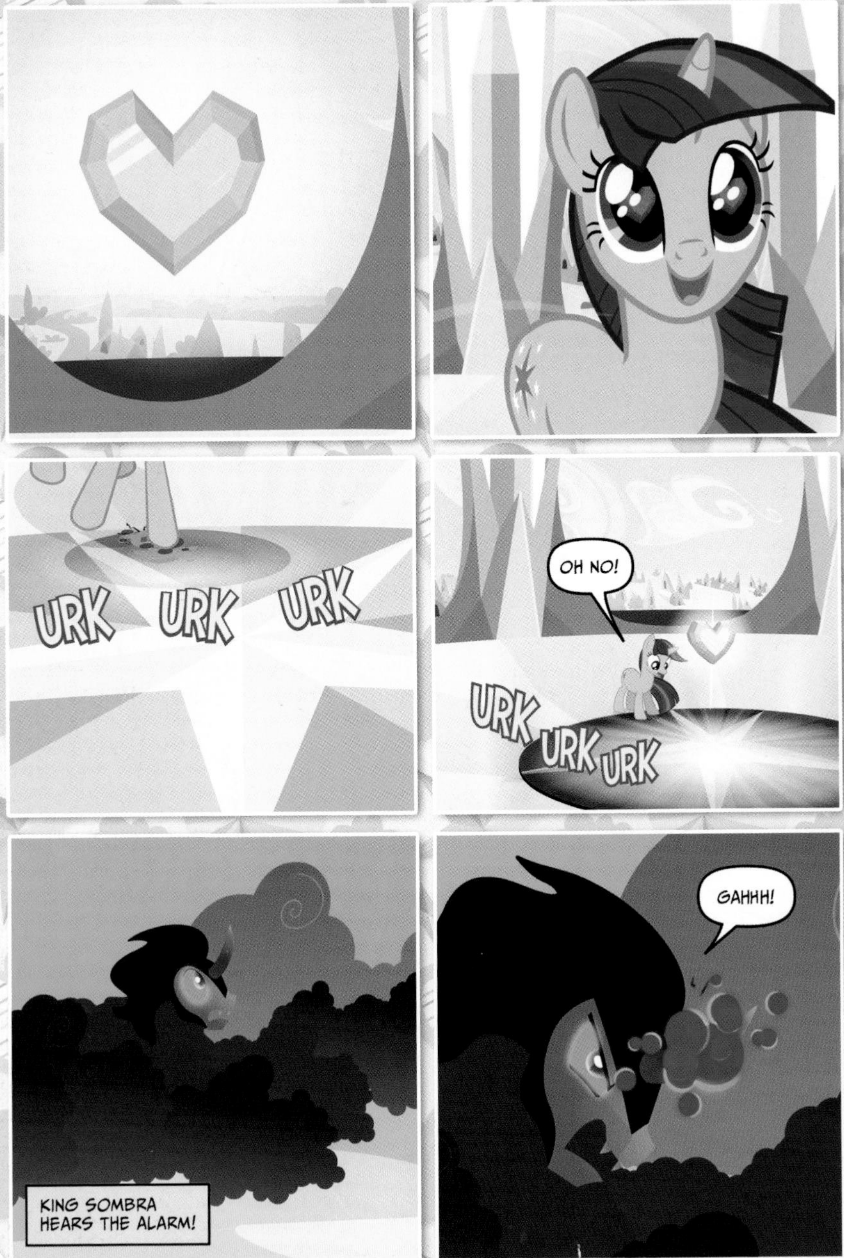
URK
URK
URK
OH NO!
URK
URK
URK
KING SOMBRA HEARS THE ALARM!
GAHHH!

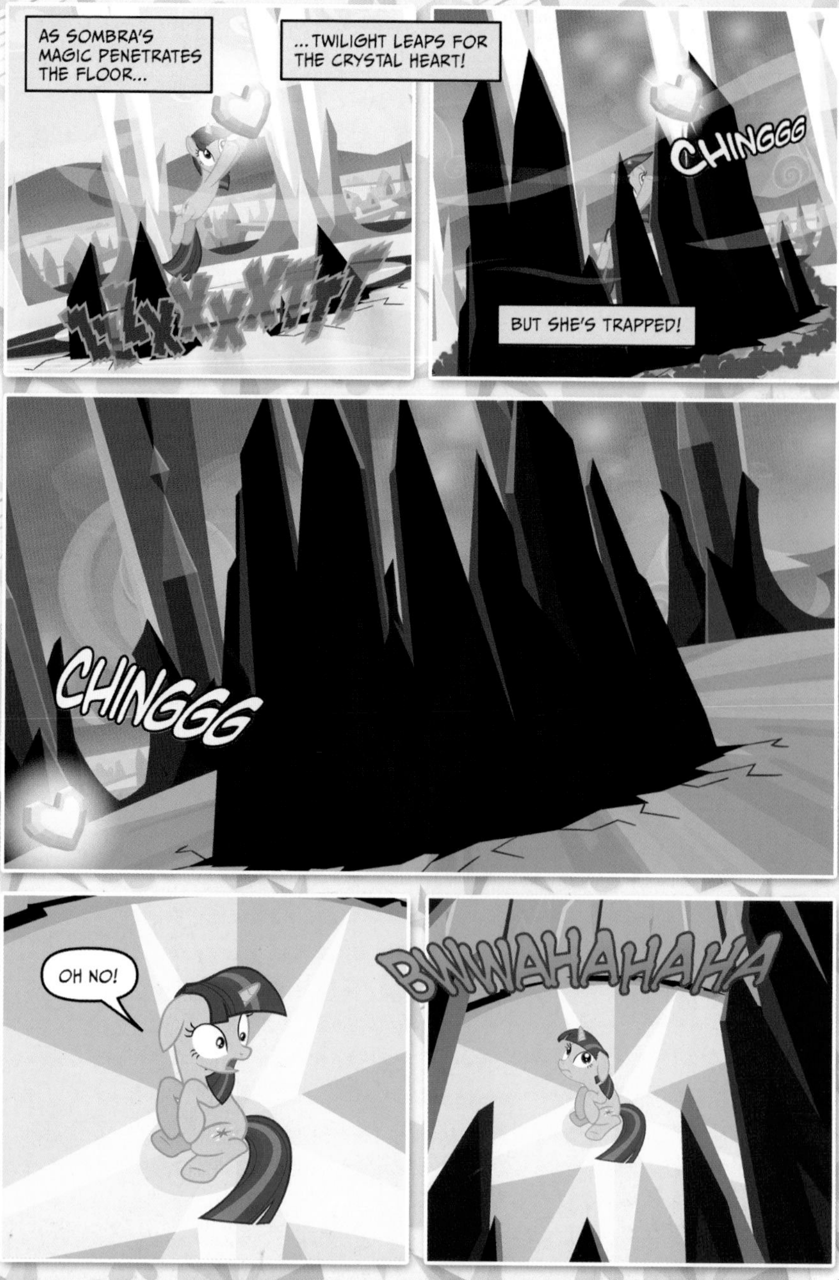
AS SOMBRA'S MAGIC PENETRATES THE FLOOR...
TLLKXXXTT!
...TWILIGHT LEAPS FOR THE CRYSTAL HEART!
CHINGGG
BUT SHE'S TRAPPED!
CHINGGG
OH NO!
BWWAHAHAHAHA

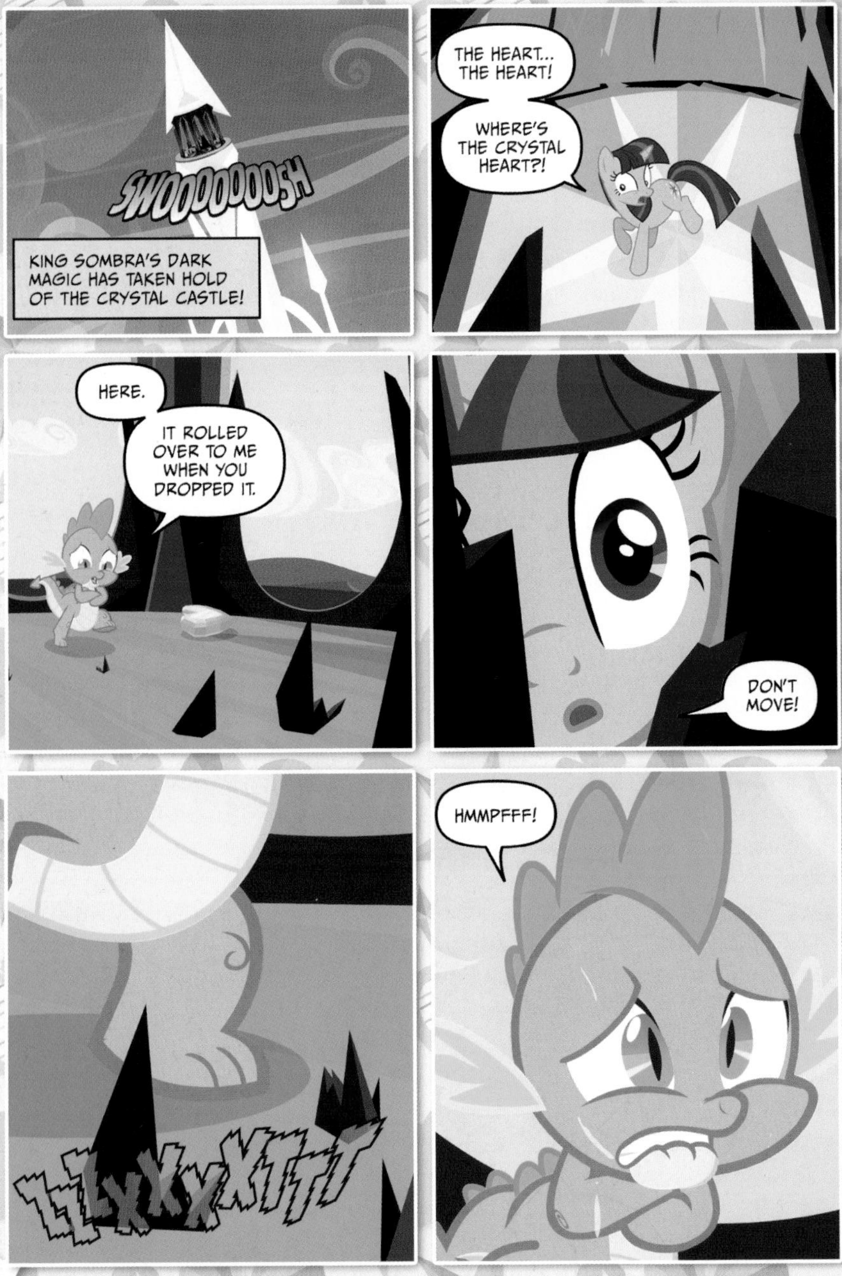
SWOOOOOOOSH
KING SOMBRA'S DARK MAGIC HAS TAKEN HOLD OF THE CRYSTAL CASTLE!
THE HEART... THE HEART!
WHERE'S THE CRYSTAL HEART?!
HERE.
IT ROLLED OVER TO ME WHEN YOU DROPPED IT.
DON'T MOVE!
HMMPFFF!

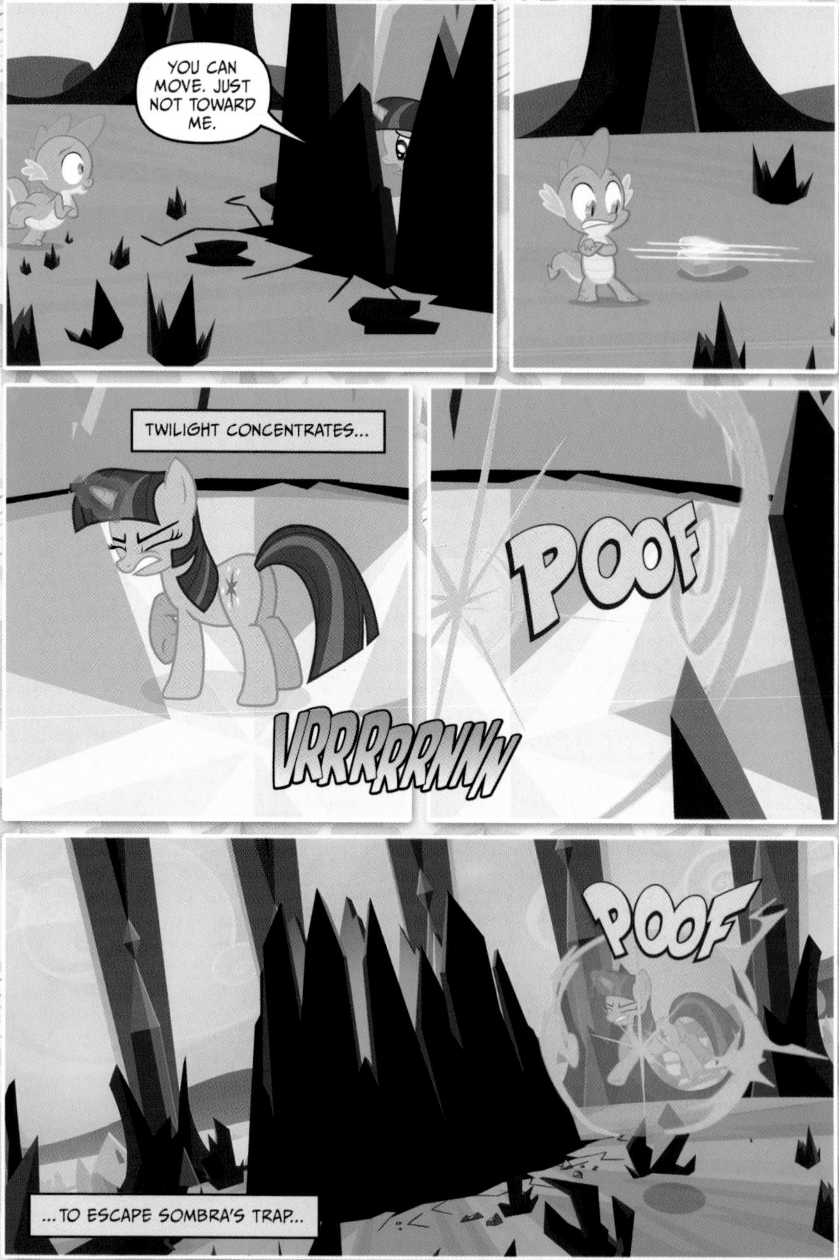
YOU CAN MOVE. JUST NOT TOWARD ME.
TWILIGHT CONCENTRATES...
VRRRRRNNN
POOF
POOF
...TO ESCAPE SOMBRA'S TRAP...

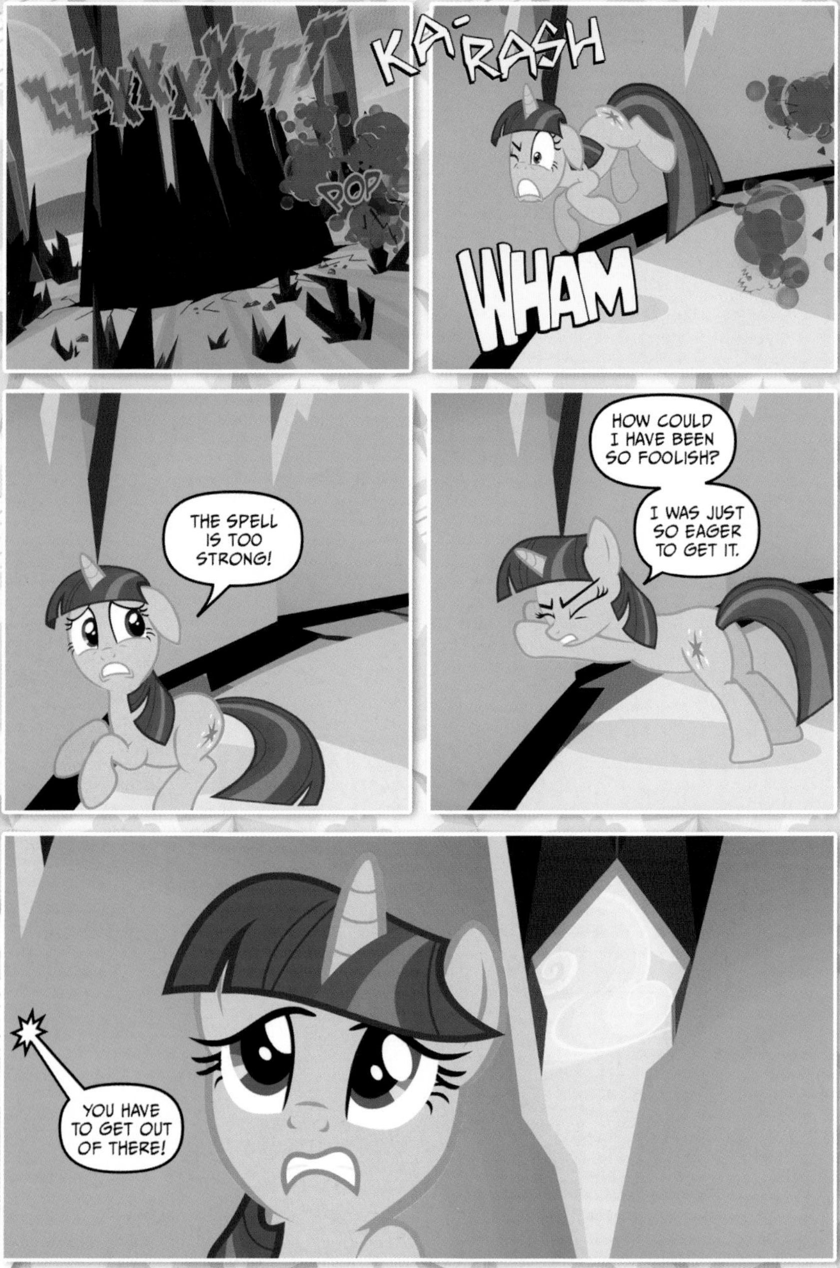
ZZZKKKKTTT
POP
KA-RASH
WHAM
THE SPELL IS TOO STRONG!
HOW COULD I HAVE BEEN SO FOOLISH?
I WAS JUST SO EAGER TO GET IT.
YOU HAVE TO GET OUT OF THERE!

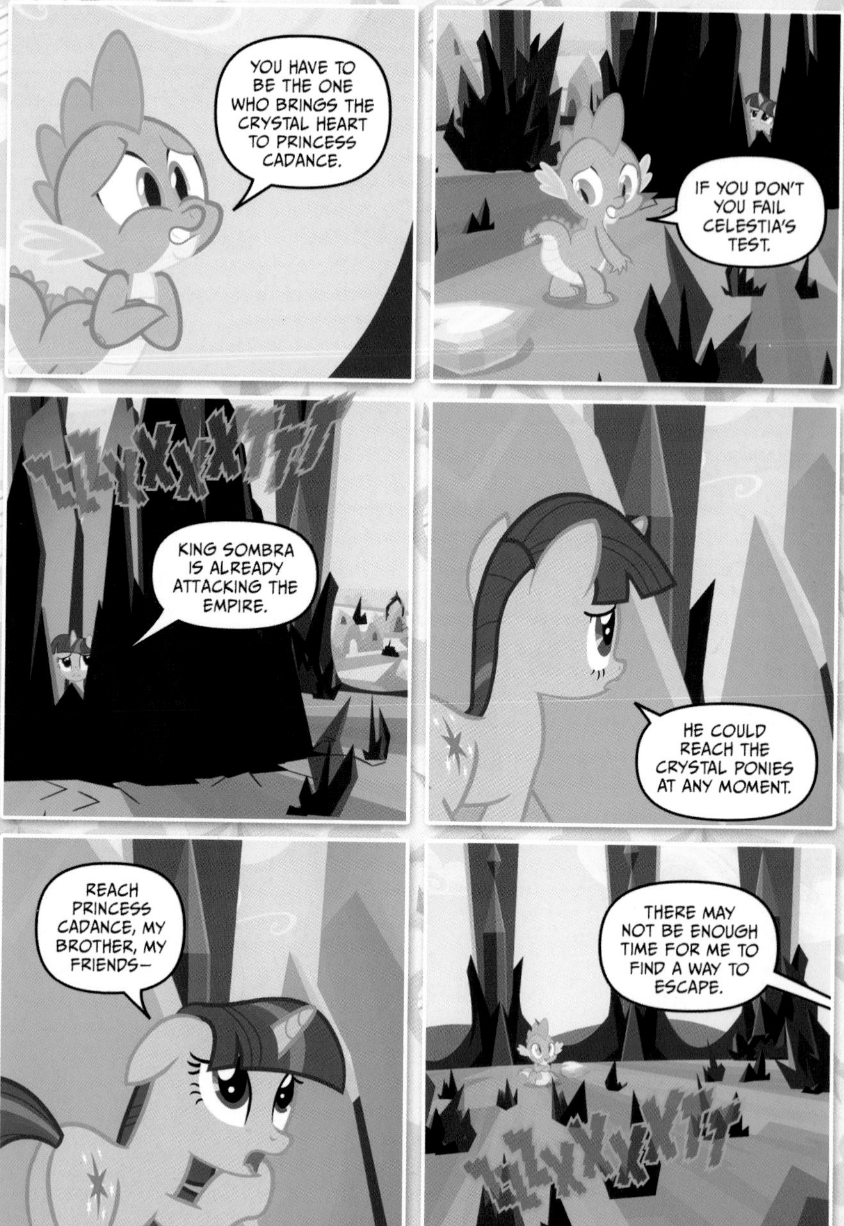
YOU HAVE TO BE THE ONE WHO BRINGS THE CRYSTAL HEART TO PRINCESS CADANCE.
IF YOU DON'T YOU FAIL CELESTIA'S TEST.
TZZXXXTT!
KING SOMBRA IS ALREADY ATTACKING THE EMPIRE.
HE COULD REACH THE CRYSTAL PONIES AT ANY MOMENT.
REACH PRINCESS CADANCE, MY BROTHER, MY FRIENDS—
THERE MAY NOT BE ENOUGH TIME FOR ME TO FIND A WAY TO ESCAPE.
TZZXXXTT!

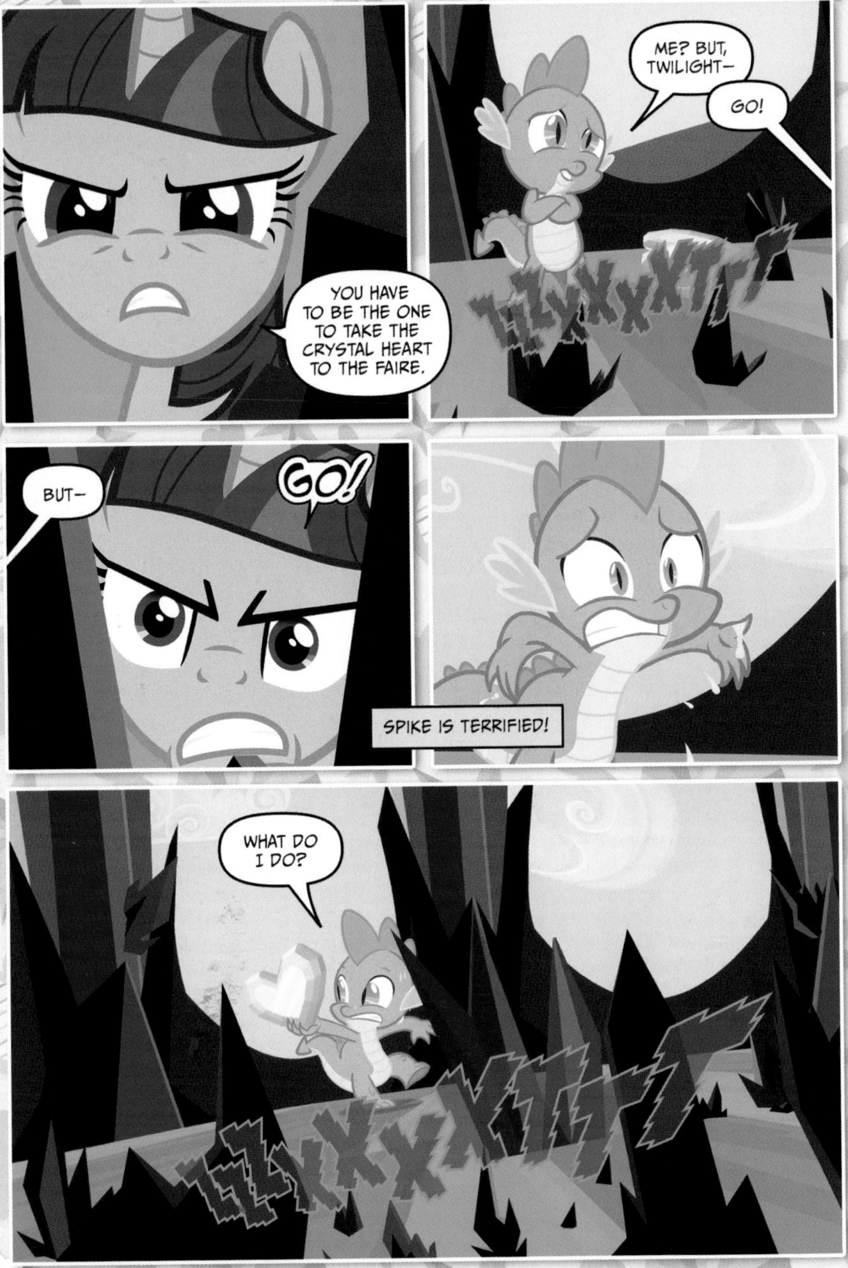

YOU HAVE TO BE THE ONE TO TAKE THE CRYSTAL HEART TO THE FAIRE.
ME? BUT, TWILIGHT—
GO!
BUT—
GO!
SPIKE IS TERRIFIED!
WHAT DO I DO?

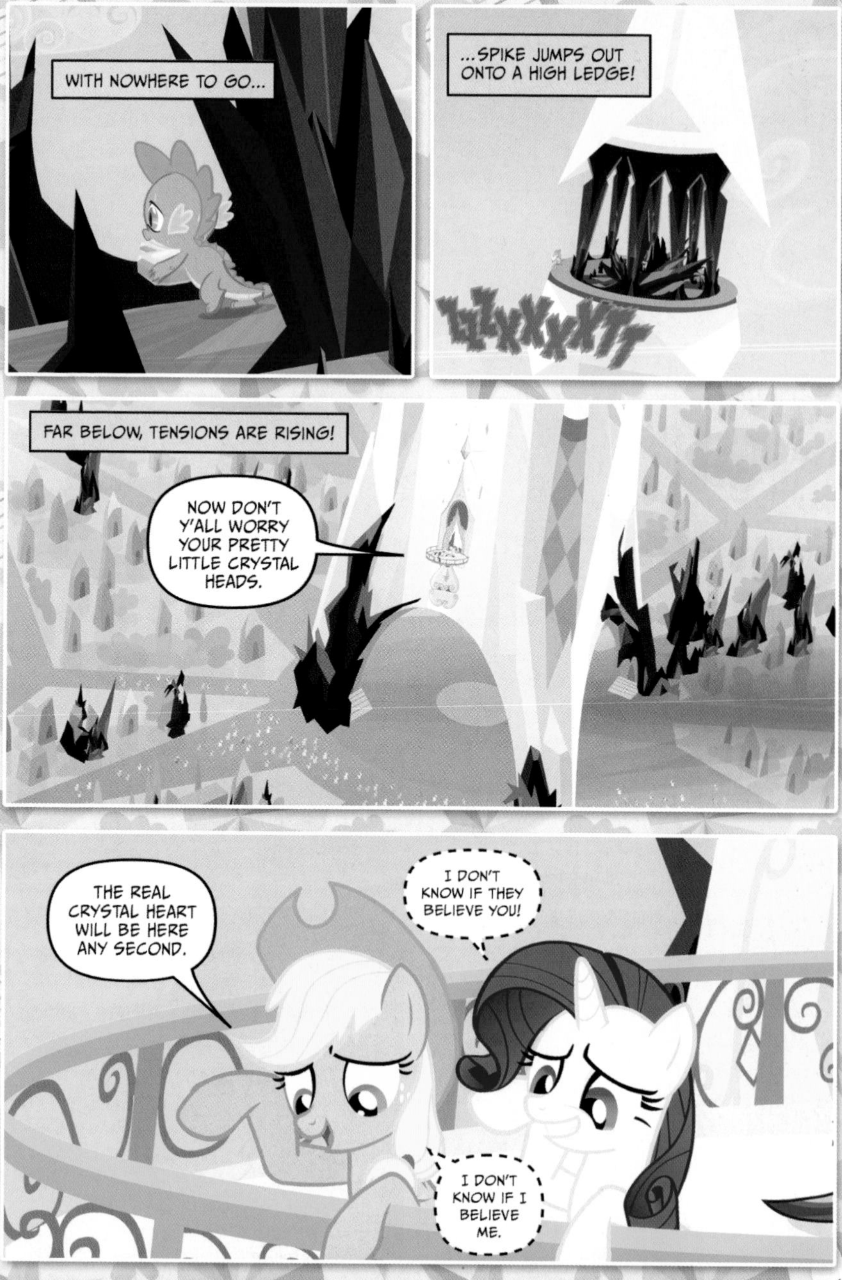
WITH NOWHERE TO GO...
...SPIKE JUMPS OUT ONTO A HIGH LEDGE!
TZZZXXXXTT
FAR BELOW, TENSIONS ARE RISING!
NOW DON'T Y'ALL WORRY YOUR PRETTY LITTLE CRYSTAL HEADS.
THE REAL CRYSTAL HEART WILL BE HERE ANY SECOND.
I DON'T KNOW IF THEY BELIEVE YOU!
I DON'T KNOW IF I BELIEVE ME.

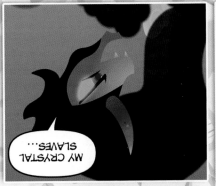

MY CRYSTAL SLAVES...

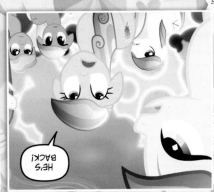

HE'S BACK!

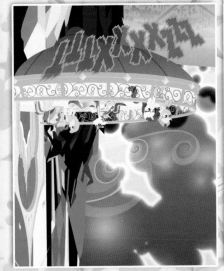

FZZXXKTT!

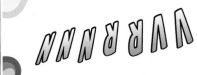

VURRNNN

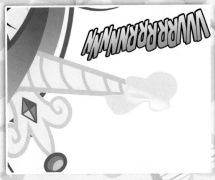

VURRRRNNNN

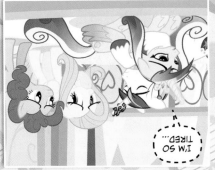

I'M SO TIRED...

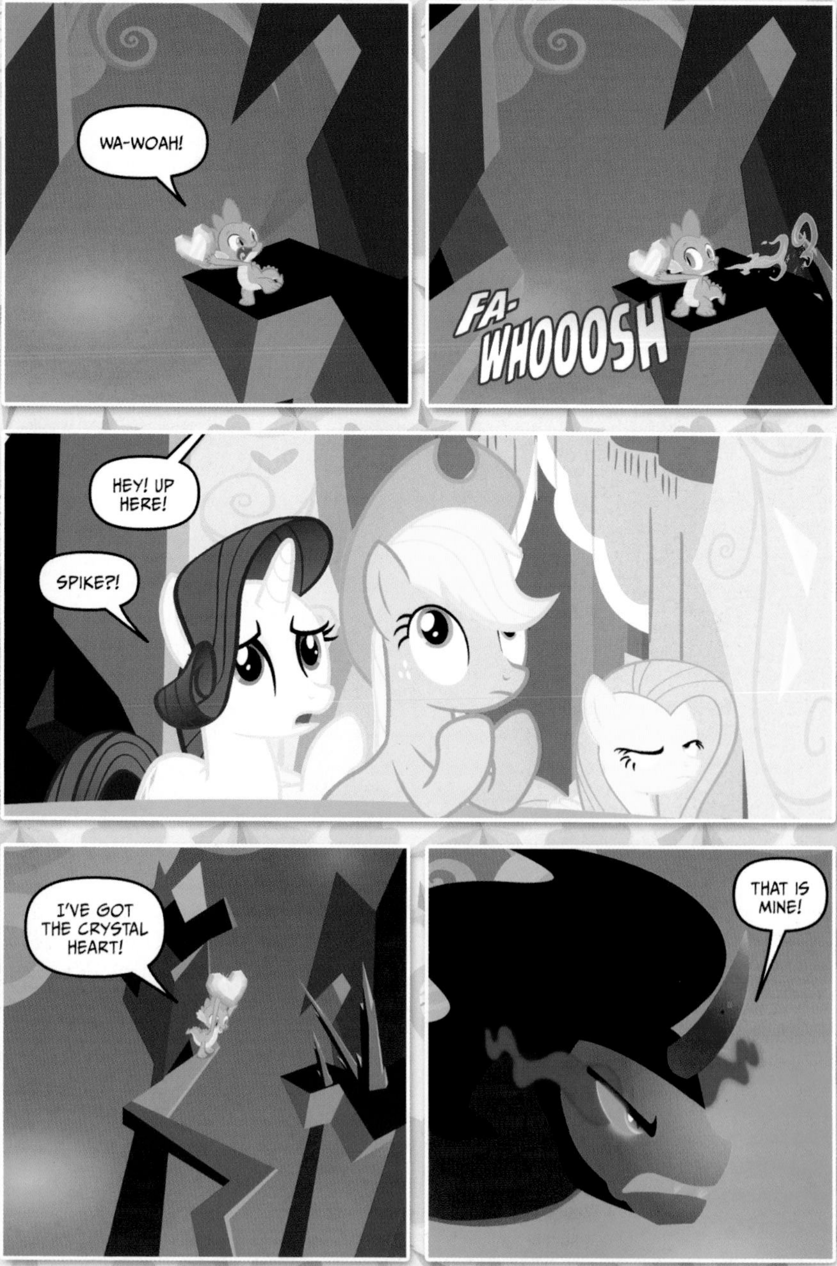
WA-WOAH!
FA-WHOOOSH
HEY! UP HERE!
SPIKE?!
I'VE GOT THE CRYSTAL HEART!
THAT IS MINE!

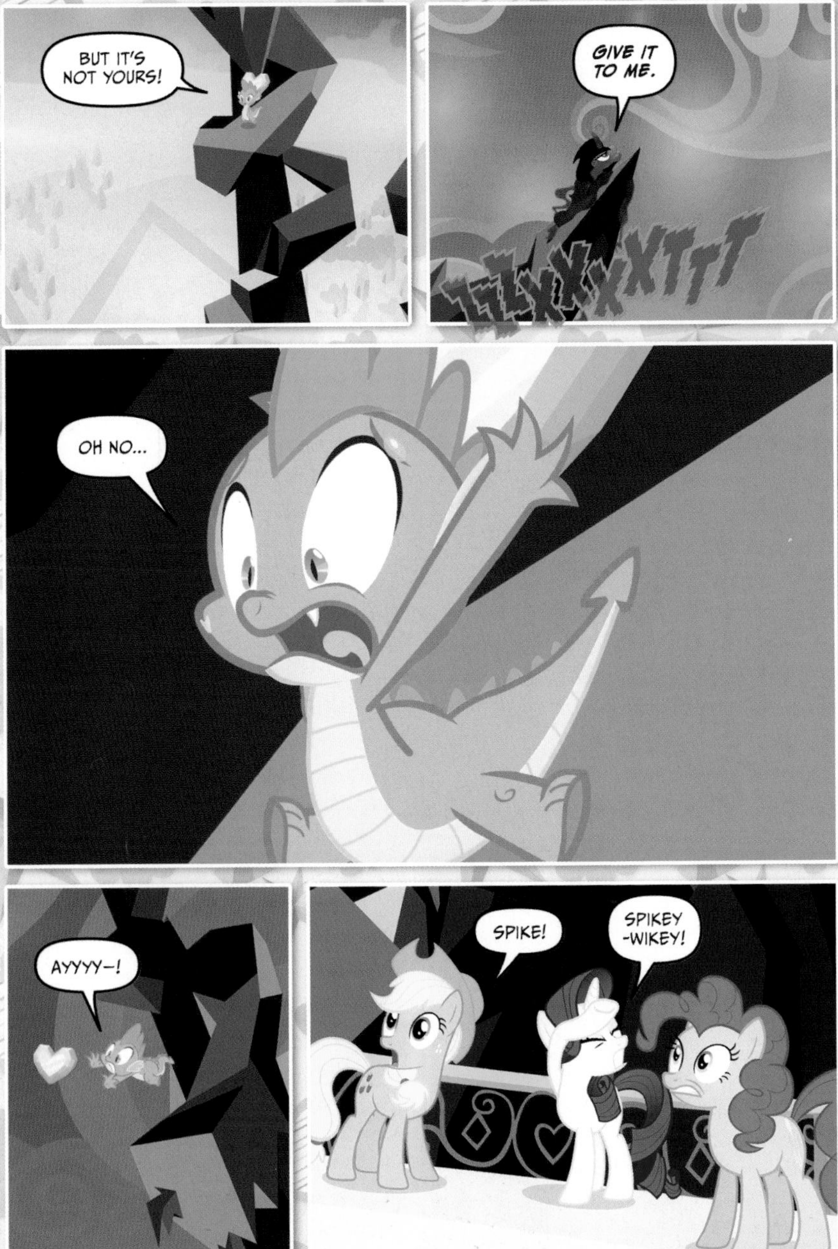
BUT IT'S NOT YOURS!
GIVE IT TO ME.
TZZKKXXTTT
OH NO...
AYYYY—!
SPIKE!
SPIKEY -WIKEY!

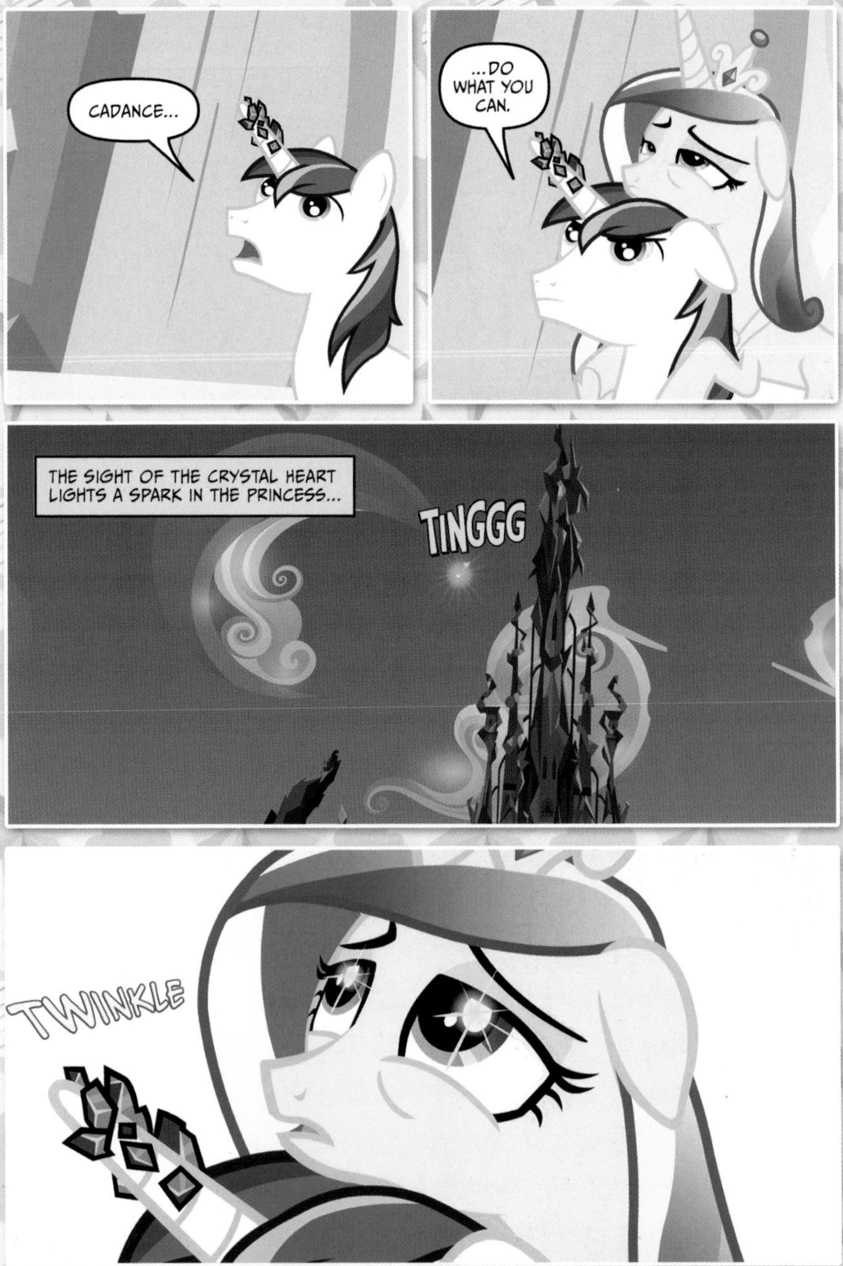
CADANCE...
...DO WHAT YOU CAN.
THE SIGHT OF THE CRYSTAL HEART LIGHTS A SPARK IN THE PRINCESS...
TINGGG
TWINKLE

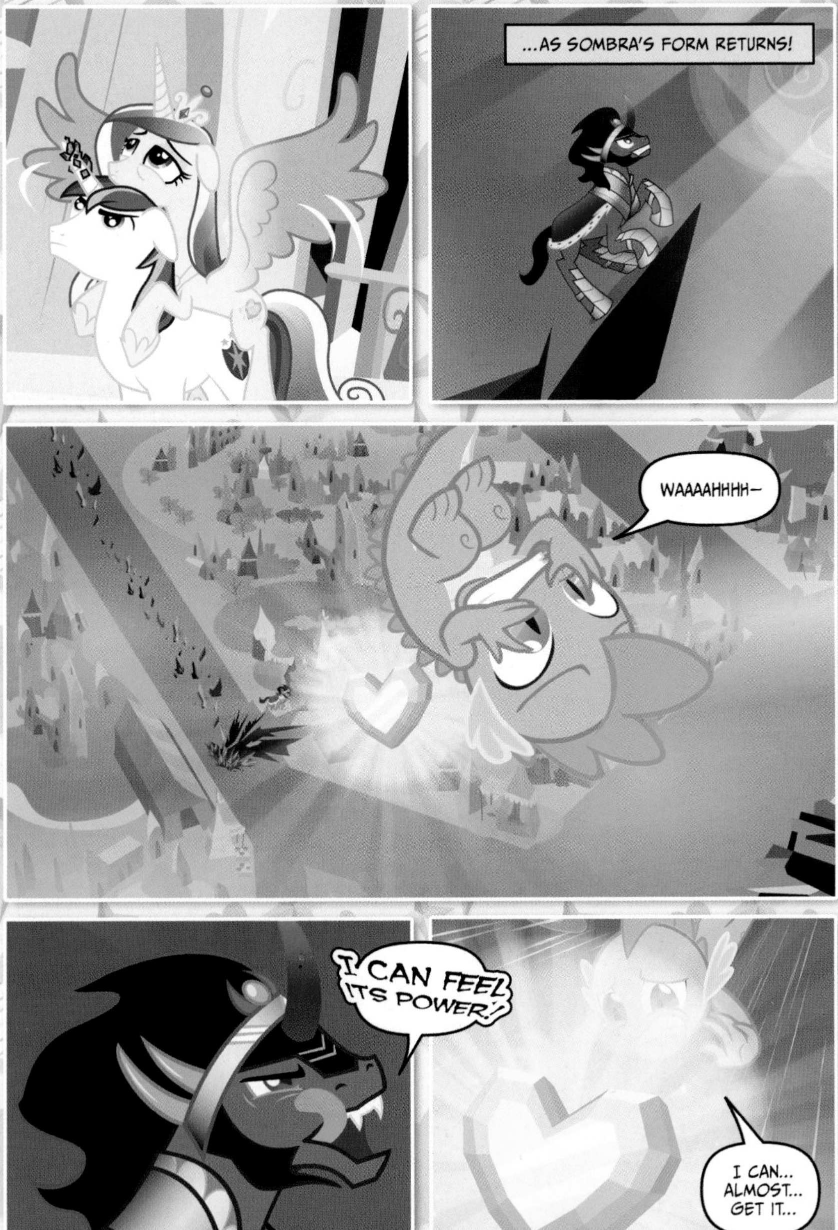
...AS SOMBRA'S FORM RETURNS!
WAAAAHHHH—
I CAN FEEL ITS POWER!
I CAN... ALMOST... GET IT...

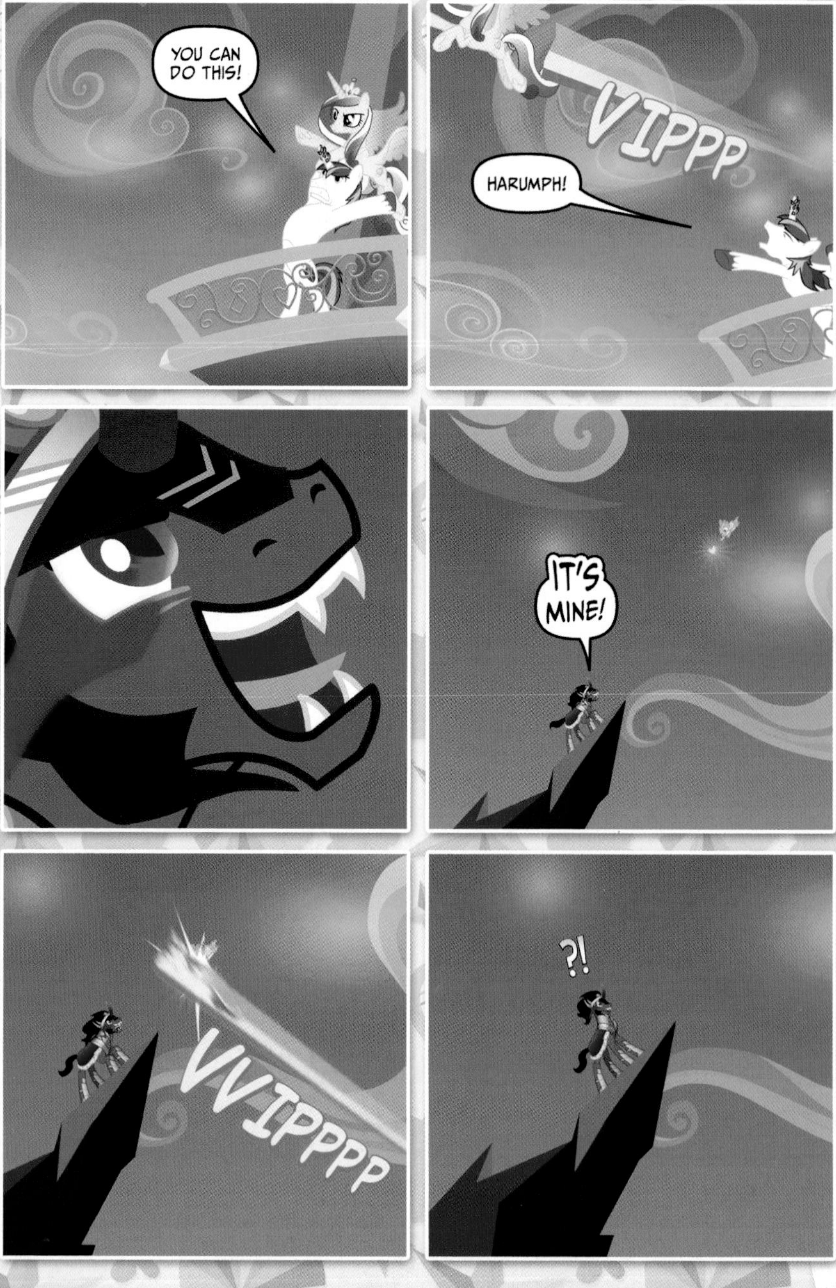
YOU CAN DO THIS!
VIPPP
HARUMPH!
IT'S MINE!
VVIPPPP
?!

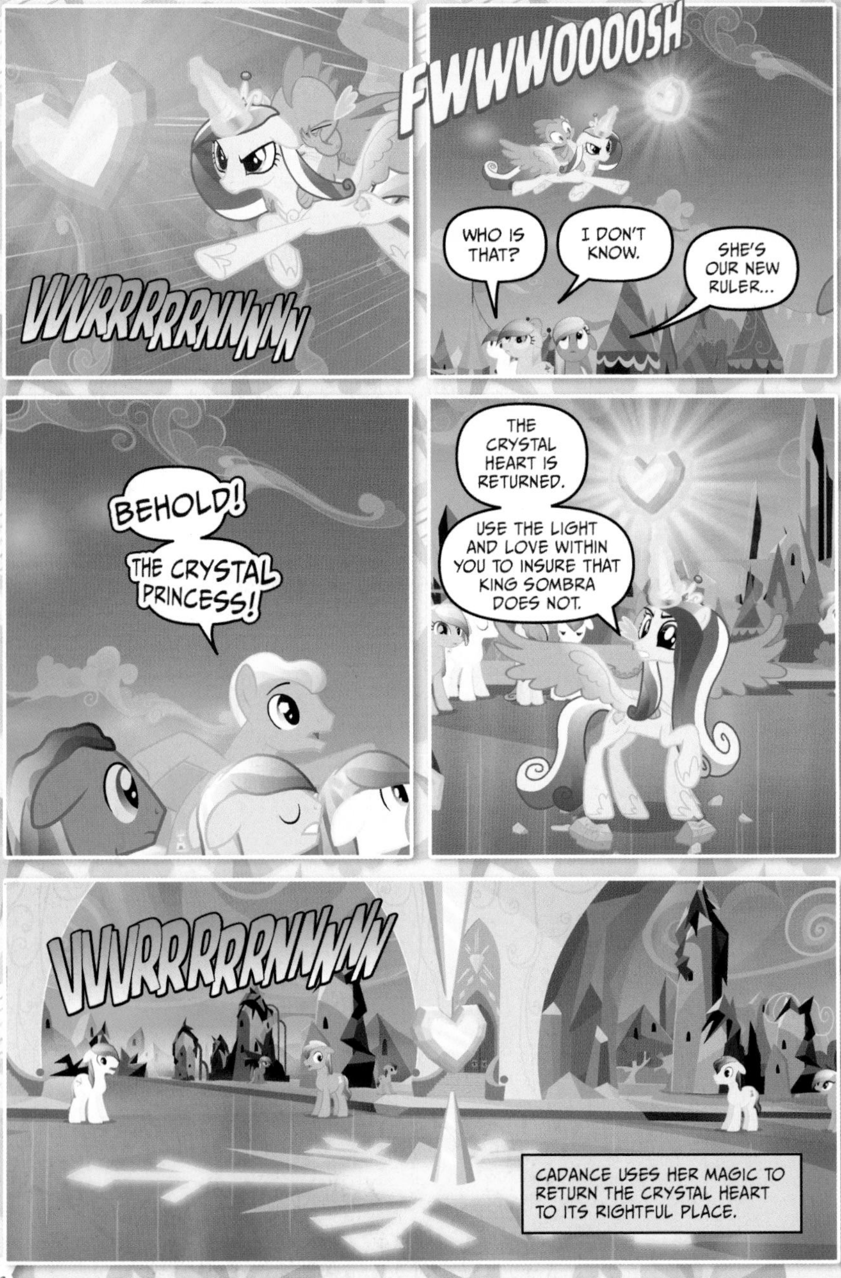
VVVRRRRRNNNNN
FWWWOOOOSH
WHO IS THAT?
I DON'T KNOW.
SHE'S OUR NEW RULER...
BEHOLD!
THE CRYSTAL PRINCESS!
THE CRYSTAL HEART IS RETURNED.
USE THE LIGHT AND LOVE WITHIN YOU TO INSURE THAT KING SOMBRA DOES NOT.
VVVRRRRRNNNNN
CADANCE USES HER MAGIC TO RETURN THE CRYSTAL HEART TO ITS RIGHTFUL PLACE.

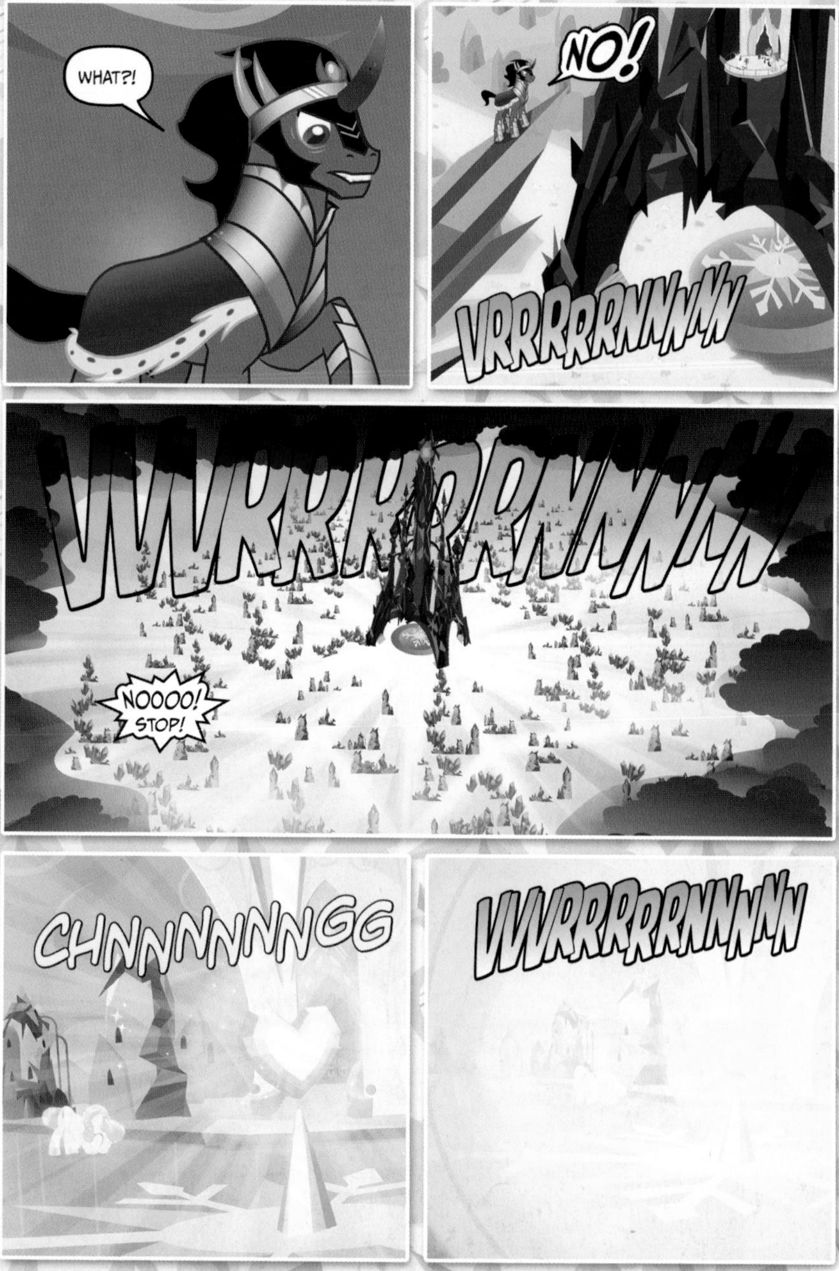
WHAT?!
NO!
VRRRRRNNNNN
VVVRRRRRRNNNNN
NOOOO! STOP!
CHNNNNNNGG
VVVRRRRRNNNNN

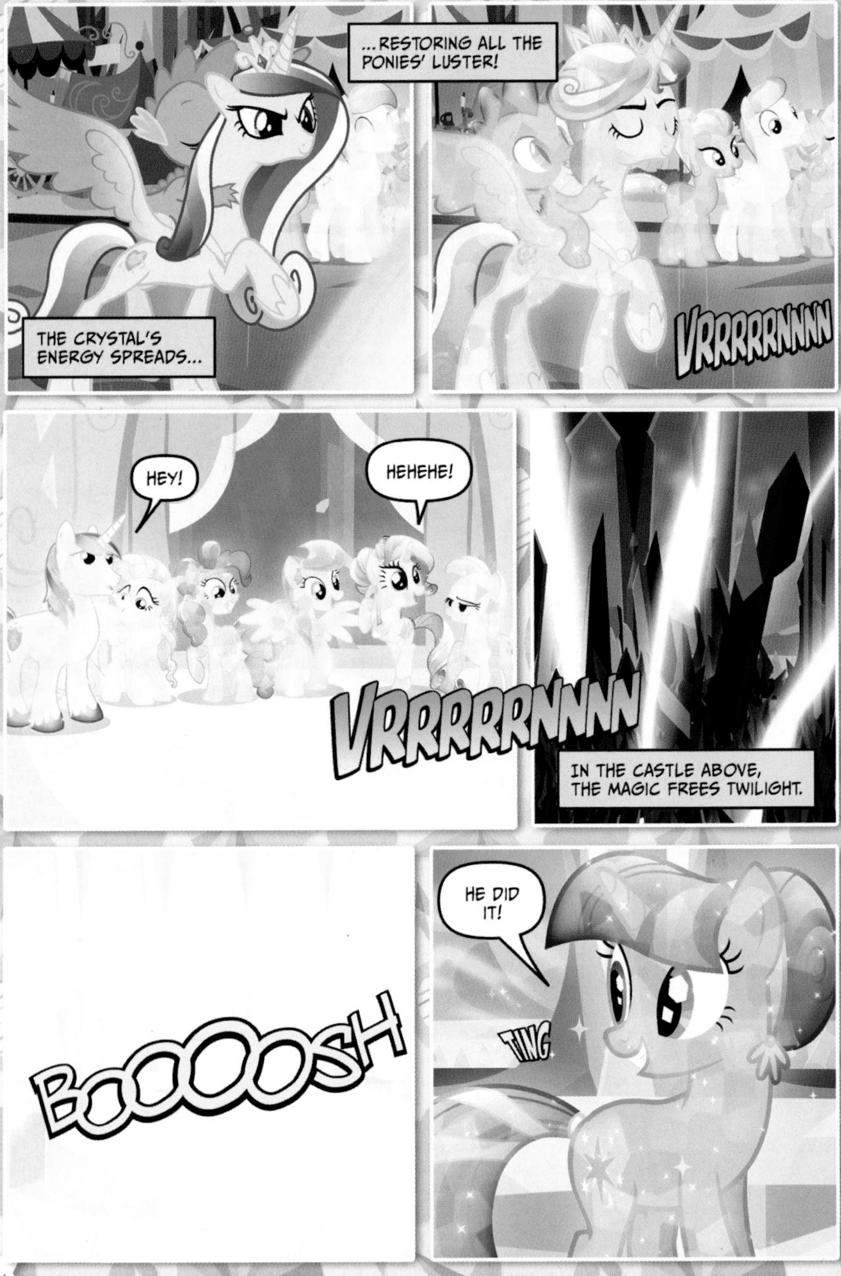
THE CRYSTAL'S ENERGY SPREADS...
...RESTORING ALL THE PONIES' LUSTER!
VRRRRRNNNN
HEY!
HEHEHE!
VRRRRRNNNN
IN THE CASTLE ABOVE, THE MAGIC FREES TWILIGHT.
BOOOOOSH
HE DID IT!
TING

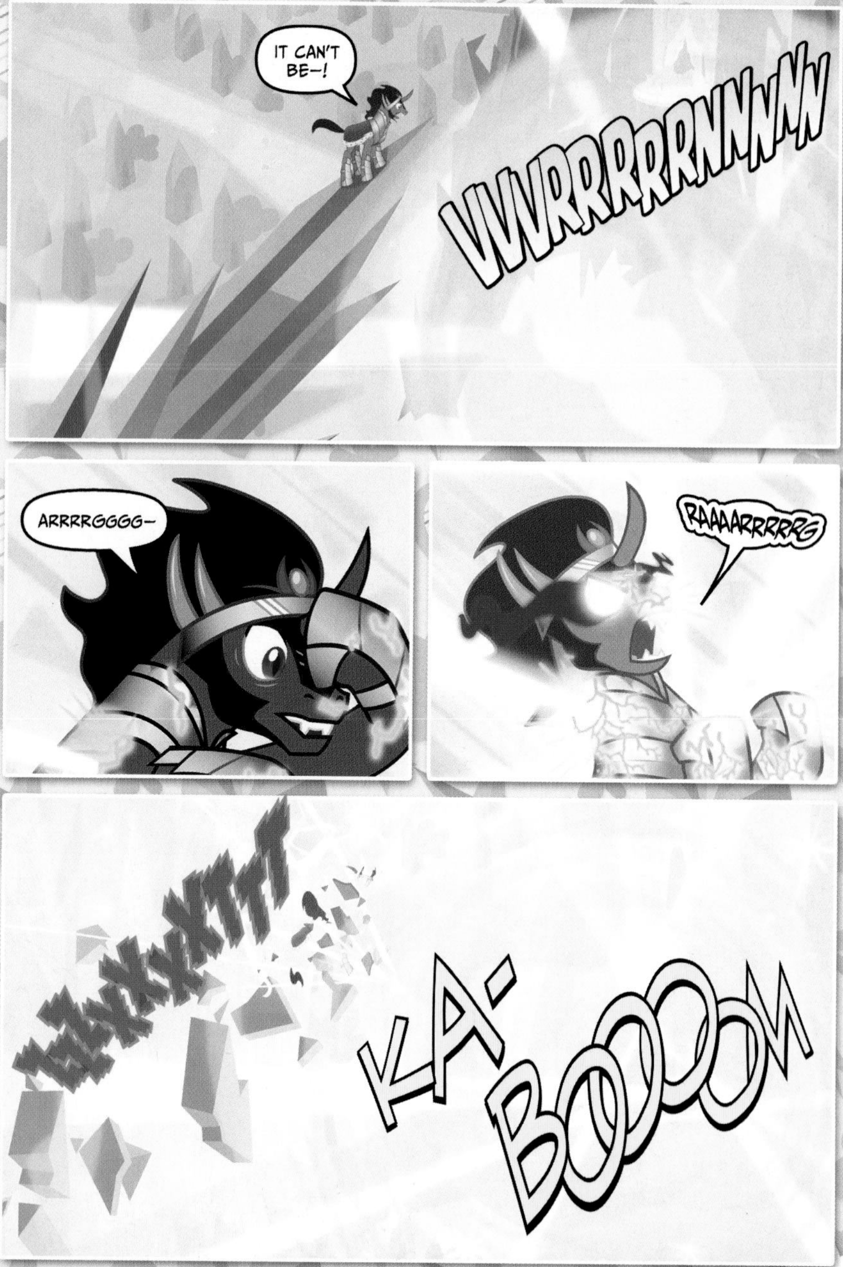
IT CAN'T BE—!
VVVRRRRRNNNNN
ARRRRGGGG—
RAAAARRRRRG
KA-BOOOOOM

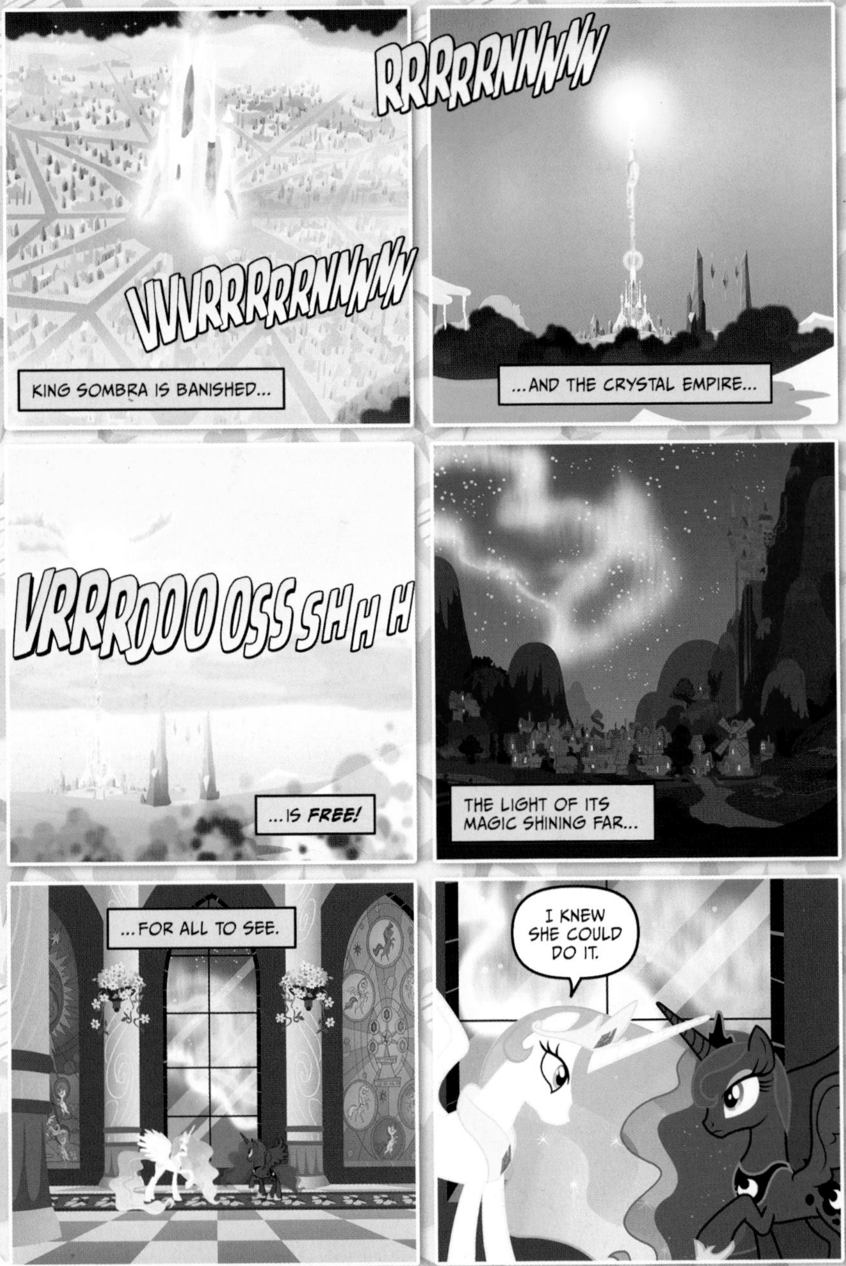
VVVRRRRRRNNNNN
KING SOMBRA IS BANISHED...
RRRRRNNNNN
...AND THE CRYSTAL EMPIRE...
VRRROOO OSSSHH H
...IS FREE!
THE LIGHT OF ITS MAGIC SHINING FAR...
...FOR ALL TO SEE.
I KNEW SHE COULD DO IT.

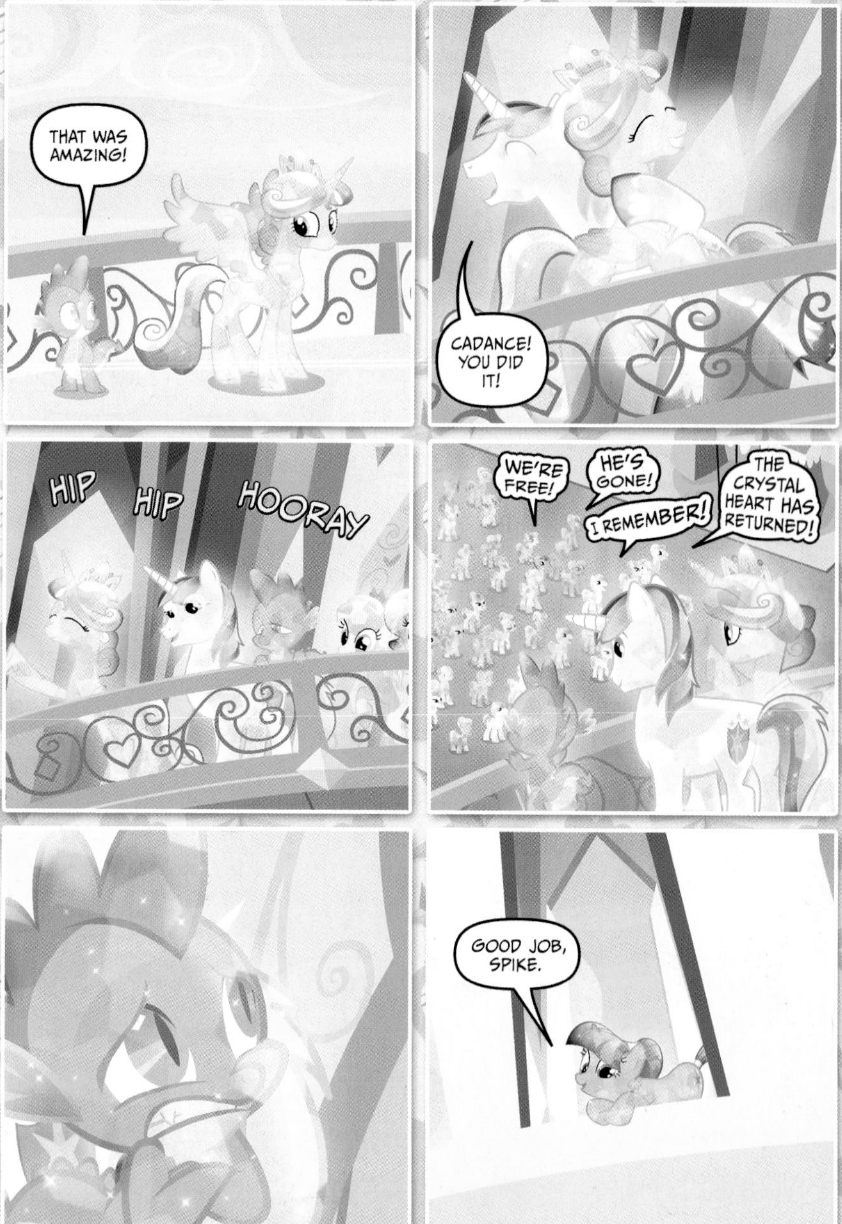
THAT WAS AMAZING!
CADANCE! YOU DID IT!
HIP
HIP
HOORAY
WE'RE FREE!
HE'S GONE!
I REMEMBER!
THE CRYSTAL HEART HAS RETURNED!
GOOD JOB, SPIKE.

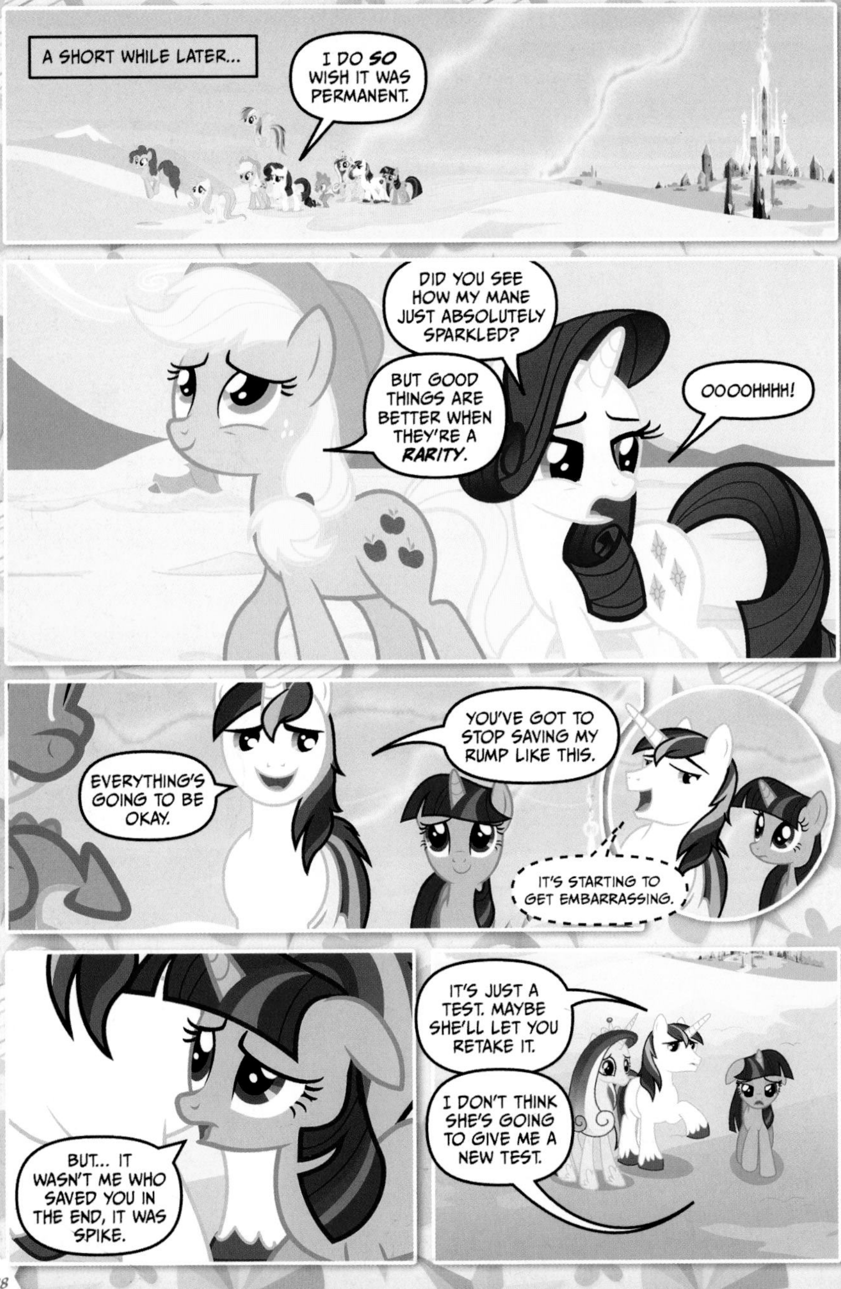
A SHORT WHILE LATER...
I DO **SO** WISH IT WAS PERMANENT.
DID YOU SEE HOW MY MANE JUST ABSOLUTELY SPARKLED?
BUT GOOD THINGS ARE BETTER WHEN THEY'RE A ***RARITY***.
OOOOHHHH!
EVERYTHING'S GOING TO BE OKAY.
YOU'VE GOT TO STOP SAVING MY RUMP LIKE THIS.
IT'S STARTING TO GET EMBARRASSING.
BUT... IT WASN'T ME WHO SAVED YOU IN THE END, IT WAS SPIKE.
IT'S JUST A TEST. MAYBE SHE'LL LET YOU RETAKE IT.
I DON'T THINK SHE'S GOING TO GIVE ME A NEW TEST.

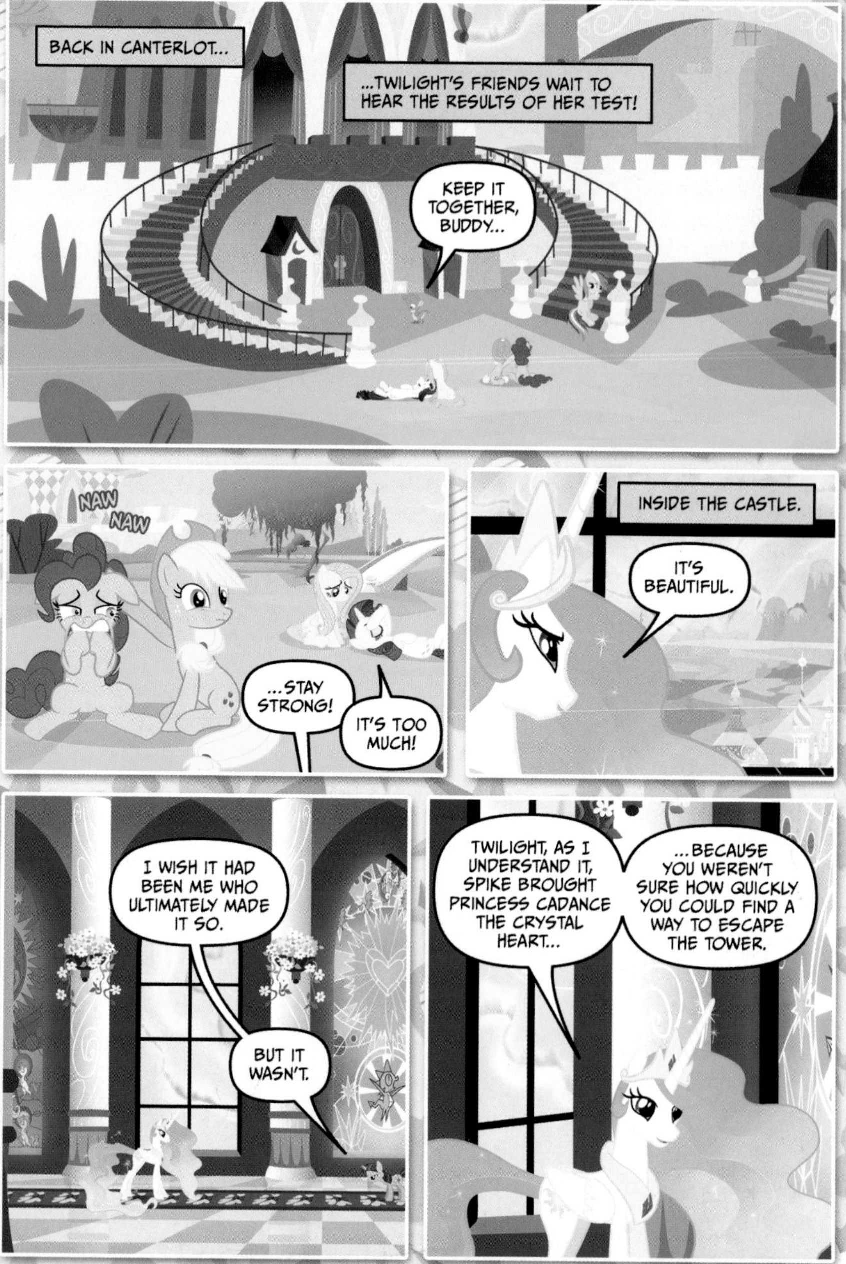
BACK IN CANTERLOT...
...TWILIGHT'S FRIENDS WAIT TO HEAR THE RESULTS OF HER TEST!
KEEP IT TOGETHER, BUDDY...
NAW NAW
...STAY STRONG!
IT'S TOO MUCH!
INSIDE THE CASTLE.
IT'S BEAUTIFUL.
I WISH IT HAD BEEN ME WHO ULTIMATELY MADE IT SO.
BUT IT WASN'T.
TWILIGHT, AS I UNDERSTAND IT, SPIKE BROUGHT PRINCESS CADANCE THE CRYSTAL HEART...
...BECAUSE YOU WEREN'T SURE HOW QUICKLY YOU COULD FIND A WAY TO ESCAPE THE TOWER.

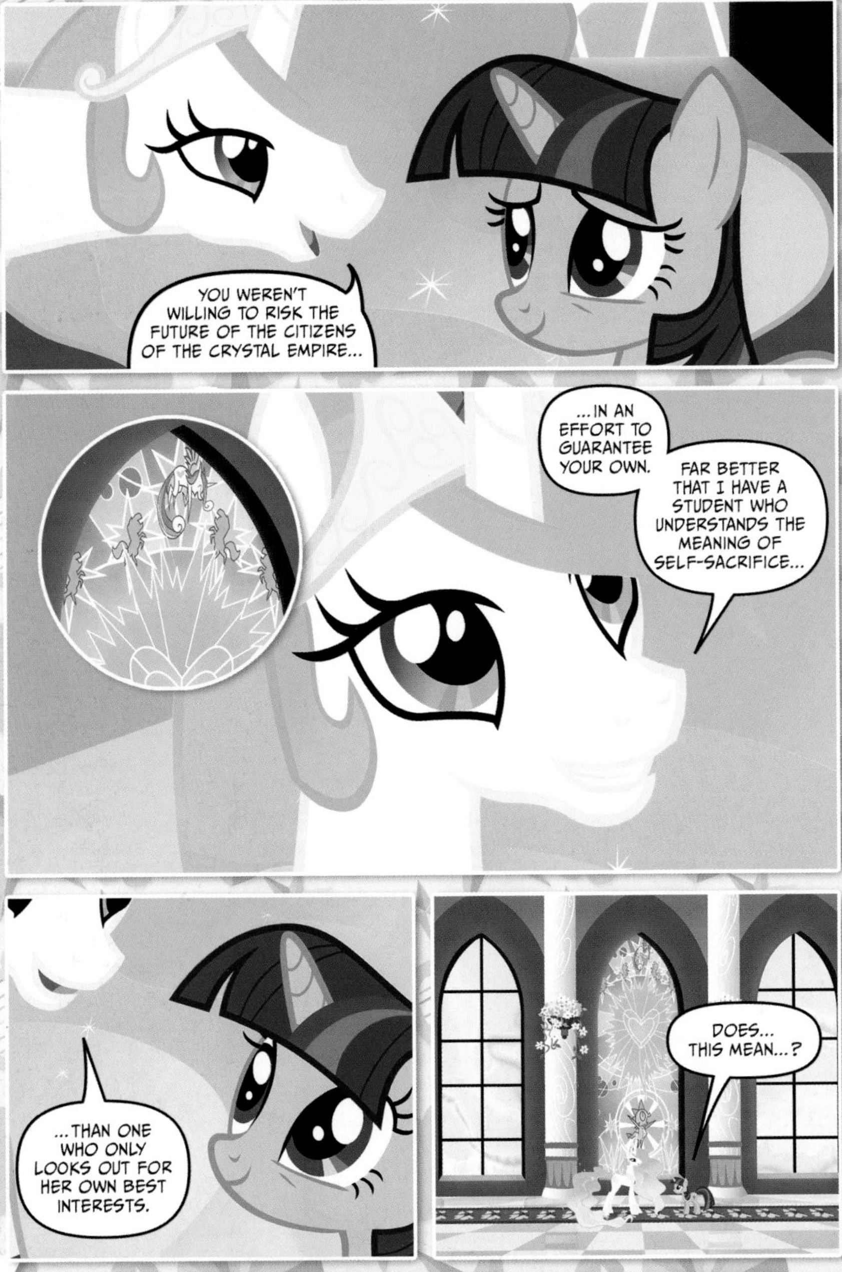
YOU WEREN'T WILLING TO RISK THE FUTURE OF THE CITIZENS OF THE CRYSTAL EMPIRE...
...IN AN EFFORT TO GUARANTEE YOUR OWN.
FAR BETTER THAT I HAVE A STUDENT WHO UNDERSTANDS THE MEANING OF SELF-SACRIFICE...
...THAN ONE WHO ONLY LOOKS OUT FOR HER OWN BEST INTERESTS.
DOES... THIS MEAN...?

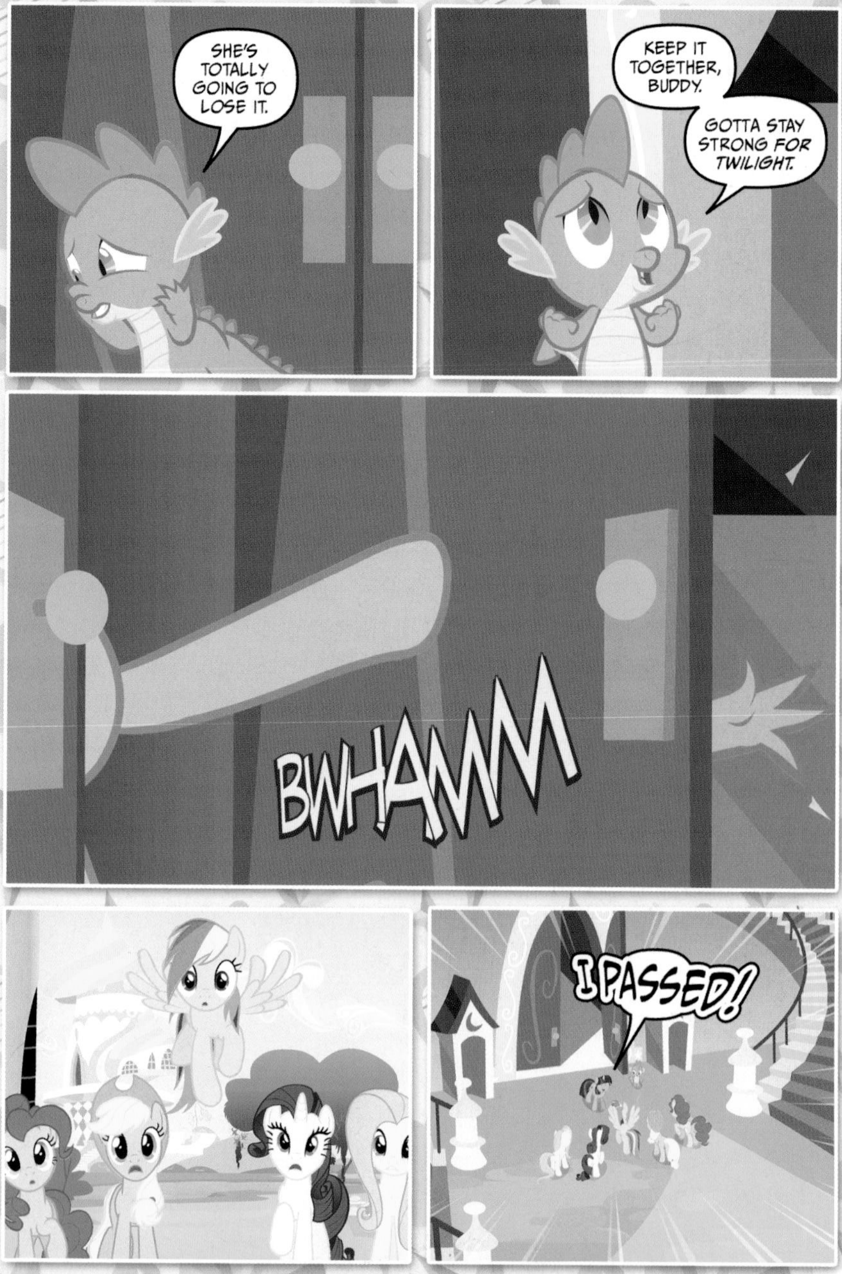
SHE'S TOTALLY GOING TO LOSE IT.
KEEP IT TOGETHER, BUDDY.
GOTTA STAY STRONG FOR TWILIGHT.
BWHAMM
I PASSED!

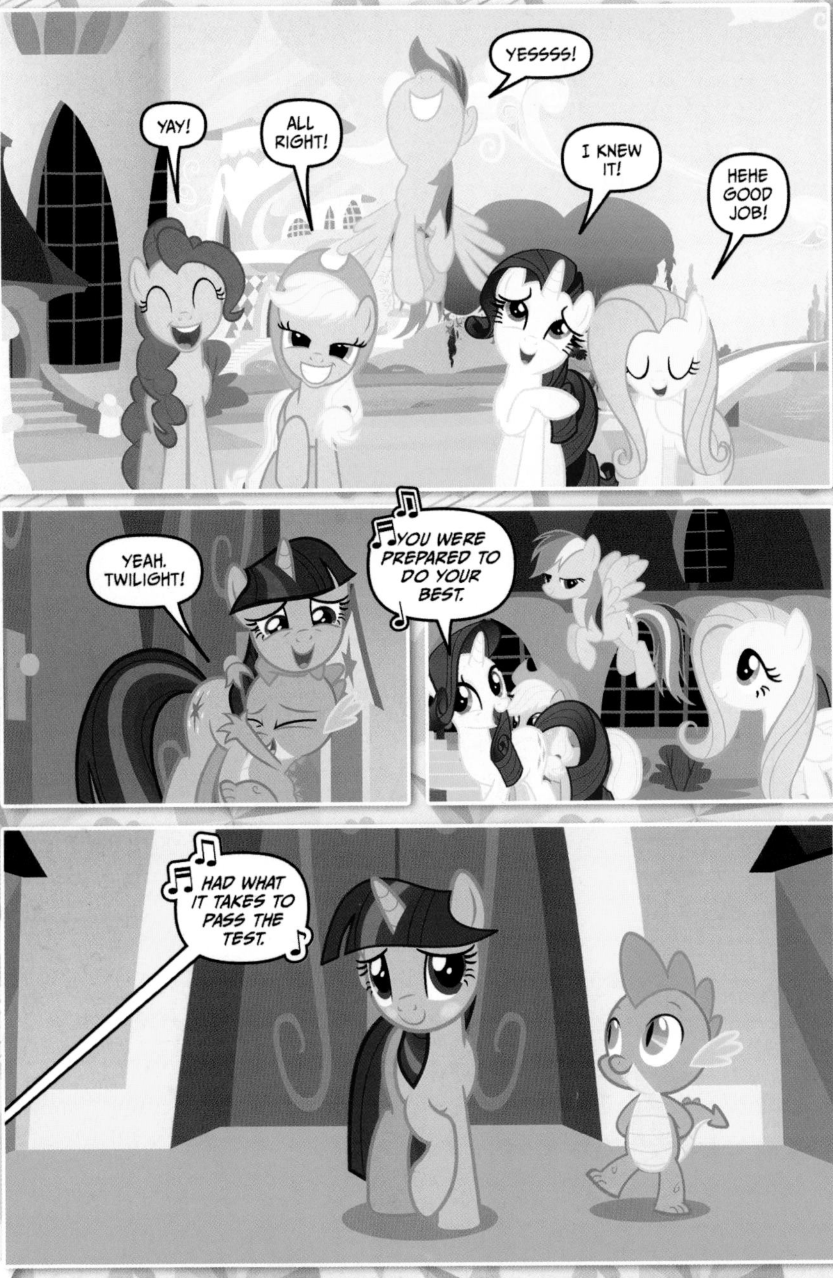
YAY!
ALL RIGHT!
YESSSS!
I KNEW IT!
HEHE GOOD JOB!
YEAH. TWILIGHT!
YOU WERE PREPARED TO DO YOUR BEST.
HAD WHAT IT TAKES TO PASS THE TEST.

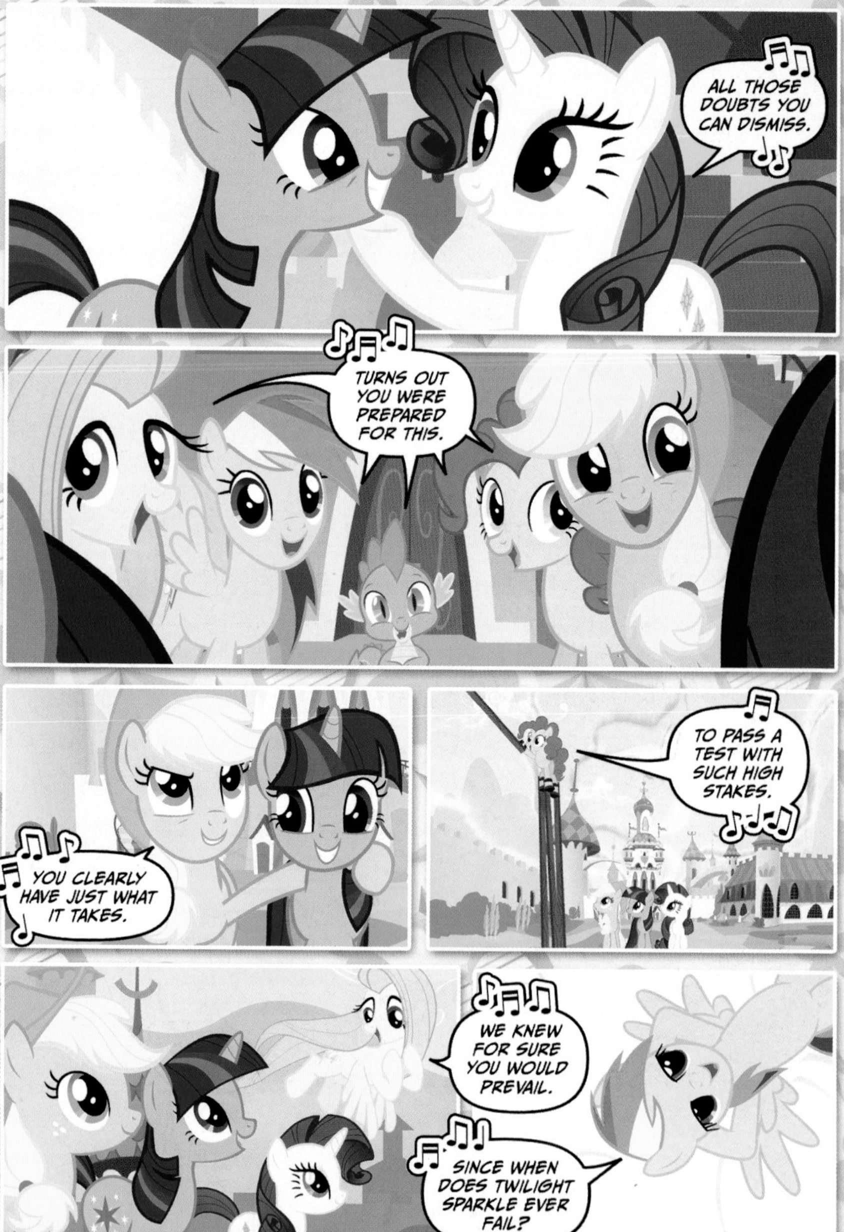
ALL THOSE DOUBTS YOU CAN DISMISS.
TURNS OUT YOU WERE PREPARED FOR THIS.
YOU CLEARLY HAVE JUST WHAT IT TAKES.
TO PASS A TEST WITH SUCH HIGH STAKES.
WE KNEW FOR SURE YOU WOULD PREVAIL.
SINCE WHEN DOES TWILIGHT SPARKLE EVER FAIL?

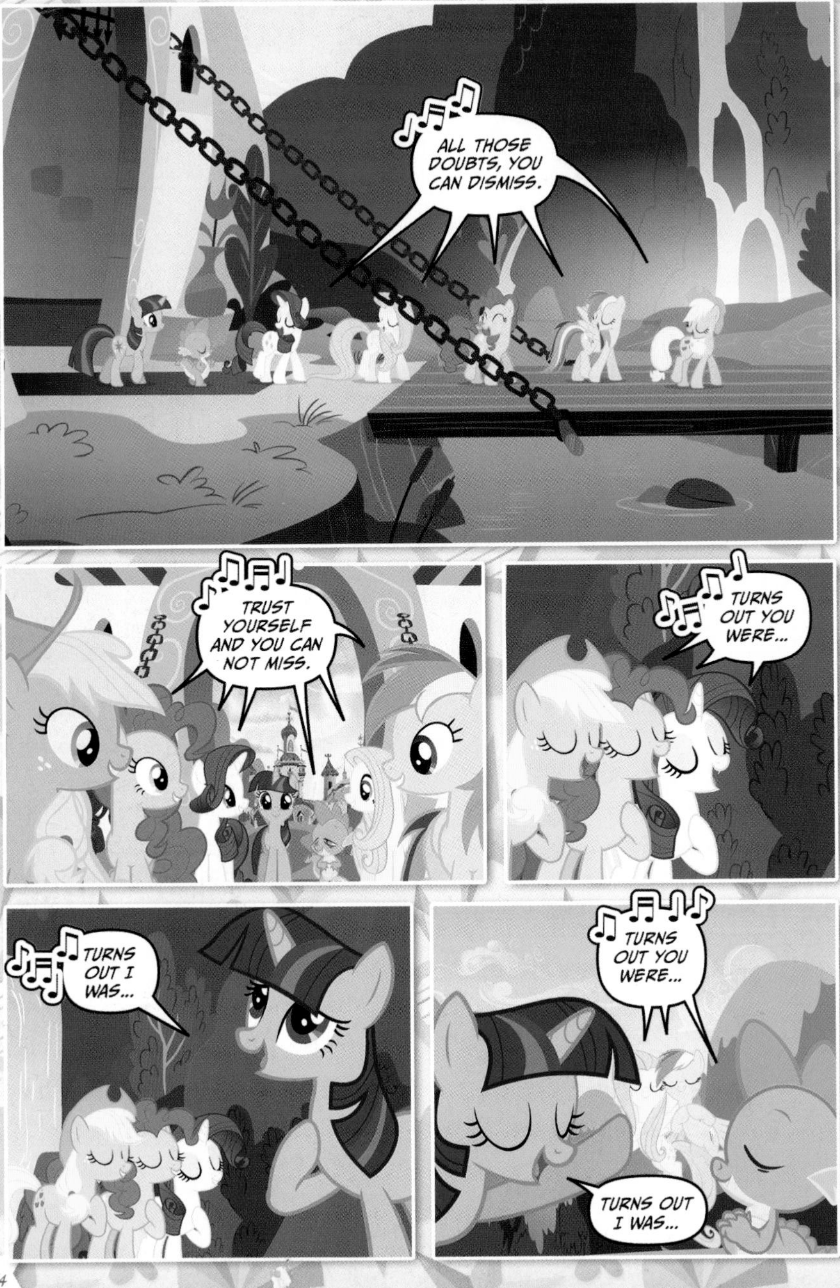
ALL THOSE DOUBTS, YOU CAN DISMISS.
TRUST YOURSELF AND YOU CAN NOT MISS.
TURNS OUT YOU WERE...
TURNS OUT I WAS...
TURNS OUT YOU WERE...
TURNS OUT I WAS...

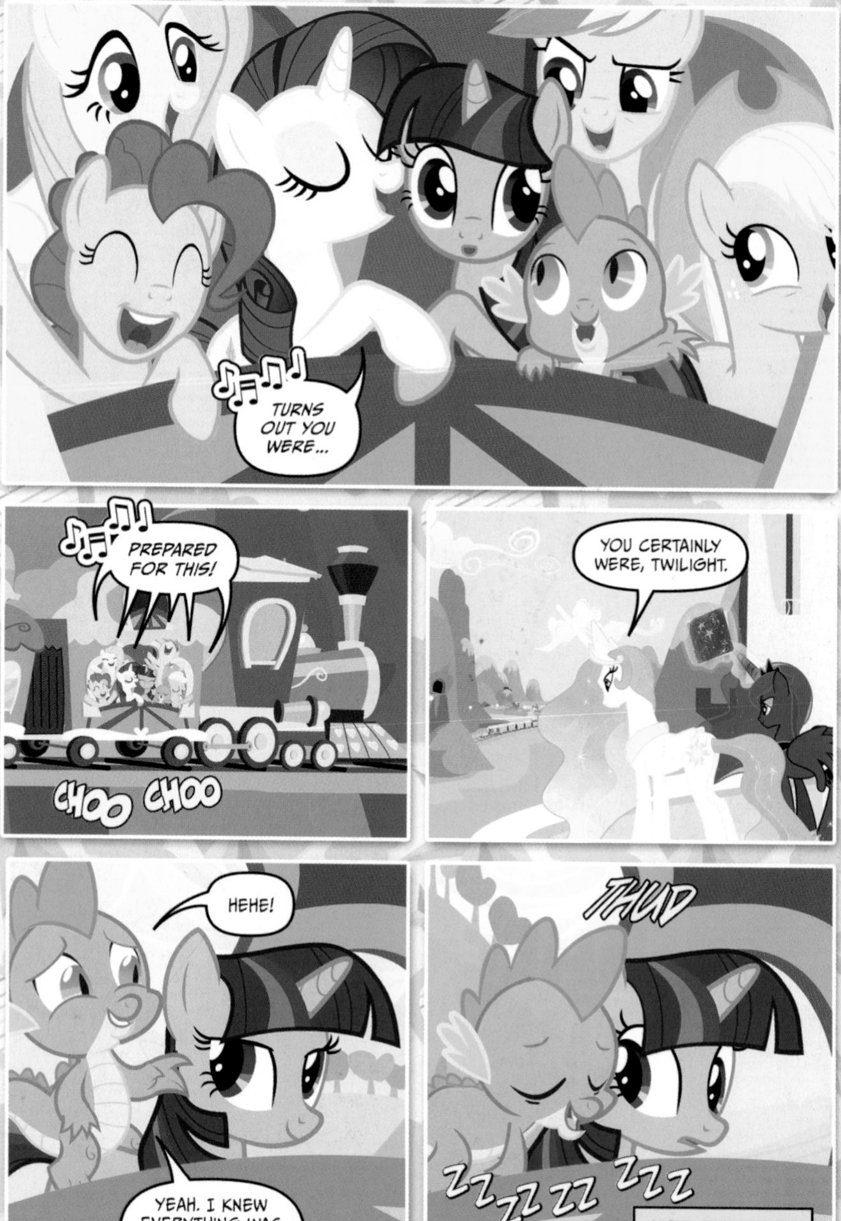
TURNS OUT YOU WERE...
PREPARED FOR THIS!
CHOO CHOO
YOU CERTAINLY WERE, TWILIGHT.
HEHE!
YEAH. I KNEW EVERYTHING WAS GOING TO BE FINE.
THUD
ZZZZZZZZZ
NOT THE END!

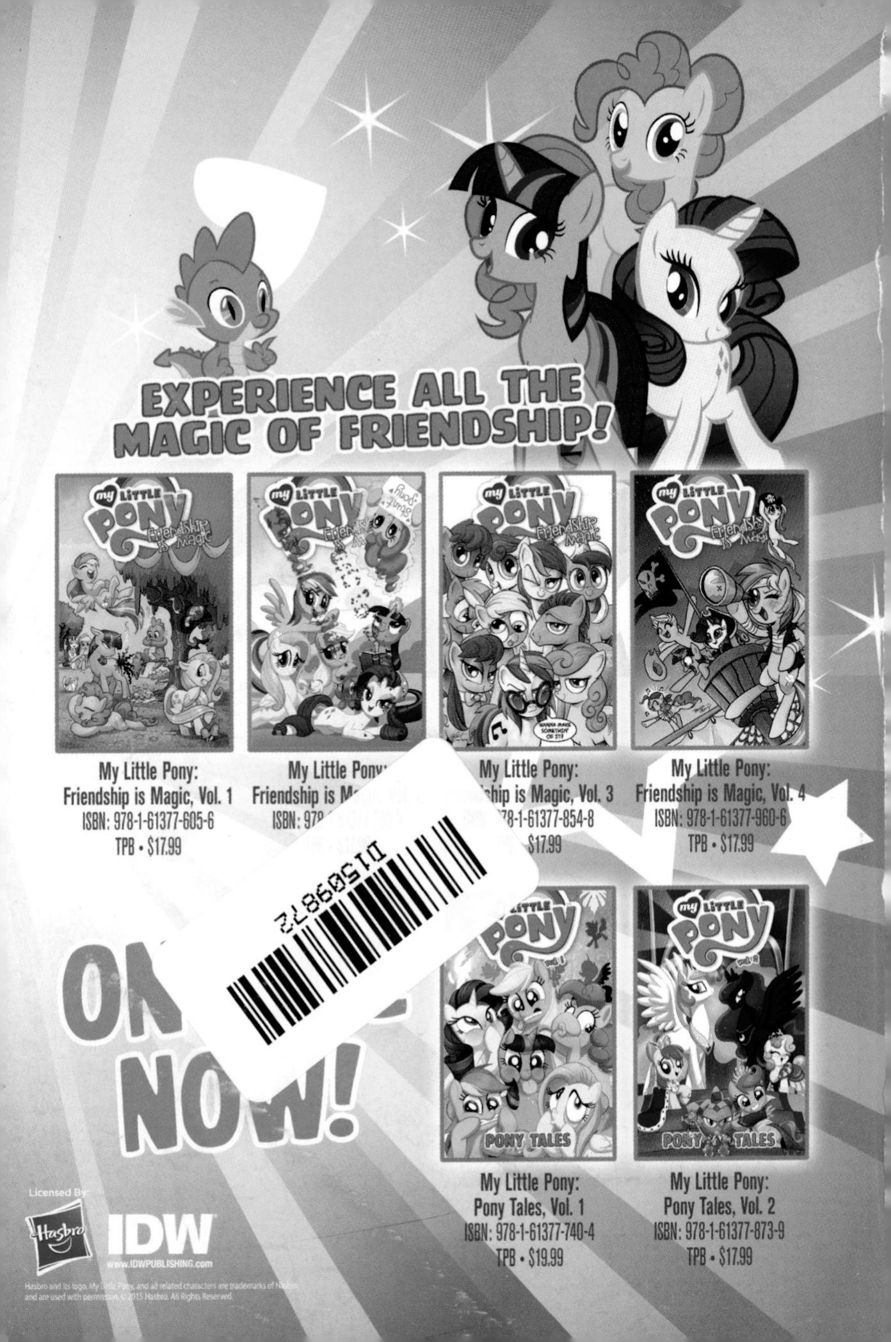
EXPERIENCE ALL THE MAGIC OF FRIENDSHIP!
My Little Pony: Friendship is Magic, Vol. 1
ISBN: 978-1-61377-605-6
TPB • $17.99
My Little Pony
Friendship is Ma
My Little Pony:
ship is Magic, Vol. 3
78-1-61377-854-8
$17.99
My Little Pony: Friendship is Magic, Vol. 4
ISBN: 978-1-61377-960-6
TPB • $17.99
ON
NOW!
My Little Pony: Pony Tales, Vol. 1
ISBN: 978-1-61377-740-4
TPB • $19.99
My Little Pony: Pony Tales, Vol. 2
ISBN: 978-1-61377-873-9
TPB • $17.99
Licensed By:
www.IDWPUBLISHING.com
Hasbro and its logo, My Little Pony, and all related characters are trademarks of Hasbro and are used with permission. © 2015 Hasbro. All Rights Reserved.